A STEEPING OF BLOOD

PRAISE FOR *A TEMPEST OF TEA*:

"A riveting page-turner, *A Tempest of Tea* is brewed to perfection: a deftly built world, a heist-fueled plot, a hint of romance, and a cast of endearing characters. Hafsah Faizal's latest novel crackles with adrenaline and charm."
—Rebecca Ross, bestselling author of *Divine Rivals*

"Slinky and witty and clever, with a lot of cosiness and a lot of claws."
—Holly Black, No. 1 *New York Times*-bestselling author of the Folk of the Air series

"*A Tempest of Tea* is a masterpiece, filled with phenomenal prose, impeccable world building, and a mesmerizing found-family cast embarking on the heist of their lives! If you like vampires, romance, and kick-ass characters with magic weapons, unique talents, and dangerous secrets, look no further and you'll be delighted!"
—Ali Hazelwood, *New York Times*-bestselling author of *The Love Hypothesis*

"All the thrills of an *Ocean's 11*-style heist, made even more fun with magic weapons, steamy kisses, and . . . vampires?! A rollicking banquet of a book!"
—Marissa Meyer, bestselling author of *Gilded*

"A wicked blend of secrets, heists, and vampires, with simmering notes of romance and a smoky foundation of revenge—*A Tempest of Tea* is a story that isn't afraid to show its fangs."
—Margaret Owen, bestselling author of the Little Thieves trilogy

PRAISE FOR HAFSAH FAIZAL

WE HUNT THE FLAME:

An Ignyte Award Winner
A *TIME* Magazine Top 100 Fantasy Book of All Time
A *Teen Vogue* Book Club Pick
A Barnes & Noble Teen Book Club Pick
A *Paste Magazine* Best YA Book
A *PopSugar* Best YA Book

★ "A fresh and gripping story."
—*Booklist*, starred review

★ "A debut series not to be missed."
—*School Library Journal*, starred review

★ "Zafira's courage will teach readers the power of the human spirit."
—*VOYA*, starred review

★ "Impressive world building, stellar cast, and intricate story."
—*The Bulletin of the Center for Children's Books*, starred review

"Faizal creates a dazzling and beautiful world that will make you not want to put this book down."
—*Seventeen*

"Delivers on all fronts."
—*Entertainment Weekly*

"Spellbinding."
—Kerri Maniscalco, No. 1 *New York Times*–bestselling author of the Stalking Jack the Ripper series

"Dazzling and magical."
—Kiersten White, *New York Times*–bestselling author

WE FREE THE STARS:

★ "A memorable story at the height of the fantasy genre."
—*Booklist*, starred review

"This Sands of Arawiya duology closer will not disappoint readers . . . Faizal's prose truly shines."
—*Kirkus Reviews*

"Those who were left breathless by the previous installment will heave a sigh of relief."
—*Bulletin of the Center for Children's Books*

ALSO BY HAFSAH FAIZAL

We Hunt the Flame
We Free the Stars
A Tempest of Tea

A STEEPING OF BLOOD

HAFSAH FAIZAL

FIRST INK

First published in the US 2025 by Farrar Straus Giroux, an imprint of Macmillan Publishing Group

First published in the UK 2025 by First Ink,
an imprint of Pan Macmillan
The Smithson, 6 Briset Street, London EC1M 5NR
EU representative: Macmillan Publishers Ireland Ltd, 1st Floor,
The Liffey Trust Centre, 117–126 Sheriff Street Upper, Dublin 1 D01 YC43
Associated companies throughout the world

ISBN 978-1-5290-9711-5

Text copyright © Hafsah Faizal 2025
Map copyright © Virginia Allyn 2025

The right of Hafsah Faizal and Virginia Allyn to be identified as the author and illustrator of this work has been asserted in accordance with the Copyright, Designs and Patents Act 1988.

All rights reserved. No part of this publication may be reproduced, stored in a retrieval system, or transmitted, in any form, or by any means (including, without limitation, electronic, mechanical, photocopying, recording or otherwise) without the prior written permission of the publisher.

Pan Macmillan does not have any control over, or any responsibility for, any author or third-party websites (including, without limitation, URLs, emails and QR codes) referred to in or on this book.

1 3 5 7 9 8 6 4 2

A CIP catalogue record for this book is available from the British Library.

Printed and bound in the UK using 100% Renewable Electricity by CPI Group (UK) Ltd
Book design by Aurora Parlagreco

This book is sold subject to the condition that it shall not, by way of trade or otherwise, be lent, hired out, or otherwise circulated without the publisher's prior consent in any form of binding or cover other than that in which it is published and without a similar condition including this condition being imposed on the subsequent purchaser.
The publisher does not authorize the use or reproduction of any part of this book in any manner for the purpose of training artificial intelligence technologies or systems. The publisher expressly reserves this book from the Text and Data Mining exception in accordance with Article 4(3) of the European Union Digital Single Market Directive 2019/790.

Visit **www.panmacmillan.com** to read more about all our books and buy them.

TO COLONIALISM:
you suck

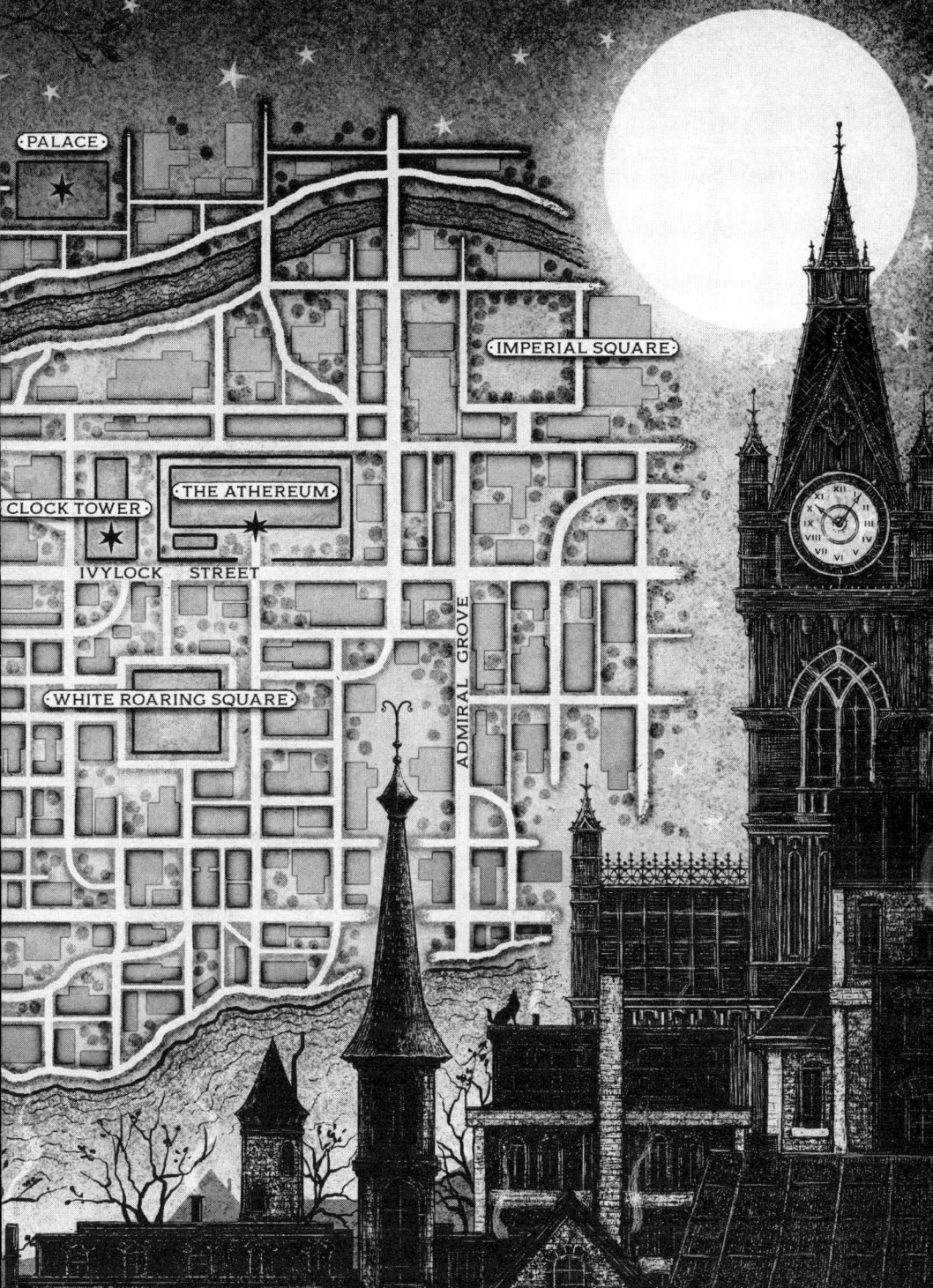

The island is Arthie Casimir incarnate. It truly is. Wild, enigmatic, and goodness does make me sweat. I can onl— hope the Siwangs will do o— bidding. I am not a viol—

vampire cells

coconuts

the dreaded laboratory

storerooms

overseer's office

chandelier

Ripper room

Armory

extra space?

the vault-like door

ACT I
A TEMPEST AT SEA

PROLOGUE

The colors Matteo Andoni used in his paintings often reflected his emotions. For years now, they were darker, more despondent, as he had long associated color with beauty, and it was hard to see beauty in a world that was so destructive.

A destruction he had both witnessed and experienced. And inflicted himself.

See, Matteo hated guns. He hated weapons. He hated violence altogether, but it had taken many years to reach that point. To brush paint across canvas with a delicate touch. To *hold* a paintbrush and not immediately see it as a weapon, and thus see himself as despicable.

Yet he had indulged in carnage tonight. If one were to walk through the Athereum's meeting hall, it would look as though someone had gone *oopsie* and knocked over several cans of paint on the well-polished floors, spattering it across the damask-patterned walls, across the bodies that had been dressed in their absolute best.

In the deepest, darkest red. It was silky, glistening, delicious.

One could ask if *indulge* and *delicious* were the right words coming from someone who loathed violence, but there was no other way to put it. Matteo lived on the edge of ferocity. He might happily wield his brush and partake in the humdrum of high society, but a single event such as tonight's could send him off, swiftly unlocking the cage where the vampire in him was waiting with bated breath.

And the vampire in him was most ardently pleased this night.

When the Ram's men came for those reporters, the selfless, brave men and women who were drawn to upholding the truth, Penn held off as many as he could using the strange and wicked power with which he had been bestowed.

Until he fell.

And then Jin fell. Flick screamed.

By that point, there were very few people left alive, very few who would have noticed Matteo's fangs extended, the blood trickling down his chin, the nails that had sharpened to claws at his fingertips. And soon, no one was left to tell the world the truth of what Matteo Andoni really was.

He never cared if anyone knew he was a vampire. But he'd lived a life so removed from true relationships that his undead-ness inevitably remained a secret. Even if word did get out, no one knew the extent of it.

For he did care about that particular bit.

Some twenty-odd years ago—he didn't like keeping count—his world turned inside out when the Wolf of White Roaring stalked through the latter hours of the night, tearing through streets and limbs with equal disregard. The Wolf was ravenous, and not for food. He was empty and hurting and hollow, and wanted so badly to fill that void, but chaos was all he knew. Savagery became the only language he spoke. He did not drink from those he mutilated. He was trapped in memories, in cruel imagery that he'd tucked away since his childhood. His mother's face contorted with pain. His father's whip lashing across his back.

Fangs, breaking the skin of his throat against his will. Draining him. Feeding—*poisoning* him. Transforming Matteo Andoni into the beast that he became:

The Wolf of White Roaring.

Eventually, bloody and beat, he had found himself in front of the lawn of a house on Imperial Square, which had been so meticulously trimmed that he had laughed at the mundaneness of it, just before he heard his name spoken with great dubiety.

"Matteo?"

He blinked back into the present. It was Penn who had spoken his name then, decades ago, but he was gone now. Now it was the girl in his arms, shivering and barely conscious. She was bleeding from a gunshot wound gaping beneath her breast. Matteo was no doctor, but she was so small and light, and her wound was so large. There was far too much blood drenching his front that he could scarcely believe it had bled out of her alone.

He threw open the front door of his house to the aghast face of Ivor. The butler stared from the bloody handprint on the door to Matteo, framed in the doorway.

"Sire? Wh-what has happened?" Ivor stammered out, already eyeing the trail of blood spattering the floor. "Is that the Casimir girl?"

"Yes. Not now, old boy." Matteo pushed past him and into an empty room, nearly snagging the end of her sari when he kicked the door closed.

He gently set her on the bed.

She said his name again.

"I'm here, Arthie," he replied. *Eternally.*

He meant that, even if he'd never say it aloud. He would goad her and tease her. He would stomach ashy tea for her and kill a thousand men for her, despite his loathing of violence. He could only hope his actions were telling enough.

"You came for me," she said softly.

"Ouch, darling. Don't sound so surprised now." He tucked a lock of hair behind her ear and swept his thumb across the soft bump of her chin. It didn't matter that the windowpane was as dark as the skies outside; she was vivid. She was the color that he had not seen in years—from the violet-gray of her hair to the bronze-brown of her skin, the deep red of her sari and the deeper red of her blood.

"How?" she asked with a wet cough. "Where are we?"

She was dying. Fading with the night.

"Hold this," he ordered, grabbing whatever cloth was close and pressing it against her wound to uselessly staunch the bleeding.

If anyone doubted the difference between half and full vampires, they only had to look at her now: Every inch of her body was fighting to stay alive. Holding on to the remnants of what made her human.

"We're at my house. After Penn—" Matteo stopped as his throat closed. There were many threads that connected Arthie and Matteo, and Penn was the strongest, wrapping around and around until their bond was irrefutable, even if Arthie had never known of it.

Penn had been the one to take him in when Matteo had stumbled onto his porch on Imperial Square. Penn was the one who calmed Matteo down, who cleaned the blood from his fingernails and taught him how to retract his fangs.

He was a father to Matteo in a way Matteo's own had never been.

"There were the gunshots," Matteo continued, "and you turning Jin, and when I saw you pick up Penn's revolver and run after Laith, I couldn't let you go alone."

"He shot me," Arthie whispered.

He. Laith. From the moment Laith had walked through his front door, Matteo had his qualms about the Arawiyan turned high captain of the Horned Guard.

But Arthie, brilliant and whip-smart, sounded as though she'd never seen it coming. Shock coated her every word. She was bleeding, *dying*. She'd seen Laith kill Penn in cold blood, and she still couldn't believe it. As if the two of them had formed some sort of bond of their own when she'd drunk his blood. Or long before then.

"Yes," Matteo said, winding his pain tight inside the word. "And he killed Penn."

"I know." Her eyes fluttered closed and then opened again. She almost looked guilty for a flash of a second.

"Is he dead?" she asked.

She wasn't asking about Penn. Was Matteo imagining the emotion in her voice? The hope that he was alive, the fear that she might have killed him?

Between the Ram barging through the doors of the Athereum's meeting hall to this moment, Matteo remembered very little. It was as if the blood he drank had crowded his vision, narrowing it and shrouding everything in a hazy, dreadful red.

But he did remember Laith.

The boy had been slumped against the wall, crimson blossoming over his white robes, a lot like the flowers he kept shoving in Arthie's face. He wasn't moving. There was clearly a hole in his chest, but Matteo didn't know if it was lethal. Truth be told, only she would know if he was dead, even before she'd fired the revolver.

"Did you want him dead?" Matteo asked.

Because if Arthie had wanted him dead, he would be.

"Does it matter?" she asked, not answering the question.

It did, but he couldn't say that without sounding selfish. He watched for her reaction, trying to decipher if the pain he was witnessing was physical, emotional, or both. Her jaw quivered. Her breath stuttered, and a soft sound of anguish escaped her.

"Your wound is fatal," he said. It didn't matter if Laith had been trying to kill her or not—she was too petite for the bullet *not* to hit anything important.

She laughed dryly. "You don't say."

Arthie Casimir might have been dying, but that mouth had never been more alive.

He froze when she looked into his eyes and said, with utter conviction: "I can't die."

Matteo knew what she asked of him. It was what he wanted to do. Desperately. Why else had he taken the precaution to rush through the night after her? Why else had he bundled her in his arms and brought her here?

It would cost him nothing to turn Arthie into a full-fledged vampire, but it would cost her everything. He looked at the ghost-white pallor of his skin. He closed his fist, still unused to the strength of his undead bones years later. He exhaled, knowing full well that even the act of breathing was something he'd selfishly held on to for no reason other than as a reminder that he'd once *needed* to breathe.

Matteo had spoken to Arthie about accepting herself, but there were days in which he wondered if he'd ever done the same.

She was half vampire, yes. She still had to drink blood like a vampire did; she still had almost every undead limitation placed upon her. But she was still half human. To be a vampire meant a life that went on forever. To be human meant cherishing its temporariness. There was value in such a thing, a certain bittersweet longing that persisted with each passing day.

The waves of her short hair were as delicate as the wheeze escaping her mouth, strands feathering the black silk pillow beneath her. He adjusted the cushions, rearranging the drape of her sari, tucking the coverlet under her side, knowing full well that each second that passed was another of excruciating pain for her. He couldn't keep stalling.

"If I do this, there's no going back," he said, needing her to understand the weight of what she was asking him to do.

"Do you think I'm unaware?" Arthie asked, the bite he so adored back in her words. "I didn't come so far to simply end up in a grave."

He couldn't stifle his surprise. "Nor does much of humanity. Is that not the ordinary progression of life?"

"Am I ordinary to you, Matteo?"

No, Arthie was about as ordinary as any other phenomenon.

Matteo rounded to the other side of the bed and climbed up beside her. He was in bed with Arthie Casimir. She must have seen the teasing on his face, for she lifted her eyebrows at him before the expression turned into a wince of pain. He knelt on the blood-soaked covers, beside the delicate length of her arm. She looked smaller without the many layers beneath her typical tailored suit, without the baker boy cap holding down her hair.

"Do it," she rasped, sensing his hesitance. "The Ram mustn't win."

Only Arthie could look at the head of an empire and say the Ram hadn't already won. Only Arthie could challenge someone like that, could think herself capable of taking down someone as distant and powerful as the masked monarch of Ettenia.

He breathed a laugh, brushing away the hair that clung to her damp skin. "My praecantrix."

She turned her head to the side, the pillow shaping to the curve of her cheek, pain momentarily out of mind. Her scorn was sharp in that dark amber gaze, for in the short time he'd been acquainted with her, he'd learned she was not fond of not knowing something.

And as much as he adored the nearly forgotten tongue and disliked disrespecting it into Ettenian, the last thing he wanted was to irk her.

"Enchantress," he translated, and with care, he reached to her other side, bracing himself over her. His hair tumbled across his shoulder, brushing her bare skin.

Her breath caught. She immediately winced and pressed a hand against her side, tilting her chin up to meet his eyes. There was anguish in hers, a bashfulness that he could tell she found irritating, but blanketing it all was her need. It had been a long time since Matteo had been needed. Wanted? Always. Needed? Rarely.

He had no right to be selfish, but oh, how he wished to be. He leaned into her, catching her scent: tea and moonlight. Blood. Like a switch being flipped, like a brush bleeding out on canvas, his zealous fangs slipped from their sheaths.

He held back a wave of sorrow.

It should be a cause for celebration: Arthie Casimir was going to live forever. It was not as if vampires could not be killed—Penn lay prone as proof—Matteo knew. But it was one thing to live expecting old age to lay eventual claim to a soul, and another entirely to exist with the knowledge that only an act of extreme violence could cause one's end.

Dark hair, brown skin, red blood. Matteo forced himself to stay present, to focus on the matter at hand. *Her.* He did this often: recited the colors around him, reminding himself that the world was not black-and-white, noting the angles and the shadows and the way the light was taken for granted.

It kept him from spiraling.

He checked her wound, her pulse. She was losing blood, but she would have to suffer longer before she could be turned. Which meant he would have to drain her himself.

"Matteo," Arthie whispered.

"Shh," he murmured, and with his nose, he brushed the hair from the side of her neck. Her pulse leaped to attention; her breath hitched. His own locked in his throat, and he wanted to savor this moment, to relish the knowledge that he had made Arthie Casimir breathless.

Gently, he ran his tongue over the skin on the side of her neck, priming it for his fangs. Vampire saliva was a strange thing. Almost numbing, almost intoxicating. Very wholly dangerous.

Matteo licked her again. Arthie gasped, grabbing his arm with both hands. He pulled back, looking for one last confirmation, and tried for a smile, hoping to convey *You'll be just fine.* He was certain it came out as a grimace.

But she smiled back, almost shyly, reaching a trembling finger to trace the curve of his dimple.

"I owe you my life," Arthie said, with so much emotion threaded into each word that it nearly made him weep.

That wasn't really her speaking. Other than mayhem to her enemies, Arthie owed no one anything.

"Hush," Matteo said, clearing his throat. "Don't say anything you don't mean and won't remember."

It was simply how the act of turning worked: Newly turned vampires remembered very little of their turning, very little of the process. Perhaps it was a curse; perhaps the body underwent so much change at once that it shredded its own memory of it.

"Oh, I always say what I mean and I never forget," she said with utter certainty, and then she threaded her fingers through his hair and pulled him to her throat.

Matteo couldn't stop himself—it was her boldness, the scent of her blood, the way he was drawn to her—his fangs went straight for her skin, piercing through her flesh. Arthie gasped, her hand slipping to the nape of his neck, nails digging into his skin.

He forced himself to ignore the way her touch made him feel, the way the low moan that escaped her lips made him want to press his eyes closed and give in to the burning desire inside of him. He drew her blood into his mouth, and it tasted like she smelled: like earthy tea and smoky nights and the enigma that was purely her.

He sucked more, goaded by her moans, by her nails digging into his neck, holding him down. He slipped his fingers through her hair and tilted her head, admiring the shadows pooling into the strain of her throat.

Sweet stars, she was divinely delicious.

He retracted his fangs, smoothing his tongue over the twin punctures before lapping even more, knowing any moment now that it would be too much for her.

As if on cue, she bucked beneath him with a soundless sigh, writhing, thrashing, and when her eyes flared even wider, he clamped a hand over her mouth to stop her from screaming. He'd already listened to one Casimir scream as they were turned today. Her teeth scraped the skin of his palm, and he tucked his leg between hers, trapping her beneath him.

This was what every vampire desired, wasn't it? An enamored thrall. An endless supply of blood. This heady, breathless, intoxicating air.

He wanted it to stop.

He kept drinking.

And then, at last, *at last* it was done.

Matteo peeled his hand from her mouth, pulled away as if not to disturb someone who was fast asleep. Arthie made no sound, no movement. Her eyes were closed, lashes damp. Her neck was jeweled in a pair of rubies that matched her sari.

Even in death she was a glory to behold.

And there, in the grim, still silence of the room, he heard her pulse. Soft, fading, a question in each faint pump. He would answer it a thousand times. He lifted his wrist to his mouth and bit down, drawing blood before pressing it against Arthie's lips. Then he pinched her nose, forcing her to draw a shallow breath through her mouth.

Matteo knew the moment she tasted it: a sick and twisted second chance at life. He felt the blood siphon out of him as she sucked in more, and more, until she stopped.

Her eyes flew open with a breathless gasp. She blinked down at his wrist, at the blood covering his clothes and hers, drenching the bed. She touched the punctures at her neck that were already knitting themselves closed and settled her gaze on his as if she'd never looked away.

There was a hesitance there, an uncertainty. At the same time, she looked as though she made good on her promise and remembered every moment since he'd brought her into this room.

Matteo didn't know what to say or ask, so he did what he did best: He deflected.

"Welcome back, Enchantress," he said with a wink, and Arthie passed out.

1
ARTHIE

The streets of White Roaring were in turmoil. Shouts, screams, protests. Arthie had heard it as she'd wavered in and out of consciousness over the past several days. She remembered waking up in a bed in Matteo's house, then flashes of a carriage. Now she was in a room she didn't recognize, not until a pang of sorrow shot through her when she caught the faint whiff of a cigar.

The Athereum.

"You're awake."

She looked toward the sound of Matteo's voice as he entered the room. He snapped the book he was carrying closed and quickly pulled a pair of dark specs from his eyes almost guiltily, as if she hadn't already seen him wearing them. He'd been a hospitable host during her horrible bouts of pain, as death tried desperately to pull her back into its depths.

"And as stunning as ever, of course."

She didn't feel stunning. She opened her mouth.

"Ah." He wagged a finger, quickly turning serious. "Before you ask, yes, they're alive. Both Jin and Flick have been found. Not together, but they're close enough."

Relief and guilt stirred inside her.

"I never thought I'd set foot in the Athereum again. What's happening out there?" she asked, nodding to the walls that rumbled from the people out on the street.

"Unrest," Matteo said, and pursed his lips. "It reminds me of—" He stopped and screwed his eyes shut for a moment, as if to regain his composure. "They're calling it the Great Press Massacre."

How original.

"The Athereum's our only refuge. It may be all but besieged, but no one can get in and it's better than my house where we have to worry about the Ram appearing on my doorstep in search of the ledger or our heads." He sighed. "I'm sorry to bombard you the moment you open your eyes. How are you feeling?"

It turned out, her magical pistol known as Calibore—the one Laith had shot her with—was far more lethal than she'd imagined. Unlike a regular weapon, Calibore could harm vampires—*kill* vampires. She knew that, but she didn't know it affected one's recovery too.

Where a newly turned vampire would be up and walking in moments, it had taken Arthie days before she could think straight. That fateful night echoed in her ears. The slaughter, the screams. The loss. She had *died*, and somehow, that was the least of her concerns.

Because she had failed.

She didn't know how to feel. She could summon so little of her pain, so little of her rage. She rubbed her knuckles over her heart, where the skin was still stitching over the wound left by Calibore's bullet, and sank deeper into the covers. The red silk of her sari had unraveled in the dark sheets, undulating like wisps of blood in the sea.

It reminded Arthie of when she'd fled Ceylan on her own, leaving her parents bloody and lifeless at the shore. She had been helpless. Hopeless.

She could all but hear Jin's voice saying *Until you found me, of course.* He wasn't wrong.

He still wasn't wrong. Because she'd lost him now, and she felt it. Deeply. She'd kept a fundamental truth from him, throwing it at him when he was breathing his last, when she was extending her fangs and turning *him* into a vampire.

The sari felt right at the time, when she and Jin and Flick were on the cusp of changing the future of Ettenia. She'd felt powerful, wearing an echo of the traditional gown her mother wore proudly to her death. In the end, Arthie had done the same.

And now she felt ridiculous.

She had failed Spindrift, she had failed her crew, but more than anything else, she had failed her past.

Matteo lit the lamp by her bedside table, then the other. The light glided over his tongue as he ran it across the points of his fangs, his eyes crimson from just having fed.

She was a full vampire now. The parts of herself that she'd refused to accept for a decade had overtaken the humanity she'd clung to for those ten years. A decade of refusing blood, subsisting on dwindling stores of coconut. It was Laith's fault. He'd shot her.

"I can't tell what you're thinking," Matteo said. He set down the book he was carrying on the bedside table, barely restraining a growl at a sudden uproar outside.

That was what she was feeling: frustration. At Laith for killing her, and if she was being honest, frustration at Matteo for saving her—even if she was the one who had asked it of him.

"I'm not thinking. I'm tired," Arthie lied.

Matteo tilted his head and drew closer to the bed, the intensity in his eyes making her feel as though he were sorting through her thoughts. She looked away.

"No, you're not," Matteo said. "You're a newborn vampire—you're not tired. I almost want to assume you're angry, but something about that emotion is different on you too."

Because that anger wasn't directed at the world anymore. She closed her eyes.

She'd kept the truth from Jin only to see his distrust as she turned him, worse than any of the destruction they'd seen that day.

She'd sent Flick to summon her mother, unaware that Lady Linden of the EJC was the very same masked monarch of the country.

She'd assumed she had a handle on Laith before he'd killed Penn and then her.

The Athereum had lost their leader. The country had lost scores of their press. The crew had lost their home. They'd failed jobs before. It was the nature of a con. Sometimes one was conned right back. But this—this had failed on every level, and Arthie could only blame herself.

The mattress dipped with Matteo's weight, and Arthie opened her eyes. He was framed in the crimson drapes of the canopied bed, as distinguished as one of his paintings, and she was reminded of the night he turned her.

He hadn't thought she would remember, and rightfully so, as vampires rarely recalled those tumultuous moments before and after the shift from life to undeath. But when had Arthie ever fit into a mold? She couldn't remember *all* of her turning, but she remembered enough—bits and pieces that made her neck feel hot.

Perhaps that was why her hand moved before she could stop it. Her fingers brushed his, stealing his attention. His gaze softened and slowly, carefully, as if she were a cat poised to run, he intertwined his fingers with hers. It sent a thrill through her arm, sharp and charged. She had touched his hand countless times before, but this was different. Everything between them was different now.

"You were my first," he said distantly.

"First what?" she asked, and as she asked the question, something inside her seemed to settle, giving him her full attention. As if she'd been running her entire life only to realize she'd been going nowhere.

He wore a freshly pressed shirt, and when he shifted to face her better, the vee of white framing the smooth lines of his chest spread wider. A hazy memory rose to her mind: her hands running up the plains of his chest, her nails digging in, her back arching.

"I'd never turned anyone before," he said, pulling her back to the present. "It was a cruel joke, having it be you. I didn't—I didn't like seeing you dead."

This was the perfect moment to thank him for saving her, but she couldn't summon the words, not when she wasn't particularly happy to be alive. Or undead. Fully undead. She cinched her jaw tight.

"I'm alive now," she managed to say.

Matteo leaned back. "Ah, so that's what it is. You're blaming yourself."

And now she was becoming easy to read. Splendid.

Still, a part of her leaped at the words, the opening, the invitation to bare her soul to him in a way she'd never felt the desire to before. Not with Jin, not with anyone. Was it because he had turned her, forging a deeper bond between them? What was wrong with her?

Images kept resurfacing in her mind: his fingers brushing back her hair with a gentleness she'd seen him demonstrate time and time again, but never on her person, never on her body. The vulnerability in his eyes as he leaned toward her, the same exuding from her own near-death state.

"I know what you're thinking," he goaded.

"No, you don't," Arthie said, cursing the breathlessness in her tone. Which was an extra level of ridiculous when she didn't need to breathe.

He propped an arm behind him and leaned back, tilting his head as if he was a king about to be hand-fed grapes. She knew to expect his cocksure drawl before he even opened his mouth.

"Admit it, darling, you feel the sudden urge to kiss me, don't you?"

She flicked her eyebrows, ready to tell him off before another idea struck. She dropped her gaze to his mouth. "And if I do?"

Matteo straightened, startled by her response. She bit back a laugh. Why had she never responded to his antics this way before? She could have shut him right up many times over.

Because I never wanted to kiss him before.

The thought alone shocked her.

She'd had little interest in love. Then Laith arrived, breaking down her walls bit by bit as he tried to get closer to her pistol, even as she did the same while attempting to decipher his secrets.

There hadn't been time to build those walls back up again.

What did Matteo want from her? It wasn't as though she could open her mouth and ask him, not without injuring her pride.

He looked down at their fingers and brushed his thumb along the back of her hand. Perhaps it was because she was hurting, or perhaps it was because she was newly turned, and by him at that, but Arthie could think of nothing *but* kissing him.

She remembered when his lips were stained dark with her blood, the cords in his arms strained from the night's battle—or from holding her down.

Arthie tugged gently on their entwined hands. An invitation. A question. A fire roared to life inside her. He obliged, still surprised by her initiation, leaning in and propping his arm on the covers beside her. Arthie caught a whiff of his scent and wondered why she'd never smelled him before: the rich, nutty warmth of the fresh walnut oil he used in his paints and something sweeter, like a blend of leather and chocolate.

She hadn't tasted chocolate in years.

It reminded her of home. Of her father bringing back rare treats that she and her mother shared because he never had much of a sweet tooth himself. Arthie pursed her lips. She hadn't thought of home that way in a long time—only the violent fragments. The chaos as the soldiers stormed the Ceylani shore. Her mother's red sari. The bullet holes. The blood.

"Arthie."

Matteo spoke her name on a hesitant sigh and pulled back. He must have seen the turmoil in her eyes now that she was so damned readable. She ran her tongue along her lips, trying to bury her memories again. Trying to bury the present and her past and everything that existed outside this room and this bed.

His eyes narrowed to slits, and with it, some part of him closed away. "There's something we need to talk about."

She waited.

"It . . . has to do with how you arrived in Ettenia," he finished, flinching when somewhere outside the window, glass shattered and people roared.

On a boat. Full of blood. Right. She'd forgotten that he knew. She'd forgotten that no one could fathom being close to a girl capable of such brutality.

Arthie wrenched her hand from his, her anger surging—*there it is*—battling with whatever raw thing was tearing through her. It was a selfish sort of pain wrapped with embarrassment.

He was rejecting her, while she was lying in this bed, looking up at him.

Everything about this moment had her positioned to be weak.

How had she allowed this to happen? She was Arthie Casimir. She rarely trusted anyone, and she'd been right not to: When she'd gone against her better judgment and trusted Penn's plan and sought out the help of the press, every last one of them had ended up dead.

What about Jin? asked a little voice in her head. She buried it deep.

She scoffed. "I know exactly how I arrived in Ettenia. There's nothing more you need to tell me about it."

The blood on her sari had dried, matting to her skin. She had no reason to stay here, not when he was spewing words like *that*.

"You misunderstand," Matteo said quickly as she began to stir.

"No, you *think* you understand," Arthie said, her voice dropping to a whisper. "No one does. No one, but—"

She stopped herself. Of the innumerable stories and secrets she'd collected in Ettenia, only one came close to hers. There were other half vampires, of course, other bouts of killing, but only one story showed her what she could have been, had her incident been on land instead of a boat stranded at sea.

She might have even been worse.

"The Wolf of White Roaring?" he asked, a stillness in his voice.

Yes. She gathered her sari and sat up straight, swaying from the blood loss, from this new version of herself. How much did he know of her? How much did he know of what had happened on that boat when she was just nine years of age?

"Wait, Arthie. Please. He's exactly whom I wanted to speak about."

"Oh, and why's that?" she asked, her back to him. She scanned the room for her pistol, searching for some semblance of herself, her *past* self. But then she remembered: It was still lying on the floor of the Nimble Street apartment, in a pool of blood with Laith.

"Because," he began, and she had the sense he was bracing himself for his next words, "he and I are one and the same."

Arthie froze, certain she hadn't heard him correctly.

Matteo was the Wolf of White Roaring? *He* was the one who had exposed vampires to the public's fear and wrath, and in so harsh a view because of a rampage in which he brutally turned the streets red? That didn't make sense. He—he was as much a murderer as she was. The number of bodies she'd mutilated was far less, but had there been more than three people on that boat, when would she have stopped? *No*, a voice reminded her, for she'd killed others too, at Penn's house.

Perhaps she *was* worse.

She turned back around to face him, regarding him anew. The delicate structure of his bones, the soft pout of his lips. The compassionate green of his eyes, now that the crimson had faded. He looked nothing like what she thought the Wolf would look like.

"But you—"

"Paint? Draw?" he asked. He laughed softly. "Come now, Arthie. You know better than that. I'm certain the evil Ram waters the peonies in her garden. Many well-mannered wives dip biscuits in their tea while dreaming of butchering their husbands. We contain multitudes."

He was prattling like he hadn't just tossed at her one of the biggest secrets she'd ever learned. She sat back down on the bed. Once, she would have leveraged such a thing in every heinous way she could. Was this why Penn had encouraged her associations with Matteo before his death? Was this why Penn had been unafraid and unaffected by her nine-year-old acts of violence?

The Ram had done this to him. That much she knew. Penn had said as much, but he hadn't given any indication that it was *Matteo*.

She was struggling to catch up. "Penn—Penn knew it was you."

Matteo nodded. "I somehow ended up on his doorstep that night. I didn't know where to go, where to turn. He took me in, knowing I was a half vampire, and eventually turned me into a full one."

Arthie saw the way his gaze flickered. Pain, shame, regret.

She could not imagine Matteo in a place so low. He was too quick to smile, to jest. He was lauded and praised; his paintings sought after by the masses. He was *flourishing*. She never would have guessed that he of all people would be the Wolf of White Roaring.

A little part of her was in awe of him, yet another emotion she rarely felt.

He'd assimilated a lot better than she ever could, but she would be naive to blame it on herself and not the social standards that praised the color of his skin.

Arthie had long believed the Wolf of White Roaring attack had been fabricated—not the attack itself but the circumstances surrounding it, and Penn had confirmed as much himself. He'd also told them who was responsible: the Ram.

"Why did the Ram choose you? Were you ill?"

Had the Ram wandered the beds of a hospital and chosen Matteo for her needs? Arthie could think of nothing else. She had been ill when the Ettenians came to her home country of Ceylan and her parents had taken her to the one "doctor" who could help, unaware that his cure would wreak a permanent change to every fiber in her being.

"Ill?" Matteo asked, and then laughed when he realized what she meant. "No. I was of perfect health, really.

"My father only ever cared about how well I was doing with my tutors, and my mother was always more concerned with how he felt than how I ever did. So I spent much of my time elsewhere. Wandering the streets, sitting under trees with a pencil and a pad.

One day, back smarting from my father's lash, I took a walk through the woods and found some sort of facility, tucked into the autumn trees. It looked like it had been placed there *for* me—I had walked that route a thousand times and never seen it before."

He picked at the lint on the covers. "I heard . . . cries from inside and knew I shouldn't be there. Instead of trying to help, I was thinking of myself, thinking of how I should run. Before I could, men rushed out of the building, grabbed me, took me in. I remember that distinct smell of a hospital ward, and something sharp pierced my neck before I was fed what I now know was blood. The last I saw was the Ram's mask, and then I woke up on the streets."

That was nowhere near how Arthie was turned into a half vampire herself.

"There have been other rampages, you know," Matteo said. "Never to the same scale, never publicized and made into propaganda either. She turned me and dropped me in the middle of a busy street for her own selfish agenda."

He sounded tired. He met her eyes, and the torment in his gaze was so great that if Arthie wasn't as grounded as she was, she would have imagined she was there with him just now. Back in his past, reliving that haunted memory. Arthie knew it could not have been easy to tell her any of this.

"Why you?" she asked.

"I don't know," Matteo said. "Perhaps I was in the wrong place at the wrong time."

No, there was more to it than that. Arthie knew how certain people worked, and as elusive and secretive as Lady Linden was, she was the sort of person who did nothing without a reason. There was always a *why*. She wouldn't have decided to turn Matteo at random.

"And mind you, she wore that mask before she was even crowned.

She was protecting her identity, playing this game of duality, *before* the Council gave her what she wanted. I just don't know how she knew of vampires when very few did. I certainly didn't. But turning me was a reckless, risky move, and she had to have had a good deal of vampire knowledge in order to do it."

"We know that people in search of power and status will use anything to get what they want," Arthie said. But why vampires when there were so many other ways to achieve what the Ram had? That, Arthie didn't know.

Matteo scoffed. "She certainly found both."

Every Ettenian, immigrant or otherwise, knew how the Ram rose to power, crowning herself as monarch shortly after the Wolf of White Roaring went on his rampage. The empire was in disarray and Ettenians were afraid. When the monarch at the time did nothing, she did. She placated the people, she promised restrictions, gave the public law and order where there was none. She had been prepared, speaking with a surety no other would, a surety that could only come from having a solid knowledge of vampires. She was Ettenia's savior, and she was rewarded with the title of monarch because of it.

"That's what the unrest out there reminds you of," Arthie said as she realized. "The days after." *After your rampage*, she wanted to say.

Matteo nodded, pursing his lips. There was a correlation there, Arthie knew. The turmoil might not have been part of the Ram's original plan, but she was certainly making use of it.

"I tried going back to the facility with Penn later, but it was gone. Empty. As if I imagined it," Matteo continued. "While she went ahead and knocked me down to climb to this empire's highest position. *I* made her what she is today. And now I learn she's Lady Linden? I *painted* for her."

Arthie had never heard such anger in his voice, so much emotion quivering in his tone.

"At some point, I went home," Matteo whispered, lost in a memory. "I killed my father. Not because I hated him, Arthie, but because he tried to hurt me. Then my mother. I couldn't stop myself. I was so painfully hungry and angry at once. It wasn't even a true hunger in the sense of the word. I never *fed*. Just craved. It was as if I was trapped inside my body—"

"Watching it happen with no control," Arthie finished softly. "I know."

"And you're the only one I know who does," he said with a small smile.

It should have stirred something positive in her. It should have deepened their companionship because someone else understood her. Instead, it unsettled her. *Because you've never had anyone like that before.*

"You see now, don't you?" Matteo asked, pinning her with his emerald gaze. "She's still our enemy."

"I never said otherwise."

"No, but you were allowing yourself to be distracted by our predicament. Blaming yourself when in truth she is wholly at fault."

Arthie didn't know how true that was, but she said nothing.

"We didn't fail that night."

Her eyes flicked up in surprise.

"I know that's what you're thinking," Matteo said. "But you're a new version of yourself. As are Flick and Jin. I'd wager even I am. As powerful as we might think Lady Linden is as both the Ram and head of the EJC, we're ignoring how powerful *we've* become. We haven't given ourselves the chance to unleash it."

Arthie's thoughts were typically separated into clear lines, each one connected to its pertinent information. They were buried beneath a fog now. She had indeed called the massacre and the days leading up to it a failure, but Matteo was right. They'd successfully infiltrated the Athereum, they'd learned the Ram's true identity, they'd successfully retrieved the ledger, the Ram's most incriminating possession. They *hadn't* failed. Admitting defeat was exactly what the Ram would want.

But Arthie couldn't shake the feeling that she had failed when it came to Penn and the members of the press who had died that night. She had failed when it came to Flick, when it came to Jin.

Matteo pulled open the drawer beside the bed and took out something shiny. Arthie's heart lurched at the sight. Calibore.

"You found it," she said, taking it from him. *And cleaned it*, she thought. There wasn't a speck of blood on its grip, the silver as pristine as the etched black filigree.

"I couldn't leave a part of you behind. Secondly, here. It's dated more than a week ago, but we were busy." Matteo handed her a newspaper and waited for her to read the headline.

LIFE WAS LIKE A CUP OF TEA: THE END WAS INEVITABLE.

It was about Spindrift. About the Casimirs who ran it, and what a shame it was that an unattended teapot had caused the fire that brought it tumbling down.

Arthie read it again. An unattended teapot. *That* was the story White Roaring would believe? That Arthie and her crew were reckless enough to let a teapot bubble over and burn down an establishment she had spent years nurturing? She read it a second time, each pass clearing the dust and grime to unearth the girl who she was on the date of the paper, rousing her anger and need for vengeance from a slumber until her mind was as clear as if she were a compass finally landing true.

"Inevitable," she scoffed. If Arthie Casimir wrote for the press, she'd have fired herself for such a headline. One, it was a grotty way to speak of her prestigious tearoom. Two, this was White Roaring. The undead removed any such permanence from endings.

Spindrift would rise from the grave, just as everything the Ram stood for became buried in another. Arthie swore upon it. With a sigh, she tossed the newspaper aside, letting it seesaw to the rug knotted in varying shades of crimson.

It settled with a whisper of a rustle as resolution settled in her unbeating heart. If only she could show Jin, to grouse and mock it with him.

"Thirdly," he said, and held out a glass. A flute, slender and crystal clear, filled to the brim with blood.

She looked away with a swallow. She hated that her stomach growled at the sight of it. She hated that she wanted it. *Needed* it.

"Drinking for your sustenance is not the same as what happened on that boat," he said, because he understood. He knew.

It tasted the same. Arthie hadn't *drunk* from any of the poor souls she had slaughtered, but their blood had spattered. It found its way into her mouth, coated her lips. Arthie knew it was sustenance; she knew it was as simple as needing to fuel herself, but she'd lost a part of herself that day—and after, in Penn's own house. She'd committed acts that defied her own logic, that ignored her own wishes. She had not been in control during those moments, and Arthie loathed not being in control.

"You drank from me," he added softly. "This is no different."

"But it was, and you know that," Arthie said, flicking her eyes to his. She drank in the heat of the moment, in the throes of death. She stared at his extended hand and the glistening glass. She spoke her next words with a promise. "One day."

He nodded, setting the glass on the cart beside him. "I would offer you coconut water, but I have none."

She would survive. She was in control now, and if she refused to drink blood, to cling desperately to the shriveling shreds of her humanity, then so be it.

Someone banged their fist on the door. "Andoni!"

With a miffed expression, Matteo rose and opened it. "What?"

Arthie could see the Athereum hall, the wallpaper and the lacquered wood. It was hard not to be reminded of Penn wherever she looked. Framed in the doorway was a vampire, silver-haired and tall.

Sidharth. One of Penn's closest friends.

He stepped inside without invitation, his grin overshadowed by the havoc in his dark gaze. "Arthie Casimir, you live!"

"Did you expect otherwise?" Arthie asked.

Sidharth sank into the armchair with a sigh. "Never. We brown-skinned folk are a tough bunch."

"Why are you here?" Matteo asked, offering no niceties of his own. "She's still recovering."

"I know," Sidharth said, looking as though he'd missed several nights of sleep, and vampires didn't even need sleep. "It's wretched. The streets are full of Horned Guard. The riots started badly enough, now it looks like the entire city is out there, and we've just learned it's not only because of the press massacre. Humans are turning up missing too."

"I wish I could summon surprise," Matteo said.

Sidharth nodded. "As of yesterday. Of all the years for Penn to die."

He spoke the words callously, but Arthie caught the crack in his voice at the end.

Matteo walked to Sidharth's side and gave his shoulder a squeeze.

"He wouldn't have wanted anyone else to take the mantle."

"You're head now?" Arthie asked.

Sidharth nodded wearily.

"Do we know who's responsible for the disappearances?" Matteo asked.

"According to everyone out there, we are. There have been 'clear indications' a vampire stole them. Since when did vampires do that? I greatly doubt he put up a sign saying I STOLE A HUMAN, TA-RA! Oh, we're also drinking their blood and killing them, I've been told. My vampires are barely leaving the premises because of the mayhem out there. Mind you, I don't know who's taking advantage of the chaos and kidnapping humans—"

"The Ram is," Arthie said.

"Whatever for?" Sidharth asked almost hysterically.

Arthie picked up Calibore and gathered her sari. "You said the streets are full of Horned Guard. She's on the lookout for us and her ledger, but is this no different than the aftermath of the Wolf of White Roaring?"

Sidharth's silence was answer enough. She didn't look at Matteo. She didn't want to give anything away.

"That was twenty years ago. Ettenia's fear of vampires hasn't been as pressing as it was then. This is the perfect moment to ramp it up again and garner support. The more the masses fear, the more they turn to her."

Fear was a weapon the powerful wielded time and time again with excellent results.

"And on the other side of it, she's using the uproar to distract everyone, more importantly, *us*."

Sidharth blinked at her. "I'm too tired to know what you mean there."

"From the vampires she's weaponizing."

He didn't look convinced. "Of everything we have going on, how can we be sure?"

The Ram might have killed scores of people that night and burned down Spindrift, but she did both in retaliation. She was hurting because she'd lost her ledger, that one book Arthie had risked their lives to retrieve from within these very walls.

The one book full of her secrets.

"Because that was the ledger's biggest secret. And when I kept it instead of handing it back, she knew we'd joined Penn's cause. We lost Spindrift because of it," Arthie said. "Along with Penn himself, Jin, and the press who gathered that night."

Outside, shouts rose like a rushing wave. A window shattered somewhere; people cheered.

Sidharth sighed. "If they're blaming that night on vampires, I wouldn't be surprised if you and your crew were named responsible too. Nevertheless, I know you were just dead, but have you a plan?"

"When have I not been a criminal?" Arthie asked. It was true, she was no stranger to being on the run and avoiding the Ram's guard, but the danger was greater now, infinitely more acute. She hadn't just snatched Calibore from White Roaring Square or decided to run a secret and illegal bloodhouse; she'd stolen something the Ram desperately needed. "But yes, I do."

Because Jin had weighed heavily on her mind even through the torment of her recovery, and with this plan, not only would she throw sand in the gears of the Ram's weaponization of vampires and expansion of Ettenia's colonies, but she'd earn Jin's forgiveness too.

"Penn said Jin's parents created the silver inoculation the Ram's using to weaponize vampires, right? We don't know if they're alive, but we—"

"They are," Sidharth said.

Arthie paused, surprised he even knew anything about them. "Penn said it was uncertain."

Sidharth nodded. "He and I were to have a discussion about them, but now we never will, eh? I'll never know what he wanted to speak of, but my understanding was that he didn't want the boy—Jin, is it?—going after them."

Arthie furrowed her brow. That was an odd wish. What sort of reason did he have to keep Jin from seeking out his own parents?

Matteo wasn't paying attention. "Find his parents, and we'll get answers that'll lead to the vampires. Find the vampires, and we'll stop the operation entirely."

"That's the idea," Arthie said.

But first, she needed the Ram's ledger. For that, she needed Flick. And Jin too, if she was being honest.

"Whatever I can provide, let me know," Sidharth said. "I won't tell you to trust everyone here, but those of us you can trust will do what we can."

Arthie's circle had tightened even more now that Penn and Laith were gone. She didn't plan on trusting Jin's parents either. She might not know under what circumstances the Siwangs worked for the Ram, but Arthie wasn't one to operate by giving anyone the benefit of the doubt.

"All right," she said, and swung her feet to the floor, standing for the first time in days. Outside, the riots echoed like a heartbeat. "Can you take us out of here? Let's please get our crew back together."

2
JIN

Sweet Poppy's Pastries was closed for the third day in a row, which didn't do wonders for Jin's already sour mood. He wanted to step through its doors and walk past the glass boxes filled with flaky, buttery goods, oozing jam and dusted in sugar and drizzled in chocolate. He knew he couldn't taste any, but a feast could be had with more than just a tongue. Or so he told himself because he was hungry and hadn't had a sip of blood since the evening he'd turned.

Like his life, White Roaring had changed. Where danger once lingered in the shadows and the shelter of night, it was now bold and loud, dealt by the hands of the angry and afraid. So many members of the press had died that night, but humans had begun disappearing off the streets too. *Missing, gone, killed*, the people were shouting. No one knew anything for certain, only that it was a vampire that had done it.

Jin could guess whether that was true.

Horned Guard were everywhere, but the Ram was letting it happen, letting anger fester. As if she wanted the people distracted, as if she couldn't care less about what was happening in Ettenia anymore.

Places like the pastry shop were closed, windows shuttered as people either hid away or marched, fists waving for answers, armed with stakes and whatever makeshift weapons they could scrounge.

It was altogether ridiculous.

The Ettenians' fear of vampires had amplified because of a falsehood: The Ram's forces had taken the lives of those reporters, not the vampires of the Athereum where it had happened. It was the Ram who had waltzed through the Athereum's doors and looked at Flick and all but said, *Oh, and here's yet another surprise: I'm your mother!* moments before she put a bullet in Jin. And the theatrics didn't end there. Miraculously, Arthie turned out to be a vampire and made him one too.

Jin scoffed. It sounded straight out of a novel, really.

Except, despite the winding, twisting, death-filled plot of this novel, the most gut-wrenching part of it was the fact that Arthie had lied to his face for the past ten years.

And he couldn't stop being so damned angry about it.

Jin rolled the crick out of his neck and flipped a chair around. The four feet thudded in the quiet of the empty classroom, dust pluming gold in the dim light of the lantern on a desk. His bullet wound throbbed dully, an ache and reminder. He sat down, adjusted his legs. Rested his arms on the back of the chair.

He was taking his time.

There was another chair across from him, with a graceless middle-aged man in a uniform that was worn and streaked with more than one patch of dirt. Jin had lured him here with small talk that had transformed into tiny threats—shiny words that were once almost second nature but seemed to be extra demanding to draw out now that this anger was running rampant in his veins.

The longer Jin took, the louder the rough ricochet of the man's breathing became and the more he strained against the ropes strapping him down. And Jin, being a vampire, could hear everything with infuriating clarity. There was much about being a vampire that Jin had not anticipated. It was known that vampires had heightened senses, but no one spoke of how overwhelming that could quickly become.

The man whimpered. Poor sod looked much like a puppy in a thunderstorm.

Jin smiled his cheeriest, kindest smile. Outside, the early winter wind slammed fists against the walls, and the unrest across White Roaring roared past.

He glanced down at the near-illegible note he'd gotten from the last bloke he'd met. Admittedly, he'd charmed the words out of that one, but his patience was wearing thin—as though he'd been at it for months and years, and not a handful of days since that night at the Athereum meeting hall.

Strictly speaking, Jin *had* been in search of his parents for months and years, but this was different.

"Coll, is it?" he asked.

Coll didn't answer. As expected. Jin had time. He laughed bitterly. He had all the time in the world now—literally.

"I was told you're one of the few people last in contact with Mister and Missus Siwang, several months ago. Do you remember?"

Coll still had nothing to say. And in the empty silence, Jin heard the blood rushing through the man's veins, a fountain of sweet nectar waiting for a pair of fangs.

Jin ground his jaw tight and straightened his cuff. He leveled his gaze on Coll again.

Maybe you ought to remove the rope from between his teeth, brother, Arthie suggested in his thoughts. *You might get an answer out of him then.*

He couldn't shake her voice no matter how hard he tried. The past seven days were excruciating enough, but having to hear her wry tone at every turn made it worse.

"What ever would I do without you, sister," Jin seethed. He was frustrated. Betrayed.

Still, he'd gone after her that night, when Penn had fallen and she'd disappeared after Laith. He was still finding his footing, his mouth too full of teeth, his body yearning for blood in a way he'd never thirsted for anything before. He had watched her die by Laith's hand, watched as Matteo took her away. Jin hadn't known she was a half vampire who could be turned into a full one. He hadn't known she was *any* percentage of a vampire to begin with.

She'd lied to him, time and time again—or omitted the truth, or whatever excuse she would use. It didn't matter what she had to say because, in the end, the fact remained: She hadn't trusted him.

He shoved her out of his mind. He had other tasks to attend to: such as finding his parents. Penn had told him they were a resource to the Ram, which meant they were likely alive, and Jin had spent the past week hunting every lead he could. He would find them, free them from the Ram's shackles and be done with it.

The Ram had taken his parents, Spindrift, his *life*, but he had been given a second chance, and he wasn't going to let her interfere in his life anymore. *Her.* He still hadn't come to terms with the fact that the Ram wasn't a faceless creature. She was Flick's mother. And Flick was her daughter, the daughter of a woman who loathed vampires, which meant—Jin wouldn't dwell on those thoughts.

He reached over and ripped the rope out of Coll's mouth, leaving it hanging around his neck.

"I don't know, a'right?" Coll sputtered, spittle flying everywhere.

The lantern flickered, sparks flying. There was a time when Jin would close his eyes and see the orange of a fire—now he saw red. Crimson that had been spilled and stolen, crimson that he craved. And to think he'd once craved pastries with that same passion, sweet treats he could still chew and swallow, if he enjoyed the taste of ash.

Jin flinched and wiped the back of his hand on his thigh. "You're going to have to be a little more specific."

"I dunno where the Siwangs are," Coll shouted. "I don't even know who they are."

"Saying it louder doesn't make your lie any more true," Jin said calmly. Coll started bellowing something else, but Jin held up a hand. "Please, Coll, stop contributing to my loss of hearing."

Coll slumped back as much as the ropes would allow.

"Let's try this again," Jin started. Normally, he would entice his marks, goad them, or finagle the response he wanted to hear. He couldn't muster any such thing now, but he would try. "You're a courier, yes?"

Coll nodded.

"And you make deliveries?"

Coll nodded again.

"Right. Then where, dear sir, did you deliver a ten-kilo parcel of liquid silver?"

His parents were scientists, ingenious and well-known throughout Ettenia. Enough that the Ram burned down their house, leaving Jin for dead. He'd spent the past ten years uncertain if they were alive until Penn told him they had fashioned a silver inoculation currently being used to weaponize vampires.

Which meant that much liquid silver could only have gone to one place: their laboratory. Wherever that was.

Coll whimpered and strained against the ropes again. The man was clearly in a rush to be somewhere.

Jin brandished a pistol from the holster at his side. He had never liked guns. He loathed them even more now that shooting someone meant he flirted with the possibility of flying into a blood-hungry frenzy.

Still, they made for a good threat, especially when a silver-tongue was in short supply.

"I—I swear," Coll belted out. The room was beginning to stink of piss, further souring Jin's mood. The man was about as useful as a chocolate teapot, and threatening him wasn't going well.

He slipped the pistol back into his holster with exaggerated movements. Coll noticed, and his whimpering slowed.

"I'm sorry, Coll," Jin said with a sigh, leaning close as if they were about to share a secret.

Coll hiccupped, confusion flashing over his features at Jin's sudden change.

"Neither of us wants to be here, eh? I know I'd much rather be at home sipping a good cup of tea or—" Jin cut himself off, looking to Coll expectantly.

"Cocoa," he contributed. "Mum makes a good cup."

He would have laughed at the portrait of the old man running home to his mother, but Jin didn't even have a home. He still spoke of Spindrift as if it stood strong, as if it weren't a pile of rubble at the top of the street.

"Mum's cocoa," Jin continued with a nod. "But I'm not allowed to leave until you tell me what I need, and *you're* not allowed to leave until you tell me what I need. It appears we're both in the same predicament. Help a bloke out, will you?"

Coll processed his words, searching for a lie before he nodded. "I—I was told to hand the package off to a woman at White Roaring Square. She never arrived."

Jin waited.

"I know nothing else, I swear," Coll said. He tried for a feeble smile. "Sha—shall we go get warm, then?"

There was more to his answer. Jin heard the *however* in his tone, heard the way he was abusing Jin's kindness, and so, his patience shriveled into the cold again.

Jin sighed and rose, glancing back over his shoulder when he heard a sound at the door to the schoolroom, instinctively concerned Arthie had found him. But Arthie had her ways, and Jin knew all of them. He glanced over his shoulder again.

Almost all of them, anyway.

The fright returned to the courier's face, nothing compared to the ugliness thrashing inside Jin. A writhing thing of rage and pain, betrayal and the need to do *something*. He picked up his umbrella, twirled it. He waited. One beat, two. Coll remained silent.

Jin slammed the umbrella into Coll's foot.

There was a sickening crunch before the courier screamed.

He could very nearly hear Flick's gasp. *That was positively diabolical!* she would say if she were here, but she wasn't here to keep him tame. And Coll worked for the EJC, the shipping conglomerate working side by side with the empire, stealing land, resources, and artifacts, uncaring for the ruin they left in their wake.

Pity was hard to scrounge.

Jin bent to meet Coll's eyes. "I heard this was the same foot you used to kick your daughter when she didn't dance to your tune. Oh, don't look so surprised. I'm a Casimir, Coll. Can't expect me not to know. Is that why you're back with Mummy? Because your wife had enough?" He moved his umbrella to the man's other foot, resting the point over his laces. "Care for another?"

It was a question he would ask patrons in Spindrift with a pot of tea in his hand.

"No! Please, no, Mr. Casimir!" Coll shouted. "After the woman didn't show, I took the package to the address myself, and it was empty, yeah? Completely empty. A big old warehouse with nothing in it? I thought, hmm, that's bonkers. It looked like they left in a hurry too. Rubbish everywhere. But I wanted to get paid, so I looked around and just when I gave up, I found a scrap of paper on the floor with another address."

To empty out an entire warehouse and move locations *was* strange, unless one was in danger of being caught, unless . . . *the ledger*, the Ram's personal agenda where she recorded her every move, from names to transactions. It was missing for far longer than Jin and the others had taken possession of it. Of course she would be making strides to change locations and distract from whatever her own notes might reveal.

Jin could only hope that didn't extend to his parents.

"And?" he asked.

"It was the address to their new place. They're—they're doing something in there. Something bad."

Jin paused. "In where?"

"I heard crying. No, no. What's the word—keening? I heard keening," he continued, gasping along the way. "Like the people inside were in pain. That's how I knew I wasn't supposed to be there."

The missing vampires? Jin didn't know, so he glanced to his right before he caught himself. He had been looking for Arthie. To share a glance in which they would have an entire, wordless conversation.

He ignored the pang in his chest.

"Was it a laboratory?" Jin asked.

Coll shook his head in tiny spasms. "It was a—an EJC shipping warehouse."

Jin's hope spiraled again. He forced his thoughts afloat to keep them from drowning.

Shipping warehouses didn't store, they shipped. There wasn't room for storage when White Roaring's ports were so busy, cargo moving in and out within days, sometimes hours.

If Coll delivered liquid silver to a shipping warehouse, that meant . . . that meant it was being sent *out* of White Roaring.

"Are you certain it was a shipping warehouse?" Jin asked.

Coll nodded. "I saw them loading a container and coming back with empty carts. They were shipping all right."

Jin bit the inside of his cheek. It was no wonder he hadn't found his parents. They weren't even *here*. Ettenia might not have been large, but he could count on one hand the number of times he'd left White Roaring.

"Where are the goods being shipped? What city?" Jin asked.

The courier was rocking back and forth as tears streaked down his freckled face. There was a time when a sight like this would stir pity and sympathy. That was before Spindrift was burned to the ground, before he'd seen death sweep across a room, before he'd woken up in a pool of his own blood and the streets had turned angry.

Jin set the umbrella on the man's foot once again.

"I don't know where! Delivering the silver was the extent of my job, a'right?"

Just as Jin knew that was the extent of what he'd get out of the courier.

"Good man." Jin circled behind Coll, slicing a knife through the ropes binding his wrists. "Much obliged."

Jin picked up his things from the dusty table he'd dragged over to their interrogation area. Coll wasn't the first one he'd bound to a chair in his search for his parents. And there were no limits to what he would do to find them. When Jin was dying and Matteo had come asking if he wanted to be turned, Arthie following swiftly after to complete the deed, Jin had only agreed *because* of his parents.

And Arthie. Because she needs me, said a voice. He buried it deep.

Coll looked up at him. "What about my foot?"

"What about it?" Jin asked. "You've got another, haven't you? And I'm getting hungry now, so I suggest you leave."

Coll stood on trembling legs with a muffled cry. He took a single, hobbling step and turned back to Jin. "I—"

Jin bared his fangs.

It was the cure Coll needed. He sprinted with the vigor of a man half his age and with two working legs, huffing out the door without a backward glance.

And then Jin was alone.

"Now what, sister?" he asked in the silence.

Arthie didn't reply.

He sighed. He almost wished, just then, that she would outsmart him as she always did and step through the doors with that devilish glint in her eyes. He ran his tongue along the points of his fangs, and a thought he'd been avoiding snuck through the noise in his head once more: What did Flick think of him? She had been raised with a strong dislike for vampires. She was the daughter of the woman *weaponizing* vampires.

No. That was unfair to Flick. It was why she'd chosen a name of her own. To be her own person, to draw some semblance of a divide between herself and her mother. Jin didn't think she'd fully realized why herself. If his mother was both head of the criminal EJC and monarch of the colonizing monstrosity otherwise known as home, he'd probably do the same.

Flick! That was it. She was the one he needed. Flick had been tasked with protecting the Ram's ledger that night. If there was any way to find out which city the silver was being sent to and where his parents were being kept, it was there. There was always the chance the

Ram might have moved them, but if Coll could sleuth and find what he needed, Jin could do the same. He might not know what Flick thought of him, but there was only one way to find out.

He slid his tinted specs over his eyes and popped his collar, opening up his umbrella as he stepped out into the evening fog. He kept his head low, ignoring the mobs.

"To the Athereum!" people were yelling.

"Join our cause, lad," someone shouted at him.

Jin pretended not to hear. Someone who should not be in possession of a machete was waving it around, and Jin narrowly avoided a slice through his sleeve. Beside him, a woman pumped a wooden stake in the air. Jin kept his mouth closed and his fangs out of view, surprised by a sudden rupture of fear in his veins.

He could die for no fault of his own. He could die because of a description of what he was. He could die because of someone's misplaced anger, because they believed a lie, and it was a harrowing thought indeed.

3
FLICK

In a tea shop not far from the scorched remains of the Casimirs' once-prestigious establishment, Flick sat in the shadows with a terrible cup of tea and a purring kitten, ever watchful.

She read the invitation once more, running her fingers over the gold edges. Days ago, against her better judgment, she had followed a carriage that was dropping off a neat and glamorous card at each house on Admiral Grove, nearly running straight into a throng of Horned Guard gathered at the end of the street. And criminal that she now was, she stole one.

A Tribute to the Written Word, the card announced. *Join us in honoring our fallen heroes and celebrating a vicennial of our monarch.*

It was just over a week from now, at Ettenia's palace north of here. She'd read of vicennial celebrations in history books, an event where long-standing monarchs reminded the rich and the powerful of how great they were and why they ought to remain in power.

She scoffed at the timing. Her mother had been busy in the scant days since the massacre. She was already making her next move, stirring her citizens while planning to honor the fallen members of the press that *she* had killed.

Flick sighed and tried another sip of her tea. *Blech*. Tea-flavored water was what it was.

The shop was equally drab, void of life in a way Spindrift had never been. She drummed her fingers on the side of the teacup, watching the liquid ripple like fear had across White Roaring, leaving it rife with tension in a way Ettenia's bustling capital never had been in her lifetime. Some hurried to wherever they needed to be, voices hushed, children clutched close. Others were pumping fists into the sky, waving wooden stakes, shouting at the top of their lungs. She couldn't decide which was worse: the angry mobs, the increase in Horned Guard, or the Ram's black-clad men.

Everything was terrible.

Flick wanted to tell those people her mother didn't care that they were hurting and mourning. She didn't care for their safety any more than Flick thought the vampires were out to attack them.

There were no limits to what her mother would do, Flick knew now. She saw the Ram's black-clad forces in every shadow, heard the screams of the reporters who had gathered for the truth, tasted the metallic tang of blood in the air as the Athereum meeting hall turned red.

They had been following her ever since that night.

At a different point in her life, she might have run straight to the nearest Horned Guard—which wasn't far, considering how many of them were patrolling the streets since that night—but life was different now. Flick wasn't as naive, nor innocent. The Ram employed them both: The Horned Guard might not kill her on sight like the black-clad forces, but Flick wouldn't be surprised if the Ram had given them instructions to apprehend Flick and bring her in.

"More tea, miss?"

She startled at the waiter's voice. She sensed his judgment of her: a young woman dressed like a boy, sitting in a dark corner with a gray-splotched white kitten in her lap. The place was empty, outside of her. Most businesses were. A string of human kidnappings had made the papers recently, claiming vampires were behind it. In Flick's experience, vampires drank blood, they didn't steal humans away. She wouldn't be surprised if her mother was the real culprit—she had always been good at riling up the crowds with campaigns for her business, why wouldn't that extend to the promotion of fearmongering?

"I would say yes if you actually served any," Flick replied, and immediately resisted the urge to slap a hand over her mouth and pluck the surly words right out of his ears. That was not the speech of a respectable lady. Sometimes, more often than not as of late, a bit of Casimir slipped out of her.

"I beg your pardon?" he said with a sniff.

Flick tipped the teacup. It was too late to retract her statement now. "This barely constitutes tea."

With a *harrumph*, he swiveled on his heel. In her lap, Laith's kitten straightened, lurching her head to watch as he stomped down the stairs. She turned her ice-green eyes to Flick when only the two of them were left.

"I believe you're right, little dollop," Flick said with a sigh. "We really must leave."

This was their life now. Every few hours, they'd relocate to a different coffeehouse or pub, keeping the ledger safe, integrating into the crowds before finding an inn to spend the night, the difference between her mother's estate and the rented room glaring. She kept her head low and senses vigilant as she traversed the streets, avoiding the Horned Guard and shadows alike. She'd exchanged her pastel gowns for loose trousers and shirts in sorry shades of brown that she was slowly beginning to like. Today's outfit was caramel and chocolate, purchased a few days ago on the Linden line of credit before she realized word would reach her mother.

For there was no telling what was being tracked. And Flick had spent long enough here.

One might tell Flick to loosen up and worry less. It had been a week, and surely the Ram had better things to do than hunt for a girl with nothing.

Except she *had* something: The ledger they'd spent days planning and plotting an infiltration into a glittering vampire society in order to steal. It was why Flick had it open in front of her just now. It incriminated the Ram, Laith had told them. It might even contain worse, but among the half thoughts, abbreviations, acronyms, and references to names and places Flick knew nothing about, the majority of the ledger was written in code. She had only just cracked it this morning, the sight of her mother's script making her breath tight.

She'd had a week. Seven excruciating days.

Seven days since she'd discovered her mother was far worse than the head of the colonizing East Jeevant Company: She was the masked monarch of Ettenia too, her influence over the empire and its economy running deeper than any citizen knew.

Seven days since Jin had died and returned as a vampire, then disappeared. Since Laith had killed Penn. Since Matteo and Arthie had gone after him, and Arthie, well—

Arthie had died too.

The teacup rattled when Flick pushed her chair against the table with half a sob. She had tried to understand why Jin would abandon her, but anytime her thoughts went down that road, it ended with pain, so she'd stopped.

Maybe he was different now that he was a vampire. Vampires didn't remember the moment of their turning, but maybe his memory loss extended beyond that. Maybe he'd forgotten their kiss and every whispered word they'd shared. Maybe he'd restarted his search for his parents now that he'd learned from Penn that they might truly be alive.

Flick swiped at her eyes.

She refused to cry.

So much death had been dealt that night, so much heartache. It was as though Spindrift had made the Casimir crew invincible, and without it, without that tether, they had crumbled.

Now Flick was alone, the hole in her chest stretched wider by their absence. And if she was being honest with herself, by the truth of what her mother was too.

Being an only child, she'd always been lonely, but she'd also spent most of her life in a veritable cage, and imagination often made for a good companion. As she had gotten older and her mother had grown more distant, the promise of a world outside the Linden estate had kept the despondency at bay.

But she'd seen the world now, she knew how eager it was to swallow dreams whole. How quickly bitterness swept in and filled every crevice. Flick had tried to remain hopeful, to keep alive the optimism that lived in her soul, but it faded more and more with each passing day.

"Hold on there," she said to herself, rereading her mother's looping, harried scrawl and matching the text with the code Flick had scribbled on a napkin.

What had Jin once said his original surname was? She was highly certain it was Siwang, which meant that—

"Ow!" Flick said as the kitten launched off her lap, claws digging through her trousers. "What is it?"

Footsteps were pounding up the stairs.

Flick shoved the invitation between the pages to mark her place and threw the ledger in her bag. She pulled her tweed hat over her curls and slung her satchel across her chest, then she snatched up the kitten against her protests, trying to find comfort in the bundle of warmth.

She turned and froze, her thoughts rushing to the day the Horned Guard had appeared at her mother's door to whisk her away. That had been terrifying, but only until she'd stumbled into the Horned Guard's carriage and into Jin's lap, someone who was decidedly as far removed from a guard as one could be.

This was nowhere near the same. These were not guards, and the Jin she knew certainly wouldn't be among them.

They were covered in black, unidentifiable but overly conspicuous, and armed to the teeth—she saw the waiting hilts of blades strapped to their arms and legs, the guns holstered within reach.

Her mother's men. Seven of them.

All she could see of them were their eyes, staring at her through the slits in their masks, but she knew they were here for her. So many days of hiding, of constantly looking over her shoulder, and not once had she stopped to plan what she would do if she *did* get caught.

What would Jin do? she asked herself. No, Jin was too suave and too charming to find himself in a situation like this. He would have talked himself out of it already.

Look sharp, came Arthie's voice in her head. Arthie wouldn't see seven assailants and panic. She'd be smug. Seven men for one girl? That meant they thought she was dangerous.

Flick lifted her chin, meeting the eyes of the man closest to her, trying her hardest not to tighten her hand around the bag by her side where she'd kept the ledger safe since she'd been entrusted with it that night. It was almost as impossible as doing up one's own corset laces.

"Where is the ledger?" the man asked.

Don't panic, don't panic.

"The tea is fairly bland, if you were contemplating some," she said.

"It will be easier if you come with us quietly," the man said. His slate-gray gaze was hard and remorseless. He turned to the man at his right. "Apprehend that thing."

She should have been relieved he was more concerned with Laith's cat than the ledger, but she knew what these men were capable of.

"*That thing* is a kitten, and she has a name," Flick said, aggrieved on the babe's behalf. There was power in a name. Identity. Admittedly, Flick hadn't decided on one for the kitten yet. She'd plucked the ball of fur up while fleeing the Athereum meeting hall with the ledger, and though she belonged to Laith, Flick had grown ever more fond of her every day since. "It's—it's—"

"I don't care," the man said, and gestured to the others. All six of them swept forward.

Two grabbed for the kitten, but she leaped from Flick's arms with mystical fluidity, scurrying back against the wall and hissing up at the men.

"It sounds like a bloody snake!" one of them exclaimed, shrinking back.

A *snake*? No, she was too precious of a gem to be likened to a snake. She was a gem! What was the name she'd considered that night? Pearl? Diamond? No, no—nothing so pompous. *Opal.* Yes, that was it. Opal was the perfect name for her.

You're distracting yourself again.

"Leave her alone!" Flick shouted.

They didn't seem to hear her. She took a step back as the other four stepped toward her. She had no pistol or knife—nor did she know how to use either. She didn't even have her lighter anymore.

She gripped the dusty chair rail behind her and tried to kick the man closest to her, but she was still so new to wearing trousers that when she swung out her leg, she forgot she wasn't kicking through the many layers of a gown and nearly teetered off-balance.

They didn't even laugh. She felt their pity, heard it in their silence. When they began working for her mother, had they ever thought they'd be in a position where they had to apprehend her own daughter?

Had her mother thought that? Did they even know who the Ram really was?

The questions flooded her with a barrage of emotion, drowning the resistance out of her.

She didn't fight as they clamped hot fingers around her arms, whirled her around and gripped her wrists. She didn't fight as they cornered her precious kitten—her Opal—and dropped her in a basket, throwing the lid on tight before she could escape. She didn't fight as they shoved her down the stairs and dragged her past the smug-faced waiter to the doors of the tea shop.

Two frosted-glass doors, almost and yet nothing like the doors of Spindrift, that place that had slowly been on its way to becoming home. That crew that had slowly become family.

It didn't matter what her mother thought.

Flick couldn't go without a fight. Not this time. She planted her feet on the floor and pulled back against the men, yanking herself out of their hold because they weren't expecting it.

No one ever expected much out of Flick.

Except Arthie and Jin and the rest of the crew. She wasn't the same girl that was apprehended in the Linden estate and taken away like a common criminal.

That was Felicity Linden. This was Flick.

She staggered away as the men shouted, and turned a frantic circle around the room, searching for another way out. The waiter locked eyes with her and must have seen something in her gaze, for he yelped and hurried into the kitchens. She fought against the panic slowly crowding her senses. *Smell.* She inhaled that bitter, sorry excuse for tea.

Feel. She felt hot. *Taste.* She tasted the sweat trickling from her brow. *Hear.* She heard the roar of her pulse pounding in her ears.

See. She saw the seven men assessing her like she was a cornered animal.

Two of them lurched toward her and she dropped to the ground, unsure of what to do next. The others surrounded her, leaving the pair with the basket by the doors. *Stop thinking, love.* Jin's voice in her head was a welcome distraction, and not exactly new—she would be lying if she said she hadn't had a few conversations with him that way. *They're strong, but you're small.*

She crawled beneath their grasp, shot to her feet, and squeezed between them, dashing toward the pair of men carrying Opal, ducking when one of them lunged. She went straight for the basket in the other man's arms, but his grip was steely and Flick felt silly for thinking she could snatch it from him. He threw the basket to the other man. Opal's cry went straight through Flick's resolve before she heard another, more terrifying sound: the hiss of a blade being pulled out of its sheath.

"We're meant to bring her in alive!" one of the men shouted.

The man in front of her dipped his chin, his voice a rasp. "Alive doesn't mean we can't scratch her up."

He swung his knife. Flick jumped back, bumping into another one of the men who made to grab her, but she ducked again, digging into her bag for anything she could use against them. It was mostly stationery, pens and paper pads, along with a box of razor blades that she used to sharpen her pencils. And the ledger, of course. She pulled out a bottle of water and threw it at the man nearest her. It crashed against his nose and fell, shattering when it hit the floor. Water and glass sprayed the floorboards. He slipped and fell, tripping another one of the men in the process.

Flick quieted her triumph. She wasn't delusional—she couldn't fight them. She needed to run. She leaped for the man holding Opal's basket. She didn't bother trying to wrench it free; this time, she tore off the lid.

Opal hopped out with a low-pitched yowl, ears flat against her head. The glint of a knife came arcing toward Flick, and she threw up the rattan lid at the last second. The blade ripped through and caught the inside of her arm, tearing past her sleeve and straight down her skin. Blood spilled free, drenching the fabric.

Flick screamed. A few of the tea shop's staff were screaming too.

As the men looked to their leader for direction, Flick stumbled toward the door and yanked it open, ears ringing as the sweep caught the broken glass with a high-pitched screech.

Opal darted out into the street, and Flick followed her into the cold Ettenian winter, arm pinned to her stomach. People stopped what they were doing and rushed out of her way. Nearby members of the Horned Guard leaped to attention, shouting at her to halt. Flick ducked past them, heart pounding. Arthie wasn't here to save her. Jin wasn't either.

In front of a florist, one of the Horned Guards caught her, his arm slinging around her middle. "Stop!"

Flick screamed and sank her teeth into his flesh, tasting the salt of his sweat, watching Opal get farther away. He released her with a howl, and Flick didn't pause—she kept running, shoes pounding on the cobblestones. She could barely think past the pain, past the blood staining her clothes, making everything that much worse.

She kept running, eventually reaching the side of White Roaring where the cobblestones were crumbling, the buildings just the same. The midday sun tucked behind gauzy clouds and smokestack exhales. The mobs echoed in the distance, trying to storm the Athereum walls. She glanced back; the men were still on her heels.

She'd seen what they'd done to the reporters in the Athereum meeting hall. She'd seen what they'd done to Raze and his foundry. On her mother's orders. *My mother is a monster.*

And that was when she smelled it: fish.

It assaulted her like a brick, strong and almost putrid. Flick gagged, but Opal perked up, darting straight for an alleyway between two dilapidated apartment buildings faster than Flick could keep up. She didn't think it was any safer than the men chasing them out in the open, but she couldn't bear to lose Opal either. She ran after her, hissing when one of her shirt buttons poked at the wound.

It didn't take much to find Opal. She was a pristine white ball of fur in the middle of the shadowed passage, and she was biting into a fish, eyes narrowing when she straightened to chew on her catch.

Odd.

White Roaring was a city by the sea, yes, but Flick didn't think that warranted a fresh, whole fish in the middle of a dark alley several streets from the docks. No, this was too out of place. Almost . . . almost as if it had been placed there deliberately.

A trap, Flick realized a moment too late.

The fish moved, as if dragged on an invisible string. Flick squinted into the shadows—not invisible. It *was* being dragged away, and Opal, the wretched babe, was following it with a playful warble.

"Opal, no," Flick whispered as loudly as she could, her heart sinking as the kitten kept going.

Her arm was throbbing and bleeding, sweat pooling down her back and her brow despite the chill.

She raced after the cat, aware of the men approaching from behind. If this alleyway was a dead end, Flick would soon be too. The fish bounced along the ground, Opal bounding to keep up, until it slammed against a wooden door.

The door opened a smidge and the fish disappeared.

Then it opened again, and Flick dove for Opal, her hands closing around air as the kitten disappeared too. And before she knew what was happening, *she* was being dragged inside. A hand clamped around her mouth and the door closed again with a soft *sitch*. Flick struggled, trying to make sense of where she was. It was too dark to decipher anything. It smelled of fish and rotting wood, like a place that had been abandoned. It didn't sound anything like it though. There was a cacophony of hushed voices and movement.

And then she was dragged to a halt into what felt to be the center of a room.

"Who—"

"Hush, love," someone said. The voice came from somewhere ahead of her. "Don't want Mother Dearest finding us."

Flick's heart leaped. She knew that voice.

A match hissed in the sudden silence and a lantern came to life, illuminating a room full of barrels and cargo chests. In the middle, legs dangling from either side of a crate, was a boy with ink-glossed hair and dark eyes, clothed in a tailored suit.

"Hello, Felicity," Jin Casimir said, sly, smooth, and stunning as ever. "I've missed you."

4
JIN

The floppy, stinky fish had been Chester's idea. While Jin was on the streets beating information out of every lead he could find, the three pint-size lordlings of Spindrift—Chester, Reni, and Felix—had been hard at work locating Flick. As well as Jin, and even Arthie.

Someone had to take charge, Chester had said with his arms crossed, when Jin snuck out of the empty schoolroom where he'd interrogated Coll and found the three of them waiting outside. They nearly caught the side of his umbrella when he thought they were Horned Guards.

You left us for an entire week, Felix added.

Alone, Reni said hollowly.

They'd been in the dark since that night at the Athereum hall, and had taken matters into their own hands.

As guilty as the words had made Jin feel, it wasn't as though *they* had gone through what he had. They looked at Jin as if this was just another Wednesday, when in reality, he had died.

He couldn't look at the sky and celebrate a rare cloudless sky anymore. He *needed* Ettenia's usual gloom. He couldn't take a stroll and follow his nose to fresh, buttery pastries and sweet jam, no. His food was inside people.

He winced at that image. The last thing Jin remembered of his life was agreeing to become a vampire and Arthie sinking her fangs into his skin. When he woke on the Athereum floor amid fallen reporters and vampires and black-clad attackers alike, he was alone.

Arthie was gone. Matteo too. Flick and Laith and the kitten were nowhere to be seen. He was overwhelmed and ravenous, but the Athereum vampires were there.

They'd turned up their noses at him, except for Sidharth, Penn's second-in-command. He'd helped him get clean and eventually fed. Jin didn't know if he liked it. He could barely remember the night, but he hadn't had another sip since.

"Jin?" Flick asked, aghast in the reeking storeroom.

She was different too. Jin had always thought Felicity Linden dazzled in a gown, but Felicity Linden in trousers and a shirt with neat lines? Wicked knives, it was something else. The tweed clung to her curves, pleats following the lines of her thighs. He would have expected every button of her shirt to be closed, but the top two were undone, framing a tiny splotch of her dark skin between the cream-colored fabric.

He couldn't look away. He wanted to sweep toward her, hold her shy gaze, and lower his lips to that skin she'd bared to tease him. He wanted to feel the lush press of her lips against his again. To press his brow to hers and ask if she had missed him.

Chester cleared his throat.

Right.

"You're bleeding," Jin said, holding himself back from going to her aid. He didn't trust himself yet. *I'm not some feral beast.* No, but he also didn't know this new body as well as he would have liked. His strengths were still surprising him. On the floor between them, the kitten rolled over with the fish in her claws, back thumping against one of the many old crates stacked about.

Flick reached for her bleeding arm. He heard the hitch in her already labored breathing when she remembered. That he was no longer human. That he was a vampire. That he was what her mother absolutely loathed.

Reni understood, being a young vampire himself. "I have a kit. Sit, my lady. I will tend to it."

It should have made Jin feel better, seeing how sure Reni was that *he* wouldn't drink her dry, an indication that one day he would reach that point. But when Flick glanced at Jin with hesitation, it made something spike within him, a feeling he couldn't quite place.

And to think, he would have known exactly what it was like to live and act and function as a vampire if Arthie had just thought to open her mouth and trust him.

Flick finally sat on one of the crates, the wood creaking under her weight. She tossed the curls out of her face and lifted her gaze to his. "You're all right."

Jin nodded.

"I—" She paused, and Jin thought her lips were closing around the letter *m*, closing around the word *miss*, but she stopped herself. Her eyelids fluttered. "Good. I was worried."

"It'll take a lot to keep me down," he replied, but with only half of his usual charm because he had missed her too. Terribly.

"And Arthie—" She stopped, unsure how to phrase her next sentiment.

"She's not dead. She's a vampire," Jin said, and paused. "Too."

Something flickered in her dusky eyes at the addition of *too*. He didn't know what he'd meant by it. Was he asking her if she accepted him? Was he trying to remind her of what he was now, in case she'd forgotten? In case she didn't recall watching him die by her mother's hand?

In the week they'd spent apart, the threads between them had frayed. As if their burgeoning bond was a house that they'd been polishing and furnishing before they'd disappeared, leaving dust to settle and cobwebs to collect in the corners.

She licked her lips and he wondered if she remembered their kiss.

His last kiss, drowning him in that meadow of wildflowers and sunlight, before he'd died. Reni returned with a tin case and bent beside her to inspect her wound. It wasn't deep, Jin surmised with relief.

"Wasn't she one before?" Flick asked, nose scrunching with confusion. "She's the one who . . ."

Who turned you, she wanted to say.

"She was half a vampire," Jin said. "Not that she told me so herself. It's what I've gathered."

Flick nodded carefully. "My mother—I don't know what to call her anymore."

Jin looked away. There he'd been, concerned about how she felt about him when her entire life had been upended.

"Whatever you like," Chester piped up. Jin had told him, Felix, and Reni everything. "You can call her a bad egg or a hornswoggler, maybe. I called my mum a ratbag for abandoning me by a fishmonger. Your mum is a lot worse, and the possibilities really are endless."

Flick laughed, the end of it teetering to half a sob. "Her men have been after me ever since that night," she said finally, and Jin didn't know if she spoke the words with blame or if he was simply feeling the guilt of it. She sucked in a breath as Reni swiped a cloth down her arm. "They won't stop. And when I can get away from them in the shadows, I have to worry about the Horned Guard in broad daylight."

Jin nodded. "You'll be safe with us."

"With you?" Flick asked plainly, looking about the room. Jin saw her point. "White Roaring is in shambles."

Her throat bobbed with a swallow, as if she was trying hard to keep it together, and Jin realized she'd never seen the chaos that he and Arthie did on a regular basis. To go from none to this level of unrest could not be easy—it was tumultuous enough for him. But he would keep her safe. So long as she was by his side, he would make sure of it.

She closed her eyes for a moment and opened them again. "What have you four been up to?"

"We just found 'im," Chester proclaimed. "We've been looking for the three of you for days now. I know we lost a lot, but we can't give up."

"No one's given up, Chester boy," Jin said, and then answered Flick's question. "I've been dodging that mess out there and following leads on my parents. It didn't cross my mind that there might be clues in the ledger."

Understanding flickered across her face, followed by hurt. "And that's why you came looking for me."

Jin clenched his jaw. He'd considered looking for her, hadn't he? But he'd been so lost in his thoughts, in his anger, in his pain, in trying to understand this new craving for blood that he simply hadn't gotten to that point yet.

He'd been so concerned that she might hate him now that he was a vampire that he hadn't even thought to give her a chance to prove that herself.

And if he'd dallied any longer, the Ram might have kidnapped her. Killed her.

"Jin knows you're not a damsel in need of saving," Chester said matter-of-factly. "And besides, he needed us to find you."

Jin could have kissed Chester just then. He didn't feel any less guilty, but the words drew a small smile out of Flick.

"Whatever would I do without you?" she said to Chester.

"I missed you, Flick," Chester said. His white-blond head bounced from her to Jin as Reni tied off a bandage around Flick's arm. "Well? Shall we get moving, then?"

"Oh? And where to?" Jin asked, suddenly wishing he was alone with her.

"To the Athereum, of course. Ivor said that's where Arthie and Matteo are. You didn't think we were trading Spindrift for an old fisherman's storeroom, did you?"

Flick scrunched her nose and opened her mouth, looking as though she was about to agree.

"We're doing no such thing," Jin said. "They're my parents, and we don't need Arthie to find them. We're going to do it ourselves."

No sooner had the words left his mouth than a knock sounded on the wooden door of the storeroom.

Chester looked at the floor, drawing a line in the dust with the toe of his shoe.

Jin sighed.

5
ARTHIE

Arthie had always known that her brother was resourceful, but she hadn't anticipated that he would find Flick before she did, although she supposed it was a matter of who Chester had gotten to first, the little bugger.

Her chest rose as she steeled herself.

"He's your brother," Matteo said. "There's love at the heart of his anger and pain, or he wouldn't feel either."

The care in his eyes unsettled her. A question bubbled to her lips: *What do you want in return for your kindness?* But something held her back. That same something sent a rush of warmth through her instead.

"All right?" Matteo asked.

Arthie nodded.

And in true, never-one-to-shy-away fashion, Jin opened the door, the look on his face telling her that he had known she was on the other side of it.

He was alive. Whole. She could still picture the smoke wisping from the bullet hole in his chest. A knot loosened in hers. It wasn't as though she hadn't seen him open his eyes after the Ram had shot him and Arthie had turned him, but so much had happened that night that Arthie hadn't realized how terribly she wanted to see him until now.

"Never thought I'd find you in a place this stinky," she said before she could stop herself. She pinched her lips together.

This was new, having to consider her words before speaking to him. Jin was the one constant in her life; he'd been a part of her world longer than even her parents had been. How had they reached this point?

Because of me. That tiny inner voice had gotten a lot louder lately.

He gave her a mock laugh, more than one emotion playing behind his dark eyes. He looked her over, and she wondered if he was assessing her or searching for her fatal wound. "Back in a suit, I see."

Her armor, each layer protecting her heart—even from herself. She'd been left bare a week ago, as exposed as the thin sari she'd wrapped around herself. No more. In the holster at her side, Calibore's presence reassured her as Jin once did.

"As much as I'm not looking forward to being surrounded by so much fish, can we come in now?" Matteo asked beside her. "My arm grows tired."

He was holding an umbrella over both his and Arthie's heads, shielding them from the Ettenian sun. There wasn't much to shield from, but shield he did.

"Come in, come in!" Chester said grandly, and Arthie had the sense he was pretending to be Matteo's butler.

Arthie stepped inside, Matteo closing the umbrella and the crumbling wooden door behind them, gagging throughout.

"Why are you here?" Jin demanded, as if they were intruding upon his fishy kingdom. He looked straight at Arthie. She wasn't sure if he was ignoring Matteo, or if he was angry enough with her not to have even noticed him.

Arthie swallowed. What was wrong with her? She was usually quick with her responses, rarely letting anyone sway her. She prided herself in being resilient, unwavering. She was made out of stone, but wasn't he the one who had fashioned it around her? Who was she without the one she'd built herself up with?

"The same reason you are," she finally replied. "For the ledger."

"Arthie!"

Flick rounded the half wall and threw her arms around her. Arthie stiffened, before some part of her relaxed. Flick was an entirely different girl than when Arthie had first given her Matteo's address back in Spindrift. Her wide-eyed innocence was gone, as were her pastel gowns and unblemished skin.

In the dim light, Flick pulled away and met Arthie's eyes with a shy smile. "I—I thought you were dead."

"I was," Arthie replied, as if it happened every day. In reality, she had been terrified. She'd long considered herself unafraid of death, but Matteo was right. She had much to do, and she couldn't die just yet. "For a few seconds. Matteo brought me back."

Arthie found it suddenly impossible to look at any of the others. She rapped her knuckles on the crate beside her. "Right. On to business, we—"

"'Brought me back,' eh? That's one way to word it," Matteo said, his gaze heavy on her. He might as well have been undressing her for the way he stared. Arthie felt her skin tingle in response.

Flick made a surprised yelp, no different than the high society ladies who tittered at the sight of an exposed ankle. Arthie met his eyes, waiting for that spike of irritation, that irked tick that should have risen in her blood. Instead, she was suddenly shy.

"What's that supposed to mean?" Jin growled at him, and the kitten stopped her chomping and flattened her ears against her head. *That* was when Arthie felt a spike, only it wasn't irritation or anger, it was satisfaction. Like she was a child who'd done something forbidden and her elder brother didn't approve.

In answer, Matteo found himself a rickety chair and sat back like a pleased and pompous king. He propped his elbow on the arm of it, never once taking his eyes off Arthie.

Flick looked between him and Arthie and opened her mouth. Whatever she was about to say, Arthie decided she did not need to hear it.

"We didn't reunite for small talk, did we?" Why was her voice more hoarse than it needed to be? "Can we redirect our attention to that ledger?"

And not what I might have done with Ettenia's most eligible bachelor in a bedroom of his own house.

"Oh, Arthie," Flick said with the edge of a smile. "I missed you too."

Matteo laughed, and it sent a shiver up Arthie's spine. She was losing it, she truly was. She crossed her arms, but Arthie *had* missed her. And the crew when they were together.

And Jin.

Who was now most certainly pretending not to pay attention. He had every right to be angry at her—unless, of course, he was angrier after what Matteo said. But could he understand that she'd kept so much of herself from him out of fear? Out of a loathing for herself and what she'd done before she'd pulled him out of that fire?

"We *were* focusing on the ledger before you two interrupted," Jin said.

And Arthie, try as she might, couldn't fling a response back quickly enough. No, she felt as though she really had interrupted them. Matteo was watching her as though he knew what she was thinking. As though he had been there, a silent part of her years with Jin.

"Now we all can," she finally said.

Jin rapped his umbrella on the dusty floor. "Well, long story short, the ledger is rubbish. The Ram's already emptied at least one warehouse."

"No—" Flick started.

Arthie snorted at his quick dismissal. "So you've decided it's completely useless because of a single warehouse?"

"Maybe out of—"

"Oh, are you the only one who can make educated guesses based on the facts we pick up?" Jin snapped.

"I've been reading—"

"I came here because of your parents," Arthie seethed.

"And I should fall at your feet, is that it?" Jin seethed back.

"*Enough*," Matteo said over them both. "Poor Flick hasn't been able to get a single word in. This won't do." He pointed from Jin to Arthie. "Can we agree that the Ram is our enemy?"

Arthie felt like a child being scolded, but she nodded. Jin did too.

"Right, and can we agree we need to find Jin's parents, for you, Jin, of course, but also to strip the Ram of, essentially, her allies?"

Jin laughed without mirth. "Because there's always a reason for what Arthie does."

"Are we to assume you don't care for the same?" Matteo asked, still in his chair.

Jin eyed him. "Let's not forget that the Ram killed me, Andoni." He gestured in Arthie's direction. "And since when do you speak for her?"

"Since your spat began to affect everyone here. We're going to need to work together, so get yourselves in order."

Jin scoffed. "You were barely invested when we *were* working together."

"A proper investment takes time," Matteo said, and then his

features darkened. "Let's not forget she killed Penn, and I—"

He stopped when his voice cracked. Chester widened his eyes in the silence. Outside, the winter wind howled.

"You what?" Jin pushed.

"I have a past with her."

"*With* her?" Flick asked. Arthie almost snorted.

"Not like that! How long do you think I've lived for?" Matteo's eyes widened at her expression. "I don't want to talk about it."

Arthie would have allowed the secret, once, but Matteo was a part of their crew now. He was invested, as he said himself, and so were the others. They deserved to know about the night he walked through the trees.

About the Wolf of White Roaring.

"*You* know though," Flick said to Arthie. "Don't you?"

Arthie bit the inside of her cheek. Life had been a lot simpler when she was in charge and no one asked questions, but their dynamic had changed that night. They had become less of a crew and more of a family. More attuned to emotions, more charged.

"She's right," Arthie said softly. "They deserve to know."

One relationship had already been torn apart by a secret.

Matteo sighed, but it was more theatrical than truly upset. "Well, sit down, because this will blow you away."

Flick didn't need to be told twice.

Jin didn't move.

Matteo waited with a pointed look, and after working his jaw and burning holes through Matteo with his glare, Jin finally sat down, wrinkling his nose at the smell.

"You may know me as Ettenia's most prolific painter," Matteo began, "but when I look in the mirror—"

"You can't see yourself in the mirror," Chester quipped, plopping on top of one of the crates with his chin on his hands.

"In the figurative sense. Don't interrupt me." Matteo drew in a careful breath, the first sign of real emotion.

Arthie held herself still against the sudden desire to step up to him and comfort him.

"I'm the Wolf of White Roaring."

The kitten continued tearing at her fish in the deafening silence. Jin let out a croak. Flick matched it. Arthie didn't know why she was relieved to see that Flick didn't scamper away in sudden fear. As if it was *her* secret he'd just shared.

Chester sat up straighter than a child's pop-out toy, eyes lighting with excitement. "Is that not aces?"

Matteo responded with a shaky laugh. He was looking at Flick and Jin, and for the first time, Arthie realized he *cared* what they thought. At some point between them showing up on his doorstep with threats and now, he'd begun to value their opinion.

"The Wolf of White Roaring," Flick whispered.

Arthie was waiting for Jin's response.

"And?" he finally deadpanned, in a tone so far from that deep, inquisitive interest he once exuded that it made even Arthie flinch.

"And—and I've killed scores of people," Matteo said. "I've—" he stopped. Arthie could very nearly hear his throat closing up.

"I know what the Wolf of White Roaring did," Jin said.

Flick gave him a glare and then looked at Matteo, choosing her words carefully. "Not—goodness, not to write away the deaths that happened that night, but if I'm to guess, my mother's to blame, isn't she?"

When Matteo didn't answer, Jin took a deep breath.

"We know how the Ram rose to power," Jin said. "Penn himself confirmed the Wolf's massacre"—he had the decency to look apologetic when Matteo winced—"was brought about by the Ram, no?"

Matteo looked at the floor.

"You're still the same crucial member of this crew you always were," Flick said softly.

"It changes nothing," Jin added. "I don't know if I'd call it aces, but I'll be judging you the same way I always did."

"With scorn?" Matteo ventured.

"Of course," Jin replied loftily.

Matteo couldn't hide the hint of a smile. "Much obliged."

And suddenly, Arthie felt as though she was watching the conversation from the outside, as though they had formed an understanding and acceptance she couldn't comprehend. She *wanted* Flick and Jin to accept Matteo, but seeing it was different. Seeing it made her wonder if she should have allowed Jin the opportunity, at least, to accept her.

"But why?" Flick whispered.

Matteo glanced at Arthie. "I've been thinking about it since you asked me, and now that we know *who* the Ram is, I might have an idea. Lady Linden was in the papers because of a scandal surrounding her family years before that night. Her father had been exposed for having an affair with a high official, and everything they had—their ventures, their social standing, whatever else—came crashing down. Her mother killed him and shortly spiraled, leaving Lady Linden to pick up the pieces."

Flick stared in wide-eyed shock. She hadn't known.

"Murder runs in the family," Jin said.

"Indeed. I'll never know for certain, but my mother was once an official. She took leave from her job shortly around the Linden scandal. I often wondered if she was the one Lady Linden's father had that affair with, and it seems more plausible now. By choosing me to become the Wolf of White Roaring, Lady Linden was enacting some form of twisted revenge," Matteo explained.

He remained unsure, but to Arthie, the Ram choosing him arbitrarily was less believable than the Ram enacting vengeance on the child of someone who had ruined her own childhood.

"She was in the papers often as she restored the family name in the years after."

It was no surprise, then, that Lady Linden remained obsessed with her image to this day.

"Gathering what she needed for her rise to monarch, no doubt," Arthie said. "You were the last piece of her plan."

"And I'd had no hope of retaliation until the lot of you turned up," Matteo said quietly.

It was Chester who reached for him first. He squeezed between the others and threw his arms around him. Jin exhaled through his teeth; Flick looked at her hands. Arthie thought of her last moments in Ceylan.

The Ram had hurt them all.

"And retaliate we will," Arthie said, before she tilted her head at Matteo. "But is it retaliation that you want?"

Matteo thought on it for a moment. "I suppose I want peace. I want to live again." He lowered his voice, directing his next words at her alone in a tone that was pensive, imploring. "With you. For you. And if retaliation is what *you* want, then I want it too."

Arthie swallowed, breaking away from the ferocity in his eyes, heightened by the knowledge that the others were watching. Did she hear him correctly? Did he want what she wanted, simply because she did?

"Which is to say, we need to find your parents, Jin," Matteo said, granting her relief. "I'm sure you've seen the streets. Horned Guard are everywhere, fear mounting against vampires once again. She's riling the people up, turning them into vigilantes. Worse, she's done kidnapping vampires alone; she's taking humans too."

"I heard," Jin said, pinching his lips. "Was destroying half of White Roaring's press not enough?"

"The more anger toward vampires, the better," Arthie said. "We were there that night. She doesn't care for humans any more than she does vampires. We're the same to her."

"If the Ram knew to turn you into the Wolf of White Roaring, how do you think she knew about vampires before the public did?" Flick asked, clearly still tangled in the history she'd learned.

"I don't know," Matteo said quietly. "I've often wondered that myself. Pondering over the Ram can be infuriating at times."

"We have more pressing matters to attend to," Jin said.

Matteo nodded. "Now that we know your parents are alive and a part of the Ram's operation to weaponize vampires, they're a crucial part of taking her down."

"Are they?" Jin asked. "Penn only said they created an inoculation for humans that was being used on vampires. We don't even have confirmation that they're *alive*."

"Penn got confirmation," Matteo said. Arthie didn't know if she wanted Jin to know that so soon.

"So he lied?" Jin's brow furrowed, then he shifted his umbrella from one hand to the other, his next words a whisper. "They're alive." He turned to Arthie and looked away. "They're—why would he lie to us? After the trust we ourselves placed in him?"

Arthie had wondered the same.

"I don't think blaming him will do us any favors," Matteo said. "Is this not a good thing? You almost sound like you're trying to argue against finding them."

"I'm against *using* them," Jin snapped. "You're referring to them as if they're round two of the Ram's ledger, as if they're an inanimate object we can retrieve and use to do our bidding."

"They're as much a tool to the Ram as the ledger was," Matteo countered. "A far more substantial one at that."

"And you're deciding to make this about you," Arthie said to Jin.

Jin went perfectly still. The lanterns set on various crates cast his unmoving shadow along the wall.

"Yes, I think I am," Jin began before Matteo lifted his hands.

"What did I say *only* a moment ago?"

But Jin wasn't finished with her. "Just as you made the past ten years about yourself."

His tone was so curt it was almost comical. Somewhere in the fishy mess, Chester chortled, but Arthie didn't think it was funny.

"Everything we did over the past ten years was for *us*," Arthie flung back. "Spindrift, our cons, stealing Calibore. Did you not benefit as much as I did?"

There was more she wanted to say. More that bubbled to her lips but she fought down, like how she'd spent just as much time trying to find his parents, following leads, reaching out to people she could trust, if only because of the blackmail she had on them. How Spindrift had started as a way to distract him, not her.

"I'd know how to answer that if I knew you," Jin replied.

Any response Arthie could have thrown back shriveled in her suddenly parched throat.

There was no one else alive who knew her as well as he did, but how could she tell him that? How, when his eyes were bright with anger, when everyone was staring at them, waiting to hear what she would say next?

"Maybe I was right not to trust you," she said instead. "Look at us, now that you know the truth. We've never been further apart."

Jin snorted, as if he'd been waiting for something more. "Of course you'd say something like that."

"What's that supposed to mean?"

"You only ever deflect and hide and swallow how you truly feel. All that talk of vengeance and getting back at the peakies for what they'd done to you? It's become your shield. A drug you keep taking to numb everything else."

Arthie pulled back as if he'd slapped her. She tried to do what he said she did best: to tamp down her emotions, to bottle them back up, but she was beginning to spiral; that bottle was starting to fracture, leaking from every crack.

They'd fought before. They might not have been siblings by blood, but they were in every other sense of the word. They'd fought over everything and nothing. None of those fights made their bond feel so fragile; none of them made the act of amending seem so distant.

None of those fights had ever been so loud and truly, terribly angry.

"I almost died that night because of this shield," she said, and then her voice dropped. "You didn't even come to see if I'd lived."

A line feathered along his jaw at that. "As if you did much more than turn me and flee. You might as well have left me for dead."

Arthie stared at him. "Left you for—"

"That's enough!" Flick snapped, stepping between them. The storeroom fell silent. She was breathing hard, her blood roaring under her skin. Arthie could hear it. "Stop. Both of you. I know you're hurting. I know you're angry, but haven't you always said, Jin, that Arthie has her reasons? And haven't you, Arthie, always said that Jin felt more deeply than anyone else you've known? Is that not enough to understand each other?"

Jin crossed his arms, his answer spelled out clear as a rare, cloudless Ettenian sky.

Flick sighed and waved the ledger between them. It was open to a page marked with a card, the ribbon fluttering loosely.

"As I've been trying to tell you both since we reunited: I found something," she said.

The change in Jin was instant, like a rubber band snapping loose, allowing the air back into the room.

"About my parents?" he asked.

Flick didn't respond, only turned away and walked over to an old chair where she proceeded to make herself comfy with the kitten curled up along one side of it. The others moved closer too, and Arthie remained where she was to slump against the wall.

Was what Jin said true? Was she hiding behind a shield? She wasn't naive; she knew she masked much of what she felt because emotions existed to drag her down and nothing else, but was there more to it than that?

"We could be in the comfort of the Athereum right now," Matteo groused. "And safety, mind you."

But getting back inside the Athereum was as difficult as it was getting out—regardless if one was a member or not. The mobs were packed tight against the walls, some trying to climb the gate, the guards doing their utmost not to incite violence upon those who were inciting violence.

Arthie willed her feet to move her closer to the group. Jin avoided her. Matteo gave her a small smile. The three of them gathered around Flick as the kitten leaped onto her lap, her dove gray tail more luxurious than a high society lady's hair.

Flick picked her up with a little laugh. "I've named her, by the way."

Arthie half expected Laith to walk through the door and pick up the kitten. To rub at her chin and glance at Arthie, somehow seeing straight through her mask to her eternal disquiet. When she blinked, the vision disappeared. In its place, Arthie saw blood blossoming across his chest, unfurling like delicate crimson petals over the white of his robes.

"Opal," Flick said, brushing the kitten between her eyes. A purr started in her throat.

Chester *ooh*ed.

Matteo gave her a nod of approval. "It suits her as well as Flick suits you."

Flick ducked her head with a smile, and when Opal hopped to the floor, Flick turned back to the ledger, readjusting the collar of her shirt and rubbing her injured arm with a wince for the umpteenth time. She didn't appear to have acclimated to her new attire just yet.

"Now," Flick said, gesturing to the book. "The reason why I don't think the ledger is rubbish is because the majority is written in code, and very well hard to crack. I'm sure Penn might have been deciphering it, but I didn't find any of his notes, so I've been deciphering it myself over the past week, mainly using my knowledge of my mother's handwriting to do so."

"So she might have moved certain warehouses and smaller operations to throw us off her scent," Matteo said.

"Precisely," Flick said with a nod. "Now, on to what I've found. How likely is it that the Siwangs are in the same place as the East Jeevant Company vampires?"

Arthie narrowed her eyes. "Is that even possible? Are you talking about the vampires the EJC has been weaponizing? They're being shipped to battlefields everywhere, are they not? The Ram hasn't once stopped colonizing since she became monarch."

Flick shook her head. "Not according to her notes. It appears they're being shipped to one place. They're dated differently, and the quantities vary, but the cargo routes are the same. There's no indication they were moved after either."

"Strange," Arthie said. "I assumed she was already utilizing them."

"That does tally," Matteo offered, glancing over. "Vampires have only recently been going missing. The operation must still be in its early stages."

Arthie didn't know if she should have felt relief then, that the vampires weren't being weaponized just yet, or worse because that meant the kidnapped vampires' suffering was being prolonged.

"Penn told us the vampires are administered one dose of the silver inoculation to immobilize them," Matteo continued. "*Then* they're starved."

"None of this confirms my parents are with them," Jin said.

"A gamble, but isn't it unlikely that the Ram would trust anyone other than the ones who know the inoculation inside and out?" Matteo countered.

Inoculation. It was a disheartening reminder that the Siwangs' discovery for the betterment of people, to protect them, was being abused in such a way.

Jin shook his head. "I'm not—I refuse to go off of anything that isn't certain."

Arthie recognized that wariness in his eyes, the set of his jaw. He had spent far too many years tracking down leads that resulted in dead ends. He couldn't handle another.

Flick flipped another page of the ledger and froze. "Jin, what are your parents' names?"

Jin leaned over her shoulder. "Shaw and Sora, why?"

She swallowed, clearly flustered at his proximity, but Jin was too frazzled himself to notice. She showed him the page, and Arthie watched the color drain from Jin's face, something she didn't think could happen to a vampire.

"*SS and SS to administer before release,*" Jin read. He looked up, his eyes meeting Arthie's first before looking away. "And here—*Siwang*. That's them. Shaw Siwang and Sora Siwang. It was dated less than two months ago."

That was clearly not the response Flick was hoping for. Her face fell. *Shipped to one place*, she had said. That meant they were being sent *out* of the country.

Arthie went still. "They're not in Ettenia."

It was no wonder none of her leads had ever amounted to anything. It was no wonder Jin had searched and searched to no avail. His parents weren't even *in* Ettenia.

"Where are the vampires being sent?" Arthie asked.

Once the words left her lips, she felt a chill roll through her body, as if she knew the answer before either of them could say it. As if she'd known her life would always take her back to where it all began and ended.

Flick lifted her head. "Ceylan."

6
FLICK

It wasn't Flick's first time riffling through the Ram's ledger, but time hadn't made it any easier. The sight of her mother's script transported Flick back to the Linden Estate, where she would try to catch her mother's attention for a conversation over tea or breakfast or anytime, really, while Lady Linden jotted away at something or another. The vanity in her words leaped off the page, the self-importance loud in the way she had signed off on the documents that were folded and tucked into the ledger.

Everywhere Flick looked was another reminder: Her mother was not a good person.

The signs had been blatant since Flick was imprisoned inside her own house, but a part of her had known long before she'd even begun forging out of her bedroom. She'd simply never pieced together the sentence. She'd never thought the words with such certainty and finality until now.

And it made Flick utterly sad.

Lonely too, in a way, until the emotion was washed away by a sudden presence drawing near, sifting through her thoughts.

"Close it, love," Jin said beside her gently. Neither Matteo nor Arthie were paying them any heed. "That's it."

She dropped the cover and immediately felt a knot loosen in her chest.

"Better?" he asked.

How did he know she was struggling? That she saw her mother on every page? She tilted her head back, and when her curls fell away, it was to find him close. Her lips parted in surprise, and his eyes followed the movement. His features softened, the anger in his gaze that he'd held since their reunion slipping away until it was just him again.

The old Jin.

The one she had kissed in an alcove of the Athereum meeting hall. The one she had watched from afar for weeks as she worked with the Casimirs, wholly aware of his reputation with other girls across White Roaring even as she wished he would notice her. She had missed the way he said her name, the way it rolled off his tongue with ease and slammed to a halt at the end, as if he was holding it back, as if he never wanted to let her go.

I'm sorry, Flick wanted to say. *It's my mother's fault you can never enjoy a pastry again. It's my mother's fault you died.*

"If anything, learning she's the Ram is a good thing," Jin said, and *goodness*, she had forgotten what it was like to hear the dips and rises of his musing tone.

Still, she furrowed her brow in confusion.

"It's ever more obvious that someone like you can never be associated with someone like that," Jin explained. "You're too good for her."

She ducked her head, her neck aflame. What a delight it was, to be seen. His words wrapped her in an embrace she'd craved since that night as she had huddled in silence and isolation from place to place.

"All right?" he asked, leaning closer. His hair fell over his eyes, the tattoo on his neck catching the lantern light. *Little heron*, he said his parents had nicknamed him as a child. Was he anxious to see them? Were they the same people as when he was younger, or had they, too, changed like Flick's mother?

"All right," she whispered. She only needed to tilt her chin up a little higher to close the distance between them and their lips would touch.

She didn't dare move.

"—really, Arthie," Matteo was saying before he turned back to Flick.

She pulled away from Jin with a quick breath. Her pulse raced like a hummingbird's wings, and when he cast her a sideways glance, she knew he had heard it.

"Ceylan as in the island?" Matteo asked. "Surely you're not serious."

Jin straightened, and Flick felt the warmth dissipate, along with her embarrassment. She was almost grateful for the distraction. Almost.

"Do any of us look like we're having a grand time right now?" Jin asked. "Of course she's serious."

Between them, Arthie looked stricken, hollow. She hadn't looked great since her argument with Jin, but now she appeared worse.

Flick remembered that Arthie had fled from Ceylan years ago. What would it be like to return to a graveyard of one's past self? That was how she imagined going back to the Linden Estate would be—and she had only been away from it for weeks.

A slow and lonely leak in a corner of the storeroom plinked in the heavy silence.

Jin was at war with himself. Flick could see him wanting to say something and holding himself back by gritting his teeth. Matteo, surprisingly, shared the same uncertainty. Flick saw him step to Arthie's side and reach for her before dropping his hands to his sides, fingers flexing as if he was fighting the urge to touch her. As if he had no qualms himself but wasn't sure how Arthie would react.

Did Flick not feel the same? Every fiber of her being craved that nearness, to be close to Jin, to touch him, to make up for the excruciating days they'd spent apart.

"Did you know that the peakies wanted control of Ceylan because of its prime position in the ocean? Almost every trade route runs through there, granting an easy refuel port to every kingdom, country, and empire we know of," Arthie said. She sounded like she was reading from a schoolbook.

"Boss?" Chester asked finally, reaching for her hand.

Arthie swallowed. It was business to the Ram, duvin to be had. For Arthie, it had been home.

"Right," she said, though she still sounded distant. Detached from herself. Her hand strayed to her pistol and stayed there. "I—I wasn't anticipating needing to leave Ettenia, or even White Roaring."

Let alone go to Ceylan.

Flick heard her unspoken words, but as she watched, Arthie rearranged herself. As though she were breaking off pieces of herself and tucking them away, out of sight and thus out of mind.

"Yet, here we are," she said, her tone resolute, and Flick could have imagined they were back in Spindrift, in control of the situation and resources, their future gripped tight in Arthie's hand as she spelled out the perfect plan. "That's why Penn didn't tell us Jin's parents are alive. He knew we'd go to Ceylan. He knew *I'd* go."

She stopped and dropped her gaze before she could say any more. Penn had been trying to protect them. Had *he* been trying to retrieve Jin's parents himself before his untimely death?

Arthie walked over to one of the crates, and the others gravitated toward her as if they had no choice in the matter. She pulled out a card from her jacket and set it down on the mottled wood, the edges foiled in gold. It was the invitation.

"Someone at the Athereum had this. Several someones. Lords and ladies, of course, ones I didn't even know were vampires," Arthie said, tapping it on the crate. "Apparently, only the upper echelon of White Roaring will be in attendance. We're barely just bouncing back after a week, and the Ram is already making strides. First a headline blaspheming Spindrift, now this."

Jin took it, reading through. "She's hosting a tribute to the fallen press that she herself obliterated? What a woman."

Flick wasn't particularly proud of the way his words stung.

"And we're going," Arthie said, sitting on the crate.

Matteo was studying her. "You think it's a cover."

"Indeed, and if she wants to make a show of herself in front of high society, I want us all there. We'll give them a show."

Flick heard the promise in Arthie's voice. She didn't know what Arthie had planned—she didn't think Arthie herself knew just yet, but there was no refuting the certainty in her tone.

"But first, Ceylan," Arthie said. "The island might be smaller than Ettenia, but we know little of the Ram's actual operations, neither the layout nor locations. Flick, keep reading through the ledger. Tell me everything."

"Nor can we verify that my parents are truly there," Jin reminded her, sitting down and setting his umbrella across his legs.

"As of six weeks ago, the Siwangs were in Ceylan," Arthie said, gesturing to the ledger. "When Laith came to us with the deal, the ledger had only just been stolen by Penn. That was less than a month ago. Enough time to change warehouses, perhaps, but an operation in a different country? Unlikely. We still have reason to trust the ledger—especially considering the fact that the Ram hasn't stopped hunting Flick since that night. *And* let's not forget she burned down Spindrift for it."

Arthie had a point—several points, really.

"What's our plan for the Siwangs?" Matteo asked.

"*SS and SS to administer before release*," Arthie repeated. "That's clear enough for me to assume they're a step in whatever the Ram needs done."

"Are they the good guys?" Chester asked dubiously.

Flick didn't know if one could work for the Ram for a decade and still remain a good guy. There was a pause, as if everyone felt the same but was collectively waiting for Jin's input on the question. He clenched his jaw and said nothing.

"It doesn't matter," Arthie finally said. "We'll swoop in and snatch them away. It'll put a stop to the process, even if temporary. Then we'll bring them here and take a page out of Penn's original plan of gathering proof. Like the ledger, the moment they're with us, they work for us."

She waited for Jin's protest, but he remained quiet.

"We're going there for the missing vampires too," Matteo reminded, looking up from the ledger. He was holding Flick's cipher in one hand. "There's still no mention of the vampires being deployed to the Ram's battles, which means they're on Ceylan. We can't just leave them there."

Flick thought he had a point.

Emotion coiled in Matteo's exhale. "Many of those missing vampires are my friends, but beyond that, they're reminders that I could have been snatched from the streets myself. Any of us three could have and still can."

Flick did not want to think of that reality. She felt for the missing vampires, but realizing it could have been one of them, one of her closest friends, or *Jin*, sent her pulse into a frenzy.

"You're right," Arthie said. "We can't leave them. But whether we'll return them to White Roaring too—or simply free them from whatever confines they may be in—remains to be seen. We need to be open to the possibility that they may not be as receptive as you think. We don't know what state they're in." She rose to her feet and pocketed the invitation. "But if we're to make it back in time for the tribute, we need to move quickly. We'll need provisions, supplies—"

"And a ship?" Reni asked, his eyes as doleful as ever.

Arthie nodded. "A large one at that, if we might possibly bring the vampires back with us."

"An EJC ship," Matteo said with dark glee. "That fleet is full of the largest ships there are, and it'll be the most poetic."

"We're not trying to make a statement," Arthie said.

"Oh, we are," Matteo countered. "She's making plenty of her own, is she not?"

Arthie didn't argue with that.

"An adventure!" Chester exclaimed. "Oh, I'm chuffed."

"Save your chuffing. You're not going," Arthie said. "Ceylan is too far away, and as crucial as it is to bring back the Siwangs and the vampires, we'll need to do far more to take down the Ram. Some of us will need to stay here."

"That won't be me," Jin said, eager to see his parents.

"Or me," Arthie said.

Jin didn't look too happy about that, but he didn't voice a protest. He knew Arthie needed to be there.

"I'll stay," Matteo said. "I never did grow sea legs."

Flick crossed her arms. "Neither Arthie nor Jin have been vampires for very long. You're going with them."

"Are you ordering me, Flick?" Matteo asked in surprise. "I never thought I'd see the day."

Flick ducked her head before straightening again. She *was* ordering him. She didn't yet know who she was, but she was getting there. It felt as though she'd been running a jagged blade along the roots connecting her to her mother ever since she'd left, and until she was free of them, she wouldn't be *able* to be herself.

"Which leaves me," she said finally. "I'll stay."

Jin's eyes snapped to hers, and it gave Flick a little thrill. *I'll miss you*, she wanted to say, but didn't know how in front of the others, so she kept her lips closed, breaking away from his gaze first.

"Oh, but Jin doesn't like that," Chester pointed out for them both.

Jin cracked a smile. "You're breaking my heart, Felicity."

"Good thing it doesn't beat anymore," Matteo quipped, wrinkling his nose when Opal tore at the fish and a piece landed beside his shiny shoes.

"Is that true?" Chester asked, aghast.

"Not if I drink some of his blood," Jin said darkly. "Vampires can have a pulse if they drink enough."

"Is that a threat, Casimir?" Matteo asked.

He was toying with Jin, Flick knew, but she'd seen them fight on the steps of Matteo's house and wasn't eager to witness that again. She stepped closer to Arthie, as discreetly as she could. The last thing Flick wanted was to make Matteo feel as though she was scared of him because she'd learned his secret. She wasn't scared of *that* in the slightest, but caution was a good thing, wasn't it?

Not counting Chester and Felix, Flick was the only human among them. Her pulse spiked, sending a rush of fear through her veins. Did the others smell it in her blood? It was a startling thought, even if she wasn't afraid of them. How far she'd come, from having never seen a vampire to being involved in their affairs.

"Back to the matter at hand," Arthie said over them, riffling through the ledger. "If we're taking an EJC ship, Flick will need to stay regardless."

"Why?" Reni asked, reaching carefully for the kitten's tail as she thumped it on the floorboards.

"*Because* it's an EJC ship. They'll know where their ships are at all times. Flick will need to forge documents to make sure we don't get caught," Arthie said, shutting the ledger again. "According to this, they send a particular line of ships for Ceylani routes, and several had departure dates as little as four days apart, which means it's no more than a two-day journey each way, possibly shorter if the ship remains at port for maintenance." She made a face. "Or longer if we hit stormy waters. There's no telling how long we'll need on Ceylan itself, but here in Ettenia, the Ram will need to believe everything is running without a hitch."

"How will a piece of paper make up for a missing ship?" Chester asked, brow pinched.

"We've been importing tea for years," Arthie said. "We rarely saw superiors getting their shoes dirty at port. The laborers report to the foremen, the foremen report to the dockmasters, and on and on until the boss finally catches wind of it. Flick will only need to intercept messages before they get that far."

"I can forge documents," Flick said, "but if she's storing vampires to ship them, she's bound to notice they're not being shipped."

"Not unless she thinks they're being shipped, while her dockworkers think she wants them to stay put," Arthie said. "Again, a letter to each will do the trick."

Flick released a careful breath. She hadn't forged anything without the company of the Casimirs since the signet ring that resulted in her life falling apart. This time, the Casimirs wouldn't even be in the same country as her. Opal bounded over and leaped into her lap again, smelling like a basket of fresh laundry, despite having chomped on a fish the past hour.

"Won't there be vampires on the ship?" Reni asked.

"If the ship's stocked, I'll have it cleared," Arthie said, as if she'd already considered the possibility and had figured out a way to avoid it. "If they're being treated like cargo, they'll be returned to a warehouse. We'll tail them to whatever new warehouse they've been relocated to, and free all of them."

"That easy, eh?" Jin asked. "How are you going to have a stocked EJC ship cleared?"

Arthie prickled. "I'll do my job; you do yours." Before Jin could counter her, she continued. "But the EJC vampires will need to remain there until our return. I'm not risking our element of surprise."

"Sidharth can handle it," Matteo suggested. "We'll put him in charge of them and tell him no movement until we return."

"Good," Arthie said. "Moving on. Chester, you and the boys will intercept the messages. Give them to Flick for the appropriate response. Flick, make sure you track down the foreman's penmanship too. Keep the ruse going for as long as you can, understand? If you have to write letters yourself, do it."

"You trust me to?" Flick asked, surprised. She'd only ever forged and written what Arthie had dictated.

"Of course. In the meantime, keep studying the ledger for anything that might help us. On the tribute, other secrets, further plans."

"Maybe even the real reason why she might be kidnapping humans off the streets," Matteo suggested.

"I wouldn't be surprised if it's solely for the reason of creating more chaos," Jin said.

Arthie didn't look so certain, and Flick marveled at how quickly Arthie had learned Flick's mother. "She's desperate, but she's not typically one to waste a resource. Once we bring back Jin's parents, the show will have only just begun. Treat the Ram and Lady Linden as two separate people. We're going to bury them both so she has no way of clawing her way back up again."

Flick held back a smile. She was well aware Arthie was talking of her mother's demise, but she sounded like herself again. Passionate. Whip-smart.

Alive.

"Make that three," Arthie corrected with narrowed eyes. "The Ram has three parts: monarch, businesswoman, and lady. Each needs stifling, or she'll assume duties as the other. Take down the Ram, and the EJC will still flourish. Take down the EJC, and the Ram will still rule."

"How can we do that?" Matteo asked.

Arthie drummed her fingers on the crate. "Ceylan is a centralized refueling port for much of the colonies. To get from Ettenia to wherever else, ships need to stop in Ceylan. I don't yet know how we'll smother EJC operations, but I'll know it when I see it. I'll make sure I leave my mark. On the other hand, simply by removing the Siwangs from the island, we'll put a dent in the *Ram's* plans for weaponizing the vampires and expanding her colonies. We also have her ledger, which we know she's been fairly cross about since we stole it."

"That leaves the lady," Flick said. *My mother.* "The one who revels at events like the tribute."

Arthie's head snapped up. "The one who cares for her image. That's it. The Ram is inviting people across high society for the tribute, a select list of people she wants there to see her carefully curated image."

"You want to unmask her," Jin said, catching on begrudgingly.

"Precisely," Arthie said.

"If she's inviting a select list of people, I can add to it," Flick said. "I know of several lords and ladies she's not fond of who are equally not fond of her. I can make sure personalized invitations get in their hands."

"Clever girl," Jin said, and Flick cracked a shy smile.

"I can also scope out the location of the tribute while you're away," Flick suggested, even though every part of her wanted to do no such thing. "See if I can find anything on what she might truly be planning?"

Arthie shook her head. "Keep the ship's ruse going, first and foremost. Forge the invites. Stay safe. I don't want you dealing with your mother, all right?"

Flick bit her lip and nodded, pretending a wave of relief hadn't just washed through her.

"Or," Jin began, "we could wait until a ship is stocked and ready for Ceylan and sneak aboard it. It might mean waiting an extra day until it can set sail, but we'll avoid stealing an entire EJC ship, and leaving Flick to keep the ruse."

"I would think Flick can hold a ruse if it means yet another ship of vampires doesn't get sent over," Matteo said.

"He's right," Arthie said. "We don't need to transport another load of vampires when we're aiming for the opposite, *and* the tribute is in eight days. We don't have time to spare. Flick?"

"What?" she asked. "Oh, yes, I agree."

"It's settled. Flick will stay behind. Matteo, Jin, and I leave for Ceylan."

"When?" Jin asked.

Arthie looked among them. "Tomorrow. Matteo, escort everyone back to the Athereum. Jin, Flick, see what more you can find in the ledger about what's happening on Ceylan. There's bound to be clues that will help us. I'll head to the docks now and secure our ship"—she gave Jin a pointed look—"an empty one."

Flick opened the ledger and picked up her cipher. Instead of an influx of sorrow this time, it calmed her nerves. She had a task, she was a part of something again, and she would give the Casimirs her fullest.

7
ARTHIE

As Matteo took the others to the Athereum—a grumpy Jin included—Arthie headed in the opposite direction. She had always walked the streets of White Roaring with the knowledge that people didn't like her. They stared as if she were an insect under a glass. As if it was acceptable to gobble countries like hers whole, but how dare she deign to walk and live and breathe upon theirs. She had always marched with a sense of caution, but now she was surprised by the unease that accompanied it.

For she was a vampire too.

Matteo spoke of unrest, the papers spoke of anger, but really, the people were afraid. When vampires were being kidnapped, the threat was nonexistent, the act almost deserved. With scores of press dead, and humans disappearing off the street without a trace, the fear had become a real, almost tangible thing. Protesters were hoisting crude weapons and baring their teeth, and Arthie kept her distance, for there was no telling what a cornered animal might do.

She tucked her mauve hair beneath her cap, aware she had three foes: the Horned Guard, the crowds, and the Ram's black-clad forces. One was for the law, one was in pain, and the third had crushed their moral compass beneath their boots in order to carry out the monarch's dark bidding. There was every likelihood the Horned Guard was given instructions to apprehend her after that night, and there was every likelihood someone in the crowds marching the streets might recognize her as the once owner of Spindrift with its open secret of a bloodhouse.

Arthie drifted to the shadows, away from the crowds, away from the Horned Guard, and tightened her hold on Calibore. If the Ram's black-clad men came, she would be ready. She passed old textile mills and piles of stinking rubbish, edging out of the thick of the city with each step. She stayed vigilant, even if her emotions at the sight of Jin and their ridiculous argument were quickly overtaken by Flick's discovery and now she could think of nothing else.

Home. Ceylan. That place she'd left, bloody and chaotic.

And the ship she would soon be on. In truth, Arthie wanted as few people on that vessel as possible. As few *humans* as possible, for she did not want a repetition of the first time she was on a boat. She was different now, in tune with her emotions, aware of what she was, but that did little against the overwhelming memories of what she'd done to those people, trapped on a tiny boat, a cage in every way. She did not want to be on a boat, even if, deep down, she'd always known fate would take her back to Ceylan.

She cleared the cluttered alleys and neared the residential streets, where the breeze was crisp and the crowds were thinner. She was about to brave the open air when a hand gripped her arm and pulled her deeper into the shadows. Arthie had Calibore cocked and aimed in heartbeats, ready to blow out the brains of whichever of the Ram's men dared to touch her.

"I would die for you, darling, but not like that."

Arthie blinked as Matteo emerged from the darkness, out of place in a setting so dilapidated. "You were supposed to take the others to the Athereum."

"We met Sidharth on the way. He's taking them."

She narrowed her eyes. "Are you following me?"

"Can we have this conversation without a pistol in my face?"

She didn't move. "You brought it upon yourself."

Matteo sighed. "I save her life once, and this is what I'm rewarded with."

"Poor vampire. Were you expecting a kiss?"

"As a matter of fact, yes," he said, and he swept closer, straight into the barrel of her gun. Goodness, he was tall. The evening air slipped between them, and she smelled that alluring blend of chocolate and nuttiness, that warmth that reminded her of Spindrift. Of her parents.

This wasn't the first time his lips had parted so closely to hers. This wasn't the first time she'd wanted him to close that distance between them, with a growing impatience thrumming through her veins.

"Well?" she asked. She could manage nothing more than a tight whisper. "Have it, then."

"Arthie Casimir, giving something freely?" he replied, and he leaned in until his lips were a hairsbreadth from hers.

And stopped.

"I think not," he whispered.

She smelled blood on his breath, heady and intoxicating. He had just fed. She wanted to lick it off his lips, devour every last drop along with his kiss. It took all of her power to peel her gaze from his mouth.

"Does this bother you, Arthie?" he asked in a voice of deep, dark indulgence. Amusement sparked in his eyes. "I am a vampire, if you recall. I have an eternity, and I do like a good tease."

Before she could piece together a reply, he tilted his head and pressed a kiss to the side of her neck, teeth grazing her skin, making the entirety of her body go weak.

He pulled back, tossing hair from his brow, and Arthie wished it was her fingers that had mussed the dark strands. She swayed, oddly bereft. *You have a job to do*, she reprimanded herself. Normally, that was enough to keep her focused, her attention razor-sharp. Now she could think of nothing but grabbing a fistful of his shirt and kissing him.

Something was truly wrong with her.

Perhaps it was her death and the reminder of how fragile life was. Knowing she was an immortal vampire did little to change the fact that she remembered, vividly, the scrape of each breath as she desperately held on to life. Her skin burned now, where he had kissed her. Her lips hummed with the promise he'd snatched away.

"I'm leaving," she snapped.

His grin widened. "May I join you? I can help."

"You'll do no such thing."

"You wound me, darling."

She whirled away with one last glare in his direction.

Ceylan. Jin's parents. The Ram. With each one, Arthie sobered a little more. She had a job. She couldn't keep thinking of Matteo's mouth and his long fingers and the way his lips crooked.

She needed a ship. Yes. And for that, she needed the cargo inspector. She wasn't fond of how she felt Matteo's absence, but she needed to step out of the shadows and couldn't dwell on her feelings just now. They could wait. Houses spread out down the street. They were empty of crowds, shooed away by the Horned Guard patrolling the tree-lined walkways.

She squinted at the nearest house across the street, trying to read the number. *519*. She pressed her lips thin. The house she needed was farther down at *529*.

Arthie knew she could have waited until the cargo inspector was back at his office before making her demands, but people were different in the comfort of their own homes. More malleable. Arthie popped her collar and lowered her chin, waiting until the guards marching in her direction turned before she crossed the street to the cover of a lone carriage.

She counted an entire minute before the trio of patrolling guards would make their rounds and see her. One minute before they'd see her standing at the door to the inspector's house. With her back to them, would they recognize her? She didn't want to find out. The moment they turned, she hurried past the houses to 529, rushed up the stairs, and knocked on the inspector's door. Down on the sidewalk, one of the guards burst out laughing at something another said. Arthie looked at the door, willing it to open. If Jin were here, he would have already deciphered the maker of the lock and asked if he should pick it, if only to irk her.

But Arthie wasn't here to meddle, only dangle what she needed to get her own work done, and her task for Willard Otis was quite simple: Present the dockworkers with an impending inspection. They'd argue otherwise, but his document would be freshly signed and dated by the crown—which was, of course, Flick. Once he moved the ship to an inspection berth, Arthie and the others would be free to sail away.

That was the downside to having an operation as large as the EJC: The bigger the distance between the lowly workers and their couldn't-be-bothered superiors, the more they relied on documents and letters.

Arthie glanced back at the guards and then at her watch. Fifteen seconds before they turned. *Fourteen.* Arthie stared at the door, willing it open. She tried to make herself small, to blend into the shadows cast by the awning above her. The guards were bantering now. Distracted, hopefully.

At last, the door opened to a young man in a tailcoat, and she was momentarily flung back to Spindrift as Reni welcomed patrons through its frosted doors. Her anger burned a bright and vibrant red, as bold as fresh blood. And to think, just a day ago, she hadn't been able to figure out how she felt.

"Can I help you?" the butler asked, his dark features framed by the glowing parlor behind him. It almost hid the bewildered look in his eyes. He kept running his hands down his tailcoat, straightening invisible wrinkles.

He's green. That could be a point in her favor.

The guards were turning back up the street.

Arthie made a show of patting at her suit jacket, then her trousers. "Can I come in?"

The butler narrowed his eyes at her. "Who are you?"

Can I come in? wasn't precisely a trustworthy opening, she admitted. "I appear to have forgotten my calling card. Forgive me, sir. I'm here to see Willard."

The butler blinked. "*Sir Otis* can be met at his office by appointment. He doesn't conduct business at home."

The level of snobbery coming out of this bloke's mouth wasn't befitting how clearly new he was to the position.

So Arthie smiled and pulled out her pocket watch. "I do have an appointment, in fact. It was moved to the house, and it's—oh, it's in exactly two minutes."

The boy's mouth opened and closed. He pulled out a tiny pocket agenda and began rummaging through it with no clear direction. Arthie wanted a moment to enjoy his discomfort, but the guards were going to spot her.

She leaned closer, keeping her voice low. "I'll be late."

"Right, right," he said, flustered. "May I have your name?"

"Arthur," she said. The less people who knew Arthie Casimir was toiling about, the better.

The boy's brow furrowed, but when she moved to pull out her pocket watch again, he scrambled to invite her inside just as Arthie heard one of the guards notice her. A voice rose, but she didn't wait, she hurried through the entrance and shut the door before the butler could, giving him a tight smile in response.

"My appointment?" she asked. There was little likelihood the guards would come to the door, but Arthie didn't want to risk it by standing here.

"Right this way," the butler said, leading her into the house. Willard's foyer was lavish, but decorated in a sparse way, as if he'd suddenly been thrust into wealth and didn't quite know what to do with it. His wife stood in the back of the room and waved as Arthie passed, her cheeks rosy and eyes kind. They stopped at a door with a sign that read WILLARD OTIS, INSPECTOR.

The majority of Arthie's books that archived secrets and blackmail had been stored in a hidden room in Spindrift. They were gone now, burned to ashes with the rest of the tearoom and bloodhouse. Still, Arthie had enough tucked away in her head that it wasn't too wretched a loss.

The butler ushered her through the door and closed it behind her, and Arthie could at last breathe. The room was as quaint as the rest of the house, with modest furnishings and a window with laced curtains that looked as though they'd never been drawn. The inspector was in no hurry of his own, sealing off an envelope with leisure. At last, he looked up from his desk with a small smile.

Arthie almost glanced behind her, certain his kindness was misplaced. She pulled off her hat and shook out her hair before repositioning it again.

"What did I tell that boy about scheduling appointments when I'm at home?" he said by way of greeting. Then he frowned, sliding stray papers out of the way to reach a calendar. "That said, I don't believe I have any other appointments today."

"You don't," Arthie said simply.

Willard laughed. "Of course not. He's new to the job and already well on his way to proving himself incapable. And who may you be, come like the reaper? Outside of that hair, of course."

He spoke the words almost endearingly, like a doting grandfather, and Arthie wasn't wholly sure how to react.

"I need a ship," Arthie said, making herself comfortable in the chair across from his desk.

"Well, I'm afraid I'm not the office for such acquisitions."

Arthie nodded. "I'm in need of a particular ship. One already in use by someone else. It's my understanding that an inspector can stop a ship from leaving port and order its crew to both unload and disembark."

Willard opened his mouth, and Arthie had the sense she was about to receive an education on how cargo inspections functioned.

"At will," she added.

Willard narrowed his eyes, setting down his pen and giving her his full attention. That was better.

"I should hope you're not suggesting theft, miss . . ."

Arthie replied with the truth this time. "Casimir."

His eyes flared in recognition, but she wasn't worried. He was about to be a part of the job. *Her* job.

"And no, not theft," she said. "I'll only borrow it for a short time."

He sat back with an uneasy laugh, chair creaking. He couldn't decide if she was being serious; though she did nothing to suggest otherwise.

"The ship belongs to the EJC," she added, and his graying eyebrows shot up.

"I'm having a troubling time understanding how casually you're speaking of treason, young miss. You are aware I can have you arrested by the Horned Guard, are you not?" he asked, trying to assess her.

I've killed a Horned Guard, she thought.

And kissed one.

Yet when she thought of the word *kiss*, her mind conjured another face. More aristocratic and cocky, more apt to laugh at the law with a paintbrush in hand than enforce it. And far less likely to point a gun at her.

"I am," Arthie replied.

And now that he'd threatened her, it was time to lay out her cards.

"But did you summon the Horned Guard when your son decided to steal money from the academy where he taught?" she asked. "Where he verbally abused several children and used that very same money to keep their parents quiet?"

Willard Otis knew, then, how to look at her. To call her a reaper wasn't too far a stretch.

"You do not understand the trials a father must endure for his children," Willard said.

Arthie shrugged. "Maybe I do, and that's why I don't have parents."

A notch appeared between Willard's brows. "I would like you to take this matter seriously."

"Seriously?" Arthie repeated, her voice dropping to a deathly note. "In that case, let's discuss *children*. They are easily impressionable, gullible, guileless. What we learn as children remains with us forever. Every last coin out of Ettenia's coffers couldn't salvage the damage your son has done to those children. So don't talk to me about what you've endured to protect him when he deserves none."

To his credit, Willard did not appear proud.

"And I hear he's now headmaster of the academy," Arthie added. "He works fast."

Willard released a careful breath, and Arthie took that as permission to present her plan. "Pull one of the ships in for inspection, give me time to use it for my needs, and then you can return it back to the EJC."

Willard looked as if he were in pain. "I don't know why you believe I can procure what you need. I *am* an inspector, but the EJC works with the monarchy. Their ships have always passed inspections. Hard not to when they come with documents already signed by the crown allowing them through. We have no reason to inspect them, and with such scrutiny, I can't pull one in for you simply because you're blackmailing me."

Arthie wasn't surprised. The EJC didn't only work with the monarchy, it *was* the monarchy. If Lady Linden could pass as the Ram, two powerful people in their own right, everything else she did was likely a walk through her gardens.

"Follow my lead, and you can. I'll only need you to sign a few documents and cordon off the pier," Arthie said. "I'll handle everything else."

"My job—"

"Won't be at risk, unlike your son's until this is over," Arthie assured. "Though if I were you, I'd ask him to quit the position myself."

But Arthie wasn't here to meddle.

"Have we a deal?" she asked.

Willard sputtered a shaky laugh at her use of the word *deal*, but he nodded. Good man.

8
JIN

Jin had thought sneaking into the Athereum when they needed to steal the ledger was difficult, but it wasn't much easier even with the newly minted head of the society escorting them. He was thankful for the shadows as they steered clear of the crowds stomping their feet and shouting at the top of their lungs. He had to stop himself, more than once, from reaching for Flick's hand to pull her close and out of harm's way. They snuck through the buildings behind the Athereum, navigating the narrow backstreets guarded by Athereum vampires until they reached a tunnel. It was still dropping clods of dirt as protesters stomped their feet aboveground, but it took Jin and the others within the gates without being seen. Chester was having fun. Flick nearly lost control of Opal more than once.

"Should have thought of this when we were breaking in during the Festival of Night," Jin remarked, ducking beneath the low opening.

"Yes," Sidharth said just as lightheartedly. "Not a single vampire would have heard you digging away."

"You're no good at sarcasm, by the way," Chester said.

"Not one bit," Reni added.

"They're right," Jin said.

Sidharth gave Jin a look with a quick raise of his brows. "I make up for it in other ways."

That was not the direction Jin wanted their conversation to go.

Between them, Flick cleared her throat. Reni shook his head in disappointment. Even Opal looked at Sidharth with scorn.

"Forgive me, my lady," Sidharth said, leading them through the doors and immediately into the locked corridor Arthie had gone through great lengths to infiltrate many nights ago. A couple of vampires turned their heads at their arrival, and Jin saluted them as if they were old friends. He only assumed they could be trusted because Sidharth nodded at them as they passed.

"The Athereum! Can you believe it, boys?" Chester said, nudging Felix and pointing to everything Jin and the others had spent days figuring out how to manipulate for the Festival of Night, when the crew was stressed and tense, but had yet to be defeated.

Arthie had yet to be defeated.

As angry as he was, when Flick had announced that his parents were on Ceylan and Arthie's gaze had shattered, it was a blow to his stomach. Arthie had relegated the island to her past, and now she was being forced to confront it again. Acknowledge its existence beyond importing tea and coconut.

Wicked knives, he was still growing accustomed to the fact that his parents were alive—truly alive, and not just a hopeful notion—but on an island far from the shores of Ettenia? On *Arthie's* island, no less. It was hard to believe how much of their lives were intertwined so deeply.

Sidharth took them to a wing of the Athereum with a spacious hall leading to various rooms. "You're safe from the mobs here, but I suggest making yourselves known as little as possible. We haven't weeded out every traitor within our own walls just yet."

The dark way in which he spoke made Jin think he had found some of them, and they hadn't met very good fates.

"Any word on the missing humans?" Jin asked.

Sidharth shook his head. "We've scoured a good portion of the city, but as far as we can tell, Arthie's right. Vampires aren't responsible, and the Ram may well have taken them herself. We'll keep looking. You've got enough to handle." He unlocked a door and gave them each a key. "I'll let you know if and when the others return." Then he gestured for Chester, Reni, and Felix to follow. "Right this way, lads."

With a wave at the boys, Jin closed the door behind them, and when he turned around, it was to find Flick standing stock-still in the center of the wide room as Opal leaped from her arms and ran for cover.

Jin came alert in an instant, grip tightening around his umbrella. "What is it?"

She sounded small. "It's a bedroom."

Oh. Jin immediately felt his guard relax. He couldn't remember the last time he'd laughed, or felt joy, for that matter. "A lavish one at that."

Flick looked about but said nothing. The room served as both parlor and bedroom, with a canopied bed to the right and a seating area to the left, and a desk against the curtained wall. It was dark and sultry, the kitten's fur bright as she explored the space.

"Is that a problem, love?"

She swallowed, glancing into the attached bathroom. "N—no. Of course not."

Clearly anxious for something to do, she pulled the ledger out of her satchel, but not before Jin saw the tremor in her hands.

"We need to see what else we can find. Before you—before you leave for Ceylan. It's hard enough on Arthie as it is." Then she paused and narrowed her eyes at something on the bed. "Are those our things?"

"You know, if you want me in your bed, there are better ways to go about it," Jin teased.

Flick ducked her head. "I'm serious!"

Indeed, she was. Jin picked up his bag, riffling through his extra clothes and belongings, what little he owned now that Spindrift was gone. Something small and brass glinted at the bottom of his bag, and Jin felt a flutter at the reminder. He'd picked it up what felt like forever ago, after he'd noticed that Flick had stopped carrying around that infernal lighter.

He glanced at her buoyant curls falling over her face as she looked through her own bag, still wishing they weren't leaving her behind. *Why?* he asked himself. What was it about Felicity Linden that made her different from the long line of girls he'd kissed and left in the past? What *wasn't* it was the real question—to him, she was everything every other girl was not. What did every other girl in the world need to do to hold a candle to Felicity Linden, was what he should have asked.

She turned to him and, finding him watching, shied away from whatever she'd been about to say. He saw it in her sweet smile.

"You can still join us," Jin said. "Come now, Felicity. A holiday courtesy of Arthie Casimir herself."

She laughed at that, and his ears rejoiced at the sound, a rush of warmth coursing through him that was not unlike when he drank blood for the first time, nourishing every part of him.

"I have a little something for you," he said. "Because I noticed you're not carrying your lighter anymore."

She stiffened. "I gave it back to the person who gave it to me."

Ah. Her mother, then.

"That could not have been easy," Jin said softly.

Flick gave him a little shrug, clearing out a decorative dish and pouring water into it for Opal. Out in the hall, he heard Chester scolding Felix, and Reni placating them both.

Jin held out his hand with the small gift nestled in his palm. "Brass knuckles. Not nearly the same as a lighter, but it's small and brass and may potentially save your life."

"Oh? How would it do that?" she asked, and he realized she'd never seen them before. She was still new to the streets. To crime and grime, and the tools they used on the other side of White Roaring.

Before he could think anything of it, he took her hand in his, and every nerve ending in his body stood on end at *her* reaction. Not because she gasped or froze, but because of her pulse, pitter-pattering like the rain outside.

She met his eyes in a flare of uncertainty. He started to pull away, but her fingers tightened ever so slightly, gripping him in place.

There was that boldness Felicity Linden only rarely portrayed. And it made Jin bold in turn. With a swallow, he lifted her hand higher, higher, holding her gaze until her hand was in line with his mouth. Ever so slowly, he brushed his lips against her skin, pressing a kiss between her thumb and forefinger.

And then he made the mistake of inhaling. He didn't smell the sweet sunshine of her skin anymore; he smelled her blood. It danced beneath her skin, a scent as earthy as tea, as delectable as the drizzle of icing on every pastry he could no longer eat.

A strangled sound escaped her throat and Jin realized his eyes had fallen closed. When his eyelids fluttered open, it was to see her own fighting to stay open.

"Jin," she whispered, both a whine and a plea in her voice.

"Yes, love?" he whispered back, before a single question rose louder than his thoughts: What would her blood taste like?

He lowered her hand with a clench of his jaw. Confusion flashed over Flick's features, but she said nothing. If he'd pulled her close and lowered his fangs to her neck, would she let him? Would she turn him away with the same disgust high society gave vampires?

He was too cowardly to find out.

"H-how does it work, then?" she asked, a little too loudly and with very little subtlety. "This weapon you mentioned."

Jin almost laughed.

"You take it like this," he said, and carefully splayed her fingers by sliding his between them. How did such a thing feel so indecent? Her breath hitched before he carefully dragged the weapon snug over her knuckles. "Fits well, doesn't it?"

Flick swallowed. Her gaze darkened, and Jin knew she was not thinking of the fit of the brass dusters.

"What are you thinking?"

"That—that they're not exactly comfortable," Flick said, flexing her fingers against the brass.

Liar. Jin gave her a pointed look but couldn't torture the poor girl any longer.

"Nor will a fight be," he said, closing her fingers around them and resisting the urge to kiss her soft skin. "These are unassuming and easier to hurt someone without hurting yourself, because no one really talks about how much a punch hurts both parties. Leave them in your pocket, and you'll always have a weapon handy."

He paused then, wanting to ask her if he could show her how to use it. Did she want that? Did she want to stand this close to him? Since when was Jin so unsure of himself?

"Once we go through the ledger, can you show me how?" she asked hesitantly.

"I was hoping you'd ask," he said with as carefree a grin as he could muster.

9
FLICK

I was hoping you'd ask. The words were an endless cycle through Flick's mind as she flipped through the ledger. What did that mean? Did it mean Jin was as interested in her as she was in him? *Never mind that,* Flick scolded herself, as she realized that asking him to show her how to use the brass knuckles also meant asking him to touch her.

She focused on the words in the ledger again, using the tribute invitation as a guide beneath each of her mother's lines, and to remind herself of how little time they had before the event.

Beside her, Jin was carefully decoding segments of the ledger into Ettenian using her cipher. It was hard not to watch him work, the way his eyes narrowed in focus, the way he murmured beneath his breath, his lips a sullen pout, and the ease with which he gripped a pen, dipping it into an inkwell like a master.

She glanced at the brass knuckles again, remembering his mention of her lighter, reminding her yet again that others might not notice her, but Jin did. He always did.

And at some point between bringing her on board to help them infiltrate the Athereum and the catastrophe of that night where everything had fallen apart, he'd gone and bought her a gift. She hadn't thought he'd ever properly looked at her lighter. He'd always see the fire and seize up until she'd tried to stop fiddling with it whenever he was around. But the brass knuckles were the same finish, with little grooves she could run her nails across whenever she was feeling anxious.

For as proud as she was for giving the lighter back to her mother, she also missed its reassuring weight in her pocket and the distraction its many textures provided.

Did he know he was giving her more than a way to protect herself? She looked up to find him watching her, his expression soft, as if yes, he did indeed know.

"Did you find something?" Flick asked.

"I think so," Jin said. "A fortress. They just recently finished the construction of it on Ceylan. By they, I mean the Ram. It would be a good place to store vampires, no?"

Fortresses were meant to protect assets from outsiders. It was absurd for the Ram to build a fortification on an island she had colonized, stolen, and plundered for her own needs.

"Arthie won't be too happy to hear that," Flick said.

"No," he agreed, "she will not."

"But a fortress would be massive. If the vampires are there, how would you even find them?"

He pushed the ledger toward her. She'd memorized the cipher by now, and barely referenced it as she read through the portion Jin pointed out, trying her best to ignore his eyes on her. She ran her fingers over the ridges of the brass knuckles.

"Ah, there's a facility inside the fort," Flick said, gesturing to the text. "A sanatorium. See: *Deliver to Siwangs at sanatorium.*"

"A what? How did I miss that?" Jin's eyes widened as he reread the lines. "Felicity, you are a master. The sanatorium, then."

Flick pressed her fingers against her lips before they could flare in a smile that was far too wide to be decent. His expression faltered, a weight settling above his brows. He was worried about his parents, she knew.

"Is there anything more? Since I apparently can't read?" he asked, masking his anxiety.

Flick skimmed a little further and shook her head. "Nothing more on the sanatorium, no. There are several guard stations within, however, so it won't be an easy entrance and exit."

"It is a fortress, after all," Jin said. He didn't look fazed or concerned—no, he looked like he didn't want to dwell on that just yet. He glanced at the time. "We'll let Arthie know. Shall we work on those brass knuckles, then?"

Oh. Was *that* what he wanted to do instead? Flick bit her lip.

He laughed and rose to his feet. "I'll take that as a yes."

Her cheeks burned as she followed him to the bed where he stacked the pillows to create a makeshift training dummy.

"It'll take a lot of practice, but in a pinch, something is better than nothing, eh? Mainly of note: The power of a blow isn't fueled by your arm or your hand." He curled a fist and dropped it as he moved closer. She saw the bob of his throat before his hands settled on her waist. Flick forgot to breathe. She felt each press of his fingers as acutely as though her skin was bare, burning hotter and more satisfying than any flame from her old lighter.

"It comes from your hips, from the weight of your body," he said, and she didn't know why, but the way his voice grew hoarse and cracked in the end filled her with utter delight.

He guided her movements, instructing her to twist forward, sliding his hand down the length of her arm, straightening her wrist before he closed her fingers into a fist. Where was she supposed to find the strength for a blow when she could barely stand on her own legs that were suddenly made of jelly?

She mimicked his movements, her fist connecting with the stacked pillows with a fraction of his force.

He stepped behind her, his form molding to hers. She felt his words against her ear more than she heard them. "Harder, love."

The tiniest whimper escaped her, and she could have sworn she heard his lips curve into a grin. How dare he! She made another fist, but simply knowing he was behind her made it impossible.

She whirled around to face him. "I—I can't do this right now."

Was it the light or were his eyes darker? Did his grin look sharper and a lot more wicked?

"Oh?" he asked, a slow drawl stretching his words. "And why's that, Felicity?"

How was he suddenly *this*? He was just as hesitant as she was a little bit ago, but that disappeared when . . . when she'd become flustered.

Perhaps Flick just needed to be like him.

"Because," she said, straightening her shoulders, and she saw him swallow again. *Delightful.* "I'm not in the mood."

He shrugged and slipped his hands into his pockets. "Fair enough. I've trained a few of the others, if you prefer learning from someone who isn't as distracting."

Flick harrumphed. Jin's grin widened. How she ever thought she could possibly distract Jin more than he distracted her was beyond her.

"But just remember. When you land that blow, wherever it is, pull back," he said. "Do you understand? Don't pity the man; don't freeze. Pull back and ready yourself for the next move. Imagine you're coiled like a spring."

That was when Flick realized it: He *wanted* to be distracted. He was worried. He was afraid to leave her behind. And as alive as his teasing made her feel, as much as she enjoyed the warmth that pooled low in her belly at his dark words, this warmth was different. It was cozy, promising to keep her warm and secure for far longer.

Did it make her weak to want someone who worried for her and wanted to protect her even though she was capable of fending for herself?

She didn't feel weak. She felt special.

He fluffed the pillows back on the bed. Seeing him doing something that mundane and domestic made her heart flutter. "I know you need to keep going through the ledger, but I don't like that you'll have it with you. It makes you a target, and I'd rather not have that."

Flick tamped down her smile. "And why's that?"

Jin paused, mid fluff. His answer was stilted. "Because you're the best forger Ettenia has. After me, of course, because I'm good at everything, but I'm technically dead."

"Of course," Flick said, entertaining him. She knew for a fact he'd never forged in his life. He was Arthie's inventor. He didn't replicate. "But it really is safest with me. And I'm her daughter; I'm a target regardless."

He didn't press, and that was how she knew the difference between being made to feel weak and special. He trusted her, he *believed* in her, and that was plenty.

"It can't be easy for you, I'm sure," he finally said. "Talking about taking her down, and seeing her pay."

Flick shrugged, and not in dismissal. She didn't yet know how she felt. Her emotions were a tangled mess, and a shrug truly encapsulated it best.

"She brought this upon herself."

That, at least, Flick knew for certain.

10

ARTHIE

A *fortress*. Arthie could think of nothing else since Jin and Flick told her of their findings the night before. There was no such monstrosity here in Ettenia, in a place the Ram truly had dominion over.

"Are you sure you don't want several more?" Sidharth asked, dragging her back to the situation at hand. They were nearing the docks. He'd lent them a carriage, making their long trek from the Athereum to the port easier without the fear of eyes tracking them. "Athereum members are snobs, but they can hold their own in a fight."

"The less people to account for, the better," Matteo said with a shake of his head. "We're trying to save enough vampires as it is. Just make sure your men are here to take the rescued vampires in when we arrive."

A gloom drifted across the skies. Seagulls called in the distance, dockworkers shouted over the breeze, and the waves crashed against the shore with a zeal Arthie felt in her bones as she and the others neared. She'd brought Chester and the boys too, in case they needed a distraction from the Horned Guard squadrons stationed at every bend, yawning and looking as though they wanted to be anywhere but near the chill of the sea.

"Once we're through here, I want you back in the carriage with Sidharth, understood?" Arthie asked Chester, Reni, and Felix.

"I might—"

Arthie cut Chester off. "*Yes* is the only appropriate answer when the Ram's kidnapping humans off the streets and doing who knows what."

Chester dropped his head, and Felix did the same beside him. "Yes, boss."

The port was quieter than usual, with the bulk of people either huddled in their homes or rioting outside the Athereum. But business never stopped, crates shuffling to and fro, bills fluttering as they were rushed from hand to hand.

Arthie glanced at her pocket watch—it was nearing ten bells. The inspector would be arriving soon.

"Are you certain you don't want to take the ledger with you?" Flick asked.

No, Arthie was not. She wanted to keep it close because her instinct, as always, was to trust no one but herself to keep anything safe. But at some point in the past decade, Ceylan had become foreign and Ettenia her home. She didn't know what lay beyond these shores and didn't want to risk taking it with them.

"You and Jin found everything you could on the trip ahead, didn't you?"

"As much as we could," Jin said. "Flick's fast. I'm the one who needs to reference the cipher every three minutes."

It wouldn't be hard to find an entire fortress, or even a sanatorium within it. Flick had scoured the rest of the pages for more relating to it but found nothing.

"You know her words better than we do; keep at it. The ledger might not have anything on the tribute, but the vicennial has to have been in the works for longer," Arthie said. "Find what you can. Every little bit will help."

The Ram's tribute was in seven days, and Arthie could only hope this voyage wouldn't take that long. She wanted them back with enough time to form a plan, Jin's parents in tow.

The pier was full of EJC ships readying to sail to every colony the Ram had her horns in, a reminder of how large and far her reach had become. A reminder of what Arthie and the others were up against, with vastly fewer resources at hand. She wasn't wide-eyed and green. She knew putting an end to colonization was well-nigh impossible. It was a monster in motion, gaining momentum for longer than she'd been alive, but that was it, wasn't it?

She was alive now, alive forever, and she would tear down every pillar hoisting up that monster. She would watch it come crashing down, and let them struggle to rebuild with the fear that she might tear it down again. And she would. Gladly.

That began with rescuing Jin's parents.

For Jin, of course. But like the ledger, snatching the Siwangs from the Ram's clutches would be severing another limb from the masked monarch, and the EJC too, really. The vampires, her sleeping army, would be next. Soon, only Lady Linden would remain.

The five of them meandered through the hubbub. Jin waved away a newsboy. Arthie turned her nose from the vendors selling fresh fish to a sparse crowd, her gaze set on the ship in the distance, the one they'd sail to Ceylan. It loomed, almost ominous in front of the storm-battered sky.

"I hope we're not intending to sail that beast on our own," Matteo said.

"I thought you were a man of many talents," Arthie said as the salty breeze greeted her.

Matteo's jaw dropped open. "Are you *flirting* with me, darling?"

Jin flicked a brow. "Don't get your hopes up."

"Oh, they're up all right."

"That better not mean what I think it means."

Matteo gave him a wink, green eyes dazzling in the meager light. Jin growled, and Arthie thought it was sweet that he believed she needed protecting. For someone dedicated to ignoring her, he still clutched his status as "elder brother" tight.

"I don't know what that means," Flick said, an innocent babe.

Nor did Arthie think she could explain it to her without Matteo's smug smile spreading wider and Arthie's recently acquired reserve curling her into a ball.

It was Sidharth who saved her the unease, nodding at a group of men waiting in the distance. "An undead crew, at Arthie's behest."

"Vampire sailors," Jin said. Each of them carried an umbrella by their side. It was a droll look entirely.

Arthie nodded. "I'm not risking it with a ship full of starved vampires."

She was aware she spoke of the starved vampires as though certain of their rescue. From the way Flick glanced at her, she could tell she thought the same.

"The crew belongs to that dignified fellow in the middle with the tricorn, goes by Silas Vane. Once a naval captain, now an Athereum official," Sidharth said, his dark eyes on the man. "You can trust him."

"I never knew the ships were so large," Flick said as they drew closer.

"No better way to transport her stolen goods," Jin said, grim.

Flick made a face as though she'd swallowed something sour. The girl had been on her way to separating herself from her mother quite well, until they'd learned Lady Linden was the Ram. In Arthie's eyes, that should have only deepened the divide between them, but she supposed it would take time. Arthie's own parents had been dead for ten years and she still thought of them.

As promised, Willard was waiting near his office. He tipped his head when Arthie approached with Flick's forged letter. He read it, and Arthie saw his lips purse as he did. He was impressed.

"The dockmaster's just arrived," he said, making no mention of the forged letter and assessing the others as he spoke. "I'll hand this to him, convey that the ship is due for inspection, and clear the deck. Then you and I are finished."

"I want the ship emptied too, if you recall. You'll also put a hold on any and all documents pertaining to the vessel," Arthie reminded him. "Send word to my colleague here, and do as she asks."

He looked at Flick. "Her?"

Out of the corner of her eye, Arthie saw Jin stir, about to blow the entire operation to the sea before Matteo held him back with a subtle shift of his shoulder in front of him.

"Yes, *her*," Arthie said, surprising herself with the confidence she had in Flick.

"Very well," Willard said, and nodded to his men who were waiting just out of earshot. They leaped to attention, quickly unwinding a length of bright rope to cordon off the pier.

Arthie pulled the others off to the shaded cover of freshly netted shipping crates.

"How did you get an inspector in your pocket?" Matteo asked. "They're typically as clean as they come."

"He is," Arthie admitted. "But his son isn't."

"No one we need to take care of, is there?" Matteo asked, a flash of darkness zipping through his green gaze. He traced down her form with concern. And Arthie, well, Arthie looked away because she didn't hate it.

"Shh," Jin hissed. "The dockmaster."

Arthie leaned close to the edge of the crates as the dockmaster shook Willard's hand and gestured to the ship. "Apologies, inspector. This one's already checked and approved."

Willard nodded, touching the brim of his hat. "It's dated a month ago, good sir. Policies are changing, and I've begun a series of exhaustive inspections after certain hooligans ran amuck a few weeks ago."

The dockmaster laughed. "This is an EJC vessel, sir. I can assure you no one runs amuck."

"I'm aware," Willard replied, pulling out the folded document. The dockmaster scanned it, and Arthie saw his gaze drop to the bottom, where Flick's forged signature burned bold with instructions to vacate the ship and berth until further notice. "By order of the Ram."

The dockmaster scratched his scruff. "I'll need to write to the head office."

Willard paused and wet his lips. Arthie waited, jaw set. She was more than happy to expose the junior Otis, but she needed that ship.

"No need," Willard finally said. "As part of the reworked policies, I will reach out to the EJC offices directly. Oh, and if you can sign here for me, that will cover it."

"What am I signing?" the dockmaster asked, barely reading it over.

"Simply a disclosure saying that I informed you of the inspection and the next steps in the process."

After a moment's hesitation, the man scribbled his signature. It was a sham, more so Flick had his signature to add to her records, but also in part so the dockmaster would sleep easier knowing he'd signed away the responsibilities.

He gave Willard a tight smile. "Right, I'll clear it out."

"Much obliged," said the inspector, and it wasn't long before the dockmaster cleared both the ship and the pier, not noticing when one of Sidharth's runners trailed the cargo route, scratching his scruff again when the inspector told him he would berth the ship elsewhere for the duration of the inspection.

He looked ready for his part in this to be over, which Arthie took as another good sign. Though the more seamlessly this went, the more dread pooled in her stomach.

"It's yours," Willard said, coming over to them. "Crewless and cargo-less. I don't know what you're planning, Casimir, but I want no part in it."

"You won't have any part in it," Arthie replied. "We have a deal, and I keep my word."

It was too late for him to back away now, and with a grimace, he realized it too.

"Safe travels, if only for the sake of the ship," he said.

Arthie said nothing as Willard Otis strode away, leaving them to their devices. Good man. Sidharth went to Silas Vane with final instructions as he and his crew boarded the ship.

"Right, Jin—" Arthie stopped, but he wasn't by her side. She turned in a circle and spotted him a short distance away, like a scene from a play. Jin was on the pier, his brow pressed to Flick's as the sea tumbled beyond them, the wind whipping their clothes. His eyes were closed, pain crowding the plains of his face.

He pulled away while she watched, and Flick took a tiny step back, as if it physically hurt to do so.

"You'll be missed, Flick," Arthie said as she and Matteo joined them.

Flick turned, her eyes bright with tears. "As will you, Arthie."

They'd come a long way since Flick had walked through Spindrift's doors and Arthie had recruited her services, knowing full well she had wanted to double-cross them for her mother. Now she was a part of the crew scrambling to take *down* her mother.

"Keep them safe, Matteo," Flick said.

Jin made a sound in the back of his throat, and turned toward the ship without a word. It would have appeared rude if Arthie didn't know otherwise: If he stayed here any longer watching Flick's tears, he might never board the ship.

"I promise," Matteo said with a tiny bow, and hurried off to Jin.

When it was just the two of them left, Flick picked up a tiny case. "Oh, and here. A gift for you three. But—open it later."

"I'll think about it," Arthie teased, taking it from her. It was fairly heavy, interestingly. And then Flick threw her arms around Arthie, holding her tight. The pitter-patter of Flick's heart raced against Arthie's rib cage until she finally pulled away. "Don't scout out the tribute site. We'll be fine. I'll protect him. *You* stay safe, and we'll reunite at the Athereum."

Flick nodded. "Seven days, Arthie."

Arthie didn't need the reminder, but she took it as Sidharth returned, silver hair shimmering in the light. He gave her a small salute with another promise to free the vampires housed in the warehouses here in Ettenia, and then it was time.

Arthie paused before the ship, heart lodged in her throat. It was only a ship; it was only the sea. She had a job, and that should take precedence as it always did.

But it didn't.

A shadow fell over her, and she dropped her eyes to the ground, not wanting Matteo to read her, but read he did.

"You can do this," Matteo said softly.

Arthie drew a breath and walked the gangway, gritting her teeth as the ground bobbed beneath her and the memories threatened to drown her whole.

"Let's not forget the satisfaction to come when we surprise the

Ram, eh?" he asked.

Arthie cracked a smile at that. If Matteo could go from Wolf to prolific painter, Arthie could brave the seas. And after? The Ram would foot the bill.

The EJC ship was beautiful, more extravagant than Arthie had thought it could be, varnished and detailed. *A beautiful grave.* For the ship was one of many the Ram used to transport her unconscious vampires, soon to be weaponized, exploited, and killed for her purposes. No, there was nothing beautiful to it.

Captain Silas Vane and his men untied ropes and loosened sails and set off without a fuss, and as the ship slowly drifted from the port, Flick shrank smaller and smaller. She waved one last time, and Arthie and the others waved back. Arthie heard the tremor in Jin's exhale, but she felt nothing of the sort herself, encased, instead, in a sense of numbness.

The seas were calm, as if waiting with bated breath for Arthie to do as she'd done the last time she stood among the waves.

But she wouldn't. She was different now. Right? She tried to find comfort in the fact that there were no humans aboard. Not far from her, Jin clutched the railing, staring into the churning waters and looking sicker by the second.

"It helps to not stare at it," she said, and he began turning his head in acknowledgment before thinking better of it.

Arthie sighed.

Matteo squeezed himself between them with a look to either side. "I knew joining the Casimirs would be an adventure, but I never saw myself leaving Ettenian shores with the pair of you."

Neither Arthie nor Jin responded.

Matteo sighed. "Good talk." Then he peered into the sloshing waves. "It's a pity vampires can't swim."

That piqued Jin's curiosity. "They can't?"

"Supposedly," Matteo admitted with a shrug. "I've never tried it myself, but I can see why it's not recommended. One, there's no cover from the sun, and I know there's no sun at night, so that brings me to point two: Swimming has been known to do wonders to heart health, increasing blood flow to arteries and the like. Excellent for humans, not so much for vampires. The better our systems work, the faster we run out of blood and can potentially starve."

"Which won't kill you—us," Jin said. Arthie had resigned herself to never hearing that tone in his voice again. That curiosity, that deep-in-thought interest. She thought it had crashed and burned with Spindrift.

Matteo shrugged. "Well, one might argue that the inability to die is worse than death. Imagine being suspended in a state of being barely alive. To drown endlessly or starve without end. Regardless, don't get any ideas."

Arthie's mother once said that to be Ceylani was to be one with the sea that cupped the island in its jeweled blue palm. Arthie had learned how to swim before she could walk. Could she still be considered a Ceylani if she couldn't wade the waters beneath the heavy weight of the sun?

"We need to discuss our next course of action," Arthie said, quieting her unending, spiraling thoughts.

"On the island? I thought we didn't know what to expect," Matteo said. "Oh, she's looking at me like I suggested she ought to start walking on her hands. Jin? Assistance, please."

"Arthie always has a plan. She doesn't cross the street without one,"

Jin explained, before realizing he had just aligned himself with her and turned his head away again.

She barely stopped her eyes from rolling.

"Forgive me, darling, for I have transgressed," Matteo said, lowering his head.

"The sun's getting bright; I'm going below," Jin said, rubbing at his exposed skin. The burn was a gradual thing, a discomfort that slowly shifted into an itch. It was no different than the living being afflicted with sunburn, only for a vampire, that process was sped up.

Jin paused at the hatch.

"Well?" he asked coldly when neither Matteo nor Arthie moved to join him.

Arthie didn't know why she was watching Matteo so closely, why she was hoping he would be disappointed to not have time alone with her.

At last, his lips jutted in the slightest pout. Arthie prickled with pleasure.

He said he wanted to tease her? Two could play at that game. She brushed past him, making sure she swept a finger across his middle, dipping to the button looping his trousers in place, underestimating how excruciating it would be for herself, as every part of her ached for more. A strangled sound escaped his throat before she yanked up the hatch and followed Jin below deck.

"I don't even want to know why you've got that grin on," Jin said tiredly when she stepped through the cabin's doorway. He was leaning against the wall, arms crossed, half bathed in shadow.

Matteo followed her in and sank into the chair that was bolted to the floor, ignoring her. "This place"—he paused and cleared his throat—"forgive me, this place is almost as lavish as my house."

"Your modesty is unmatched," Arthie said, unable to hide

the gloat from her tone.

"I try," Matteo said.

"Right, so our plan," Jin said pointedly.

"What plan? We have a list of unknowns, no?" Matteo asked. "We don't know where your parents even are."

"We do," Arthie said. "Flick and Jin discovered last night that the Ram recently finished construction of a fortress on the island, along with a sanatorium where the vampires are being delivered."

After a moment, Matteo spoke slowly, as if treading a dangerous line. "And, you might have considered this already, but do we know which side the Siwangs work for?"

"The right one," Jin snapped. "Ours."

Matteo didn't brush off Jin's anger. No, his voice was gentle when he spoke. "You're not new to this, Jin. You know anyone can change sides."

Arthie wondered if he spoke of Laith, or Lady Linden, who was revealed to be the Ram. Arthie remembered he had painted for her too. Whatever his reasons, Arthie was at once struck by how different he was from that first moment she'd stepped through his doors.

"Don't question my parents to me," Jin said through gritted teeth, but Arthie recognized the undertone to his words. He had asked himself the same question, and he was already afraid of the answer.

"It doesn't matter," Arthie said. "If they're on our side, they'll assist us. If they're on hers, we'll use force. Regardless, we will not only rip out a crucial cog of her operation, we will end it."

Jin was still trying to convince himself that they weren't what his gut was saying they were. "They were recognized by the Eagle long before the Ram came into power. They're well-known in high circles. Trusted, even."

If they still were. Arthie wasn't so certain, but their resources were dwindling, and if it was a possibility, she would take it.

She opened her sack and pulled out a small box she had brought with her. Inside were two revolvers and bullet belts. "I know neither of you are particular about guns, but this trip isn't about what we like or don't."

Matteo made a face as he took it gingerly, but she saw the way he released the cylinder to see if it was loaded. He caught her looking. "My father was a marksman. He insisted I learn, unfortunately."

"My father hates guns," Jin countered, securing his belt and holstering the revolver.

Arthie snapped the case closed and tucked it away. She didn't think her parents had ever seen guns before the Ettenians came to Ceylan.

"The Siwangs are our priority," she said, moving on, "but once we find them, we'll find the vampires too. Shall we scope out the ship? Judging from the size alone, I'm sure a good number of them will fit, should they decide to join us."

"They might be dangerous," Jin reminded.

"We're aware," Matteo said. "We don't know the state of anything on the island. They might not even be conscious."

Arthie had known Ceylan like the back of her hand, once. The Ceylani treated their land differently than Ettenians did their own. From the sea to every part of the coconut, from the gems buried deep in the earth to the wildlife that called the tropical paradise home, the Ceylani were one with their surroundings.

Jin gave him a look.

Matteo sighed. "I don't mean to be curt. I don't think many fully understand that we're not talking of stolen cargo or resources, but living people."

"Living?" Jin asked, and Arthie snapped her gaze to his, but it wasn't a retort. He was genuinely curious. For his own sake, it seemed.

"Of a sort, if I'm being honest. I do believe that when one takes away the promise of death and the prospect of aging, people can change. The longer one lives, the less we pay heed to consequence and the more morals fade away," Matteo mused.

"Then there are vampires like Penn," Arthie added.

"Nuanced as those who are alive, I suppose," Jin said, and it sounded as though he had thought long and hard about this. Was he questioning his own morals? Was he afraid of what he might become? "But the fact still stands that they're being seen as inanimate objects, that they're being treated as though they deserve no say in their lives."

"We'll give that to them," Arthie promised. "Whether that means returning to Ettenia with us or remaining on Ceylan is up to them."

Matteo nodded, pleased.

"But as Jin said, we still need to be open to the possibility that we'll have to point Calibore at them."

Arthie was surprised to find herself more concerned with whether they were to be trusted than she was about locating them. She might know where they were, but she hadn't *seen* the place herself, and that didn't make this voyage any less mired with unknowns. Still, Arthie was beginning to realize she didn't need to scope out a place to scheme. She felt as if she'd done this before, as if every job she'd pulled since arriving in Ettenia as a little girl had prepared her for this moment.

"I almost forgot," Arthie said, picking up the case Flick had given them. She glanced at Jin before they could leave the cabin. "A parting gift from your beloved."

Jin's brows flattened. "She's not—Flick?"

"I didn't realize there were other possibilities," Matteo said with a sideways look.

Jin scowled.

Arthie unlatched it and found a note. "*Sidharth promised they were freshly bottled. Drink up!*" A sinking feeling settled into her gut. She peered inside to find three slender glass bottles. "Blood."

"Oh, good," Matteo said, taking one. "I was famished." He looked between Arthie and Jin and gestured to their gift. "Well? Don't defy the lady's orders, now."

Jin moved first, picking up his bottle, touching the note with a dark gleam in his eyes that made Arthie wonder if he would have preferred to drink straight from Flick. He unscrewed the cap without a sliver of the hesitation Arthie had exhibited for the past decade of her life. No, to him this was another form of sustenance. He'd always been partial to food; why was blood any different?

He caught her looking and her shoulders seized, waiting for his glare. Instead, she was surprised to see a flash of trepidation. She was wrong. He *wasn't* without hesitation. He wasn't disgusted either. No— he hadn't fed since the night she'd turned him. He was afraid, nervous of taking that first sip and tumbling over the edge.

Arthie felt that in her soul, but she felt more than that too: He was her brother. She'd spent the past decade avoiding the consumption of blood as much as watching over him at every turn, keeping him alive and ensuring he was safe.

That was what made her pick up her bottle.

That was what made her unscrew the lid.

In an instant, the smell of blood assaulted her—sharp and metallic. Heady and honeyed in a sickly sort of way. It reminded her of what she'd done, and the swaying of the ship beneath her didn't help.

Jin was watching. Matteo was too, but this wasn't a moment between him and her. This was Jin's.

"It's nowhere close to coconut, is it?" he asked softly.

She made a sound. "Not one bit."

Heart in her throat, Arthie stared at the bottle, at the liquid inside that sloshed with a consistency thicker than water, in a color that was rich and jeweled, no different than Spindrift after-hours. In the hushed silence of the crashing waves, Jin's stomach growled.

He was starving.

With a stuttering inhale, Arthie lifted her bottle to him. "*Dulce periculum?*"

He lifted his eyes to hers, held them. For longer than a second, for the first time in what felt like a breathless forever. *Are you sure?* his gaze asked.

She dipped her chin in answer. She had never felt more sure, because the emotions coursing through her veins just then were elation, excitement, hope—because of *him*.

He didn't ask again. He clinked his bottle against hers and lifted it to his lips, taking a swig just as she did, nostrils flaring as he swallowed.

Feeding when one was turned was one thing, but choosing to drink when a vampire had their wits about them was different. It was a deliberate act. A choice. Jin had just made his.

And Arthie—well, Arthie had done the same. When the first syrupy drop fell upon her tongue, it was as though a switch had flipped within her. She was hungry, starved. It was nectar on her tongue, sweet and wretched, and she downed the bottle within moments, each sip coating her tongue, her throat, searing a line through her insides until the bottle was empty.

Arthie pressed her eyes closed and opened them again and it was as if she could see once more. As if a vibrancy had returned to the world around her, a clarity that had been muffled by her hunger for far too long.

She had fed from Laith in a moment of weakness and passion. She had fed off of Matteo, too, when he turned her.

Despite both of those moments, Arthie counted this as her first since she'd sworn off blood as a young girl. When she'd sworn to preserve the remnants of her humanity.

Jin could barely tamp down his smile as he tucked his now-empty bottle away. "I must admit that was good."

It *was* good. It was especially good to have shared that moment with *him*.

"Well, well, darling," Matteo said, grinning from ear to ear. "Now that you understand what Spindrift was about, shall we return to avenging it?"

"Spindrift after-hours," she corrected.

"You served blood after-hours, but you served that"—Matteo stopped and gestured to her—"at all hours. Those emotions, that contentment. Tea, blood, human, vampire, regardless of whether one walked in the shadows or the light, you gave them the sustenance they craved." His eyes were bright with intent because he understood her hesitance. "Is that not a fundamental part of being human?"

She'd never considered that. She looked away. How had he known her humanity was the reason she'd refused to drink blood?

"Both of you did," Matteo added, opening the cabin door. "Together. And that's how we'll waltz in, grab our people, and waltz out. It'll be a breeze."

"That easy, eh?" Jin snarked as they closed the door behind them, sidestepping the narrow passageway lined with cabins. "Like any other job, certainly."

Yes, Ceylan was another job, nothing more, she reminded herself. *But is it?* Ceylan was also home. *But is it?*

She didn't believe in talking to the dead, in saying farewell to her parents who were now long gone. She didn't want to scout out her old home and walk through its tiny rooms. Some other family likely lived in it now. Life carried on, even if it came to a halt for some. And even if she wanted to do both of those things, there wasn't time. They had a job and a time limit.

Nor did Arthie have anyone left. Her deepest connection to the island was the tea the Ettenians had planted in scores.

She had spent the last ten years in White Roaring ever aware of how she stood out and couldn't fit in, but not once had she considered that every day she spent assimilating into Ettenia was a day she spent whittling away at the ties that tethered her to Ceylan.

She belonged nowhere, and it was a very lonely place to be.

They fell quiet when the narrow passageway opened to a larger hall-like space. It was dimly lit, the central portion wide and empty. She was surprised by how clear her vision was, how much *more* she could comprehend. The space smelled sterile, metallic.

Like blood.

Arthie stopped.

"I was expecting cells," Matteo whispered.

"Me too," Jin murmured. "Chains. Imprisonment."

Instead, there were shelves upon shelves, empty, rising to the ship's ceiling, each wide and tall enough to fit one particular style of cargo: coffins.

To prove her assumption, there was a single, empty coffin at the end. When she'd described the ship as a beautiful grave, she didn't expect to find a literal *tomb* in its depths.

"I—" Matteo stopped and cleared his throat. "This is worse than throwing a vampire in a cell. Imagine traveling across the ocean in a *box*."

It was true the kidnapped vampires had little control over themselves, but Matteo was right—this was worse.

"It's an entirely more efficient method of transport," Arthie said, feeling sick. Jin looked equally ready to hurl the contents of his stomach.

Matteo's mouth tightened. "I'd wager the coffins are lined with spikes too. As an extra level of precaution."

For a moment, none of them said a word.

"Well," Jin said finally. "It's a good thing we were already angry, eh?"

11

FLICK

Flick clutched the hat Arthie had given her to lend her *some* protection from prying eyes as tightly as if it was her rampant heart. She was alone. As the stolen EJC ship drifted away, a gaping emptiness stretched inside of her. *Naronic*, the ship was named, painted in ivory along its dark bow. Several of the letters weren't straight, the kerning slightly off, and Flick couldn't look at them for long without turning antsy.

Better that than sad, she thought. When she had first begun working with the Casimirs, she'd never anticipated missing one so terribly to the point where it hurt to breathe.

Sad and *afraid*. She had waved Sidharth off when he wanted to leave before the ship disappeared from sight, and now she was beginning to regret it. The threat of her mother's men surged again without the Casimirs' presence to dull it, along with Arthie's warning to Chester and the boys about the missing humans. Would the Ram kidnap her? It wasn't as though her men knew Flick was her daughter.

Willard Otis handed her an address. "Meet me at ten bells tomorrow. That's when my runner will bring around any new paperwork."

Delightful, Flick didn't say, taking the card from him.

He glanced at her dubiously one last time, his eyes brightening a fraction in what Flick feared was recognition. She whirled away, and after a moment's pause, she heard him step into his carriage. Flick exhaled as his tawny horses trotted him away into the midday traffic, and then the dockworkers were rolling up the ropes that had cordoned off the pier.

"Want us to follow him?" Chester asked. "Make sure he stays quiet?"

"Arthie already took care of that," Reni chided.

"Get back to the Athereum," Flick said.

Felix frowned. "But—"

"Nope," Flick said. "I've got work to do, and don't tell me Arthie didn't give you a list of tasks to do yourselves."

"She's right," Reni murmured, guiding the younger boys away. "Be careful, miss."

"I will," Flick said with a nod, watching them weave through the square and into the street in the direction of the Athereum.

And then she was alone.

She sighed. It wasn't that she didn't want their company, but she was like Arthie and Jin and Matteo—recognizable. The last thing she wanted was to be responsible for them getting caught.

She couldn't stay here forever, tucked into the shadows of the port offices, but she wasn't particularly keen to venture back into the open either. Horned Guard were everywhere, their uniforms in every shade between white and black to indicate rank. Flick wrapped her arms around herself, wishing she had little Opal with her at least, but she'd left the kitten in the safety of her room back at the Athereum.

Flick tightened her hand around the satchel by her side and glanced back toward the expanse of the sea, as if Jin and the others might have already returned. "Now what?"

Now you sit and recollect every feature of my face that you adore, and why, Jin said in her head, most matter-of-factly.

Of course he'd say such a thing. Goodness, he had *just* left and she was already having make-believe conversations with him.

The ledger weighed heavily beside her. The tribute was inching closer. She had work to do.

The Athereum was much too far away—she didn't want to risk such a long trek with so many guards present and so few crowds to blend into. She pulled her knit cap tight over her hair, ignoring the errant curls that tickled her neck, and stepped from the shadows, hurrying past the graveyard and through the thick of White Roaring until she found the shady grove near the portside of White Roaring Square where she would sometimes sit to collect her thoughts. Her heart pounded, muffling everything else.

Despite the trees shedding leaves and turning bare throughout the capital, this grove was lush, foliage teeming beneath her feet, branches swaying with the breeze. It looked as untouched as the days when she would run to its shelter to get away from her mother.

A different time, a different Flick.

Now she had a mission. Making sure she was alone and out of sight, she pulled out the ledger from her satchel to thumb through what she'd tabbed that could potentially give them an upper hand for the tribute. If such a thing as an upper hand was possible. *Arthie says it is.* That had to be enough.

But Arthie didn't know Flick's mother. Arthie didn't know how ruthless Lady Linden could truly be. Flick closed her eyes for the briefest of moments. She couldn't dwell on that. She couldn't allow herself to spiral. If her mother truly was that terrifying, Flick needed to do what she could to give them that upper hand. To make sure they won this time.

For good.

She could scout out the site of the tribute, but Arthie had told her not to. Flick would focus on other tasks first, like the personalized invitations she needed to send. She had a list of names that she was almost excited to contact, for they weren't fond of Lady Linden, but they would be most eager to be a guest of the Ram's. They didn't yet know there was no difference between the two people.

Their scorn was just what the crew needed to help ruin the Ram's image. But Flick was quick when it came to forging letters in her mother's hand. It could wait for now.

She opened the ledger with a sigh. She'd read much of the book already, but her earlier sleuthing had been for clues on Ceylan and the Siwangs, not the tribute and the Ram's plans outside of the weaponized vampires. Home wafted through the pages as she turned them, that unique smell that could only spawn from a culmination of other scents, from the soil used in their indoor plants to her mother's perfume. Flick ran her fingers over a page, feeling the imprint of her mother's words, wishing she didn't feel a spike in her heart at the sight of them.

The others were sailing off to an island. Deciphering a book and forging documents were the least Flick could do.

12
JIN

Jin had lived in a constant state of breathless anticipation since he had died. Even now, as he stood aboard the EJC ship, his insides were churning, roiling, and it wasn't because the sea was doing the same beneath him. He wanted to dig his hand into his pocket and toss a clove rock between his teeth. He wanted to lick raspberry jam off his fingers. He wanted to look at Flick's sunshine curls and calm himself.

He felt incomplete, something he rarely ever experienced when it was him and Arthie against the world.

He still tasted blood on his lips. In reality, Jin didn't mind his new sustenance. He was surprised by how strangely sweet it had tasted. It wasn't as though he hadn't tasted blood before. He'd nicked enough fingers and sucked on enough wounds in the battlefields that were both inventing and running the streets, but it tasted different now. Better. Sweeter, yes, but with distinct notes if he really sat down and allowed himself to savor each sip, and Jin had always been known to savor.

Two paces and a million miles away, Arthie gripped the rail and stared into the distance, the billowing sails casting her in shadow. She held her hat tight against her head, the mauve swoops of her hair rippling with the wind. There was something more she hadn't told him. He'd seen it in her eyes when she'd lifted her bottle to his in the hold of the ship.

Arthie had always been small for her age, but he'd never seen her actually *look* it. As if the world had grown larger since she'd been turned into a vampire and she wasn't so sure of her place in it anymore.

He took a step closer, and her head whipped toward him. The look on her face, raw and open, was so deprived of her usual mask that it gave him pause.

"The last time I was at sea, I killed people."

Jin froze at her words.

Her voice was eerie, distant in a way Arthie rarely ever was. She turned to face him fully.

"Remember when Matteo said I came to Ettenia on a boat filled with blood? It was the blood of the people I killed."

One of the crew spotted them and started walking their way for small talk. Jin shooed him off with his umbrella.

Arthie didn't even notice. "There were only four of us on that boat. Fleeing. They'd done nothing to hurt me, but if there had been more, I likely would have killed them too. Penn took me in when I set foot on shore, and I killed some of his staff too. I was a half vampire, like the Wolf of White Roaring. Like Matteo."

Jin had not known any of this. *That* was the reason for her pause, the reason she'd drunk nothing but coconut water, eagerly gobbling it up when they'd met for the very first time.

Which meant—

"You drank that blood because of me," he said.

She lifted a shoulder. "Eh, I was hungry."

A corner of his lips hitched in a smile. Hers matched.

"Do you see why I couldn't tell you? I couldn't simply say, *Jin, I'm a vampire*, and let it be. I was going to give you the whole truth or none of it," she said, and for a beat, there was no sound but the waves crashing against the ship.

"You could have though," Jin finally said. "You could have told me and I would have understood, because I know *you*. I've known you from the moment you took my hand in front of my parents' burning house. Nothing would have changed that."

If anything, Jin thought this new information helped him understand her better.

Her anger, her deeply ingrained need for vengeance, her pain that she allowed no one else to see.

"I trusted you with everything," he continued. "I only wished for the same in return. I had no one but you."

She said nothing.

That was that, he supposed. He inhaled deep, remembering when Matteo had alerted him to the fact that he didn't have to anymore. Jin couldn't see a world where he didn't breathe—unless he was completely, utterly dead. He joined Arthie at the rail, facing the sea. After a beat, he placed his hand over hers. She glanced down and then at him, a little hopeful and a little dubious.

"We're all right, Arthie. If I'd massacred a boatful of people myself, I wouldn't want you knowing either," he drawled.

Arthie rolled her eyes. There she was, that tempest in a bottle he knew so well. Shouts rose from the crew as they turned course, and Jin watched as Arthie's gaze drifted across the deck.

"He's not here," Jin said.

"I wasn't looking," she lied.

"Sure." Jin nodded. In the distance, he saw a tail disappear into the ocean. "So, the Wolf of White Roaring, eh?"

"What's that supposed to mean?" she asked with a sideways glance.

Knowing that Matteo was the Wolf and knowing what Arthie had done herself . . . their bond made far more sense. Even if Arthie wouldn't give into it or admit what it meant.

The hatch creaked open and Matteo climbed on deck, looking

between Jin and Arthie when they fell silent.

"Talking about me?"

"No," Arthie said at the same moment Jin said, "Maybe."

Matteo cracked a laugh. "For two of White Roaring's most notorious criminals, you're terrible liars."

"Only for you," Jin said, and it was true.

Arthie was struggling to hide it, but she was flustered, her composure nowhere near the calm, cool, and collected mask she usually plastered on herself. It was yet another reminder of how much they'd changed. Arthie, Matteo, Flick.

Jin didn't want to think about what lay ahead. He had his umbrella and his just-reconciled sister, but that didn't relieve as much stress as he would have liked. He had only what the ledger said to guide them.

"We'll find them," Arthie said quietly.

Because that was what Arthie did: followed through, and that fact was perhaps what Jin was most concerned about. He'd spent years wanting to find his parents, and now that he was finally headed in that direction, now that they were finally attainable, he found himself wavering.

Were his parents the same people that they were a decade ago? He certainly wasn't. He wasn't even alive now, and that—that was the core of it, he realized. He could understand Arthie and her reluctance to tell him the truth just then. Because he was a criminal, a vampire, nowhere near the high society boy his parents had raised, and he didn't know if they would want him anymore.

"Thank you," he said at last. "For doing this. I know it's not easy on you."

Arthie pulled a face. "It's nothing. Besides, I owe it to you."

"No, you don't."

She smiled. "No, I don't."

13

ARTHIE

After two days at sea, Arthie still had to remind herself that she was in a ship, not a tiny boat again. Every blink conjured blood sloshing against her bare shins, moving with the ocean's current. The skies had split open after she'd done what she'd done, and no matter how much water pooled inside her tiny vessel, she hadn't sunk.

She had wanted to sink. To drown. She wished the sea would swallow her whole.

In the years since, Arthie hadn't allowed herself to recall these long-deemed "moments of darkness"—not until she had retreated back into them after the Great Press Massacre.

If not for Matteo, she would have entertained them longer in the shelter of his canopied bed and the Athereum one after. She would have folded further into herself.

"That's enough," she told herself, and rose from the crate she was sitting on in the dark corner of the captain's cabin.

"There you are."

Matteo sidestepped the wide slant of light on the floorboards cast by the sun through the window and sat on the floor in front of her, propping an arm behind him.

"You're hiding."

"Am I?" she asked, pulling on her suit jacket.

"Unless you're here protecting your skin from the sun, yes."

She snorted. "I might be a vampire, but I'm no peaky. The sun doesn't hurt me as much as it does you."

"Arthie, Arthie," he said with a sigh. "*I* might be a vampire, but you're always finding new ways to stake me through the heart."

"As you can see, I'm getting ready to leave," she said, but when he looked at her, his teasing replaced with something earnest, she sat back down on the crate with a sigh.

Waves lapped and crashed in the silence between them.

"I can't stand up there and relive it over and over again," she said eventually.

"Understandably. One isn't out at sea very often," Matteo said. "I couldn't walk the streets of White Roaring for the longest time myself."

His gaze drifted to the dust stirring in the light of the window. Arthie never thought she'd find anyone like her, and she appreciated when he opened up to her, trusted her. She couldn't say she liked doing the same, but she tried. He made the words easier. He was forced to be a monster, and he knew what it took to be peaceful.

"Ceylan will be a test, but you will ace it," Matteo continued. "I know it."

"I left right as the Ram was sinking her claws into the island," Arthie said. "I don't know what she's done to it."

Outside of what she'd heard about Ceylan—and almost every country Ettenia had colonized really—she knew little for certain. From the streets near Ceylani and Jeevani shops, she'd heard snippets about streaks of poverty brought on by the newcomers and dwindling resources. She'd heard of deforestation, and the way it had permanently altered, *butchered*, the very earth that made up the island. She'd seen the skilled and the talented arriving on Ettenian shores for the promise of a "better life"—handing over their expertise to a place that had ruined the better life they already had.

The real and true happenings of other countries and kingdoms weren't written about in Ettenian newspapers. Not enough cared.

"Whatever she's done, you're planning to undo, remember?" he asked.

There was no undoing what had been done, but he was right. Arthie would make change happen.

"And after? What will you do once you've saved the vampires and the Siwangs and dismantled the three parts of the Ram's reign?" Matteo asked, tilting his head.

"What do you mean?" she asked, but a part of her knew what he was asking.

Matteo held her eyes. "Do you mean to kill her, Arthie?"

Arthie was no innocent. She had blood on her hands, and she wasn't about to forget that fact. She'd never outright set out with the intention of ending anyone, but the Ram was different, wasn't she? She'd meddled in and destroyed Arthie's life. She'd stolen her childhood, her home, her *humanity*—and Matteo's too. Even Jin's. She deserved to die in the worst way possible.

So why, then, did Matteo's question give Arthie pause?

Arthie hadn't even realized she'd tightened her grip around Calibore until Matteo reached for her hand, as if he knew she was looking for comfort, as if he knew how to provide it, entwining his fingers with hers. Her hand felt small in his, sheltered. Safe.

Perhaps she'd hit her head and boggled her mind, because when had she ever cared about feeling sheltered and safe?

She yanked her fingers from his and pulled out her pocket watch, flustered yet again. "The captain says we'll arrive any moment now."

"Oh really?" he asked.

"Yes. It's already—"

He snatched her watch from her hand, using the chain secured to her vest to pull her close. Arthie was not proud of the yelp that ripped out of her.

"Don't rush me," he whispered, catching her by the waist and cinching the remaining distance between them. She gasped, grabbing ahold of him to halt her fall.

His green eyes were hooded, bleeding to inky darkness as they traced her face, settling on her mouth and lighting her aflame. She might not have a pulse on a regular day anymore, but in that moment, she felt it all over. Pounding through her, an incessant drumming she couldn't tame.

"Arthie, Arthie, Arthie," he whispered, and she followed the sensuous curve of his mouth. "Go on now, tell me what time it is."

Her watch was swinging back and forth against her leg, but she made no move to obey. He ran his hands up her sides, one settling at the nape of her neck, the other brushing the hair from her face.

He lifted a brow in question.

"Don't tell me what to do," she said.

"I believe I will," he said darkly, leaning closer. "What time is it, Arthie?"

She gritted her teeth. He smiled as lazily as a lion regarding a mouse. He wasn't going to let her be until she told him. She reached for her watch, shakily, and when she leaned to her side, exposing her throat, she felt the brush of his hair against her skin.

And then his lips.

He kissed her neck, pulling away and dropping another an inch higher, then another. Arthie thought she would combust.

"Well?" he asked on a scraping exhale she felt more than heard.

She struggled to thumb the latch. He watched her, drinking it in, enjoying every second of this torture. She needed only to turn her cheek and she could kiss him.

What's stopping you?

Nothing. Nothing was stopping her. She was Arthie Casimir, and she seized what she wanted, no matter what was in her way.

Arthie turned her cheek. The warm lacquered wood framed him in opulence. She dropped her watch, threaded her fingers in his hair, pulled him to her.

And then she kissed him.

The most glorious groan escaped him, and she swallowed every morsel of the sound before he kissed her back. It was as intoxicating as the moment he turned her, as decadent as sipping blood, as victorious as pulling off a job.

His lips were soft, his kiss firm. He was cool to the touch, as vampires were wont to be, but he smelled the opposite, sending warm shivers down her spine.

He took command of her the way she imagined he commanded a canvas before him, painting a portrait of lust in shades of red and crimson, deep strokes of violet and amaranth. He bit down on her lip, drawing blood. He rasped at the taste and she wove her fingers tighter in his hair at the sound.

He gripped her waist, just one of his hands wide enough to span the width of her back, then he dropped his hold even lower to her thighs, igniting her. She released his hair and reached for his shirt, doing away with the few buttons he'd bothered to fasten. He lifted her up, grinning against her mouth until she kissed him into another groan. She kissed him passionately, ardently, hard enough to bruise so that he would remember her forever. She wrapped her legs around him, belatedly realizing the position that put her in.

She ground her hips against him with a gasp.

"Praecantrix," he moaned against her mouth, as she shoved her hands into his shirt and traced the lean lines of his chest.

Shouts echoed above deck. He set her on a crate and every inch of her protested, but he pushed closer again, capturing her lips in another kiss until Arthie pulled away with great reluctance. He pressed his brow to hers. His eyes were darker than she'd ever seen them.

Land ho! the watch called.

It took Arthie a long, drunken moment to make sense of the words: They had arrived. Footsteps pounded up above, in time with her roiling, burning need.

"Who knew Arthie Casimir was such an expert in matters of kissing," Matteo said, his voice hoarse.

She jumped off the crate, doing her utmost not to watch him button his shirt back up and adjust his trousers. Her insides burned. Every part of her wanted to turn back to him, fighting the dread that wished so desperately to leave now that they had arrived.

"You know I excel at all that I do," she managed to say, and couldn't decide if she was thankful or not when Jin threw open the hatch and called her name.

14

FLICK

It was two days before Flick could return to the grove after spending the entirety of yesterday running back and forth to meet with the inspector and hand him the multiple forged documents he needed: One was a letter from Willard's own desk signed by the Ram approving an extended hold on the vessel Arthie and Jin had taken. On the second one, Flick simply had to sign a letter from the foreman looking for confirmation that the EJC ship did indeed get berthed in the first place. The third was a letter explaining why the ship might have needed to be moved from the berth should anyone inquire about its whereabouts.

That particular letter took her far too many tries to get right. She might be a forger with an extensive vocabulary, but she was also a girl and not a disdainful official.

And then it was done.

She was free to focus on the ledger, and was so deep within its pages that she jumped when the Old Roaring Tower began to toll. She straightened a crick in her neck and stretched her arms.

"Three bells?" Flick counted in surprise. "It's been hours!"

Jin and the others should have arrived in Ceylan by now, if their calculations were correct.

And Flick had progress of her own to show for it: She hadn't yet forged the invitations, but she'd taken pages and pages of notes, from details she was able to decipher and expand upon to various affairs here in Ettenia that her mother was involved in as both the Ram and the head of the EJC. Flick closed her eyes to clear the many lines and slashes of her mother's code and reopened them to give her notes a proper read.

Every bit of it was horrible.

The Ram extorted and monopolized several exports and imports, successfully—and gleefully—depleting the coffers of long-standing high society names. She had detailed how, too, from securing contracts with the EJC, and thus, herself, or by racking up fees and absurd fines until profit margins weren't feasible in any way for anyone, even high society folk. Then there were plans for how she might influence the pricing on medical amenities—from medications to doctor visits and facilities—that Ettenians would be too desperate not to drop exorbitant amounts of duvin to attain.

Arthie had told Flick to find anything and everything that would help them bring down the Ram, but Arthie didn't have to tell her that it needed to be something of substance. Something loud. As heinous as weaponizing vampires, as heinous as stealing humans off the streets.

Like the real reason why.

"Like you," Flick said to a page in the ledger, smoothing it out. She'd marked it because of how it stood out to her. It featured a building of some sort. An entire segment of the ledger was dedicated to it, including several drawings, a skill to which Flick knew her mother was typically averse.

In the margins, her mother had scribbled something about needing more trials and incubation periods, at the end of which read, *to shift at fortnight*, whatever that meant. Flick didn't know how long ago that fortnight had been, but was it a base for the Ram and her men? There were far too many disparate details written, it seemed, as they struck her mother's mind.

The building's layout was as detailed as could be, considering the lack of artistic talent. It spread wide and long and was a single story as far as Flick could tell, with an open area at its center and several rooms and halls fanning from it, including a large one with a strange set of . . . pill-shaped objects spaced out within. Was her mother creating a new ingestible way to subdue vampires?

The longer Flick looked, she found more questions and fewer answers. She set aside her notes and flipped back through the ledger to study the original drawing again.

"Why, hello there," she murmured to an inset at the corner of the drawing. It nearly blended in with the text. A series of lines were sketched inside a circle, some intersecting, others cutting diagonally. Flick rotated the ledger, studying it every which way, but couldn't tell what it was. Distracted doodles? The method the Ram had used to come up with her code?

Flick rotated the ledger again, and a number of the scraps tucked inside slipped out. Flick growled and began shoving them back inside, pausing when she found a map of the world. She saw Ettenia and the Eastern Colonies, Jeevant Gar and Ceylan. Qirilan and Arawiya. Some were shaded, others not, and Flick realized the shaded countries had been colonized. Some parts of Qirilan too. Not an inch of Arawiya, the kingdom Laith had come from, with its vast expanse, had been touched.

Yet, a voice warned her.

She couldn't worry about that.

"That's it!" Flick exclaimed, studying the inset with fresh eyes. She dug through her satchel for the kit that she carried everywhere, undoing the elastic loop and riffling through her stack of carbon paper, notes, and—*aha!* a map of White Roaring.

The inset was a bird's-eye view of a cluster of streets.

Flick unfolded her map and laid the semitransparent sheet over her mother's drawing, sliding it around while hoping and wishing it was in White Roaring, and not another country again. Like Ceylan, or someplace even more unknown to them.

At last, it matched up. With a relieved laugh, Flick pulled it away and studied the location. Her breath caught. It was certainly in White Roaring, just beyond the river, a side of the capital she rarely visited. Flick studied the corner more closely, trepidation settling over her like a cloak.

Near the palace. Where the tribute was to be hosted.

That, Flick thought, was not a coincidence.

She was suddenly hot and cold at once, knowing she needed to see this place for herself and figure out what her mother had planned. For all their sakes. Arthie had specifically told her not to, but Arthie was also sailing to an island where she didn't know what to expect. If she and Jin and Matteo could do that, Flick could do this.

Besides, this wasn't the location of the tribute, which is what Arthie had forbidden, but it was close enough to be concerning.

She folded up her map and notes. These she would keep with her, tucking them into her satchel, but she couldn't tote the ledger around too.

She wrapped the book in a swath of cloth, then in the weatherproof sleeve Arthie had made her store it in, and with a wince, Flick began digging into the dirt, moss, and loam and deteriorating twigs clinging to her fingers and finding a home beneath her nails—a sight she'd never seen, or felt for that matter, before. She grimaced. She tucked the ledger into the dirt and covered it back up again, patting the soil tight and layering as much of the salvaged moss back over it.

Dusting off her hands, Flick hurried from the grove to White Roaring Square, almost forgetting her predicament and the need to keep her head low until she dunked her hands into the fountain and scrubbed away the dirt. *There*. That was better.

"Penny for a paper, miss?" called a newsboy as she crossed the street. Even the newsboys were different since that night. Jittery and skittish. They jumped at every carriage that turned their way, fearful they were next to be kidnapped. Eyes that were once eager for coin now darted for danger.

Flick shook her head at him, heart in her throat as she rushed for cover when a group of Horned Guard turned their way. She didn't want to read another newspaper flaunting the Ram's plans to protect Ettenians from the ever-growing dangers around them. The members of the press who were on Arthie's side, the ones who were truly interested in the truth, were dead. Now the printers ran for the highest bidder, and there was no question who that bidder was.

What are you planning, Mother?

The sketches burned bright in Flick's mind, along with Arthie's disapproval, but Flick would be careful. She *had* to be careful when she had both the Horned Guard and the Ram's private black-clad army to worry about. She hailed a cab to shield herself from prying eyes and watchful guards. The timid driver ushered her inside, and Flick was only happy to oblige as the crowds shouted and stomped their feet not far from them.

With the curtains closed and her hands fisted in her lap, Flick struggled to breathe as the cab trundled through the street, wishing she could silence the mayhem out there. How could her mother let this continue?

The salt of the sea was barely a lick in the air as the carriage took Flick closer and closer to the palace. She didn't have to glance out the window to know where they were as they passed the Athereum and the ruckus surrounding its walls rang loud.

Eventually, the streets turned quiet as they left the thick of the capital and only the clip of the horses' hooves echoed as they passed over the bridge and the river whispered down below. After a few more turns, the carriage came to a halt.

The cab driver opened the door. He looked concerned. "Here, miss?"

Flick peered out at the empty road. The palace loomed in the distance, the Horned Guard headquarters not far to its left. It was past business hours, and there were no people here. His horses snorted in the quiet. The sun was inching below the horizon, and only a few gaslights had been lit.

"Yes, sir. Thank you," she said.

With another look to see if she was going to meet someone, perhaps, the cab driver nodded, climbed back on and drove away.

The skies were clear here, free from the roiling gray of the smokestacks, the air fresher. The last of the sunlight glinted off the palace up ahead, washing the beige stone in gold. Flick kept to the shadows as she turned up the street. The houses here were towering, sprawling with turrets and large windows, with frills and gilded lines beautifying them further. Each had a sign posted out front—they were offices, she realized, each one standing on a meticulously trimmed, vast lawn.

She drew her coat tighter around her and glanced at her map again. She hadn't wanted the cab driver to take her too close to the location. It was near the palace, and there was every possibility that it was guarded and protected; she didn't need clomping horses to give her away.

Goodness, am I really doing this?

Voices rose in the quiet, and Flick froze. They were heading toward her. She ducked her head and tiptoed backwards until she was tucked beneath the cover of a skeletal rosebush. Horned Guard. A squad of them—were they headed in the same direction as Flick? Or back to their headquarters?

Instead of turning left, toward the place her mother had drawn in her ledger, they kept going forward, in the direction of the palace. Of course. The Horned Guard wouldn't be privy to a secret location described in the Ram's ledger. It was her mother's black-clad men who had chased Flick, the black-clad men who had stormed the Athereum meeting hall and murdered the reporters that night. They worked for the Ram alone—a private group of mercenaries for hire, if Flick were to guess—and while the Horned Guard worked for the Ram too, they did so because they worked for the good of Ettenia first.

When the guards disappeared, she ventured out of the shadows and hurried across the street, slowing her footsteps as she neared the bend where the place would be. A house? A storeroom? A warehouse? Flick didn't know, and the anticipation had her heart in her throat. She wasn't far from the palace now either. The sun had disappeared, the quiet deepening as she rushed onward. Why were the locations so close together? It was just beyond the brick wall up ahead. She held her breath and stepped past it, her footsteps light on the leaf-littered cobblestones, and froze.

Nothing.

There was nothing.

That couldn't be. Flick glanced back down at her map, then at her sketches. This was where it should have been. The building, the house, *whatever* the place her mother had drawn. Instead, all that stood before her was a sea of trimmed and manicured grass. Up ahead, the palace wall rose, threatening in the darkness. She could hear the chatter of Horned Guards patrolling its perimeter.

No, she was missing something. She had studied the ledger, she had scoured its pages for hours, *days*, and then studied her notes after. The truth was here. *Something* had to be here, or her mother wouldn't have drawn it to begin with.

That was when she heard it: footsteps. Behind her.

Always trust your instincts, Jin's voice echoed in her head from days ago, and with an overwhelming sense of calm, Flick knew it wasn't the Horned Guard or a lady and lord out for a stroll.

Don't let them know when you know, Jin had also said. *Always keep your composure.*

Flick resisted the urge to reach for her satchel. The ledger wasn't there, she reminded herself. It was safe. She couldn't call out to the guards. By the time they got to her, she'd be dead. She exhaled slowly, moving her hand as casually as she could to her pocket, where her brass knuckles sat. The weight in her pocket was a semblance of comfort. As if Jin was beside her, his umbrella rapping along their path, punctuating his every bold statement.

But he wasn't.

She pulled her hat off her head, suddenly warm, and sucked in a breath as black-clad figures converged from her surroundings. The Ram's men. And this time, Flick didn't think she was getting away.

Her breath clouded in the air. She didn't know how many there were, only that her vision was starting to blur. She tried to feel a sense of pride for hiding the ledger away. For doing as a Casimir would. *Fight, love.* Her fist tightened around the brass knuckles, but what good would it do? She could give one of them a bloody lip or a bloody nose, only to get her weapon ripped away.

No, if she was going to be taken away, she was going to remain armed.

Flick straightened her shoulders and lifted her chin. "What do you want with me?"

Did they know who she was? Was she going to be snatched away like the other unsuspecting humans who had disappeared over the past week and been taken who knows where? Or were they here for the ledger?

"The ledger, and you can go free," one of the men said.

There was her answer.

Flick didn't believe them one bit.

Good girl, Jin said in her head.

She shrugged. "I don't know what you're talking about."

The men looked among themselves, and the one closest to her mimicked her shrug. "Is that right?"

Flick swallowed the fear rising up her throat, refusing to give in even as he strode closer. She took a step back, only to bump into another man behind her. She tried to duck away, then attempted to make a run for it.

But they held her fast, their gloved hands rough and unyielding.

And pulled a sack over her head.

No, no, no. She needed to find out what the tribute would truly be about. She needed to forge invites. She needed to meet Willard in the morning, to keep the ruse of the missing ship going for as long as she could. For Jin's sake. For Arthie's sake. For Matteo.

"We'll jog your memory, worry not," the same man promised.

The cloth was rough and musty, pulling her hair tight against her head and over her brow. Flick suddenly imagined others being apprehended the same way, girls like her, boys, women, men. Kidnapped for her mother to stoke false fear into the hearts of her people, and then possibly killed after. It was getting harder to breathe. To stay awake.

Flick was prodded forward, half dragged. She had the sense they were leading her away from here, but not far enough that they had to hail a carriage. What would Arthie do in this moment? Thank them for saving her the time, really.

Flick couldn't say the words, but she tried her best to feel them.

15

ARTHIE

One might not have been able to tell from the outside, but inside, Arthie was a tempest at sea. She didn't look to the Ceylani shore when she emerged on deck. She went straight to Vane to instruct him to berth away from prying eyes. But he was one step ahead of her because he didn't "quite like the look of the people at shore," the ship turning as she strode toward him, forcing the island in front of her.

Her island. Her home. The sticky heat she had once attributed to her daily life was as foreign as the first time she'd set foot on Ettenia and the cold, dry air had scraped her skin. It might not have been an Ettenian climate, but the sight of the harbor could have fooled her.

There was nothing Ceylani about it.

Colonizers had torn up the trees and shanties and erected a miniature White Roaring sea port, with cargo stacked high beside branches of popular Ettenian shops. There were even a number of horse-drawn carriages in a land full of thatched bullock carts, and for what? As if they needed to be reminded of home while they pillaged and looted every resource they could find a use for.

She didn't see a fortress and wondered for a moment if that was a worse truth, for it meant the fortress was elsewhere, that the Ettenians had constructed far more throughout the island.

Why have you returned? the sea seemed to ask her as it rushed against the sides of the ship. *Why are you here?*

It was so ridiculous that it was maddening. Some strange and twisted hallucination that couldn't possibly be real. How *could* someone take over another land and live guilt-free? How could they destroy and pillage and act as if it was wholly natural and their right to do so?

All she saw were Ettenians, their skin a lot less peaky and a lot more golden from the sun. She had expected it, hadn't she? Ceylan was now an Ettenian colony, but how were there more of them than there were brown-skinned Ceylanis?

"Wicked knives, it's hot," Jin exclaimed as he joined her, shaded by the canopy of his umbrella. He stood close. Their earlier conversation had smoothed some of their wrinkled bond, but only time could mend the rest of it.

His lips tightened as he took in the view just as the ship completed its turn and lanky tropical trees crowded their view. Matteo was just as speechless beside him, anger pulsing at his jaw. His umbrella was a deep shade of crimson, casting a shadowed, reddish hue over his face. There was a familiarity to this moment. She'd stared into another pair of vengeful eyes before. Only this time, *this* anger was stirred because of *her* pain, because of how the scene before them affected *her*, nothing more. It was a strange distinction, indeed.

"You will leave your mark," he said quietly, reminding her of her own words.

"How? By tearing down every Ettenian building standing proud on Ceylani soil?" Jin asked, scorn at the sight before him apparent in his voice.

"Retribution needn't be so loud," Matteo said. "Spindrift wasn't."

But this wasn't the same. This required something loud. A statement, as Matteo had said when he wanted them to steal the EJC vessel.

He was watching her. "Or maybe we can destroy their ships on our way out, possibly even dump their cargo into the sea."

Those were two solid ideas.

The ship wrenched to a halt.

"A port would have been safer," Vane said apologetically as his men extended the longest plank they had.

Arthie shook her head. "We were right not to trust them."

It didn't look entirely safe, but the twisting trees were less risky than showing their faces to the Ettenians at shore. Their ship had been spotted, and no doubt a scouting party would venture this way soon enough to see why they'd berthed so far away, but Arthie and the others hadn't been seen, and that was enough. Besides, she didn't think she had to worry much about an Athereum vampire who also happened to be a naval captain. He could handle his own.

"Best of luck out there," Vane said as Arthie stepped over to the plank, Jin and Matteo in tow. "We'll circle and keep out of sight until your return."

"That's a good man," Matteo observed as soon as they were out of earshot.

Arthie glanced down. The rocky shore was far below, bordering a sea of green leaves—one misstep and she would break her neck. She didn't want to know what that would be like as a vampire.

Matteo gulped. "I'm not too fond of heights."

"Neither am I, which is why I'm not yapping," Jin snapped, his jaw cinched tight.

Arthie raced to the bottom and hopped off, the leafy covering softening her landing as the heat layered her like a coat. She pitched open her umbrella and glanced up at them wobbling and hobbling and bickering their way down. "Any day now."

At last, the doddering men joined her, and Vane's men retracted the plank. Arthie started through the trees without comment, both Jin and Matteo muttering complaints as they dirtied their shoes.

Until a terrifying shriek echoed through the jungle—a bloodcurdling screech. The two of them froze.

"What was that?" Matteo asked, his voice tight.

"Arthie?" Jin whispered.

"A devil bird," Arthie murmured in response, searching the trees. "They're usually only out at night. They say a devil bird's cry portends death."

"How sweet," Matteo said with false cheer.

"Simply wonderful," Jin added.

Arthie ignored them, trekking ahead. She used to be afraid of the bird's shrieks in the dead of night as a little girl. Now there were scarier things in the world. She studied her surroundings. She didn't know where she was. A decade ago, the world was larger, and she really only knew the places she frequented. Under the shade of a towering tree, Arthie swatted away mosquitos as she waited for Jin and Matteo, a familiar scent tickling her nose. It was faint but unmistakable. She glanced up: coconuts. They clung beneath the fanning leaves, ripe for the picking.

When she was younger, her father would knot up his sarong and shimmy up to the top, hacking away with his machete until the entire bunch came loose. He'd shimmy back down and free one of the heavy fruits to create an incision along the top with that same, broad machete and hand it to her with a sweaty brow and a proud smile. Arthie would flip the coconut over into her mouth, lapping up the murky water and the sweet white flesh, though her favorite was when her mother would stir it up with a fresh squeeze of lime and a dash of sugar.

Arthie ached at the memory. She had gone from that—relishing coconuts as a treat—to needing them to survive. *Not anymore.* She glanced at Jin as he and Matteo joined her, remembering the bottles they'd clinked aboard the ship.

No, not anymore, she told herself. And perhaps one day she would go back to that time of her life, to relishing coconuts as a treat.

Goodness, she was beginning to plan for the future. Arthie tried her best to view this like any other job, trying not to let the trees, the heat, and the memories weigh her down. She passed a startled palm civet and beckoned Matteo and Jin to a vantage point on a hill.

"I couldn't spend another second in those trees," Matteo said with a sigh.

"I was melting," Jin agreed.

Arthie sighed. "Men."

In the distance, coconut trees leaned toward the sun, monkeys darted into the foliage. She could hear the trumpet of an elephant, the snorting of oxen. There were hens and cows loitering down one of the dirt roads that wound toward houses, and a river where women were gossiping while washing clothes. She glanced down at the shine of her polished shoes, her tweed suit, the thread work that was Ettenian through and through. Even the hat on her head was more Ettenian than she could ever be. More Ettenian than she ever *wanted* to be.

And to think, she had regretted wearing a sari that matched her mother's. And to think, she had, in some minute way, attributed her failure that night to her heritage. She clutched her anger as if it was a rope and she was hanging on for dear life. Better anger than sorrow. Better rage than pain. Better vengeance than anguish.

Ettenia had forced its way upon her. She never asked to be taken away to Ettenian shores. She never wanted to forge a life for herself in a foreign land. She never asked them to destroy her life and her country.

"Thompson & Thompson Grocers?" Jin sputtered and listed out the rest of the Ettenian storefronts he recognized. "Edith's Spools, Beautiful For Ever—they've gotten comfy."

Arthie said nothing. Beyond the shops and Ettenian replications, there were stacks and stacks of crates waiting to be loaded into the ships crowding the harbor. She could read the name spelled across a fanciful banner even from a distance.

EAST JEEVANT COMPANY GOODS

"Are you all right?" Matteo asked.

"Just fine," Arthie said, her tone clipped as she refused to dwell on her emotions, refusing to do anything but focus on their goal.

Still, she made the mistake of meeting his eyes. He stepped closer, enveloping her in his scent. "If you could use a distraction, just let me know."

Arthie glared, drawing a laugh out of him that she devoured as eagerly as one who was starved.

Jin was watching the exchange but knew better than to voice his thoughts. "I don't see the fortress. Maybe we deciphered it wrong?" He froze and panic flared in his gaze. "What if Flick's cipher is wrong? What if some of her other findings are wrong too? What—"

Arthie pulled him down to a crouch. "Beyond the trees. There."

She gestured to the massive, sprawling stronghold farther inland, just behind the port city, gray-brown stones rising at a slant to parapets. It was difficult to see at first, blending into the wildlife, but once one saw it, it was impossible not to.

The fort was built along the adjacent sea line. Cannons jutted out of windows, ready to protect what was theirs. She bit back a snort. A lighthouse rose toward the sea. Closer, a clock tower with a face in bold black counted away the minutes. Flags had been planted at intervals along the parapet. Not a single one of them was Ceylani.

"It's a lot larger than I thought it would be," Matteo said. "Then again, I'd never seen a fortress."

"And a lot more fortified," Jin said. What did either of them think a fortress would be? "Perfect place for a sanatorium to house vampires—if one escapes, they can cordon it off."

"How do you reckon *we'll* get inside it, then?" Matteo asked.

As they watched, gates rattled open for a line of carriages and a bullock cart. Each was blanketed in black coverings, rocking beneath weighty contents. The Ram wouldn't have built the fort for the vampires alone. It was *massive*, and she wasn't one to waste an opportunity. The place likely housed everything she wanted protected for her colony. The silver sigil embroidered on the carriages was familiar, as were the men in charge: *Horned Guards*.

They inspected each one and the gates immediately rolled closed once they'd passed within.

"That's how we'll get in," Arthie said.

Jin twirled his umbrella. "I've always wanted to commandeer a carriage."

16

JIN

Jin thought Arthie's plan was simple enough, but the heat made everything sound laborious: Track down a Horned Guard carriage, commandeer it, sneak through the fortress gates. Still, he couldn't complain, for it served as a grand distraction from Flick, and the deep-seated ache he felt from being so far from her.

He had vowed not to worry for her welfare, but that didn't make it easy. She was capable, and she was armed, he told himself. She could handle whatever was thrown her way.

They stumbled down the hillside—he and Matteo did, anyway. Arthie navigated the brush like she had lived in it her entire life. Half was just as long, he supposed. As they neared, the township seemed to grow exponentially, spanning roughly a quarter of the size of White Roaring.

"I could probably pick the gate's lock if we can't find a carriage," Jin said. He'd picked all sorts of locks. There was even that one time on Imperial Square where, long story short, a wealthy—for it was always the wealthy—lord had locked him in a cage in his bedroom.

"I'm sure we can ask the guards to hold on while you do," Arthie said cheerily.

"Oh, how I missed your commentary, sister," Jin replied.

"A tea shop!" Matteo said. It was more of a hut, really. And not even staffed by a Ceylani. He grimaced. "Truly puts Spindrift to shame, eh?"

As if conjured by his words, Jin could smell a perfectly brewed cup of Lady Slate with a raspberry streusel on the side. He ignored the flop in his stomach. He didn't need a reminder of what he couldn't consume anymore.

He spotted another shop tucked farther ahead. "Do they take duvin here, you think?"

"Unfortunately," Arthie said dryly, her umbrella washing shadows over her like a gown.

He dragged them over to a peddler with fewer options than he would have hoped. "Good. I think I'm in need of a hat."

"Are you?"

"I'd say the three of us marching with umbrellas is a tad too conspicuous, eh?"

Arthie pursed the side of her mouth in agreement, eyeing him as he tried on different kinds. "A bowler hat?"

"The boy can't look in a mirror to know," Matteo reminded her.

Jin paid the man and pulled the hat snug over his head, closing up his umbrella and testing out the sun. Not bad. "Someone who knows they look good in anything and nothing doesn't need a mirror."

Arthie followed suit, repositioning her baker boy hat and tugging on a pair of gloves. Matteo had neither a hat, gloves, nor enough buttons on his shirt, so under his umbrella he remained.

"Still no sign of a Horned Guard carriage," Matteo said.

"There," Arthie said, pointing to a trio of guards marching up the street. They were laughing, rifles nowhere to be seen. "No weapons; they're off-duty. Not captains, though it'd be ideal if we found one so we'd have a better chance of finding something important. Follow them."

"To?" Matteo asked, but Jin knew better and tailed Arthie as she rushed up the hill.

She came to a halt when they reached the paved road. Jin didn't know if she was reliving a memory or seething just then, but she blinked and the line of her brow smoothed as she tucked away her emotions yet again with a hand on Calibore. They darted up the cobblestones to the edge of a newly built, still-vacant shop, and crouched beside the cover of the shrubs lining the side of it.

"To their haunt," Arthie replied, nodding to the bright red pub. "And there's our carriage."

It was sitting across the street. The Ram's sigil was emblazoned on the side, silver bright on the black covering.

"The guard's inside the pub," Arthie said.

"How do you know?" Matteo asked, and Jin was reminded that Matteo had never been on a job before. The Athereum infiltration, yes, but never a street job such as this.

"Because the carriage is parked in front of it," Jin said. "And you can see a number of Horned Guard through the frosted glass."

"As I said, it's their haunt," Arthie finished. "Let's go. Matteo, you first. Jin, we'll—"

"Oi, he's already going," Jin said before she could finish her instructions. He straightened, the two of them readying to run after him when the pub doors swung open, the jangle of the bells reminding him of Spindrift. "Well, and there's your captain."

Who began walking toward the carriage.

Matteo heard it too. He was already beside the carriage and rose on his toes, glancing over it and then back at them with growing panic. And instead of running away or acting like he was lost, Matteo Andoni opened the damned carriage door and snuck inside.

"No, you fool," Arthie whispered beneath her breath as the carriage took off with a whinny from the horses.

With a growl, she shot to her feet and ran after it, still in the cover of the foliage lining the road. Jin crashed through beside her, scowling at the branches poking at him.

"He's a painter, not a criminal," Jin reminded her.

The carriage turned from their tiny road onto a larger, busier one, and the two of them wrenched to a halt.

"It's—" Arthie stopped, aghast.

"*Busy*," Jin said, stumbling after her. He hadn't realized there would be *this* many people here. The traffic was bustling, carriages trundling in either direction, people calling out to one another. What had he expected? More than Ceylanis lived here now.

He hurried after Arthie, but they were losing ground, and fast. He glanced at her to say as much, only to find her scanning the street and eyeing a carriage up ahead. He knew what she was about to do, and when he found himself attuned to her scheming, a part of Jin settled. Like a coin that had been spinning without end and finally, finally came to a satisfying halt.

Right now, Arthie was going to requisition another carriage.

While it was in motion.

She ran into traffic, her trajectory curved, ignoring the shouts of the drivers behind them and the horses protesting the sudden yank of their reins. And then she leaped, Jin on her heels, the pair of them grabbing the handhold on either side of the carriage frame.

Jin placed a finger over his lips.

"What was that?" the carriage driver shouted. Jin and Arthie ducked as the curtain inside the carriage swept open and a woman's face peered out, looking everywhere but straight below.

"What about her?" Jin hissed, but Arthie was already eyeing another carriage. Was she—

She was. She leaped for the next one without hesitation, almost missing the hold. One second too late and she would have tumbled to the street, trampled by the horses stomping ahead.

Vampire or not, that would hurt.

Jin clenched his jaw, readied his footing, and leaped after her, wind rushing through his hair and nearly stealing his hat. He landed on the carriage's foothold and nearly yanked open the door in the process before slowly sidestepping to the front, where a pair of men with rifles were having a heated conversation.

"Oi!" they yelled in unison.

"Sorry, lads, don't mean to interrupt," Jin said over the hot, roaring air. He hooked the end of his umbrella around the first man's neck and threw him off. The man rolled off the street and leaped to his feet with a snarl the wind greedily snatched up. Jin almost felt sorry for the fellow.

But then he remembered he had no sympathy for colonizers.

The remaining man was frozen, unsure of what to do. His rifle leaned against his shoulder, the reins clutched in his hands.

"Let me help you with that," Jin said, waiting until they neared a patch of grass before he yanked the reins from him and kicked him and his rifle off. The carriage teetered, the horses whinnying, as they trundled toward the carts parked on the side of the road. "Whoa now."

Jin plopped down on the seat and steered them back to the road as Arthie climbed up beside him, her hair a tangled mess.

"The carriage," she shouted over the wind. He followed her line of sight. The Horned Guard carriage carrying Matteo was turning up ahead. Jin spurred the horses faster, cutting off another carriage and then a smaller cart. "Get me closer."

Jin caught up to the Horned Guard carriage, glancing over at the wild glaze in her eyes. "You're not going to jump, Arthie." Too late. "Arthie!"

She jumped, gripping the door handle. The curtain inside swept open, Matteo's eyes widening when he saw Arthie hanging off the edge, the wind ruffling her clothes and her hair; it was a wonder it hadn't snatched her away.

Jin kept one eye on the road and one eye on her as she carefully made her way to the captain at the front.

"Who are you?" he heard the captain sputter.

"Whatever you call a thief who steals from another one," she said, and Jin watched her slam the butt of her pistol against the captain's skull. He slumped forward. The reins fell from his hands and the horses stumbled, screaming without direction, excited at the chance of freedom.

Arthie pitched forward, grabbing the reins and regaining control at the last moment. Jin should have trusted her to do what needed to be done. He should have kept his eyes on the road.

And maybe then he wouldn't have crashed.

17
FLICK

Flick did her best to keep silent and listen well, but the scratchy, thick cloth over her head made it near impossible to hear the men and potentially track where they were taking her. It almost felt as though she was walking in circles, heading in one direction before moving in the other. She laughed at herself—quietly, of course. Who was she trying to trick, acting as though she knew the streets? Who did she think she was? Arthie? Jin? *Chester?*

The Linden girl, the men called her. She didn't dare dip her hand into her pocket, but she pressed her wrist against it, the ridges of the brass knuckles reassuring her. They hadn't thought to search her, or perhaps they expected little of Lady Linden's sheltered adopted daughter.

Flick needed to use that to her benefit.

The men slowed and the one holding her released her, only to pat her down. Flick held her breath, hoping he would dismiss her brass knuckles for a fancy part of her coat. He paused at her pocket, then patted it again.

"What, you think she can fit the ledger in there?" one of the other men asked.

He snorted. "You're right."

Flick exhaled when he stood up with a grunt, and she struggled to keep her breathing neutral when he dragged her by the arm again. She stumbled and nearly tripped on the threshold of a doorway. It couldn't have been more than five minutes since she was caught. Where was she? One of the posh and ornate offices that looked like houses? The palace? No, it was neither of those places. Wherever she was, it was large, judging by the echoes, with a bone-chilling cold. Like a tomb.

She was yanked down several more turns before she was pushed through a doorway and shoved in a chair. *At least they didn't bind me to it.* No sooner had the thought occurred than someone came back over and bound her wrists behind her. Voices rose, ricocheted; a door clicked closed.

And then it was quiet.

She strained against the ropes, but they were thick and chafing. The binding didn't budge. Her breathing echoed in what felt to be a fairly empty room, and she had a sudden, startling thought: If something happened to her, if she *died*, no one would know. No one would know where to find her body, or what had happened.

Stay calm, Jin had told her. *We're more doomed to fail when we're in a panic.*

It was strange, she supposed, to go from a life where death was something far out of reach, not as imminent as an exquisite new gown or a walk through the gardens, to this. Death had never weighed at the forefront of her mind before the Casimirs.

The door opened and closed again, and Flick cinched her thoughts, willing her mind to quiet and her pulse the same. A single pair of footsteps rang dully along what sounded like hollow floorboards, more like a storeroom than an estate or anyplace fancy.

Flick gasped when the hood was ripped from her head without warning.

As her eyes slowly adjusted to her new surroundings, she noticed that she was wrong: She hadn't been alone in the room. There were two black-clad men near her. Had they been hoping she would talk to herself? Rat herself out somehow and make their lives easier?

Focus.

Her mind wasn't racing because of the men; it was racing because of the third presence. That single pair of footsteps that had entered, a pair as familiar as her own name.

Lady Linden. The Ram.

Flick met her mother's eyes, those blue eyes she thought so remarkable. The rest of her features were hidden by the gilded mask of the Ram.

The last time Flick saw her, it was at the Athereum's meeting hall. She'd watched her mother sweep into the room, and then her men follow. She didn't flinch as they murdered those people.

Flick hated the fear that flooded her. She wasn't in any more danger than when she was apprehended, so why did she fear her mother?

Maybe because I've lived with that fear my whole life.

That stopped now.

Flick chewed on the inside of her cheek. She felt, suddenly, like a bottle of fizzy water that had been shaken up and the cap popped off, everything roiling and roaring and eager to lash out.

Hello, Mother, she wanted her to say. *Take off that mask; you're fooling no one.*

Flick bit her tongue and swallowed her words, thorns and all. But why? Those were the actions of the old Flick. This one had learned she owed her mother nothing. This one had learned from Arthie Casimir to keep secrets close until it was time to exploit them.

"What do you want?" Flick asked. The room was fairly small, void of furnishings except for Flick's chair in the middle of it and a single chest in the corner. The walls were gray, the floorboards wide, unlacquered planks.

Flick didn't have a clue as to where she was.

Her mother's eye twitched. Strange, she'd never had an eye twitch before. Was she bothered by her daughter being apprehended? Flick almost cracked a laugh. No. Her mother was content enough to lock up her daughter in her own house.

She held out Flick's satchel, turned it upside down, and emptied its contents onto the floor. Flick's supplies, from her pens to her notebooks and even her map, tumbled to the ground. The Ram bent down and picked up Flick's notes on the mystery building.

Damn it all, Flick.

"Where is my ledger?" the Ram asked. Her voice sounded different through her mask, rougher and more modulated. She could pass for a woman or a man. How much effort did she have to put into being the monster that she was? And Flick had thought Spindrift had their hands full transforming from tearoom to bloodhouse every night.

Her eye hadn't twitched because of how Flick had been treated. But because of how Flick had acted: her gall, her continued escape from the Ram's forces, her possession of what was the Ram's.

The Ram didn't care a lick about Flick.

"First you misplace your ledger, then you misplace your foes. What's next? Your mask?" Flick said, barely holding back a smirk. This time, she let the words bubble out of her. "You've become awfully irresponsible lately, Mother."

The air siphoned out of the room. The men blinked in confusion, looking between themselves and then at the Ram, and ultimately at Flick.

As though what she said was impossible to believe.

The Ram clucked her tongue. It was the same sound she would make when Flick had done something wrong and she was left to clean it up. *Look at what you've made me do*, it said.

She turned, and before Flick could fully comprehend what was happening, two loud pops ricocheted in the room. The men fell. They did not move. They did not breathe.

Gunshots. Her mother—her mother had killed the men.

For a moment, the Ram stood still. Flick was frozen. A croak escaped her lips. As if her mind wanted to scream, but her heart knew better than to be shocked.

The Ram tilted her head, clearly wishing she could somehow make Flick forget who she was. Or, she was contemplating her death. Flick wouldn't put it past her. Flick stared at the dead men until they began to quiver in her vision, until her entire body began to shake.

"Don't do that again," the Ram said as simply as though Flick had left food on her plate, and the Ram had been forced to go through the trouble of cleaning it up.

Flick refused to let her see how much the men's deaths had affected her. She willed her rushing thoughts to settle, her limbs to ease, her clenched teeth to relax.

My mother just killed two men.

"I recognized you the moment you walked into the room that night," Flick said. "And I want to say I didn't recognize the woman who murdered those people, but I—I can't." She sniffed, looking at the men. "Have you no heart?"

The Ram took off her mask, and a pang shot through Flick's chest.

She was back home again, vying for her mother's attention, eager for every meal they shared, every walk they had through the gardens, every outing for jewels or ribbons or purses.

You have a new home now, she reminded herself. It might not always share the same walls, but it did have the same faces: Jin, Arthie, Matteo, and the entirety of the crew.

She straightened her spine.

"I will ask you again, where is the ledger?" the Ram asked, making no effort to answer Flick's question. Making no effort to mask her apathy toward the men lying dead on either side of her. She held up Flick's notes. "I know you have it because you've barely bothered to hide the fact that you've gone through it. Tell me, Felicity, were you trying to find this place?"

This place?

It *was* a place, but how had Flick gotten the coordinates incorrect? She'd matched up the map precisely, stood at the crossroads her mother had drawn in her ledger, but she'd seen nothing. Had the Ram changed locations? Was Jin right, and the ledger was rubbish now?

Goodness, they'd sailed across the *sea*.

"You know you could have just asked me," the Ram said, dropping Flick's notes. She knocked on the door twice. Hard. It opened right away, two men entering without preamble to drag the dead bodies away, leaving a trail of blood behind them.

They didn't flinch; they didn't pause. They knew they were expendable. And Flick couldn't decide if her being brought here was a good thing.

Say something. Don't let her get you afraid. "It's nice to see you too."

"Oh, do not act as though the distance between us isn't due to your own reckless actions," her mother replied. How easily she spoke after having just killed two men. She had even tucked her pistol away as if it was a pencil she'd pulled free to jot down a quick note.

Was she referring to when Flick broke into a vampire's mansion? When she helped infiltrate the Athereum? When Spindrift had gone up in flames? Or when she'd stood in the midst of a massacre of her mother's own making?

"It's peculiar for you to sound disappointed in my actions when you're diddling the entire empire, Mother," Flick said, relishing the dregs of satisfaction when her mother winced at her choice in language.

"I always assumed the EJC straddled moral lines, but I didn't know how far that went. I didn't know that when I learned you were abusing vampires, I could be horrified by anything more, and then you walked in wearing that mask. And now you're kidnapping humans too."

Flick stopped there, despite the lengthy list she wanted to run through, calling out what her mother had done. Whatever she did say, the Ram did not refute, not even the kidnapping of humans off the street. Flick didn't know why she was surprised: The Ram had just killed two men in front of her, simply because of something Flick said.

"Come back home," her mother said, almost tiredly.

That wasn't the response Flick was expecting, not in the slightest. She regarded her mother with suspicion, even as the instinctual responses bubbled up in her throat.

Yes.

I'm sorry, Mother.

I'll return to you.

"Please, Felicity," her mother added.

Instinct disappeared and disgust took its place. The sound of her name out of her mother's mouth was what had made Flick want to change it—even before she'd been locked in her own house like a prisoner. The beseeching was a farce. There was another reason her mother was as close to begging as she'd allow herself, and it had nothing to do with Flick's run from home.

"Why?" Flick asked, and it felt like a transgression somehow.

Lady Linden—the Ram, her mother—blinked, because Flick rarely questioned her.

"I'm your mother, Felicity," she said, taken aback. "Your real family. Do you not miss me?"

Flick considered the question. She missed what she thought she had, and if she'd never had it to begin with, was there anything to miss?

Everything motherly about her mother had been whittled away to reveal the mask beneath—an ironic thought. Flick had always believed her mother had slowly lost interest in her, as one did when a shiny toy became dull with age, but was it Flick who had changed?

Her mother made a sound in the back of her throat. "What have I done wrong to deserve this? Your behavior is utterly atrocious."

"Utterly atrocious?" Flick almost burst out laughing, but her mother was oblivious.

"I fed you, clothed you in the best White Roaring has to offer, hired the best tutors, but time and time again, this is how you treat me, Felicity."

That bit was true. Flick did get the best. She was fed and clothed and sheltered in one of White Roaring's best neighborhoods. Arthie had never had such a thing. Jin had it taken from him.

She ought to be grateful. Flick looked into her mother's eyes and saw a shift from imploring to satisfaction, as if she was guiding Flick in a direction of her choosing.

Did she not recall using this tactic before? She'd made this very same attempt to guilt and persuade Flick into believing that no one but her mother truly cared for her. And if Flick did that, well, she'd be trusting her mother. She'd be willing to tell her everything.

"What do you mean?" Flick asked in the most coy manner she could summon. "How have I treated you?"

Her mother blustered at the question. "Ungratefully! You behave like a rebellious child. It is unbecoming."

What was really unbecoming was the snort Flick just held back.

Her mother was meandering woefully off script, and it had only taken Flick talking back. It was almost *fun*.

"What could you possibly have out there that you don't have here with me?" her mother asked, and she sounded on the verge of tears. If

Flick hadn't been bound, her first instinct would have been to go over to her and offer comfort. A hug, or a pat on the back. Something.

No, no, no.

"Mother, I—"

"You what, Felicity?" Lady Linden pressed.

Why are you doing this? Flick wanted to ask. But what reason could ever be enough to justify her atrocities? Greed had no fill. Greed was a bottomless pit, and Flick wouldn't contribute.

"You act as though you missed me, as though you *love* me, but over the past few years, you've barely treated me as a daughter," Flick said.

"Grudges are never good, Felicity. Don't bring up the past."

The woman was insufferable.

"Is the passage of time forgiveness?" Flick replied. "You want your ledger. That's why I'm here."

"Among other things. I want you back too," Lady Linden replied gently. That was a bald-faced lie. An afterthought, at best. "That Casimir girl is dead, as far as I know, isn't she? As is that boy you fancied. In all honesty, Felicity, it's presumably a good—"

"He's not—"

Flick stopped the moment the words blurted out of her, but it was too late. Never before had she wished oh so dearly to reel back time. Mere *seconds* would have been enough.

Understanding crossed her mother's face, and Flick realized with bitter dread that she was right. This entire conversation *was* a farce. She had been luring Flick with words, trying to get her to speak and reveal where the others were and what they were up to. This wasn't a mother asking her daughter where she'd gone wrong; this was a woman questioning someone she saw as inferior.

Someone with whom she shared no ties of kinship.

This was an interrogation of a prisoner, and Flick, despite knowing as much, had failed.

"He's not dead," Lady Linden said, in a tone that said she should have known.

"No, I was going to say he's not the boy I fancy," Flick corrected, but it was too late to fix her mistake.

Lady Linden latched the door closed and set her mask on the chest. "You never were a good liar, dear."

How did her mother know of this? How did she know that Arthie had died to begin with? No one but Laith and Matteo had been there when it happened—and Laith was dead. Wasn't he?

Her mother slowly turned back toward her, and Flick swallowed as fear lifted the little hairs off the back of her neck. If she thought her mother had been cold before, she was mistaken. Her eyes were now devoid of life, heartless in a way that made Flick shiver.

"Where are they?" Lady Linden asked. No, she wasn't Lady Linden anymore. She wasn't her mother anymore.

This was the Ram.

Flick didn't know how to respond—insist that they were dead? Say she didn't know? Lie and say . . . what?

"I told you—"

The Ram cut her off. "It would be best if you didn't waste my time, Felicity."

The twin trails of blood gleamed by the door, threatening her. Flick wouldn't fall for it.

"Don't call me Felicity," Flick said as carefully as she could, struggling to stop seeing the woman in front of her as her mother.

"Oh?" the Ram said. "Is that not your name anymore? Did you forget who gave—"

Not this again. "Even if I had wanted to, I could never forget anything you've given me."

And Flick didn't know if she wanted to. Arthie had been through trials and struggles of her own, and she was better for it. Her every hardship had made her stronger, smarter, more brilliant in every way.

"You should put your mask back on," Flick goaded. "Go on, hide yourself from the people whose praise you strive to receive."

She didn't know why, exactly, but it filled Flick with immense joy when the Ram's mouth tightened and she glanced over at the chest to make sure her mask was still there and not somehow in the hands of the girl bound to a chair in front of her.

"I don't believe you understand the gravity of your situation," the Ram said. "You're alone. They don't know where you are. They can't swoop in to save you."

Flick furrowed her brow and looked into the Ram's eyes. "I wasn't hoping to be saved. I didn't realize I needed to be afraid for my life. You"—she added a stutter for good measure—"you're my mother."

The Ram stared back for a long, unending moment in which Flick's heart threatened to leap out of her chest.

"Then you will tell me, your mother, where they are."

There was no point in trying to pretend her tongue hadn't slipped anymore. Flick needed to make sure she didn't do it again. Arthie and Jin were trusting her.

"They're as angry with me as you are," Flick lied. "No one tells me anything."

"And Calibore?" the Ram asked.

Flick blinked at her. "Calibore?"

Her answering sound of exasperation was no different than when Flick took too long to dress before an outing. "The pistol the Casimir girl carried with her. Where is it?"

Flick narrowed her eyes, taken aback. She assumed she was here just because her mother wanted the ledger, but why the sudden interest in Arthie's pistol? Did she know it was capable of killing vampires? Of course she did. Penn had died in front of her—in front of all of them, when Laith had squeezed the trigger.

Or did she know it was more than that? Arthie told them Laith had come for the pistol on orders from his king, who was slowly gathering every magic-imbued Arawiyan artifact that had been spread throughout the world. Did the Ram hope to utilize it against the desert kingdom?

"How would I know, Mother?" Flick asked.

The way Flick said *Mother* was how her mother said *Felicity*.

That was why it irked her so much, Flick realized. She hated the way the syllables dug into her eardrums, the way the name sat over her like an ill-fitted coat.

The Ram's lips thinned. She snatched up her mask and secured it over her face, pulling up her hood to cover her tightly bound hair before wrenching open the door and barking orders in the hall that Flick couldn't make out. And then the door clicked closed, a promise of more to come hanging in the air.

The island is Arthie Casimir
incarnate. It truly is. Wild,
enigmatic, and goodness does
make me sweat. I can onl[y]
hope the Siwangs will do o[ur]
bidding. I am not a viol[ent]
m...

Map labels:
- vampire cells
- coconuts
- the dreaded laboratory
- storerooms
- overseer's office
- chandelier
- Ripper room
- extra space?
- Armory
- the vault-like door

ACT II
AN UNASSAILABLE FOE

18
ARTHIE

Arthie steered the Horned Guard carriage to the side of the road, and when the infernal horses came to a stop, she yanked on the brake and leaped off the side. Matteo opened the carriage door, staring as she ran in the direction they'd come.

Toward the midday Ceylani traffic. Toward where Jin had gone and crashed a carriage of his own.

"Apprehend the captain," she shouted back at Matteo without breaking stride.

"With what?" he asked.

"It's a guard car, Matteo! Check the trunk, find some rope. Get creative."

She had a fool of a brother to save. She rushed down the grass to where Jin had crashed, fear compounding at the throng of people gathered around the wreckage up ahead. A simple crash wouldn't hurt him, but a crashed carriage provided plenty of sharpened stakes she didn't want to worry about just now.

As she approached, she heard words of alarm, whispers, murmurs. In Ceylani.

She saw brown faces. She saw saris, batik dresses, sarongs. She saw hair as dark as hers had been before she'd dyed it mauve. And in between each Ceylani, she saw Ettenians, two or three to every one. There were more of them than there were of the people to whom the country belonged. Arthie wanted to stop it, change it, *fix it.*

She shook the ringing from her ears and dove into the crowd, pushing through until she stumbled to the ruined carriage. Its undyed covering fluttered in the humid breeze. Arthie's heart clamored to her throat, but at last the rubble shifted and Jin rose, unscathed except for the dust he was brushing off with a frown. He was holding the warped carriage door over his head to shade against the sun and tossed it away as he dropped to his knees.

Fear clenched Arthie in a vise, but no more than a second later, Jin rose to his feet again.

"Found my hat!" he shouted, waving it in the air and meeting her eyes across the fray.

The crowd cheered. Arthie sighed.

He hopped over the wreckage, and the two of them squeezed back through the crowd, Jin tossing "thank yous" and "oh, it was nothing" as he strode through them like some sort of hero. Arthie all but dragged him out before someone could call him back for questioning.

"You're looking chipper," he said when they were alone.

Arthie paused beside a stone wall erected by a house. "Next time you might be dead, I'll plaster on a grin."

"I was never in any danger. I'm a vampire now, remember?"

"You're immortal, not unkillable," Arthie reminded him. "Now come on."

Imitating her seriousness under his breath, he followed her to the Horned Guard carriage where, in the shadows of a few teetering coconut trees, Matteo was making good work of binding the still-unconscious captain's wrists behind his back. There was a strip of rope knotted around his mouth too.

"I didn't mean this creative," Arthie said. "Can he even breathe?"

Matteo frowned. "I was being careful! I think he can breathe."

"Nope," Jin said with a shake of his head, while polishing the handle of his umbrella to a shine.

Matteo loosened the knot by a smidge. "Better?"

"Perfect." Arthie glanced back at the carriage and then at the captain. "Now undress him."

"Darling, when I'm right here?" Matteo asked, eyes wide.

Arthie glared, surprised by the heat that flared in her cheeks. The smell of the coconuts didn't help, goading her to let down her guard and relax.

"One of us is going to need to pose like a guard if we're going to get inside," she said.

"That would be you," Jin said to him.

"Me?" Matteo asked with a pout.

"Neither of us is a peaky, and Arthie's too short."

"That last part wasn't necessary," she said, but warmed at his teasing.

With a dramatic sigh, Matteo crouched and untied the guard to peel off his shirt with Jin's help before moving to the trousers. Jin riffled through the shirt pockets, pulling out a set of skeleton keys, a pair of calling cards, a miniature portrait of what appeared to be the man's son, and then a folded note.

Matteo took the shirt and buttoned it over his clothes, following with the trousers. "How do I look?"

Dashing, Arthie was about to say before she paused when the light dappling through the trees shone on the sigil embroidered on his shirt. It reminded her of another Horned Guard captain's uniform, more Arawiyan than Ettenian, but the same rich shade of gray-white.

"Oh, she's speechless. It's all right; I have that effect on people."

Arthie sniffed. "I was only keeping quiet for your sake, really."

His grin drew a dimple in his cheek. "Don't limit yourself on my account, darling."

She opened her mouth to respond, but Jin croaked. It was a wretched, terrible sound that anyone else might have overlooked, but not Arthie. Every inch of her came alert. She whirled, hand on Calibore, to find Jin was quite safe.

But he had unfolded the parchment from the captain's pocket.

"They're alive," he whispered. "This is my father's handwriting."

But something was wrong.

"And? What is it?" She snatched it from him, scanning the neat, slanted script. It was a list of tasks for the Horned Guard captain, but Arthie paused at the bottom.

To be added to Bloodworth's report: Despite numerous attempts, patients refuse to cooperate. More corpus required to continue our efforts. The Ram would be pleased to hear we are making progress on Rippers, as intended. Send our regards.

Sincerely, S. Siwang

Arthie met Jin's eyes. Beside her, Matteo read *more corpus required* aloud and choked.

"They work for her," Jin whispered, but he sounded as though a part of him had expected this.

Arthie wished she was surprised. For his sake, she had held out a sliver of hope that they could have been blackmailed, or biding time, or—Arthie didn't know.

"You've only ever looked for confirmation," she said softly. He'd been fighting for the opposite outwardly, but she had seen the resignation in his eyes whenever he spoke of his parents. For he himself had changed, undeniably, *thoroughly*. "This changes nothing, right? Our plan remains the same. Jin, look at me."

He dropped the letter and crushed it under his foot before finally looking up at her. "Right."

"Now get in the carriage," Arthie said, staring at the fort looming ahead.

If they could infiltrate the Athereum when it was a den of elite vampires poised to kill, they could handle whatever these outside-of-their-element peakies threw at them too.

This was her country, after all, even if it didn't feel like it just then.

19
FLICK

When Flick was younger, her mother would often get angry and leave Flick to stew in her own thoughts, until everything she hadn't said bubbled up in tears. This room was cold and empty, trying to squeeze the same emotions into her as the hours ticked on and on, but Flick refused.

Instead, pride simmered in her chest. She was learning her mother, and in doing so, she was learning herself. Perhaps. She didn't know for sure. She was trying to stay positive while her eyes remained glued to the door.

What she needed was to escape. She didn't have a watch, nor was there a window to see if the sun had risen, but it felt as if an age had passed. Had the Casimirs made their way into the fort? Into the sanatorium? Were they safe?

Focus on yourself, Flick, she scolded. She strained against the bindings around her wrists again, but they wouldn't budge, and her hands wouldn't stop shaking enough for her to properly figure out where one knot ended and the other began.

Flick slumped back in her chair.

Those twin streaks of blood shone bright against the floorboards. She was grateful Chester, Reni, and Felix hadn't been with her when the Ram's men found her. Right now, Flick was certain the one thing keeping her alive was the fact that she had the ledger—and perhaps the fact that she was the Ram's daughter.

Seeing her mother as evil was harder than she thought. Her entire life, her measure of good was tied to how her mother felt. If her mother was happy, that meant Flick was good. If her mother was upset, Flick had done something wrong.

Flick had always been an obedient daughter, but if her mother wasn't a good person to begin with, what sort of scale had Flick followed her entire life? And to think, she'd once been ready to undermine Arthie and Jin simply for her mother's pleasure.

She looked up as the doorknob rattled, and she imagined the revelation rattling into her just the same: Felicity Linden would be obedient no longer.

But when the door opened, it wasn't only her mother who entered. Four black-clad men followed her inside, and the wan light of the lamp they set on the chest glinted off her mask.

No one spoke.

One of the men brought in a small silver tray, something like pens clattering atop it, another carried a heavy crate that Flick thought safe to assume wasn't full of pastries. A pang shot through her, and the weight of her brass knuckles pulsed in her pocket.

"It's been a day since your arrival, Felicity. Have you anything to share?" the Ram asked.

Flick said nothing, but she felt a lick of pride when the Ram didn't look surprised. Her resilience was gaining a reputation, at least. But goodness, a *day*. That meant the Casimirs had been on Ceylan for at least as long.

"The manacles," the Ram demanded, her eyes locked on Flick. "I've been told she forges for the Casimirs. She values her hands very much, and I don't see her using them to the fullest extent after this."

It took everything in Flick's power to keep the emotions from showing on her face. *My hands.* She had a job to finish. She had invites to forge before the tribute.

"Unless, of course, you share the answers I seek," the Ram continued.

Flick held her breath quick before her fright could betray her. At the Ram's nod, the men swept toward her. She felt powerless, helpless. She wanted to shout at the men that they would be next to die, but they knew that already. She could see it in their eyes. What would Jin do? He'd goad the Ram, even as he was strung up, even when hope was in short supply.

Flick was not Jin. And yet, the words trickled out of her anyway. "Whatever will the people think when they learn the Ram is torturing a young girl for information you only assume she has?"

There's a time and place to fight, Jin had said.

This was the time for fighting. Flick waited until the men made her stand, waited until their grip on her eased when they thought she wouldn't fight back. She ripped her hands free, wanting to pull her brass knuckles over her fingers and punch something. Something told her to save them—she couldn't best four men on her own. Instead, she kicked at the crate they'd brought in that had seen better days. It rammed against the nearest man's shins, but where could she go? What could she do?

She hadn't found the place she'd sought out—she'd been dragged here. She hadn't found the answers she wanted—she was trapped in a room with four trained men and her mother.

The fight drained out of her. The men clamped metal cuffs around her wrists. They were wide and heavy, the chain fat. Flick wasn't breathing so much as gasping. They kicked the crate back toward her and shoved her on it.

The Ram marched closer. "Where is the ledger?"

Flick found no remorse in her mother's eyes, no sympathy, and she did her utmost to not give her any emotion back.

"The Casimirs took it from me," Flick said. Had she somehow planted a seed of worry in her mother by revealing that Jin and Arthie were alive and well?

The Ram didn't believe her. She waved a hand. "Hang her up."

Nothing else mattered then. Not the plan, not the Casimirs, not Flick being a bad daughter or a good one.

Only the fact that, without a doubt, she was going to suffer.

"You will pay for this," Flick said, but her voice was small. Her strength had scattered into the recesses of her mind.

The men looped the chain to a hook in the ceiling, forcing her to extend her arms as high as they would go. The links slid with eerie, haunting clinks until it was done. Flick's arms quivered in protest.

"Stop," she whispered. "Please stop."

The men stopped in some semblance of pity, but when they glanced at the Ram, she only nodded, and Flick knew the worst was yet to come.

Then the men pulled the crate out from beneath her feet.

A scream tore from Flick's lungs. She gasped for air as the ground disappeared. Her shoulders shrieked. The metal cuffs dug into the bones of her wrist, the knobby bones of her thumbs, her skin. She was suddenly lightheaded, and she wished she could hold back the tremors that ran through her, to stop herself from shaking and her wrists from chafing.

She was hanging.

Please, was what she wanted to say. *Stop this*, she wanted to beg. *I can't take it*, she wanted to admit. But Flick refused to beg even as she whimpered.

The Ram tilted her head. "Such steel, Felicity. And for what? For a pair of orphans who haven't even come to your aid."

"Better an orphan than an unwanted child," Flick said, her voice strained.

She had been wanted, once. She wasn't a child the Ram birthed; she was chosen by her. Adopted, for some reason, before the Ram decided she didn't quite care anymore.

The men likely assumed she was prattling nonsense because of the pain. Flick didn't know if she meant the words, really, but she felt them just then. She wished, more than anything, that the Ram had never been her mother, and when she looked into those blue eyes now, framed with gilded metal, she saw that it didn't matter whether Flick believed it.

Her mother did.

And the satisfaction that washed through Flick, from her stretched and aching arms to the tips of her toes, was insurmountable. The Ram turned on her heel and stormed from the room. The men looked at one another and a pair of them left while the other two remained, taking up position by the door.

Tears streamed down Flick's face, hot and angry and spurred by the pain. No one was coming to save her. What would Arthie do, or Jin? What would—why could she not do anything herself? Why did she need them? She craned her neck up as much as she could. The hook suspended from the ceiling didn't snap closed. It didn't have a lock or closure. It was open, ending with a sharp curve, made for easy use. *And you only need the manacle chain link to jump the hook, love*, Jin said in her head.

That was exactly what she needed. If only she still had that crate beneath her to use as a launchpad to leap off. It would be a lot easier to throw up her arms and get the chain over the hook then.

You wouldn't be in this situation either, came Arthie's words in her thoughts.

And Flick realized: Arthie's and Jin's voices in her head weren't memories or things they'd said to her before. They were Flick's own thoughts. She wasn't incapable of functioning without them. She'd *learned* from them. She'd taken the best of Arthie's and Jin's cunning and strength and made herself better in turn.

Having their voices in her head made her a little less lonely, really, and there couldn't possibly be anything wrong with that.

She tried shuffling the chains as best as she could through the pain numbing every inch of her form, until her arms quivered even more and she couldn't muster the strength to keep craning her neck upward.

The men were watching her.

"Are you going to just stand there and stare?" she snapped.

They turned their attention to the floor.

Flick blubbered. Her arms were going numb now. She could barely feel her thumbs. The Ram had said she wouldn't be able to use her hands all too well if she was ever freed, and Flick sincerely hoped that wasn't true.

Another sob lodged in her throat. She wanted to sink into a ball on the floor and weep. No, she wanted to thrash; she wanted to scream.

And perhaps because she was alone and there was no one to stop her, or because she was angry and hurting and had come to so many realizations at once, she did just that. Flick screamed.

It wasn't smart, she knew deep down inside. She should have reserved whatever energy she had left, but she couldn't.

Flick screamed again, a sound unlike any other she'd made before. She thrashed, the clinking chains a melody to her voice, and then she slumped forward, empty of life and breath, and everything went dark.

20

JIN

Jin hurried behind Arthie into the Horned Guard carriage and closed the door behind them, leaving the unconscious captain behind. They had little time to waste. The carriage dipped to one side and straightened as Matteo got in the driver's seat outside, quickly joining the line of carriages waiting to pass into the fort.

Jin was numb. Arthie had told him nothing changed.

The plan was still the same, because she had planned for this.

Jin wanted to lash out and say she was wrong. That they—*he* hadn't seen this coming, but *my parents could be on the wrong side* had been a prevalent thought since he'd begun his search anew. Perhaps they were being blackmailed or were biding time, but did that make their actions any different? He felt the sharp points of his fangs—that he still hadn't mastered retracting at will—and remembered his first thought: If he had changed, how could he have expected them not to?

Switching sides isn't a change, he told himself. It was a tragedy.

At his core, Jin liked to think he was still the same person that he was a decade ago. Arthie pulled back the curtain and glanced outside as an imposing shadow fell over them.

"The fort," she whispered, gaze tracking its height.

Birds cried out in the lush trees, chirping tunes he'd never heard in Ettenia. Coconut trees loomed above. They were everywhere, much like the coconuts piled in his parents' house before it had burned down.

Before, when his father had been in search of a way to improve the lives of vampires.

Before he'd joined the Ram.

She looked back at him, and he didn't need light to see the pity in her eyes. "The plan remains, did you hear me? If we have to lead them out at gunpoint, I'll do just that. If we have to knock them out and drag them, we will. But we're here to ruin the Ram's machine."

Jin wanted to hate every word spilling out of her mouth, but she was right. This wasn't about him or his parents. This was about taking down the Ram—tearing down the EJC and her crown in one fell swoop. The woman who killed him. Who treated Flick like she wasn't worthy of love. Who made Matteo into something he was not. Who ruined Arthie's homeland and countless more.

And if his parents were a part of it, stealing them away would be an even larger blow to the Ram.

"The fort is huge," Jin said, trying to contribute. "Where do we even begin to find a sanatorium?"

Arthie was still staring out the window. When the gate opened for the carriages up ahead, she pressed her face to the glass as Matteo slid open the grate and glanced inside, draped in the bloody tint of his umbrella.

"Can you see the sanatorium?" Arthie asked, just as he spoke.

"To the sanatorium, I'm guessing? There's a sign, believe it or not."

Hiding in plain sight. Like the Athereum. Like Lady Linden beneath her mask. Like Spindrift.

She nodded. "As close as we can."

He closed the grate shut again without a tease or grin. He was as nervous as they were—or as Jin was. Arthie didn't look concerned in the slightest.

The carriage rolled forward again, then again. Voices picked up, barked laughter and snide words as men tried to sound tough in the heavy heat. They were nearing the gate.

"Almost through," Arthie said, and perhaps it was her words, or the shriek of another devil bird in the trees, but dread coiled tighter in Jin's stomach.

Something was going to go wrong.

Arthie leaned back, closing the curtain and crossing her wrists, pulling on the apprehended-criminal act she was going to give the guards when they opened the door to inspect inside, and then Jin heard it: the shouts.

They were coming from *behind* them.

Arthie straightened. "Revolver?"

Jin nodded. "I have it."

Matteo opened the grate. "It's a guard. He's—oh, he's pointing at us."

"Get us inside," Arthie insisted. Up ahead, the guards were still waving the line of carriages forward. Matteo inched the horses toward the gate, halting and moving at command. Jin swallowed a growl at their slow progress. Through the window, Jin could see the spiked gate suspended just above them when Matteo halted.

That would be a terrible way to go.

"They stole the captain's carriage!" came a shout from behind them.

"I think they're talking about us," Jin said matter-of-factly. "We need to make a run for it."

"Arthie? I must say I agree with him," Matteo called.

Arthie pressed her lips thin, clearly weighing their options. The shouts were getting louder. The guards were coming toward them.

"No," she said finally. "How far do you think we can get on foot? Press on. We still need to get inside."

With a grunt, Matteo spurred the horses forward. They protested against him, and Jin spotted a number of guards crowding within the gates. Damned considerate steeds. But Matteo pressed on, nudging guards out of the way until they finally made it inside.

Jin and Arthie both jumped when a hand thumped on the carriage doors. This was not going to plan. Arthie hid Calibore. Jin folded his bullet belt under the waistband of his trousers.

The doors flung open to a slew of guards, and Arthie squeezed Jin's hand before they were dragged outside without warning. He didn't have time to grab his hat. Arthie was pulled from the other side and thrown at him. She stumbled, Matteo grabbing her before she could fall.

Well, they had made it inside the fort at least.

The stone walls rose around them. There were no shops or houses here. It was a compound, full of Ettenians and Ceylani walking to and fro, either in the uniform of a guard or a worker, accepting packages or running duties or loading weaponry. Women in saris carried baskets overhead, delivering food. Coconut palms fanned the dusty ground with their leaves, and horses loitered with oxen.

Here, under the archway that seemed to run along the fort's perimeter, Jin gripped his umbrella tight, ready for a fight, but the guards had surrounded them. Even if the three of them managed to overcome this cluster, they were inside and the gate was shut. Guards were everywhere.

They couldn't fight their way out of this.

One of the guards snapped his fingers in front of Jin's face.

"Care to tell us why you stole my colleague's cab?" he asked. He was dressed in the same-colored uniform as the captain they'd apprehended. That was likely why he was looking at Matteo with an extra level of disgust.

"Can they understand us?" another guard murmured.

"Is it stolen if it's in front of you?" Arthie replied in perfect Ettenian. A number of the men looked surprised.

"And yes, we understand ruffian quite well," Jin said, and when the rest of the guards turned their attention to the captain for his response, two of the younger guards remained staring at Jin.

The captain gave them a mirthless smile. "Ah, we have ourselves some Ettenian jokesters."

The pair of younger guards continued staring at him, murmuring to each other, studying Jin like a bug under a glass. He tried to catch what they were saying, but not even his vampire hearing was of any help. There was too much else happening at once, including a roaring in his ears, worsening his disquiet. He opened his mouth to snap at them, but when he did, one of them dropped his gaze to Jin's mouth with a gasp, as if his suspicions were confirmed.

Jin's fangs.

"Vampire!" the guard shouted, pulling out his weapon and aiming it at Jin. In seconds, the entire platoon of guards had followed suit.

Jin froze. Fear dragged a finger down his spine. As the guards circled tighter around him, Arthie and Matteo were forgotten. He couldn't see them, couldn't sense them nearby. Had they snuck away? That was a good thing, he told himself, even if it didn't feel like it.

"Do we shoot?" the guard asked, as if their guns could hurt him. They were acting like he was a rabid animal. Like he was standing here, baring his teeth.

Jin took a slight step backward. The guards followed, the circle tightening.

Only then did he notice their weapons: They weren't regular rifles. They were loaded with a strange kind of dart that was filled with a luminescent green serum. Jin didn't know how much damage it would do to a vampire, but he wasn't particularly ready to test it out.

He remembered distinctly, after he had been turned, trying to find the benefits of being a vampire. *At least I won't have to worry about dying.*

And then he'd gone and journeyed to a place where they were weakening and weaponizing vampires, and now threatening to kill one.

"No," the captain said, stepping closer. Jin weighed the advantage of pulling out his revolver and shooting him. He found none. "It's useless dead."

It? Jin snarled.

"We've got a better use." The captain nodded to a guard, and then his hands were pulled behind him and clamped in cuffs before he could react. His umbrella clattered to the ground, a piece of his heart being flayed and flung away.

"Move, and spikes will deploy," the captain warned him. He turned his head. "Get this thing inside."

Before Jin could react, the guards began pulling a sack over his head, and it took every ounce of effort not to search for Arthie in the shadows. Days ago, Jin had been ready to leave Arthie in the dust. He had been ready to leave her behind in Ettenia and sail to Ceylan himself. But he wasn't a child; he wasn't silly. He needed her, and she needed him. He was half her brain. He couldn't help her if they were separated.

"What about the other two? Where'd they go?" one of the guards asked. The captain ignored him, and another guard gestured to him to be quiet and pulled him along.

Jin stomped his feet, trying to draw their attention. It worked. Several of the guards shouted. He was whipped around, and that was when he caught one last glimpse of her under the cover of a stack of trunks.

We were made for trouble, you and me, he tried to convey with his eyes before the darkness swallowed him whole and he was dragged away.

21
ARTHIE

Arthie didn't wait for the guards' shock to wear off and remember her and Matteo—she grabbed his arm and tugged him into one of the pockets of shadow between the columns holding up the fortress's archway. There was no shortage of guards throughout the fort, and as the men shoved Jin away, Matteo choked another, smaller guard unconscious with an arm around his neck and undressed him with haste, giving the uniform to Arthie to button up over her clothes.

They hid him behind a stack of crates labeled *cinnamon* with the EJC logo branded into the wood. Arthie ignored the rage that flooded her veins at the sight and transformed Calibore into a hairpin, tucking as much of her mauve locks away before pulling the guard's cap tight over her head.

"Don't lose sight of them," Arthie whispered to Matteo, and they hurried across the yard in the direction of the wave of guards leading Jin around a bend. They kept their heads low and shoulders relaxed as though they belonged. Arthie stopped to snatch up Jin's umbrella. She wasn't going to leave such an important part of him behind.

Matteo nearly tripped, straightening with a curse as a red canister rolled to its side with a clang. "Why are there so many canisters *everywhere?*"

He was right. They lined the covered walkway that ran the perimeter of the fort, going on for as long as Arthie could see.

"Fuel. Oil, I think. For the ships that port here," Arthie answered. Jin was getting away. She tipped her hat down and kept moving. "Not now. They're going to the sanatorium."

The sanatorium looked like a miniature version of the fort with its gray-brown stone. As the guards neared, the grand doors groaned open.

"I don't know if walking in plain view is a good idea," Matteo murmured.

"We can't let Jin out of sight," Arthie said. Especially not when the men referred to him as though he wasn't human.

The guards marched into the sanatorium, prodding and pushing Jin along. They passed through the threshold, Arthie and Matteo on their heels. There were plenty enough guards marching around, making it easier for the two of them to blend in.

Before the doors shut behind her, Arthie glanced back outside to where a woman stood in a sari the color of blood. Her mother—no. Her mother was dead, and Arthie's mind was playing tricks on her.

Still, Arthie met her eyes, and the woman squinted at her through the sun with a strange expression, as though she couldn't quite place Arthie and the clothes she wore.

Why are you here? Arthie thought those eyes asked. *Why have you returned?*

And then the doors closed, sealing them inside.

"Odd place," Matteo murmured as Arthie tried to shake the woman's uncanny scrutiny from her mind. *Why are you here? Why have you returned?* Had the sea not asked her the same question when she'd arrived? She forced herself to study their surroundings.

The sanatorium was a lot smaller than Arthie had thought it would be. It looked less like a facility housing vampires and more like a bank, with a welcoming foyer, windows, and lacquered wood, complete with a vault-like door near the back wall. The ceiling pitched high, with a mural and lavish lights. Evening sunlight poured in through the windows, painting a cheery display. Out of place, stacked along the side wall and awaiting export, were crates stamped with the EJC logo.

"Tea," Matteo said beside her.

Arthie knew one of Ettenia's greatest exports out of Ceylan was tea, but it was different seeing it in person, and it wasn't until Matteo brushed a finger down her arm, sparking a current in her veins, that she released her clenched jaw.

Behind the polished counter, a stately man wore a false smile and a short top hat. He nodded as the cluster of guards continued to that vault-like door in the back, dragging Jin between them. Arthie and Matteo followed, as closely as possible. The man didn't look fazed in the slightest. He held up that fake smile and pulled a latch.

And the door began to open. It was imposing, standing with a sense of foreboding and finality. Arthie could hear mechanisms dislodging inside, groaning awake like a beast from its slumber. She quickly whipped her head away when one of the guards glanced back to the wide windows.

The door ground to a halt, and the guards continued inside in varying degrees of excitement: some hushed, some scared they'd found a vampire roaming the streets, others all but thumping their chests in a display of pride. Arthie considered thwacking one in the back of the head with Jin's umbrella.

"Onward?" Matteo asked, eyeing the door with dubiety.

"Onward," Arthie replied without breaking stride.

And the vault door shut behind them. It swallowed the last of the Ceylani sun, leaving them in wan light. A series of gears rolled and the door sighed as it locked into place once again. Their exit was barred, sealed shut like a tomb.

Arthie and Matteo exchanged a glance.

"This looks more like a sanatorium. A miserable one at that," he said, taking in their surroundings beyond the short hall.

Indeed.

The structure was even larger inside, not because it sprawled or rose high, no. It was built deep into the ground. As warm as it had appeared from the outside, the inside was anything but. It was cold, sterile, and lifeless. The very air felt forlorn, and Arthie was about to agree before Matteo yanked her into the shadows of an alcove.

"Why—"

He pressed a finger to her lips, dragging a shiver through her, and nodded to where they had just stood. A pair of guards had pulled away from the group, circling back in suspicion. Matteo pulled her flat against him, and she forced away a memory of another moment like this. Atop the Old Roaring Tower.

She shivered and craned her head back. "This was entirely unnecessary."

"Oh, does it bother you?" he whispered back, one corner of his lips ticked up, and he peeled his body away from hers just enough to create a gap between them.

Arthie felt like a magnet that had been forced to flip around, hovering close but not close enough. She shoved herself to him, grinning at the spark that shone in his green, green eyes.

"Do I appear bothered?" she asked, breathless. The guards had disappeared. "Let's go."

It took far more effort than she would have liked to pull away and step back into the hall, their footsteps light, their senses vigilant. She kept her distance, clenching her jaw when she heard the scuff of Jin's shoes while he was dragged yet again, and the snicker of the guard who did it. He was still covered by a wretched, scratchy sack, and for what? To scare him? To irritate him?

The short entrance corridor led to another, this one suspended above the underground levels. Farther ahead, a large, ornate chandelier hung from the ceiling off a thick chain, crystal shards swaying just barely, lending to the eeriness of the place. Arthie glanced at Jin's umbrella in her hand. He had snatched it from the jaws of the fire as it greedily swallowed up his past. He had carried it with him since that fateful day, for years upon years, hoping he could be half the man his father was.

Only to learn his father might have become half the man *he* was.

"Where do you think the guards are taking him?" Matteo whispered.

"They said they have use for him," she replied. "I took that to mean they'll toss him with the other vampires."

"What kind of twisted place is this?" he murmured, looking around, and then answered his own question. "A place secure enough for the EJC to do what they want, while retaining their pristine Ettenian image."

It was a concept Arthie hadn't considered: To her, the EJC was entirely evil, from its meddling in the affairs of vampires to its theft of resources across the colonies. To others, the EJC wasn't so bad. It was working *for* Ettenian society, bringing them the wonders of the world beyond its shores.

"I don't see a single exit point other than that door," Arthie noted.

The guards kept walking until the walls on either side of them gave way to cells, one beside the next. They were narrow, as far as Arthie could tell, but long, so the single light suspended from the center of the ceiling made it impossible to see all the way inside. That didn't stop her from feeling eyes on her more than once.

They turned down another corridor, their footsteps loud. Every sound was hushed. It gave her the strangest sense, as if the entire sanatorium was waiting with bated breath for a blow.

A sound stopped them in their tracks. Ahead, the guards kept moving, unfazed, snapping at Jin to continue when he too skidded to a halt. It was a keening, almost unending, utterly haunting.

Matteo's face turned grim. "Vampires. The sound of a starved man."

And Jin was about to join them.

Arthie nudged Matteo as the guards turned down the hall. They seemed to be slowing, as if they'd reached their destination. She tightened her hold around Jin's umbrella, feeling the weight of Calibore in her hair, and peered around the corner.

Only to find every single guard waiting for them, guns raised.

The captain's shrewd eyes were bright with satisfaction. "I told them this would be the best way to lure you two in when you'd disappeared."

Every inch of her itched to draw Calibore, but she knew when the odds weren't stacked in her favor. Matteo reached for her arm as if he'd had the same thought.

"Nothing to say this time?" the captain goaded. "Lock the pair up."

The cell was stifling, and Arthie was certain it was designed to be. The halls fell silent once the guards left, and Arthie had the feeling she wouldn't be seeing much of them anymore. It was clear the corridors were rarely frequented, for isolation was as much a prison as a cell.

Matteo immediately began to pace the narrow space, still dressed in the Horned Guard uniform. As was she, the smell of the guard's sweat stinging her nostrils.

The silence was deafening. She pulled the hat from her head and tugged Calibore from her hair, waiting for it to transform into her pistol, but it didn't budge. She was too worried about Jin, too worried about the island, too worried about too much. She couldn't focus on her connection to Calibore. She couldn't think straight. She wanted to press it against the Ram's temple and demand answers from her. Dangle her secrets in front of her face and watch her squirm.

"Come on, you wretched thing," she snapped, shaking the hairpin in her hands, looking away and then looking back at it again as if that would make a difference.

She stifled her scream, before pressing her back against the wall at the end of the cell, sliding down until she sat on the cold, relentless floor.

"Arthie," Matteo said with a sigh when he saw her curled into herself. He settled beside her, knees up like hers, arms crossed. He brushed his fingers along the side of her arm.

There was a time when she would have moved away and thrown him something snide. *All this room, and you decide to sit* here?

Now she leaned into his touch. She never imagined the threads that would connect them: They had suffered at the hands of the Ram, the EJC, and Lady Linden. They had ravaged their surroundings as newly turned half vampires.

And then he had turned her, kneeling over her in his canopied bed, pressing his lips to her skin, his tongue, and then his fangs.

He saw the shift in her eyes, the tilt of her chin as the memories resurfaced from that night.

"You are a naughty thing, aren't you," he whispered, brushing his fingers up to her shoulder and then lower, tracing her side, leaving a line of fire she wanted desperately to spread through every inch of her.

Arthie tracked his movement, relishing the heat of his eyes on her. He leaned closer, tilting his head to press a kiss to the side of her nose, another above her eyebrow, another at her temple. A shiver ran down her spine, and Arthie discovered that one of her favorite things was the feel of his smile curving against her skin.

She tilted her chin, meeting his lips with her own. It was a softer kiss, one laden with the weight of their surroundings, the anger and pain and hatred they shared.

"There you go," he whispered, pulling away. In her lap, Calibore was a pistol again.

Oh.

Arthie paused, torn. She had never needed anyone before. For anything. *Is it so bad to rely on others?* She shifted Calibore from pistol to dagger, black filigree shifting to the hilt, blade bright in the darkness. Calibore could only shift into weapons, bladed hairpins included, and a dagger was the closest thing to a lockpick.

"I knew getting into a cell with you wasn't a bad idea," Matteo said with a grin, rising to his feet and helping her up beside him. Did a current zap through him, too, every time he touched her?

Arthie flicked a brow. "You're so certain I won't leave you behind, are you?"

Matteo sulked, and Arthie looked away from the perfect pout of his lips.

She finagled the dagger into the keyhole, pausing when she felt something else just inside the lock. A strange mechanism, different from any lock she'd seen before, more delicate. Arthie ran the pad of her finger up the tiny panel. Fine wires were bound and wrapped inside it.

She wriggled the tip of the dagger, trying to work the pins with at least half the expertise Jin used, but she heard the rough scrape of her dagger jumping off to the side more than once.

Shouts echoed from down the hall where they'd taken Jin. Time was running out.

22

JIN

Jin hadn't known Arthie and Matteo had slipped into the sanatorium until he heard them get caught. Then a cell door creaked shut as the guards locked them away, and that was that. Jin was on his own. Undeniably this time. He twisted his wrists ever so slightly, testing the captain's claim. Sure enough, the more he moved, the farther a row of spikes ejected from the cuffs. He wasn't ready to die just yet.

The guards dragged Jin the rest of the way, one on either side of him, their arms hooked under his until they dropped him unceremoniously on the floor of a room. He had never felt so directly disrespected in his life. He was yanked and prodded, voices muffled by the rough jute cloth around his head.

The cuffs fell away from his wrists, clamps quickly taking their place, securing him like a leash to the wall. He couldn't move.

"Get this infernal sack off of me," he snarled, refusing to let his voice betray how breathless he'd become.

And they obliged. They tore it from his head, and Jin screwed his eyes shut against the blast of sterile light. It smelled just as bleak—like a hospital.

Like a morgue.

"You said you wanted more vampires to test on, eh?" the captain was saying in that smug, punchable tone. The fool could have had two more vampires but didn't even know it. He'd seen Jin's fangs and assumed that was the only tell? "We found this one loitering by the gates. It's all yours."

Jin was going to rip out the man's throat.

When his eyes adjusted at last, he pinned the captain with a glare. The room was large, as wide as a shipping warehouse, and there were various workbenches fitted with tools and machines and vials, as well as contraptions he'd never seen before, and inclined beds that looked as stifling as a rack used for torture.

The rest of the guards were already shuffling out the door, but the captain positioned a pair of them by the entrance before he left, casting Jin one last satisfied smirk.

Only then did Jin fully understand what the captain had said.

You said you wanted more vampires to test on, eh?

He had read those very words before, hadn't he? In a letter. Written in his father's hand. Ahead of him, two figures moved. He didn't know why he hadn't noticed them before. Perhaps, in the way that a mind rarely takes note of things that are familiar, Jin had allowed himself to be distracted by everything that wasn't.

He noticed now.

And that was when he saw them. A man and a woman he would have recognized blind, by sound alone.

His parents.

Alive, whole, *here*. Jin blinked wearily. His parents were standing before him.

His father was holding a needle. His mother was holding a vial full of something green—the same luminescent fluid from the darts the guards had loaded into their weapons.

They had aged, one decade older than the portraits Jin had painted in his memories. There was white in his father's hair, there were fine lines on his mother's face, but it was their eyes that had changed the most. They were not bright and full of possibility anymore; they were haunted and dark.

And for a moment, they could only stare, paling as if they were staring at a ghost. In many ways, Jin *was* a ghost. He stared back. What more could he do? His tongue refused to move, his brain refused to form words, his heart refused to stop weeping.

And he knew, without a single shred of doubt, that despite the ten years they'd spent apart, despite the endless changes *he'd* been through, they recognized him.

"Jin?" his mother whispered.

Don't say my name, he wanted to snarl, but oh, how many years had he hoped to hear his name from his mother's mouth again? He couldn't spew any of his anger at them.

Only silence.

It was confirmation enough. She cried out, dropping the vial. It shattered to the floor, glass and liquid spraying every which way. He thought, at first, that she was going to embrace him, but in her other hand, Jin saw a weapon. It looked like the grip of a pistol, as if the barrel had been sawed off. As she held it, a current zapped from one side of a prong to the other, to and fro with unimaginable speed. In his father's hand, a matching one buzzed.

They looked dangerous.

Ten years apart, and the parents who loved him, birthed him, raised him, were going to hurt him.

Jin felt numb.

His mother almost looked apologetic as she approached, one side of her upper lip lifting higher in that odd way that it used to, making him feel like a little boy again. "Guards? Some aid, if you will."

Jin couldn't hold back his scoff. She couldn't even touch him.

"Do you want us to hold him?" one of the guards asked.

"Yes," his mother said.

When the guards reached for Jin on either side, both of his parents moved at once. Jin braced himself for whatever pain was to come, knowing it would hurt tenfold not because of the unknown weapons but because they were the wielders. His parents that he had longed for, searched for. They shoved their hands forward, and Jin closed his eyes.

The guards yelped in surprise.

Jin's eyes flew open. His parents had their weapons tucked against the necks of the guards. They were shuddering, shaking, eyes rolling to the backs of their heads, stunned with the current zapping between the prongs. They fell to the floor in twin thumps. His mother dashed to the doors and locked them tight.

Jin blinked.

He was not expecting that.

"My boy," his father whispered, setting the stun weapon on a table before he broke into a laugh. It was a sound Jin thought he'd never hear again. A sound he had placed in a glass case and attributed to the hero he'd lost as a child.

It rearranged the pain echoing inside of him; it calmed him. It was his father's voice, soothing away the years upon years of disquiet.

Jin forced his guard back up.

"You're . . . not surprised to see me," he said carefully.

His mother laughed. "No. We were waiting for you."

When Jin was a boy, his father and mother would teach him the strangest, most random bits of knowledge that one would argue a child of his age didn't need to know. How to tie a knot, how to pick a lock in case he was trapped, how to treat a wound himself. He had always been a sponge, soaking up what they taught him, but he hadn't realized his parents had been teaching him because they'd been preparing for the worst.

"Oh, she's been waiting for years," his father said, a shine in his eyes.

"For me?" Jin asked.

He took a careful step back. Had the Ram sent word to his parents? No, even if she had figured out that he and Arthie had stolen her ship, she couldn't have moved any faster than they had, and they'd wasted no time getting here.

"If anyone would save us, it would be you," his mother said, sitting down on a chair and gesturing for Jin to do the same. "We'd long wondered if anyone even knew where we were. We had hoped Penn would come for us. Do you remember him?"

Jin rubbed at his chafed wrists and sat. He tried to, anyway. He appeared to have forgotten how to do the simplest of things, struck with the surrealness of this moment. His fangs had finally slipped away but threatened to come out in full force again.

He toyed with the clove rock in his pocket, remembering Penn's visits when he would toss them his way.

"He's how I learned you were here. He's . . . dead now," Jin said. Whatever plans Penn had wanted to enact, aid or otherwise, had died with him.

His father's eyes widened in surprise before his face fell.

Jin glanced at the mostly empty room, immediately suspicious again. "Can we sit like this? Won't the captain or someone come in?"

Jin's father looked at the unconscious guards and shook his head. "The doors are locked, but they rarely come in here, particularly when we're working." He dropped his gaze to the floor. "They're afraid."

Was he *afraid of* Jin?

He thought of the captain likening him to not being human. Jin had worked with vampires for a good portion of his life—not counting Arthie herself, of course—and he'd never seen them as anything *but* human. He might have held them to different standards and understood that standing before one was always a risk, but wasn't that the case with a human too? He had simply fancied himself stronger than most of the living then, or at the very least, skilled enough to outsmart one.

Jin glanced at the locked doors. They had time for an interrogation. Good. Especially with Arthie and Matteo safely locked away in a cell. Jin didn't want to risk taking his parents to them, not yet.

"I can't believe Penn is dead," his father whispered. "He was a good man. A good leader. Is the Athereum still standing?"

It was promising to hear his father refer to Penn as a good man. How much of Ettenian affairs did his parents know? Not much, he supposed, if his father was asking about the Athereum.

"It is. One of his closest friends has taken up the mantle," Jin said.

"You know quite a bit about all of this," his father said, tilting his head.

Because at some point in time, he and Arthie had wriggled their way into the center of everything, but Jin said nothing. He was keeping his answers to a minimum, holding back any information that could be used against him and Arthie and everything they aimed to do: like destroy the pillars holding up his parents' boss.

He winced at that.

They sat in silence. Jin could almost hear the *tick, tick, tick,* of the seconds passing by. He was torn between wanting to tell his parents he needed to rescue Arthie and Matteo from the cells and not knowing if mentioning them was a death sentence. Was stunning two guards unconscious enough reason to trust his parents?

He was encased in ice, numb to feeling.

"When you were a boy, you would fold into yourself when something was amiss and you didn't want to speak your mind," his father said. "You're doing that now, Jin."

"H—how can I trust you?" Jin blurted out. He wished he had his umbrella, for comfort, but that only made him scoff because he'd carried it around for the comfort of his father. "That captain said you wanted more vampires to test on. What would you have done to me if I wasn't your son?"

His mother opened her mouth to answer, but Jin cut her off. "From the beginning. Unless we have to worry about your guards coming in to check on us."

She nodded. "No, no. We don't. From the beginning, of course. Unlike many, our work involved the welfare of both humans and vampires. We weren't strangers to criticism and angry folk, but when Penn warned us that the Ram had eyes on us, I almost want to say that we didn't believe it. And then a decade ago, we discovered that liquid silver could be formulated and used in vaccines and other protections against viruses and the like."

"For humans, mind you," Jin's father added.

"Yes," his mother said. "Shortly after, the Ram came to us promising more duvin than we'd ever seen. Silver has long been known to be detrimental to vampires. 'If the silver can help humans, it can do the opposite on vampires, yes?' but the question itself left us little room for escape. If we answered yes, the Ram would demand our services. If we answered no, we knew the Ram wouldn't let us or you live."

You. Jin had always known his parents had been stolen from their home, but he couldn't bask in the satisfaction of being right, not when their words brought a lingering question to the forefront of Jin's mind: Had his parents become traitors to protect him?

"When we wavered, the Ram burned down the estate."

The Ram had done the same to him and Arthie when they had wavered, too, hadn't she? When they'd kept the ledger one day too long, she had burned down Spindrift. The woman wasn't very creative.

"Why didn't you tell anyone?" Jin asked.

"Who would we tell?" his mother asked. "We were imprisoned, shuffled from place to place with such randomness that we dared to hope we were close to being found. The Ram wanted the inoculation refined for use on vampires, and it was a back-and-forth battle with us losing a little more every time. Sometimes tortured, sometimes starved. We had no way of ensuring you were safe, no way of reaching any of our contacts. Even if we did have a soul to speak to that wasn't a part of the Ram's cohort, who would trust the word of a pair of scientists, albeit with high standing, against the monarch's?"

"That must have persisted for—what, three years, perhaps?" his father asked.

"A little over two. Time blurs," she said with a scrape of her throat. "Look at our boy now."

Her hands fluttered in her lap. She kept leaning forward ever so slightly and pulling back. As if she wanted to reach for Jin. Hold him. Hug him.

Jin stayed put.

They were talking about the beginning of their imprisonment. In the years since, Jin had found a sister, helped her steal an Ettenian artifact she carried with her every day, and opened a successful tearoom that doubled as a bloodhouse. He'd lived long enough to become a thorn in the Ram's side and see Spindrift burned to the ground.

"And? Do you plan on accounting for the remaining eight years? What were you doing?"

His father gave a short laugh and seemed to age another decade in that moment alone. He slumped back in his chair. "Slowing the Ram down, my boy."

His mother's response was a harsh whisper. "In any way we could."

The words gave Jin pause. A flicker of hope ignited inside him, and despite the gusts of doubt, a part of him tried to keep it safe.

"We stopped being unwilling participants once we realized we could do more outside a prison than inside one. Once we committed to refining the formula, work for the Ram had just begun. This sanatorium needed to be built, the fort around it, the contraptions produced, mass amounts of liquid silver and other materials needed to be gathered. Kidnapping vampires off Ettenia was the final step in the procedure, the part we were dreading most, but at that point we had better ideas for double-crossing the Ram."

"But the vampires—I saw your letter," Jin said. "You wrote that you require more vampires to continue your testing. That doesn't sound to me like double-crossing."

"In Ettenia, the vampires are kidnapped and locked in coffins lined in barbed wire," his father said. "Once they're shipped here, we have some semblance of control. If they're in our sanatorium, we can at least ensure they're not being mistreated. We can care for them."

"Care for them?" Jin asked.

"The long-lasting effects," Jin's father said haltingly, choosing his words carefully, "of the silver are . . . still unknown."

Jin didn't quite like his hesitation, and that flicker wavered. "They're sent here to be starved."

His father nodded. "But they need to be *awake* to be starved. We created a serum that puts them to sleep, to prolong the process in which they'd be ready for the Ram's needs. We've told the Ram that awakening them from the silver inoculation can take months, but really, we're purposely keeping them asleep for as long as we can."

"I heard noises on the way here," Jin deadpanned. "They're not all asleep."

"Vampires are yet a vastly unstudied group of beings," his father conceded. "Some don't take to it, some do and don't remain asleep for long. Sora and I visit each cell several times per week, administering . . ."

"Administering what?" Jin pushed. What was he hiding?

"The required necessities. The longer they remain unconscious, the safer they are. Asleep, vampires' bodily functions are halted. They can survive. Awake, they deal with the results of the silver inoculation, and their starvation leads them to a crazed state, upon which they'll be deployed to the Ram's station of choice."

"And have they? Been deployed?" Jin asked.

It felt, to him, that he was trying, struggling, *fighting* to keep that flame alive just then. He was asking questions in the hopes that he'd receive answers that were different, better, morally perfect. But the more he asked, the worse he heard. The more they appeared simply a level above the Ram—she wanted something vile? They'd find a way to make it less so.

His father tilted his head in question.

"Have they been deployed to the Ram's stations of choice?" Jin asked again.

"No," his mother proclaimed.

His father shook his head too, though he looked a little ashamed by the pride with which she answered. As if they didn't deserve that pride. As if the good that they'd done was outweighed by the atrocious.

He turned his eyes from Jin to the floor, but not before Jin saw the look in them. His actions haunted him. There were those who did terrible things and regretted them later. Grew and bettered themselves after a time. Then there were others, like his parents, who did terrible things with or without regret, who knew they were wrong but did them anyway. But there were spaces in between too, where people like Arthie and Jin lived, perfectly capable of doing terrible things to right wrongs. Out of retribution and vengeance, sometimes for a greater good.

"For our own sanity, we needed to strive for a single aim," his father continued. "The Ram wanted the weaponization of vampires on the ground, and we needed to ensure it never happened. It's horrible for the undead, of course, but it's also horrible for the living soldiers on both sides of the battle. Even beyond that, if a vampire worked their way through those soldiers and fled the battleground, innocents would be placed in danger."

Like the Wolf of White Roaring attack.

"The Ram's wishes sound simple enough, but it has taken us a near decade to achieve what we have, and deliberately so. What would have taken six years to create, we stretched to eight, and so on," his mother said, and Jin watched his father as she spoke. Did he agree with what she said? When he spoke, it was with dismay, a man disheartened. She spoke with more embellishment in comparison. At last, she reached forward and pressed her palm to Jin's cheek.

He couldn't help it; he leaned into her touch, and it felt as if no time had passed at all. As if he wasn't a foot taller than her now. As if his voice hadn't changed. As if he hadn't gone from high society prig to undead criminal.

"You were never traitors," Jin whispered. "You—you were prisoners."

His parents said nothing. His father shifted, ever so slightly, and Jin could smell him. He could smell the *memories*, which was the strangest feeling he'd ever experienced. He smelled like comfort and coconuts. He smelled like Spindrift, a connection Jin had never made before.

His father exhaled long and slow. "No, Jin. The vampires are prisoners. Outside of our imprisonment, we've lived with some semblance of freedom within these walls the past several years, but given the chance, we can't—we couldn't leave them behind. Even without you to protect, we would have undertaken this project. For them. The Ram made plenty of threats. You were the first, yes, but after a while, it became clear to the monarch that we"—he stopped and looked away again—"we would risk our son in order to save the lives of countless vampires and the humans they'd kill. Then the threats moved to other things, our notes being shared to other scientists who would do better, our in-progress theories tested as rigorously as the Ram wished."

He stopped with a sob.

"In order to prevent one evil, we committed our own," he whispered.

What? Jin wanted to ask. There was something weighing on him, something he wasn't telling Jin, and Jin couldn't bring himself to ask. How had he expected a ten-year ordeal to be clear-cut, black-and-white, bad and not?

His parents spoke with care for the vampires—they always had. His father's work had involved bettering life for both the living and the undead, even when Jin was a boy. The coconuts scattered throughout their house had been proof of that. He couldn't believe that had changed, despite everything else that might have. He had worried they had, after the numerous changes he himself had gone through, but some things remained, didn't they?

Jin rose to his feet, wishing he wasn't so numb, so strangely hollow.

The image of his parents the morning before the fire was still seared so vividly into his mind that it was odd to see them like this. Older, wearier, the world weighing on their shoulders. He felt like he'd walked into a fortune teller's tent and stared into her glass ball. Only he wouldn't walk out of here snorting at her con. This was real.

He swallowed everything: his emotions, his questions, his thoughts. "Grab your keys."

His father blinked up at him, his eyes wet, confusion furrowing his brow. "Whatever for?"

Jin nudged the still-unconscious guards with the toe of his shoe. "To meet my sister."

23

ARTHIE

Arthie tensed when Matteo gripped her arm as footsteps echoed down the quiet hall, but when she pulled her dagger back through the cell bars and listened, she recognized that gait. That cocksure stride.

Jin came into view in the dim light, and Arthie scoured his face, looking for blood-streaked skin, carnage-bright eyes, fisted hands. Instead, he looked calm and collected. Safe.

And he was holding a key.

"Did you hit your head?" she asked.

Jin flashed a grin, and if she closed her eyes on that sight, she could have imagined she was back in Spindrift, but then she saw his gaze. Haunted.

"Hello, sister," he said quietly.

He shoved the key into the lock and turned it. He didn't look to see if guards were present, he didn't look ready to mutilate anyone in sight, and as the cell door swung open, Arthie saw two figures behind him.

The man was tall, trim, his dark hair streaked in white. Everything about him was exactly like Jin, but older. It was a surreal sight. But when Arthie looked at the woman, she saw where Jin got his crooked smile, the clever sparkle in his eyes, the jokester in his blood.

His parents.

Arthie stepped into the hall, Matteo right behind her, setting a hand on her shoulder. She didn't know what it was about the touch that calmed her—any other time, she would have shaken it off and hissed at him for patronizing her.

His parents looked at her, and she at them.

"This isn't the place," Jin said in the expectant silence. Arthie couldn't read him, and it sent a lash of fear through her. What had he learned?

He led the four of them to a room that was wide and looming, with a certain hollowness that echoed like a tomb. Jin's father closed the doors behind them, and Arthie tensed when the lock fell shut.

"Jin," she hissed.

"It's all right," he said. "This is where they brought me in."

She turned to face the approaching footsteps.

"A Ceylani girl with fairy-floss hair. You're the Casimir girl," Jin's father said in a voice that was both elegant and inquisitive, altogether a combination that made it one people would want to listen to.

Arthie pursed her lips to the side. "That's me."

"Then . . . that makes you the Casimir boy," his mother slowly began, looking to Jin.

Arthie could tell he braced himself for a scolding. It was instinct, she supposed. These were his parents. It didn't help that he'd been worried about their reactions from the moment he'd learned they were truly alive, but she hadn't imagined the Casimir reputation preceded them past the shores of Ettenia.

His mother's face softened with a laugh. "You two have been thorns in the Ram's side for years now. We hear little about the outside world, but tidbits reach us eventually."

Jin couldn't tamp down his smile at that, but Arthie would take a tad more convincing. Her hand didn't leave Calibore.

"And it's a boon the Ram didn't know as much," his father said. "You couldn't be both our son *and* a thorn in the Ram's side."

Had she known, Arthie didn't doubt the Ram would have killed

Jin—or attempted to, with a relentless passion. But she had not, and it appeared she'd threatened the Siwangs and ended it there. It seemed it didn't matter to her whether Jin was alive, only that the Siwangs believed that he lived so they remained compliant. As his mother said, they didn't have ready access to the world outside of the fort to know otherwise.

"Arthie pulled me out of the fire that day," Jin said, glancing at her. "I went through the house, looking for you both. She saved my life, and she's been saving it ever since."

"The sister you always wanted," Jin's mother whispered, her eyes welling with tears.

"I believe introductions are in order?" his father asked with a sniffle. "I'm Shaw."

"Sora," his mother said to her. "And who might this handsome man be?"

"Matteo Andoni, currently displaced and apprehended in a prison that doubles as an armory and laboratory at once," Matteo said. "So I'd rather not chitchat."

Arthie bit her lip at his curt tone.

"That's how you sound too, you know," Jin whispered to her.

"Are we to act as though everything is fine and dandy because they're your parents, Jin?" Matteo continued.

To her surprise, Jin didn't lash out at Matteo. He merely looked to the Siwangs for an explanation, and that set Arthie at ease. It meant he wasn't going to toss caution out the window because they were his parents. She didn't know why a part of her believed he would to begin with.

"No," Shaw said softly. "We expect nothing of the sort. We are indeed responsible for the vampires housed here, silent soldiers awaiting the Ram's commands for deployment."

"How many?" Matteo asked, deathly still.

"Thus far, one hundred and fifteen. We took several in for testing every year, though last year saw the vast majority. In that, we had little choice."

"There is always a choice." Matteo's voice was hard.

Arthie paused at the heat of his tone, at the anguish rolling off him in waves. The weight was almost tangible. He took the slightest step away from her.

It was a strange thing, the hurt that tunneled under her skin.

"Just as Lady Linden chose to kidnap those vampires when she could have been content with knives and guns. Just as the Ram chose to colonize what she had no right to touch. Just as she chose to make me what I am—"

"She?" Shaw asked.

Jin nodded. "Lady Linden and the Ram are one and the same."

The Siwangs gasped in unison.

"And she made me into the Wolf of White Roaring to merge the two," Matteo said.

Shaw sank into the chair behind him.

"I could have been one of those vampires," Matteo continued. "I lived every day with the fear that I was next, to be kidnapped, drugged, stuffed in a coffin and brought to your Ceylani doorstep. Is that not a result of your choice?"

Jin lifted a finger, but Matteo wasn't finished.

"I am those one hundred and fifteen vampires who suffered because you chose it."

Matteo was breathing hard. Arthie studied him, the fear written on his face, the pain that he seemed to have little control over. He'd spent the past twenty years in a cage of his own making, painting his emotions for the masses and speaking none of it, holding his truth behind debonair smiles and easy words.

And with his return to the outside world came fear, naturally amplified by decades of seclusion.

Shaw and Sora didn't try to refute him.

Arthie's voice was soft. "And now we have the choice to stop it. To find peace for yourself, the kidnapped vampires, all of us."

Matteo said nothing.

Shaw looked as though he wanted to pull Matteo in for a hug, sending a surge of bittersweet sorrow through Arthie's chest. She had long wished for her parents, and Jin had always wished for his, but who did Matteo have? His parents had been as absent as Flick's. Penn had filled that void, it seemed, but he'd gone from missing to dead.

"I don't speak to dismiss our deeds," Shaw said. "I will not dare to ask forgiveness either. We've done what we could over the past decade to defy the Ram: delaying projects, purposely failing tests, extending timelines, but at the same time, we've committed our share of evil too."

"We needed the Ram to believe us so we wouldn't be replaced by someone as heartless as she is, and with our notes in hand," Sora said. "It's true we wanted Jin safe, but we also needed to stay alive ourselves, if only for as many vampires to have the best chance at—at escaping alive."

Matteo said nothing. Jin didn't either. Now Arthie understood the look on his face when he'd released her and Matteo from their cell. There was more to this matter than good or evil.

"In truth, we could have fled many times over recent years," Sora added. "But we know the damage that would have caused—particularly after vampires were brought here."

It was how she spoke of leaving the vampires that gave Arthie pause. She spoke of them with guilt more than duty.

As though she saw Arthie's hesitance, Sora gave her a small smile. "For it was our silver inoculation that brought them to this point."

They were hiding something.

Arthie didn't know if she should care. Regardless of what they'd done, the present was still more important. The tribute would not stop, the guards here would not wait, and the Siwangs still had a part to play. They needed to move.

"We didn't come here to have a moral debate," Arthie said. "We have more pressing matters to attend to back in Ettenia, and you two are going to help."

"Anything," Shaw said. "We've—it's embarrassing to say, but to remain sane, we've been working on a plan of our own—of escape for us and the vampires, and beyond."

"Beyond?" Arthie asked.

"When we first made our discovery regarding liquid silver," Shaw said, "we were invited to present our findings to the Ram and the Council."

"The Council?" Matteo asked.

"Indeed," Shaw said. "We've long believed they're our only hope of toppling the Ram's reign."

Penn had wanted to appeal to them too. He had been searching for evidence, pooling together what he could. What larger piece of evidence could they provide than the Siwangs themselves, and work the Council already knew of?

Hope resurfaced within her, as eager as a rising tide at sea.

Jin gestured to a slender box on the table amid a medley of test tubes and notes. Nestled within was a vial attached to a capped needle. The liquid inside shimmered, molten and beautiful. "Is that it?"

Shaw nodded. "One dose of silver. Enough to subdue a single vampire."

"To ask for your trust is selfish, but may we ask for a chance?" Sora asked. Her question was directed at Matteo, but Arthie knew she was asking them all in that moment, Jin included.

Matteo sighed but eventually nodded. For her own self, Arthie much preferred not having to command them at gunpoint.

She studied the silver dose on the table, unsure what possessed her to pick it up and slip it into her pocket. Precaution, she supposed. None of the others noticed.

"The sanatorium is filled to the brim with guards armed to kill on sight. We'll have to be careful. Where is the rest of your group?" Sora asked.

"You're looking at it," Jin said.

Sora and Shaw exchanged a glance.

Matteo splayed his hands. "It's just us."

"And when have we not been enough?" Arthie asked.

"Though I'd like to preface our next excursion by saying we're typically a lot better at our jobs than this," Jin said. "We just didn't know what to expect coming in here."

"And what exactly is your job?" Sora asked as if she wasn't sure she wanted to know.

"We're criminals," Arthie said, past ready to plot their escape. "The good kind, anyway. Just as you're about to be."

24

ARTHIE

Arthie lifted a brow when the Siwangs unrolled blueprint records of the sanatorium, and even a layout of the fort. The sheets were thin and coated, stamped in the corners with the sigil of the EJC, a mighty ship in the center of a circle, the words *East Jeevant Company* running along the curve.

"Am I to believe you had these lying about?" she asked.

"This sanatorium is our domain, essentially, so we were a part of its construction," Sora explained. "I might have snuck some records away after. Shaw and I repurposed little nooks throughout as safe spaces for notes, goods we've stashed over the years, and the like."

Arthie could see where Jin had gotten his sticky fingers.

Shaw was staring at the EJC sigil. "I don't know why it came as such a shock to hear that the Ram is Lady Linden. The crown and the EJC work so closely together that I can't *not* see them as one and the same."

Arthie didn't say it was a shock to them all, even Lady Linden's daughter. When the Siwangs turned to Jin, she took the blueprints over to Matteo.

"These are excruciating to read," she said, smoothing her hand over the many layers and trying to make sense of them. She didn't need the minute details that constructing a building required, she needed something that was as easy as their Athereum infiltration plans.

She looked at Matteo. He was waiting.

"I do offer my services, for a fee," he said with a wink, his low voice meant for her alone.

Arthie chewed the inside of her lip, shutting down the prickle in her chest. Goodness, now was *not* the time. "We can discuss payment later."

"What a flirt, darling," he replied, pulling the sketches toward him and plucking a pen from Sora's desk. He paused. "There's another option, you know."

"Oh?" she asked, indulging him. "I didn't realize my scheming skills had competition."

He removed the Horned Guard uniform and folded up his sleeves to his forearms. Arthie removed hers too.

"Fight our way out," he said. "We're armed. The Siwangs are bound to know where we can find weaponry. This sanatorium is vile. Do they deserve anything less than our worst?"

A muscle twitched in his jaw. There was chaos, and then there was reckless abandon. Arthie liked to think she had a handle on the balance.

"I don't see us leaving *without* a fight, but we can't rush out of here guns blazing. We need a plan."

Matteo gave her a dramatic sigh. "As you say."

It wasn't his usual cavalier attitude. He was afraid, Arthie realized. He was standing in the middle of a place he had feared since vampires went missing off of White Roaring's streets.

But when he sat in Sora's chair and smoothed out the clean sheet of paper, a calmness seemed to come over him. His lean arms flexed as he traced neat lines, the green of his eyes intent. *That's enough of that.* She swallowed and turned to give Jin his umbrella, surprised he hadn't noticed it in her hands.

"You picked it up," Jin said.

"Of course I did."

Shaw noticed. "Is that my old umbrella?"

"It's Jin's weapon of choice," Arthie quipped.

Shaw looked to Jin for an explanation, and Jin shrugged. "You never did like guns, so I decided not to either."

His voice cracked as he said the words, and Arthie knew what he was thinking. His father hadn't liked guns because he was a man of peace. Instead, he'd come to an island where he'd done worse without one.

"Not that he doesn't know how to use one," Matteo added without looking up from his work. "He shot me in the heart."

"At Arthie's behest!" Jin protested, pointing at her.

Shaw looked among them. "I would find this raillery amusing if the humor wasn't so dark."

"He's fine," Arthie said, even as Matteo pouted. "Dark is all we know."

"Unfortunately," Jin groused. "On both counts."

Sora walked over to them. "Bloodworth will be here at seven bells."

Arthie recognized the name from the letter Jin had shown her.

"He's . . . our handler, if you will," Shaw explained. "He reports directly to the Ram, controls the guards, and the man is in a fouler mood than usual because he seems to have lost a shipment of vampires that were due to arrive today."

Jin snorted.

Shaw narrowed his gaze. "You three don't happen to know anything about that, do you?"

Jin tilted his head from one side to the other. "Strictly speaking, a ship of vampires did arrive today. They're just not in coffins, you see."

It took Shaw a moment to catch on. "You three." His eyes flew wide. "You—you commandeered an EJC ship?"

Arthie shrugged as if that was an everyday occurrence.

"Oh, Pa," Jin said. "I have so much to tell you."

"Later," Matteo said, returning to them with a neat roll of paper. "As requested, milady."

Arthie unfurled it and was transported, for a moment, back to his parlor and the warmth of his house.

"It's perfect," she said. The sanatorium was large, but not as elaborate as Arthie originally thought, with rooms and corridors arranged in a modular fashion. She gestured to the chandelier they'd seen when they'd entered the facility. "You even captured its splendor."

"Only a fraction of my art skills, darling," Matteo said. "Though I do agree that a chandelier is a peculiar addition to a place such as this."

"None of our planning will matter if we can't unlock the door," Jin said, looking over Arthie's shoulder. "It's our only exit. I didn't see it, but I heard enough to know I can't pick its lock."

"Arthie and I saw the mechanism leading—" Matteo began.

Jin's father shook his head. "Unfortunately, the door is monitored, and only Bloodworth and his trusted staff can operate it. There are master keys, but they're on Bloodworth himself. Believe me, we've tried to get them replicated."

Arthie pulled out her pocket watch. "Right, we have just under an hour before Bloodworth arrives."

"I would suggest hiding when he does, but the captain was far too excited at the prospect of having caught Jin to not tell him about a newly captured vampire," Shaw said. "Bloodworth will want to see."

"I expect nothing less," Arthie said. If he had the keys to their one and only exit, Arthie didn't want to avoid him.

"Why? What do you mean to do?" Sora asked.

"I intend to have us escape in an hour, and Bloodworth is going to help us."

As Arthie studied Matteo's sketches, she slowly began to lose focus on his neat lines and the task at hand, for now she knew how to answer that woman in the sari the color of blood who had scrutinized her. She knew how to answer the sea's whisper when she'd set foot on Ceylan's shore.

She knew why she'd returned.

The Ram would learn at some point that Arthie had returned to her homeland. And when she did, Arthie wanted the Ram to know the heart of her trade route had fallen, that her vampires were gone, that the land had been returned to the people it belonged to.

And she would be afraid.

Arthie remembered the red canisters lining the perimeter of the fort, gathered neatly to fuel the EJC ships. She was going to give them a new purpose.

"I need oil," Arthie said, standing up. The others looked at her. Jin looked concerned. "Lots of it."

"Whatever for?" Matteo asked.

"I know how I'm going to leave my mark and hurt the EJC. Jin, you wanted to free your parents. Matteo, you wanted to free the vampires," Arthie said. "I'm going to burn this entire operation to the ground."

Matteo burst into a broad grin.

"I know they're colonizers, but you can't mean to kill them," Jin said, brow furrowed.

"Oh, no," Arthie said, "I intend to drive them into the sea, as they did with my parents and my people."

"And make a statement," Matteo said. "I like it."

"They can scramble on board their ships and go back to where they came from, if they've enough fuel for it. Or into the wilderness if they so choose," Arthie said. "The fort is stone. The fire will be contained. There are plenty of shops and goods outside the fort, yes, but why have a fort if not to protect what's important? When it burns, we'll be setting them back years, from reserves to fuel, and in the meantime, my people will rebuild. If Ettenia finds itself starved of Ceylani resources, they can forge agreements, establish contracts, and act civil as civilized people are wont to do."

Arthie had not returned to leave the island as she had left it before. She wasn't a child anymore. She wasn't torn between the living and the dead.

She never felt more alive.

"Ceylan *is* the heart of the EJC's trade route. If there's one thing we have no shortage of, it's fuel for the ships, imported and safely stored here in the fort, since we're close enough to the harbor. We'll get you what you need," Shaw said with a nod.

Arthie hadn't expected Jin's parents to leap on board so quickly, but she was grateful for it. The Siwangs had said it had taken them ten years to build their way to this point—Arthie intended to bring it all down in a night.

"Now, the vampires," she continued, beckoning them closer and gesturing to Matteo's sketches.

"I must say," Shaw interjected, "this is well done for the time you spent on it, Matteo."

Matteo inclined his head. "Thank you."

"A good portion of our vampires will be angry, possibly violent," Shaw added. "We can feed them and free them, thus ensuring they're clearheaded, but many of them have been confined for a very long time."

"A number of the vampires are Athereum members who will recognize me. I can't imagine someone not wanting to side with us if we promise vengeance," Matteo said.

"And how exactly are we going to feed and unlock all the vampires at once?" Jin asked, ever pragmatic.

"Funny you should ask," Shaw said with a grin. "Actually, it's best if we show you, and it's right next door, so we won't need to worry about being seen. Grab your things."

Arthie shook her head. "We don't have time to—"

But Shaw was already unlocking a door tucked into the side of the laboratory. He stepped into the hall, peering every which way before he beckoned for them to follow.

This had better be worth it.

They crossed the short corridor and he pulled out a different key from his pocket, one that wasn't connected to the ring hanging from his side. The door swung open to a room as large as Spindrift's floor, and a scent she craved hit her like a wave.

Arthie prided herself in rarely being taken by surprise, but in this case, her jaw dropped. "So that's where they went."

25

JIN

Jin's jaw dropped beside Arthie's. This was one of his parents' stashes. The space was unfurnished and unadorned, chilling him to the bone, and like the emperor in a fairy tale hoarding gold in a room to near bursting, it was full of coconuts. King coconuts, oblong and golden.

In addition to making excellent weapons, coconuts make you happy, his father had once said, and Jin remembered he had been certain they could do more than that. He had hoped vampires could subsist on coconut, and it wasn't until Jin had discovered that Arthie was a vampire herself that he'd learned his father was right.

"They've been impossible to import for the longest time," Arthie breathed.

"I didn't know you were a businesswoman," his father said.

Of course the Ram had conveyed Jin's and Arthie's notoriety to his parents, but nothing about Spindrift.

"Among other things," Matteo said, and Jin approved of the pride in his voice—not necessarily the coy glance he slid Arthie's way though, causing her to look down. Wicked knives, was his sister *shy*?

"Well, in that case, I apologize for monopolizing the Ceylani coconut trade," his father said, and Jin watched for Arthie's reaction.

They hadn't spoken about how the lack of coconut had affected her. Before, she would ask him every few days for an update on their shipments, and Jin had always assumed it was for Spindrift's bloodhouse menu. Not for her.

He still didn't take lightly the fact that she'd drunk blood for him.

"I've been slowly accumulating the fruit and preserving it to the best of my ability. Early discreet tests have indicated that it can reverse the effects of the inoculation," his father said.

Matteo looked impressed at the lengths they'd gone. "It might have been easier to feed the vampires what they typically drink, no?"

"So we assumed," his mother said. "But it's not nearly as easy to gather and accumulate fresh blood for over one hundred starving vampires, especially without the Ram's men finding out. Further, we've found that a dose of coconut aids vampire vitals and has longer-lasting effects than blood. It can keep them sated long enough to escape."

"Clever, since vampires don't need to feed daily," Matteo said.

"But if any decide to feed on the guards we might need to fight during our escape, I can't blame them," Jin added.

"And the brutes will have deserved it," his mother said.

Jin's father was aghast. "Forgive my wife. She's angry."

Arthie burst out laughing, and upon seeing the look on his father's face, Jin did too. And perhaps it was the laughter, or the spurt of joy, but Jin wished Flick was here with them.

His mother sniffed and jutted out her chin. She had always been the more fiery of the two. Where his father failed to react, his mother did. Where his mother fell too deep into emotions, his father reeled her back. But this was a situation where Sora Siwang deserved every ounce of her anger, and then some.

"That's a lot of coconut to extract in such a short time," Arthie said, powering ahead with a glance at her pocket watch.

Jin's father nodded. "That is what I had been eager to tell you. We knew we couldn't risk feeding the vampires one by one: Bloodworth or his men would notice before we made it far, because once awoken, the vampires won't sit quiet. The ruckus will draw the guards, and trapped vampires are easy targets for the very well-armed men.

"Unleashing the vampires at once is the only way they'd stand a chance, so during what little time we've had away from Bloodworth's eyes, Sora and I have been automating a way to feed them and unlock the cells from one central location in the hopes that one day we'd have a way to escape. The coconuts here will drop into a contraption that will crack them and send a measured amount to each cell. Once fed, the vampires will come to. We'll then unlock the cells. Again, there's no predicting the outcome once the vampires are out."

"They're not rabid animals," Matteo reminded them. "Especially once they're fed. I don't doubt they'd want to kill the guards on sight, but does the same apply to you two?"

Jin's father shook his head, albeit guiltily, and Jin couldn't abate his own growing apprehension.

It was his mother who answered. "They've seen us in and out of their cells, in between doses of the serum that keeps them asleep. They know us. Still, Shaw is right. There will very likely be chaos."

"And that's where the work of the scientist comes to an end, and ours begins," Arthie said. "Chaos is exactly what we need."

She gestured for the others to gather closer, and Jin caught the flare of her nostrils, breathing in the breezy, nutty aroma of the coconuts around them. It seemed to set her at ease.

Matteo pulled the sketch from her and added *coconuts* to the room they were in. His sketches *were* well done for how quickly he made them, with labels and decor, including the ornate chandelier Arthie mentioned but Jin hadn't seen on his walkthrough, likely because his head was in a sack.

"We're here," Arthie said, pointing. Across the short hall was the wide laboratory, planted in the center of the sanatorium. There were more testing rooms and smaller laboratories throughout. "This is where we were. The main laboratory."

"Where's the switch to feed the vampires and open all the cells?" Jin asked.

Sora pointed to a room farther down the hall, near the giant chandelier.

Arthie took note and traced a finger around the inside of the sanatorium. "The cells line the perimeter of the sanatorium."

"Those are a lot of cell doors we'd need to open manually if not for your automation," Matteo remarked.

Jin's father beamed at his compliment.

"The moment those doors are opened, the guards will mobilize," Jin's mother said. "They're stationed throughout the sanatorium, with more outside."

"This is a good moment to bring up that Bloodworth's guards will be armed for killing vampires," Jin's father said. "It's dangerous."

That was the first acknowledgment his parents had given about him being a vampire.

"The green darts?" Matteo asked.

He nodded.

"Created by you, I'd like to guess?"

His nod this time was far less assured. "I—"

"Needed to keep yourselves safe, I understand. I'm not unreasonable," Matteo said with a sniff. "Dangerous, yes, but a shot at an escape is better than none."

Any other time, Jin would have derided him for thinking he could speak for someone else, but he now knew Matteo saw himself as one of those vampires. He'd put himself in their shoes more than once, as if he was making up for the scores of people who didn't care for them.

Arthie skimmed through the sketches once more before she glanced at her pocket watch. "Fifteen minutes before Bloodworth's arrival."

"And how is he supposedly aiding our escape?" Jin asked.

"By letting us take the keys right off him," Arthie said. "First, our timing has to be precise—we'll face guards either way, but if Bloodworth is distracted, we'll have the element of surprise on our side, and thus extra time. Sora and Shaw, you'll be splitting up. Sora will go for the switches; Shaw will meet with Bloodworth."

Arthie looked at her pocket watch, calculating. "Activate the switches at the half hour. We'll be ready."

"Are you certain?" Shaw asked. "Bloodworth can be unpredictable."

"We'll make it work," Arthie said. "You'll meet Bloodworth with us as your prisoners. We'll apprehend him, snatch the keys, and regroup here"—she tapped at the junction beneath the chandelier—"Shaw, Sora, the vampires, and us."

"Why there and not at the exit corridor?" Matteo asked.

"At that point, we'll have a number of guards on our tail, and I aim to make that chandelier a main attraction to aid in our escape. Any other questions?" she asked. "Right. Sora, cuff us."

Jin thought it very sad indeed that they had equipment to apprehend people readily available in every room. He watched as his mother cuffed Matteo.

"I'm not fond of putting myself in the hands of strangers, you know," Matteo said.

"They're not locked," Sora said, "if that's any consolation."

"It's not."

Sora patted his cheek and turned to Jin next. "This is the last thing I ever wanted to do to my son."

Jin tried not to let his apprehension consume him when the cold metal touched his skin. They were unlocked, he reminded himself, and not prone to piercing his flesh the way the captain's had been.

But when his mother took his umbrella from him and handed it back to his father, Jin felt . . . off.

Sora turned to Arthie, who was still studying Matteo's sketches. "Why is this space empty?" Arthie asked. "If it's to scale, it's as large as the laboratory. Is it one of your secret rooms?"

"I'd been meaning to ask about that," Matteo said as he and Jin shuffled closer, and the three of them looked up when neither of his parents answered.

No, they had *paled*.

"Awfully quiet there, Shaw," Matteo said, widening his stance. "Sora."

Jin knew, somehow, that this was what his parents had been hiding from them, why his father had been unable to *not* speak with guilt and self-reproach. That numbness crept back into Jin's veins. He felt his trust crumbling again. It was a fragile tree to begin with, weak bows begging for strength.

And now it was falling.

"Sora, the switches," his father said softly. Sora nodded, slipping from the room without another word. Shaw turned to them. "Remember when I mentioned that the long-lasting effects—"

"We don't have time for this. Show us," Jin said. *I don't trust you*, was what he wanted to say.

As if he heard the unspoken words, his father looked at him, resigned and empty.

Just like Jin.

26

FLICK

Flick was in a chair. Her wrists ached more than she would have liked, but that was fine. Eyes ate more than mouths ever did, and the feast before her was delightful. The chair was quite comfortable, the round table before her laden with some of her favorite things: a slender vase full of happy sunflowers, a spread of sandwiches with cucumbers and cream—a rarity, for cucumbers were expensive and hard to come by. She could smell the tea brewing in a dainty cup.

Royal Rouge. Her favorite Spindrift blend, with rose petals and caramel. If the papers ever came to interview her at the Linden Estate and asked her to describe herself, she would say Royal Rouge. It was Flick in a teacup.

And she wasn't alone, for Flick loved companionship more than anything else.

"You look lovely today, Mother," she said. Where Lady Linden's gown brought out her remarkable blue eyes, Flick's dress didn't really complement her skin or hair or the color of her eyes, but she didn't find herself concerned, because they matched. It meant her mother liked her enough to dress alike.

"Thank you, dear. Have you tried the tea?" Lady Linden asked. "I know it's your favorite."

Flick's smile slipped before she mentally pinched herself and tacked it back on. How did her mother know her favorite tea? She'd been far too occupied with everything else to even take Flick to Spindrift, let alone learn what she liked there.

Still, Flick was always a gracious, obedient daughter. She widened her smile and reached for her cup. But her arm kept... *going*. She stretched and stretched, and when her fingers finally closed around the handle of the teacup, she was dreadfully tired. When she pulled the cup closer, the smell of it began to change. The sweet caramel turned sharper, spicier, and when she brought it to her lips, she saw that it wasn't tea that was brewing.

It was a steeping of blood. Her hand shook, causing it to splash and scald her chest.

Flick gasped, and the teacup faded away, as did the spread of food and her gown and her mother. She *felt* herself awaken—she felt herself lurching back into her body, her senses rousing from darkness, every excruciating inch of her screaming with pain. It thumped through her veins, sending echoing waves of weakness washing through her with every other breath.

The Ram was before her, cloaked in shadows, and Flick was still hanging from the ceiling, her wrists bound. In that moment, she wished she was horribly, terribly alone.

Because this was worse.

The Ram assessed Flick through her mask that was as ugly as her soul. Beside her was a tiny stool with a wicked blade resting in wait. It was long with sharp, serrated teeth. Terror shot through Flick's veins, warring with the pain.

She was supposed to find out more about the Ram's plans for the tribute. She was supposed to forge invitations and figure out what those pill-shaped sketches represented. Was she really at the location of the coordinates and had somehow gotten them wrong? Or was her mother mocking her as she tended to do?

"Enjoying yourself?" she rasped. A familiar scent tickled her nose: that spritz of lavender perfume her mother sprayed every morning. She was methodical with it, so that it never mixed poorly with her evening fragrances.

A day had passed. Or was it two? Flick had been hanging for a day. She ought to be proud of herself, but she could barely think from the pain leaching through her.

"I don't like your tone," the Ram said.

Flick laughed. It was more of a wheeze, but the Ram had lived with her long enough to know what it was meant to be. "I don't like your methods, so I suppose we're equal, *Mother*."

Flick decided then and there that she enjoyed sarcasm. Not only did it sound exquisite to her ears, but when she visualized the word, it was a lovely italicized stream of disdain that was quite joyful.

The Old Roaring Tower tolled, marking the hour, and Flick wished her head wasn't throbbing. Three bells clanged across the city. Why did it sound so far above her? Was it three at night or in the afternoon? There wasn't a window in here to tell. Years might have passed for all she knew. She couldn't remember *not* being in pain.

"Don't you have a tribute to plan?" Flick asked in another rasp. She could barely get the words out. She wriggled her fingers. They were numbed to the bone. She stifled a sob.

The Ram noticed. She strode forward and kicked the crate beneath Flick.

Flick only needed to lift her feet onto it, and she would feel relief. Her mother would feel satisfaction. *Don't do it, don't.*

Flick lifted her feet.

It was a struggle, but she did it, one after the other, touching them to the surface of the crate. Her feet felt as though they would snap as she straightened them. She couldn't hold back her sob this time. It racked through her, and the pain was almost worse as feeling slowly eked back into her limbs.

"There, isn't that better? Can you blame me for being deterred by the sudden change in my daughter's behavior?" the Ram asked. "You won't tell me where the ledger is, or where your friends are, or even where the Casimir girl's pistol might be."

Flick gave her an emotionless look. *There is good, there is bad, and then there is obedience and the lack thereof,* Flick reminded herself.

"Did you know that she's a vampire?" the Ram asked.

First the pistol, now Arthie's being undead. Where was the Ram getting this information?

The Ram tried something else. "Is it not disheartening that the family you chose over me still hasn't come to your rescue?"

Flick kept her blank gaze steady in reply.

The Ram sighed. "Felicity, you and I are lonely souls."

She didn't know why the Ram's words drew tears through the steel Flick had layered over herself. Perhaps it was because she was aching and weak, thirsty and exhausted.

And again the Ram noticed. She brought her water. Fed it to her. Flick wanted to spit it back at her and drench that detestable mask. She was too thirsty to hold her ground. She gulped down every sip, and when her mother brought bread to her lips, she ate that too, trying not to choke. She was so starved that she couldn't care for the disgraceful way in which she devoured it.

The Ram said nothing. She waited until Flick finished chewing, until her eyes flickered shut and relief washed through her.

"Do you think they like you?" the Ram asked quietly.

Flick opened her eyes. It was time to pay for her mother's kindness.

But Flick wasn't trying to be liked. She didn't *want* to be liked. She wanted to be loved, ardently, passionately. She wanted to be cared for and to care for someone in turn. And she knew, deep in her heart of hearts, that she had that.

"Dearest, the Casimirs already have others they rely upon. They will discard you the moment you are of no value to them."

Flick couldn't stand the Ram talking badly about Jin and Arthie anymore.

"They haven't come for me only because they're not—" Flick stopped herself when the Ram held herself very, very still. As if Flick were a bird she was afraid of spooking, as if Flick were a mark she was afraid would realize she was being fooled.

"They're not what? Smart enough to find where we are?" she scoffed.

"They're not here," Flick snapped.

And in that moment, Flick felt undeniably small and useless, until she saw the way the Ram reacted.

"No," she breathed. She stumbled back, her blue eyes aghast. "They're not here. They're in Ceylan."

How did she—had the Ram heard of the missing EJC ship? No, it was too soon, but her mother was smart. She knew they had the ledger in their possession and that they were aware of the weaponized vampires. It wasn't hard to put everything together. She met Flick's eyes, and Flick realized that no matter what the Ram might try to do now to stop Arthie and the others, to ramp up security in her fort, to protect her operation—it was too late. She couldn't get there soon enough if the others were *already* there.

"You deciphered my ledger, you wretched child."

Flick didn't know what it was about that phrase that made a laugh bubble up in her throat. The Ram, monarch to the most powerful empire in the world, was being bested by a *wretched child.*

There was a glint in the Ram's eyes now. It was bright and

wild—understandably. Ceylan was the heart of the Ram's operation, and the Ram knew Arthie was calculating and angry, content with hurting both the EJC *and* the crown.

Her reign was crumbling.

"It wasn't that hard, really," Flick said, unable to resist the urge to gloat.

The Ram started turning for the door, and dread sank through Flick, heavy and laden, and it had nothing to do with her aching, numbing limbs. The crate beneath her feet offered little relief. She didn't want the Ram to leave. Letting her leave meant allowing her to plan her next course of action.

"Why do you hate vampires?" she asked.

The Ram froze.

"This is because you loathe vampires, isn't it?" Flick continued. "The fearmongering when you rose to power, the kidnappings, the weaponization of them for your own needs. You raised me to hate them. You're training a whole *empire* to hate them still."

The Ram's eyes were cruel when she turned to face Flick fully. She stormed closer, but Flick wasn't afraid, even if she was chained and unable to defend herself. She held the Ram's gaze and screwed her jaw tight, challenging her.

"You're one of them," Flick said.

"What did you say?" the Ram asked, her voice deathly low.

"You see yourself as so superior, but vampires were once human, just as much as you," Flick said, drawing as deep a breath as she could muster. "You use them to advance your own interests, but you forget how similar you really are."

The Ram kicked the crate out from beneath Flick's feet without warning. Flick cried out. Her arms wrenched with her weight, and her vision began to fade black. Flick blinked, forcing herself awake.

"Do you think to lecture me, girl?" the Ram asked.

Girl.

Not Flick. Not Felicity. She was not even a *bad daughter* anymore. If Flick was having a hard time snipping away the last of the threads binding her to her mother—and only because her hands were bound—the Ram was eager to help.

"I know the tribute is a cover," Flick managed to say, trying to swing forward and—and what? Flick didn't know. "You're not as smart as you think you are."

The Ram looked bored behind her mask. "Oh? You ought to consider yourself fortunate you won't be there when I meet your friends upon their return from Ceylan. Should they return, that is, from a fortress full of my men. Did you know that too?"

"They will return," Flick swore. "They will return, and together, we will tear you down."

The Ram scoffed. "And to think, I gave you everything."

"Everything to you was still nothing to me," Flick said. "I wanted a mother."

"And I wanted a daughter."

At some point, yes. Flick believed her mother did. That desire faded with her humanity. That desire was long gone now, gobbled by her greed and hatred.

"Then I reckon neither of us got what we wanted," Flick said, and she was surprisingly content with that.

The Ram seethed, and slammed the door closed behind her, leaving Flick alone with her thundering heart. She had no way of getting in contact with Jin and Arthie, but she needed to escape. She needed to be there at the docks when they arrived to warn them.

The Ram's patience was waning. The next interrogation wouldn't go so kindly, if the blade she had left on the stool was any indication, but

Flick refused to let the Ram's tactics get to her. She had left it behind on purpose, to scare Flick.

Her body ached anew, tricked by the temporary relief the Ram had given her for a scant handful of minutes. Flick stared up. Like in her nightmare, her hands looked so far out of reach, as if they might not even belong to her.

She was used to being cared for, used to having maids attend to her every need—even when she didn't want it. Even when she'd decided to take matters into her own hands, she always knew somewhere in the back of her mind that help was waiting for her should she need it. Even when she'd broken into the Athereum, she'd walked with the reassurance that Arthie Casimir would know what to do no matter what went wrong.

This time, Flick was alone. She was here due to her own decisions, of her own volition.

No one could save her but herself. It was both a harrowing and empowering realization at once. She fought her constraints again, exerting against the cuffs before trying to wriggle the chain over the hook.

Focus, Felicity, Jin said in her ear. Right. She needed to assess the situation in front of her. Above her. And when she did, her eyes threatening to burst out of her skull for straining them so, she noticed the curve of the hook ended high up enough that the chain links would require quite a jump to leap free. It was impossible.

She squinted up at the cuffs. Her head would not stop throbbing, the skin beneath her arms aching like she had rubbed it raw with a scrubber. The brass knuckles from Jin pulsed in her pocket, almost taunting her.

The cuffs were just wider than her wrists, leaving a gap where she could only fit two fingertips. She pressed her thumb tight and flush against her index finger, tugging downward with more force. Nothing.

Her thumb wasn't getting in the way though—the cuffs kept scraping against her knuckle.

What was it that Jin had said about bones and imprisonments? No, not what he'd said, but what he'd shown her when he dislocated his shoulder to demonstrate how he had escaped from the basement of a lord's gambling den several years ago.

Flick had balked at the sight before a portion of her breakfast reversed back up to her mouth. She stared at her hands now, at that knuckle bone. With dreadful certainty, Flick knew she would need to do the same. *Works with any joint*, Jin had said, casually popping his shoulder back into place with a jaw-clenched growl.

Flick's eyes had widened at the pain in his eyes.

He responded with a shrug and a smile. *Human bones are no different than a machine socketed together. We're stronger than we think.*

She exhaled a trembling breath. She needed to shimmy herself higher if she was to escape. She had no other leverage against the weight of the cuffs pressed firmly against her wrists. She tried to wrap her fingers around the chain links and pull herself an inch or so higher, but her fingers were too weak. They faltered, sending a fresh wave of fatigue through her.

She grabbed her thumb and shoved, trying to push the joint inward, trying to pop it out of place the way Jin had with ease and precision. She cried out from the pressure. Both hands ached from her efforts. *Think, Flick*. If bones were that easy to pop out of place, it would happen by chance all the time. She needed to pull herself higher, force a gap between her hand and the cuffs that sat tight against her bones.

At a muffled thud, she glanced at the door, but the knob didn't turn and no one stepped through. Only more noises. Flick held her breath, trying to discern them. It was a scuffle. She heard a fist connecting with flesh, someone sucking air through clenched teeth. Flick might not have been a vampire, but she grew up in a house where everyone was quiet, where staff whispered about her and her mother whispered about business behind the closed door of her office.

And Flick liked to listen.

It seemed there was another prisoner, one they'd begun to use brute force upon. Flick needed to hurry. Before she could stop herself, she threw her weight to the side, swinging just high enough to throw her hand up and grab the chain. The cuff slipped down her arm with a sweaty pop. Gravity wrenched her back, teeth jarring.

"Step one, complete," she told herself.

She braced the cuff against one wrist and shoved it against her other thumb. She cried out, clamping her mouth tight to muffle the sound. If she could catch whispers of happenings outside of here, the opposite could happen too.

Again, Flick.

No different than a machine socketed together, Jin had said. She needed to stop shoving and be smart about it. With another clench of her teeth, she slid the cuff down the side of her hand, the skin now raw and starting to bruise, until it slotted beneath the joint. Then she sucked in a deep breath, scrunched her eyes tight, and pressed.

Color erupted behind her eyes, bright and blinding.

She felt more than heard her bone pop, and the cuff jerked off, forced by the weight of her hanging body, scraping her skin even further. Her arm was free. The chain clanged with joy of its own.

"Yes!" she cried out, forgetting to be quiet, before the pain of hanging from one arm shot through her, mutating her joy to a sob. "Can't—celebrate—yet."

Tears were streaming down her face, stinging her skin. It was impossible not to look at the weird angle of her thumb and retch. She swallowed the bile back down and did what Jin had done: snapped it back into place.

Returning a part of her back into place didn't make the pain, surprise, or sound any easier.

Don't think, she told herself, or she would spiral, and then she'd be hanging from a single arm. She didn't need to know bones or the human body to know that would be worse.

With a huffed exhale, she slid the remaining cuff into place and pushed against her other thumb, momentarily distracted by the fact that her seconds-ago-disjointed thumb worked as though it hadn't just been abused. The distraction helped, she supposed. She wasn't nearly as focused on her actions—the cuff yanked off.

Flick fell.

Free.

At last.

She tumbled to the ground in a heap, biting her tongue. Blood filled her mouth, dripped down her chin, mixing with the tears streaming down her face. She couldn't move. Every inch of her was wound tight, the pain so great she was seeing double.

"You did it," she whispered to herself. "You did it, Flick."

She folded into herself.

She was sore all over, *raw* all over, and—she glanced at the door when that muffled thud sounded again—she couldn't afford to rest. Her escape had just begun.

It took three tries before Flick could stand. Her legs were heavy; her arms were light. She looked at her hands with a gasp. They were pale, deathly so. Bloodless.

She needed to keep moving.

She stumbled to the Ram's chair and tried to pick up the knife, but her hands refused to work. They shook violently, her fingers so numb she barely felt the chair when she reached for it. How was she supposed to escape without the use of her hands? How was she supposed to forge anything anymore? Her penmanship—*no*.

No, no, no.

The abyss opened up beneath her, threatening to tug her into its depths. She couldn't spiral down that hole. She had people to save. She had purpose, and that was enough.

What an excellent weapon, Jin said to her, but really she was the one thinking the words. *So violent, love.*

Indeed, she was. She saw red everywhere she looked. She understood Arthie's rage. Flick reached into her pocket with shaking hands. She pulled out Jin's brass knuckles—*her* brass knuckles—and, ignoring the quiver as best as she could, slid them over her fingers.

She had thought the dusters were boxy and heavy for a hand used to sliding on dainty rings, but her hands were different now. They were raw and rough, bruised and angry.

They fit perfectly.

Then she reached again for the serrated knife the Ram had left behind, consciously telling her fingers to close around its grip, and stepped to the door, slumping against it with a sigh of relief.

"No," she told herself. "No time . . . for rest."

She pushed herself off the door and saw the pitcher of water the Ram had given her. It was still half-full. Flick dropped to her knees and gulped it down—half of which drenched her shirt because her hands refused to cooperate.

Her gaze cleared a little then. She forced deep breaths through her lungs and tried the knob, but the door was locked from the other side. She couldn't pick a lock, not with the way her hands shook. No, she would wait, and whoever came through that door would find their reckoning.

What if it's the Ram?

What did that matter anymore? In these walls, Lady Linden and her daughter didn't exist, because the Ram wore a mask and her daughter—

Well, Felicity Linden was dead.

27
ARTHIE

Arthie snatched the last pair of cuffs as they followed a defeated Shaw down the corridors. Beside her, Matteo and Jin were quiet. For two different reasons, she suspected. Arthie didn't need to ask to know they were heading to see one of the Siwangs' sins for themselves.

Her skin still crawled with that unsettling sense that they were being watched. Arthie knew vengeance well—the smell of it, the feel of it. And the eyes that tracked them from some of the cells they passed were exuding it.

"There you are."

The four of them froze.

"Overseer Bloodworth," Shaw said.

Arthie snapped the cuffs around her wrists, positioning her fingers in place to undo them and reach for her pistol at the first sign of trouble. The overseer drifted closer, and he looked just as she had suspected: an eerie man, more bones than flesh, his dark eyes gaunt. They looked hungry, and Arthie wasn't sure it was a hunger that might ever be sated.

"Where are you going?" Bloodworth asked.

"To see you," Shaw replied. "Horace said you were in the Ripper room and I had no reason to believe otherwise."

Ripper room. Arthie hadn't seen a room marked as such in Matteo's sketches, but she vaguely remembered it being mentioned in the letter they'd found.

Bloodworth hummed, circling around them. Was this what the Siwangs had to deal with for the past decade? He eyed Jin until *Arthie* felt the need to squirm.

"Is this not the one you were given for testing?" Bloodworth asked, his gaze missing nothing.

"Have you tried speaking to him directly?" Jin sniped.

Bloodworth leaned toward him. "That would be beneath me."

Arthie could see every fiber of Jin's being winding up to ram his head into Bloodworth's before he rocked back on his heels.

"Shaw?" Bloodworth asked, still staring at Jin. "I want to know why these three are here in our sanatorium, and why this one, in particular, is awake."

Arthie knew the look on Shaw's face. She'd seen it before when Jin would occasionally make calculated, spur-of-the-moment decisions he hadn't previously discussed with her. The percentile in which they succeeded was excruciatingly low.

"His vitals are far higher than the majority of the vampires sent here," Shaw said. "He's never been inoculated. Sora and I decided he's much more suited for Ripper testing."

He spoke with an alarming level of confidence. It was believable—even to Arthie's ears. Which made her wonder how much of what he had told them was actually true. But he hadn't yet outed them to Bloodworth, so Arthie held her tongue—and held her hand back from Calibore.

"Is that so?" Bloodworth asked. He scrutinized Jin more closely, looking between him and Shaw until Arthie feared he recognized the resemblance. How much of the Ram's schemes was he aware of? Did he know of Jin? "I've never seen you work with this new methodology. Locking them in canisters sounds quite like canning the fruits of the season, no? I'd very much enjoy watching."

Canisters? Shaw paled even more.

"What is he talking about?" Jin asked quietly.

Shaw turned in the direction of the Ripper room. The hall widened to the intersection from Matteo's sketches that led in four directions. Arthie glanced up to where the massive chandelier hung in almost comical contrast to the dim, forlorn cells.

Bloodworth strode behind them, and though she'd kept a close eye on him, he'd given no indication as to where he kept the key to the vault-like door. Calibore pressed against her side, and when she glanced at Matteo, he gave the pistol a pointed glance too, reminding her that there was another way out of here.

Shaw reached the doors to the Ripper room, and with a grim glance at Jin, Arthie, and Matteo, he unlatched the doors and pushed them open.

Arthie froze.

If she thought the rest of the sanatorium was eerie, compared to this, it was not. The air sent a deathly chill down her spine. As with the rest of the place, it was dimly lit, except for the glowing blue pill-shaped cylinders lining the room in rows, slanted at an angle, a faint light within pulsing as if in time to a heartbeat. Arthie counted seven.

Inside each of the seven canisters was a body.

"Are they alive?" Jin whispered.

"Yes," Shaw said, just as hushed.

"I'll be hanged," Bloodworth exclaimed. "Every time I come in here, it's a feat to behold."

The canisters were filled with some sort of fluid, and because of the angled position, the heads of the bodies within weren't submerged. They were almost entirely naked, with flesh that looked to be carved from stone.

"Vampires," Arthie murmured. Of course they were vampires.

"Ripper vampires," Bloodworth corrected.

"What are you doing to them?" Matteo asked, a frenzy in his voice.

"The Siwangs truly are the best of the best," Bloodworth touted.

Two guards stood on either side of the door. On the *inside*, and Arthie had a sinking feeling they weren't there to protect the caged vampires.

"They are no doubt brilliant, no? When the Ram asked for better, they provided. Starved vampires are an ingenious, brilliant utilization, but why settle for what's available, when you have minds such as theirs? Thus, their brilliant creation: the Ripper. An unassailable foe. I named them myself, in memory of one of my old colleagues who was ripped to shreds," Bloodworth continued.

Arthie wished she loved anything as much as this man loved to say *brilliant*.

"Creation?" Jin hissed at his father. The use of the word sounded no different from when the captain had referred to him as *it*.

Shaw's perfect composure cracked then. He shuffled from foot to foot.

Bloodworth, conversely, couldn't contain his glee. "Indeed. A newly developed serum that produces a specialized breed of super vampires."

"No," Shaw said.

A silence slithered into the room, as anxious as Shaw. Bloodworth's brow furrowed, the color draining from his face, and Arthie was surprised by the power he held over Shaw. Why else did a simple word cause such unease?

"What did you say?" Bloodworth asked.

Shaw stepped closer, not to his so-called creations, not to Bloodworth, but to Jin. "I said no."

"No, what, Shaw? No, you are not the best of the best? Or no, you did not create a specialized breed of vampires?"

"No, there is no serum."

Bloodworth looked confused, glancing at the canisters lining the room. The "specialized breed" was standing—floating—before them.

"Am I imagining them?" he asked.

Jin drew in a sharp breath. "The long-lasting effects of the silver—when you said it was unknown, I knew there was more you weren't telling me."

Arthie was beginning to piece together what the Siwangs had told them since they'd met: their guilt, Sora and his need to remain with the vampires despite the opportunities for escape, the daily visits to the cells for necessary administrations.

"Well then, how *are* these brilliant vampires being made?" Bloodworth asked.

"Through the untold effects of the silver inoculation—on *accident*," Arthie whispered, looking at Shaw. "You don't know, do you?"

It took several moments before Shaw shook his head.

"The silver inoculation triggers a mutation in some vampires that, over time, alters their brain function until only the need for survival remains," he said quietly. "They do not respond to their names, or at all. They've been stripped away of what makes them human, and with no moral boundaries, they're—"

"Monsters," Bloodworth whispered, drifting to stare intently at one of the vampires suspended in the blue fluid. "Weapons of the highest caliber. Without these supposed morals and values, they can kill without mercy. But an accident?" He didn't look angry that Shaw had lied, no. He looked excited. "By golly, the Ram would be astounded to hear this. We'll just have to starve each of your silver-injected vampires long enough to become these brilliant beasts. Immortal, impossible to injure, bones of steel."

"Since when?" Matteo asked. Bloodworth might not have even existed for the way he stared at Shaw.

"At least two years."

"Seven have mutated. So the one hundred and fifteen vampires out there and the rest waiting to be delivered from Ettenia are doomed to lose their humanity too?" Jin asked, and Arthie didn't need to hear Shaw's heart crushing. It was clear in his eyes when he saw Jin's face.

"They could," Shaw answered, his eyes flicking to Bloodworth for a moment before he decided to continue. "But we've found that coconut fights the silver. At the very least, it will delay the alteration, but blood test comparisons between those who had consumed coconut and those who hadn't were vastly different."

"Keep drinking coconut water, and it'll keep the monster at bay," Jin said. He slid a glance at Arthie when the words were out of his mouth, for that was her life for a near decade. "Literally speaking. Why didn't you tell us sooner?"

Shaw looked away. The *why* was clear enough. This was a horror of his own making, his *and* Sora's.

Shaw looked at the vampires locked in the canisters. "We were too late to save them though. We could do nothing but put them to sleep."

What were the vampires in those canisters thinking? Was some part of their brains still conscious? They looked asleep, dead. Arthie was reminded of herself, adrift in a sea of blue, afraid of the monster beneath her skin commanding her bones.

That was how she'd felt when she'd been made into a half vampire. This—this was tenfold of that.

"Save? Hold on there a moment," Bloodworth said, brow furrowed as he tried to follow along. "You and Sora—you've been feeding the others coconut water. I saw it! You've been *staving off* the effects?"

Shaw paused, glancing not at Jin nor Matteo, but at Arthie. It was a look Jin had given her a thousand times before: *Get ready*.

Good. The countdown had begun the moment they'd parted ways with Sora, and Arthie couldn't glance at her pocket watch to keep track of the time with her hands cuffed behind her.

"Why do you think they're in these canisters, Bloodworth?" Shaw asked.

"Because! The longer the better, you said during our meeting months ago. The stronger they'd be."

"The longer they stay in the canisters, the slower the silver takes over. I'm not making monsters. I'm trying to stop them."

Understanding settled in Bloodworth's form. Arthie saw how he almost relaxed with the information, as if he had long wanted, possibly even suspected, Shaw and Sora to be traitors. He toyed with something beneath the folds of his overcoat, and Arthie caught the glint of a ring of keys before he straightened his coat.

"Is that so? Oh, Shaw, I do love a good tell-all moment when I know our audience won't be able to tell anyone after," Bloodworth drawled.

Arthie caught Jin's eye, making sure he saw her unlatch her cuffs. She gestured to Matteo to do the same.

"Everyone, stop."

Bloodworth pulled out a dart gun. The guards leaped to attention with weapons of their own. Matteo froze several feet to her left, Jin to her right, and before Bloodworth could decide where to aim, Arthie drew Calibore and leveled it at his head.

"Drop it," she commanded.

"And why would I do that?" Bloodworth asked.

Arthie cocked her pistol, watching the guards out of the corner of her eye. "Because if you don't, I will put a bullet through your brain."

Bloodworth looked among them. There was a madness about him, something keen on suffering. She could tell from the loving way in which he'd regarded the vampire in the canister, from the glitter in his eyes and the vile words he'd spewed.

He would not lower his weapon, even if she threatened him. Even if she fired first. He would fire his weapon regardless.

Arthie intended to make the most of it. She took a step toward him. That took her closer to one of the canisters too.

"Stop moving," one of the guards commanded, but that did the trick: Bloodworth's aim was solidly on her now.

"Distract the guards," she heard Shaw whisper to Matteo.

"He said stop moving," the other guard shouted, aiming for Arthie.

"That's enough out of you," Matteo said, and lunged toward them. One of them fired at Arthie, but Matteo swerved, knocking him to the ground. The other pulled out a knife, slicing into Matteo's arm.

Matteo scowled. "You ruined my shirt."

The guard stumbled back to the door as Matteo stalked closer. And closer. He didn't pull out his gun, no. He *was* the gun. The guard tried reaching for the handle, but Matteo didn't let him. He ripped out his throat, drenching the floor in blood.

He—he killed him.

Matteo froze, staring at the guard's prone body. His dead body. Then he glanced at Arthie, shame flooding his verdant gaze. Only the guard who had aimed at her was dead. Only he had seen Matteo's wrath.

He had killed for her.

It took everything in Arthie's power not to waver, to keep her aim steady. It wasn't as though she hadn't seen Matteo kill before, but never so quickly, so *easily*. The other guard screamed, Shaw froze in place, and Bloodworth looked ready to give in to his own panic.

Which wasn't ideal when he was holding a gun.

Arthie didn't wait; she spoke her next words on a low breath. "Jin, the master key."

Shaw tossed him his umbrella, and Jin dropped his cuffs to the floor, diving for Bloodworth. The overseer fired, but Arthie was ready. She leaped out of the way. The tiny dart oozed out a greenish liquid when it hit the floor.

What she didn't expect was how quickly the weapon could fire. Bloodworth squeezed out another shot just as Jin tackled him to the floorboards.

The dart soared. It hit the canister.

As Jin and Bloodworth battled on the floor, Matteo met Arthie's eyes from across the room, and a fissure formed in the glass.

"No," Shaw breathed, and Arthie refused to give in to the utter terror in his eyes.

"Shaw, listen to me," she said. "Can we free the other six Ripper vampires?"

His gaze flew wider. "No! I put them in there to slow the process in the hopes that I might find a reversal to the silver; meanwhile I developed a fail-safe, a way to kill them if we could not find a solution, because once they're out—"

A bell tolled loudly as the remaining guard rose behind Matteo and yanked on a cord.

"Guards!" Bloodworth shouted, the last of it uselessly muffled as Jin clamped a hand over his mouth with a grimace.

"They're on their way!" the remaining guard shouted back, pulling out a short stake.

"Matteo!" Jin shouted.

In the same movement, Matteo turned and threw the guard against the wall. His stake clattered to the floor. He groaned one last time before he breathed his last.

Matteo wiped a smear of blood from his brow. "Much obliged, Jin."

Arthie whirled back to Shaw.

"I can't stop this one," he said. "If oxygen enters that canister, our circumstances will worsen."

"Too late for that now. Find Sora. We'll meet you at the doors," Arthie said.

"I'm not leaving you three," Shaw said with a shake of his head.

Bloodworth yowled from the floor, pinned beneath Jin's knees. Jin threw another punch and rose with the keys in his hand. Shouts echoed from afar.

"The moment the guards come in, Bloodworth will inform them that you're not on their side anymore. We don't have time." And she didn't need to worry about keeping Shaw safe too. "Leave. *Now.*"

With one last look at Jin, Shaw threw open the doors and disappeared down the hall.

Arthie turned back to find Jin rising with a bloody jaw, Matteo standing over his kill, and as Bloodworth groaned, the canister finally gave way. Glass and luminescent fluid crashed to the floor, the body of the altered vampire within slumping face-first with it.

For a moment, nothing happened. Shaw hadn't told her what would happen if oxygen entered the canister, or in their case, if its contents met oxygen.

Jin stepped closer, hooking his umbrella around the Ripper vampire's arm and rolling him onto his back with excessive effort.

"What have you done?" Bloodworth asked, horror in his voice. He scrambled to his feet and stumbled for the door. No one stopped him.

A harrowing feeling settled into Arthie's bones.

And the vampire opened his eyes.

28

JIN

Jin's first thought when the Ripper vampire opened his eyes was relief that they hadn't killed him. It was quickly replaced with panic when that fiend of a man Bloodworth staggered for the door, terror exuding from his every action. He ran without looking back.

"We ought to leave, don't you think?" Jin said as indifferently and calmly as he could.

The Ripper vampire was slowly sitting up, squeezing his eyes closed and opening them again. Arthie was carefully stepping toward the door.

"I happen to agree," Matteo said.

And the Ripper vampire stared straight at them. Jin shivered. His eyes were blue and might have made him good-looking at one point, but they were cold and cruel now.

"Run," Arthie whispered.

They bolted into the hall on Bloodworth's heels. Jin helped Arthie shut the doors, narrowly missing the Ripper's nose. Matteo tossed over the fallen guard's rifle and Jin shoved it beneath the handles, jumping away when the vampire rammed his weight against them.

Arthie was pulling out her pocket watch. "We're cutting it close. Sora should be opening the cells now. The vampires are about to be free."

Guards were shouting, footsteps thundering. The three of them dashed into the intersection between halls and stopped. The chandelier swayed above them.

This was where they were to reconvene with Jin's parents and the fed and freed vampires. That was before the Ripper room, before bloody Bloodworth summoned his men, who were now streaming from the three surrounding halls, the overseer in front of them—or behind several of them, really, the coward.

Jin wanted to wipe the smug look off his face.

The men leveled their dart-loaded weapons at them. They were an unusual shape, in between a pistol and a rifle but taller, as if the darts were stacked rather than lined in a cylinder.

There were an awful lot of guards for three barely armed vampires.

"Arthie, darling?" Matteo said, taking her hand. "We're surrounded."

Jin saw her fingers tighten around his.

"Good, we can attack in the direction of our choosing, then," she replied.

The ground began to rumble. Jin felt it in the soles of his shoes, the reverberation echoing up to his teeth. The guards glanced at one another, suddenly wary.

"The vampires," Arthie whispered. "Right on time. Shaw and Sora did it."

The coconut water worked. The vampires were awake. Matteo was grinning from ear to ear, even if that wariness was still in his eyes. As it should—there was still no telling if the vampires would side with them.

"Don't move!" someone commanded. It was that wretched captain.

"That one's mine," Jin seethed.

Gradually, the guards in the hall across from them began to turn, their dart weapons facing the opposite way as the floor continued to rumble. That was the direction of their exit. In the halls to Jin's left and right, the guards mumbled in confusion, torn between keeping their eyes on the three of them or aiding their brethren.

Arthie seized the distraction. She was already running with a glance at the chandelier. "Cover me."

I aim to make that chandelier a main attraction.

Jin and Matteo followed. They pulled out the revolvers Arthie had given them and squeezed out a round of shots as the guards moved to fire. Darts zipped past them.

One caught in Jin's shoe; one whizzed through his hair. Arthie dropped to her knees to avoid the guards' line of fire and slid the rest of the way to the opposite hall, where she pulled out Calibore, swung a wide arc to intimidate the guards nearest her, cocked it, and fired straight at the ceiling. At the ornate chandelier.

"Arthie, it's metal," Jin shouted.

"And we're on an island," she replied.

The link crumbled at the impact, rusted just enough. The chain gave way, and the chandelier rattled to the floor where it crashed, glass exploding in every direction.

The destruction rang out, casting a deafening silence for one long, excruciating moment.

Matteo reached into the mess of it—the chandelier was almost as tall as he was—and ripped one of the arms free, giving himself a mangled semblance of a spear and running back amid a spray of darts.

In Arthie's hand, Calibore became a spiked shield.

"Brilliant," Matteo said.

Arthie picked up a fallen knife. "I would like to never hear that word again. Rush them. Our exit is at the other end of this hall, the vampires too."

She charged forward, shoving her shield against the first line of guards. They stumbled, firing their weapons as they fell on the men behind them. The shield was barely wide enough for her, let alone three people, and Jin hissed when one of the darts caught on his sleeve, dampening it with the strange green serum.

"They'll surround us, Arthie," Matteo warned as he glanced back. Sure enough, guards were making their way past the fallen chandelier.

The ground rumbled louder. Shouts echoed not far from them.

Jin arced his umbrella, knocking the nearest guard's weapon from his hand. Jin caught it before it fell and shoved the end against the guard's nose. He stumbled before Jin kicked him square in the chest, knocking him into the man behind him and dropping them both.

Another guard went flying past and Matteo dove straight after him into the crowd, ramming the butt of his revolver into heads to knock them out of his way.

Shouts began anew, screams echoing from—*behind them.*

"It's him," Matteo said, breathless.

The Ripper vampire was thundering to the fallen chandelier.

Something told Jin that was a fight they could not win.

Panic spread like wildfire to the front of the guards. Bloodworth's tinny voice rose from the din, saying something Jin could not make out other than its terrified tone. No one wanted to fight the vampire, and possibly, terribly worse was the realization that it seemed no one was equipped to fight him either.

"Arthie," Jin warned.

"I know," she replied, and pushed through. One moment, her spiked shield was up, the next, Calibore became a flail. Jin ducked out of her swing with a huff.

"A little warning would be appreciated next time."

She swung it again, and Jin realized what she was doing: The guards were backing away. Arthie was clearing a path. Jin pressed close at her heels, pulling Matteo behind him and swinging his umbrella, ramming it against skull and weapon alike, until he tripped, coming face-to-face with the barrel of one of the guns, the wretched captain's face sneering behind it.

The rest of the world slowed and melted away. Jin acutely recalled this feeling before, when he was staring down the end of the Ram's miniature revolver, suspended between life and death for an eternal, insubstantial moment.

He heard the captain's finger fall to the trigger, heard the click of the metal as he pressed down on it, the compression of the springs coiling tight, the green dart readying to launch.

Not today. Not again.

He had far too much to live for. His parents, Arthie, Chester. *Flick.* He needed to return to her, and he knew he wouldn't receive a second chance.

Because that was what Arthie had given him, despite his anger at her betrayal, despite his pain at her distrust: a second chance. That decade he'd lived without his parents had been one of worry, always concerned someone would take away what was his yet again. And they had, in the end: The Ram had burned Spindrift to ashes, but it was his own fault he hadn't lived those ten years enjoying every second of it.

He was undead now, but he had every intention of living.

Jin completed the arc of his umbrella, swinging it forward, nudging the barrel out of his face as the captain fired. The dart whizzed past Jin's cheek, landing in the arm of an unsuspecting guard. Jin straightened, pulled an ugly ornament from the wall, and slammed it against the back of the guard's head.

"Now that's what it's really for," Jin said, holding it at his side. The captain fell with a groan, and Jin felt no pity.

He didn't know what possessed him to look back just then, but he almost wished he hadn't.

The Ripper vampire was staring straight through the chaos at Jin.

Arthie locked her arm around his and pulled him out of the way of an arcing blade. She squeezed out a shot with Calibore the pistol. He was surprised to see that she wasn't aiming or shooting to kill, only maim.

Together, they pushed their way through the guards until Jin fell, stumbling again headfirst toward the bare floor until someone caught him.

"I have you."

Jin looked up at his father's face. His parents were standing before him, an army of vampires behind them, each of them carrying a coconut. Some even hefted netted sacks of them over their shoulders. Behind them, the exit was still sealed.

"You're alive," his mother exclaimed.

"Not now, Sora. Jin, the keys!" his father said quickly.

Jin tossed his father the keys as the fight continued behind him. He searched the vampires' haggard faces. They were pale, bruised, tired, but they didn't look violent or crazed. They looked as though they trusted his parents. As though, despite their sedation, they knew the ones who had cared for them in their imprisonment. There was a look in their eyes weighted with familiarity.

"Oliver?" Matteo asked from behind them as he dropped a guard. Jin hadn't the faintest clue who Oliver was, but judging by the fair-haired man's poise, he was an Athereum vampire.

"Andoni? They got you too, eh?" the man called Oliver shouted back amid the chaos. "One moment we're paying top duvin for quality blood, the next you're bleeding it out on a ship."

Matteo pressed his lips thin as another guard swung a machete toward him. Jin leaped to his aid, but Arthie was there first, firing Calibore before whirling to the other side.

"We're here to take you back to Ettenia." Then he lifted his chin, calling out to the other vampires. "Stay here any longer and that fellow will rip you apart. Join us. Help us, and we'll take you home."

Home.

Jin saw Arthie's jaw tighten at the word. Ceylan had become a prison, a fortress, a drop of land in the ocean Ettenia repurposed to its liking.

That was the look in their eyes. They looked like Arthie—vengeful. Oliver inclined his head, others following suit.

"You have my fangs," one said.

"And my claws," said another.

Their anger resonated in the air; Jin felt it resonate within him too, through his weary bones. The vampires had been missing for far too long, stolen as Arthie's lands had been, control ripped away from their lives as the Ceylani soldiers in the Ettenian army had been.

The vampires closed the distance behind them, eager for a fight, but the guards were struggling to flee from the Ripper marching toward them, flinging away men and weapons as though he were batting away flies.

Jin knew his umbrella wouldn't do a thing. The vampire looked to be made of steel more than flesh. Arthie lifted Calibore. Far beyond, by the fallen chandelier, Bloodworth watched with bated breath, as did the guards.

Arthie fired. The guards froze, every eye following the bullet until it hit the vampire square in his bare chest. He staggered back, arms stretched wide as he regarded the slug.

He did not fall. He did not die as a vampire should when shot by Calibore. Outside of the surprise at being shot, the vampire didn't seem to be affected by the bullet. It looked like a burr had gotten caught on his skin and he couldn't be bothered to pull it out.

Arthie cocked Calibore and fired bullet after bullet. They were slowing him down at least, for he lurched back with each shot and inspected the wound—if it could even be called that—before resuming his stomping.

"Enough," Arthie said, until an idea glinted in her eyes. She racked Calibore again and leveled her aim lower this time, straight for—

"What are you doing?" Matteo sputtered, aghast when he followed her gaze.

"Vampires don't need their hearts as much as they need blood. How much of it do you reckon flows through the groin?"

"Arthie!" Matteo chided.

"That's sacrilegious," Jin said.

"Sacrilegious," Arthie deadpanned.

"You want to drain a man—or woman, I shan't discriminate—shoot for the thigh. There's no time or material for him to tourniquet it off. It'll siphon fast thanks to gravity."

With a sigh, Arthie lowered her pistol even more and squeezed out a shot to his right thigh. This time, the vampire stumbled. She fired at the other leg. Jin flinched. Even the guards stopped to stare as the Ripper fell to his knees. Blood squirted out in twin streams. The body only carried so much blood, and gravity demanded much of it. Jin almost pitied the vampire in that moment.

Until he stopped staring at his wounds and his gaze lifted, ever so slowly, back to Jin and the others.

"Is it just me, or does he seem angrier?" Matteo asked, tilting his head. "Imagine how this would have gone if you'd shot his manhood."

The Ripper rose with stilted movements.

And a groan resonated through the sanatorium. The seal around the vault-like door broke with a hiss of rushing air. His parents had unlocked the door. The relief in the sanatorium was palpable. Jin whirled as the gears above began to turn, slowly at first. Too slowly. The Ripper vampire was getting closer, men continuing to flee from his path.

At last, a breeze rushed through the doorway.

"Go!" Arthie shouted at the vampires.

The vampires rushed through, footsteps loud and thunderous, his parents waving them onward, helping the ones who stumbled on still-lethargic legs. Arthie squeezed off more shots, slowing down the Ripper vampire. Her jaw was tight, teeth clenched.

Jin understood the war within her—they couldn't reason with the vampire; they couldn't ask him to stop. He would fight them, kill them if he had the chance, and they had no choice but to fight back.

And to think, his father had— *No.* Jin could not think about that right now.

"Jin! Arthie!" Matteo shouted. The doors were clear.

Arthie raced through. Jin heard the jangle of heavy chains and saw several guards at the other end of the hall bracing themselves to trap the vampire.

He didn't know if they would succeed, but he wasn't going to stay here and find out. He squeezed through after Arthie and Matteo. His parents were at the other end of a short incline in an ornate foyer that Jin had walked through earlier with a sack on his head. The moon lit the dainty space with a white glow. His mother had a scratch on her face. His father's hair was more unkempt than Jin had ever seen, and— Jin blinked. There was a pistol in his hand.

"You're all right," his father whispered, pulling Jin to his side and making him feel like a little boy.

"Close the door," Arthie said.

"We can't," his father replied. "They're only operational from within."

"Then we run." She flung open the outer doors to the fort. The wildlife met them, insects chirping, birds cooing, monkeys screeching. "Oliver, I don't know you, but take up the rear and make sure no one's left behind. The rest of you, follow us."

They rushed into the courtyard, where they were met with the sticky Ceylani night. Even without the sun, the warmth clung to him like a weight. Braziers were being lit, gas lamps flickering to life as the fort guards rushed toward the commotion, shouting and tossing weapons.

"Hurry," Arthie shouted, heading straight for the gates, but Oliver stopped.

Seeing him, the others trickled to a halt too.

Oliver shook his head. "I'm not leaving that place whole for them to do this again."

At least they weren't in opposition to what Arthie already wanted to do. Murmurs of agreement spread through the vampires. They weren't even concerned by the gathering guards. Some fell, injected with green darts. Others tore the men down without hesitance.

"You're not alone in that sentiment," Arthie called over them. In the chaos, Jin caught the look in his mother's eyes. His parents wanted this too. "I'm going to burn it down."

The vampires paused, as if they weren't certain they were hearing her correctly.

"Well?" she asked the silence.

"By all means!" Oliver shouted, and the rest of the vampires roared in agreement.

"Now go!" she shouted. "Clear us a path to the ship where you'll see the show. I'll set the stage."

Jin couldn't tamp down a smile as the vampires obeyed her commands. Arthie allowed herself no such triumph. Her gaze tracked every movement around them. "If there are more Ripper vampires, we'll have a problem on our hands."

Jin's mother shook her head. "There is only the one."

His father's fail-safe had killed the other six.

"Really? We have nearly a hundred more waiting to turn," Matteo snapped.

"They will not mutate so long as they continue consumption of the coconut water."

"And how exactly are we going to get rid of the Ripper on our tail?" Arthie asked.

"It appears he's targeting you three," his mother said. "He will follow you as far as he can."

"That's not reassuring, Mother," Jin said.

"Don't you understand? We only need to get to your ship," she said. "He'll follow you into the sea."

And vampires couldn't swim. Even if a Ripper vampire could, he couldn't make it across the sea to Ettenia. It was entirely morbid, but it would have to do.

29
ARTHIE

Calibore in hand, Arthie waved the vampires through the fortress gates. They weren't in the best shape. They were pale from being starved—ghastly so, for vampires were already pale from lack of blood to begin with. Most had thinning hair and gangly limbs.

But they were eager for the same vengeance she was, and she was just as eager to give it to them. Jin and Matteo made quick work of the guards rushing toward them, but Arthie knew it wouldn't be long before they were overrun. Once the others passed through the gates and started for the trees, Oliver included, she turned to Shaw. Sora was nowhere to be seen.

She was about to ask for a torch. Shaw had something else instead.

"Take this—it's a calling card."

He held out a heavy gold coin, stamped with something she couldn't make out in the dark. Arthie glanced at him, brow furrowed before she pushed him aside and fired Calibore in the direction of an oncoming guard.

"It's one of our few possessions we kept safe and out of her sight. From long ago when we first met with the Council to show them our findings. In case we don't make it off the island, take this to a Horned Guard minister," Shaw explained, "and it will earn you an audience with them."

A guaranteed ticket to the Council. Arthie didn't know such a thing existed.

"Why are you giving this to me and not Jin?" she asked. He didn't answer, and Arthie didn't have time to wait. She pocketed it. "You're making it off the island. We still need you, remember?"

The moonlight flickered in Shaw's gaze. Appreciation shone in his eyes, for she wasn't discarding him after what she'd seen, and that meant his son might not either.

Sora joined them with a torch. "Everything is in place."

"That quickly?"

"Oliver offered to help, as did a few others. Vampires do move fast."

When Arthie took it from her, it was with a sense of reverence. It weighed as heavily as the years since she'd fled Ceylan's shores. The fort reached for the skies with a cold hand, casting its black shadow over the coast. Inside, guards shouted in Ettenian. Ceylani were in there too, but they knew the island. They'd escape. They had to.

Arthie raised the torch. *For my mother. For my people. For the tyranny that must end.* "Now."

Shaw lit the torch and took a step back. The flames flickered in his eyes. She held it high, thinking of the trees that had been cut down for Ettenia's tea plantations, spawning regular landslides. Thinking of the spices they'd snatched away, the gems they'd scoured the earth to find. The lives they'd ruined for no reason other than the fact that they could.

The flames crackled in her hand. *Are you sure?* It seemed to ask. Arthie looked up at the fort one last time. She had never been more certain of anything in her life.

"Stop!" someone shouted from the fort gates. Bloodworth. He was aiming a gun at her. "I will kill you."

The barrel of his gun looked strangely insignificant after what she'd done. She had come to Ceylan through her dread and fear, she had reunited with her brother and freed scores of vampires. Arthie wasn't afraid.

"Then bury me shallow, for I will return," Arthie said, and threw the torch to the damp earth.

It ignited instantly. Bloodworth fired, and Arthie ducked, pulling Shaw and Sora down with her before she heard the overseer's hasty retreat. So much for killing her. He couldn't even brave a little fire.

Only it was no little fire. It rose higher and higher, roaring, hissing and moaning in the salt-heavy breeze. Arthie stared into its depths, and in it, she saw Spindrift. She saw Jin's home.

She saw her parents, her life.

Her guilt that had begun as a child.

And some part of Arthie came to a sharp and startling halt. Somewhere inside of her, some deep and dark place she'd shut away and tucked beneath all her happenings, from bookkeeping to tracking inventory to keep Spindrift's doors open, from snarking at the Horned Guard to stoking her vengeance when she read the day's paper, there was a bowl of guilt. It had overflowed and turned rancid, hatred leaching into her veins and breeding a version of herself that she refused to accept.

That was why she'd survived on what meager coconut water she could get her hands on. That was why she'd opened the bloodhouse at Spindrift, lying to herself that it was for money and nothing more.

She took that bowl and turned it over, letting the flames eat it away.

"Arthie!" someone shouted. It was her mother, her father, Matteo, Jin, Shaw, Sora. The voices and faces blurred into one. She looked into the trees, into the darkness, trying to find whoever had called her, but it was too dark to see and she needed to keep the Siwangs safe, the coin in her pocket be damned.

That was when she heard it: a green dart whizzing toward her. No, toward Jin's parents, silhouetted against the shadows.

"Shaw! Sora!" Arthie shouted, and pushed them out of the way.

And then Arthie was falling. She remembered nothing else.

30
FLICK

Flick didn't have to wait long for the door to her prison to open. When it did, she was ready, brass knuckles snug over her injured fingers. She had stretched her aching arms until they didn't feel like foreign things attached to her shoulders.

She braced for the Ram, but it was one of her black-clad men. A knot loosened in Flick's chest, and she held herself very still, not wanting to spook him too soon. When he noticed she wasn't hanging from the manacles, he was already mostly through the door. Flick threw her weight against it, slamming it shut before he could back his way through.

The lock fell, but Flick wasn't worried.

He had a key on him, and she intended to take it.

Her heart was pounding in her chest. The man whirled toward her, but Flick was ready. She threw a punch, imagining Jin's presence behind her, guiding her fist, loosening the tense length of her arm, lending her the strength the manacles had stolen from her.

She hit the man square in his chin with her brass knuckles.

He sputtered. Her breathing was the only sound grating in her ears. He stared at her for a beat before his eyes rolled to the back of his head and he fell like a sack of potatoes.

That, love, is a glass jaw.

"Did I kill him?" she asked the empty room. She could feel the pressure in her chest building. Her exhales were coming out in tiny bursts.

Calm down, she told herself. *You were ready to kill the woman you once called Mother.*

And there was no time to waste. She had lost track of the hours and when Jin and Arthie returned from Ceylan; she needed to be there—*unless they had failed.*

She refused to let herself dwell on that alternative.

Arthie would claw her way out of any grave her enemies fathomed to place her in, and she'd make sure Jin was by her side. She never failed. Which was another reason why Flick needed to be there at the docks when they returned. To warn them, yes, but if they noticed she was missing, that she wasn't in the Athereum, they would rain destruction on the Ram, plans be damned.

One might have called it haughty to think such a thing, but Flick knew with utmost certainty that the care Jin and Arthie had for her warranted nothing less.

Flick dropped to her knees beside the man, and after wriggling her throbbing fingers to will them back to their original selves, she riffled through his pockets until she found what she needed: a heavy iron key.

She shot back to her feet. It took several tries to slide the key into the lock. It felt silly, unlocking a door from the inside, but locking up one's daughter ought to be silly too.

As she turned the key, an idea struck. There was an easy way to slip through this unfamiliar domain: by looking like the ones who were allowed to be here.

Flick unraveled the black cloth around the man's head, peeling back the layers over his face to reveal a boy who couldn't be much older than she was. *Why?* Flick wanted to ask him. Why did he work for the Ram to the point where he strung up a girl for no reason?

It had to be coin that forged such loyalty. Flick refused to believe they saw anything worthy in the Ram's cause. She couldn't see someone so young being so resolute and set in their ways. Jin snorted in her head. *Have you met Arthie?*

How *would* Arthie look at these men? She wouldn't see them working for coin as a thing of disgust, no.

Arthie would see a benefit.

The men having no loyalty would be a benefit. Like the head of a snake, if the Ram was out of the picture, they would do nothing.

Still have to figure out how to get *her out of the picture.*

Flick draped the head wrapping over the chair to air out before pulling off the boy's shirt. It was a struggle. An unconscious body was far heavier than she thought it could be. With a huff, she yanked the shirt free, wincing when his head thudded to the floorboards. She pulled it over her shirt that was now more grime than white, and knelt again to remove his trousers.

She unbuttoned them, thinking of Jin and the time she'd torn away his shirt to mend his wound. Heat flushed down her skin. *Undressing someone else is not the time to be thinking of him, Flick,* she chided, immediately relieved the boy was wearing drawers underneath.

She had to remove his shoes to get the trousers off him, but the job was done and she moved to winding his head wrap around her face, a job that was tedious with trembling hands and without a mirror. She straightened the shirt and adjusted her trousers before tucking that wicked knife into the sheath sewn on the side of the trousers' leg. Had his shirt been tucked into the waist of his trousers? Flick folded the hem and unfolded it, trying to picture him and the countless black-clad men she'd evaded and fought against.

How could she not have noticed something so obvious?

Perhaps because you were focused on staying alive, she reminded herself.

Flick tugged on his large gloves, wriggling her fingers to fit as best as she could and pulled on Jin's brass knuckles, immediately feeling a little stronger, a little less alone, then pulled her sleeve as low as she could to shield them from view.

Key in hand, heart in throat, Flick walked to the door. She still needed to find out why the Ram had referred to this place in her ledger with such importance, why it was so close to the palace where the tribute was to occur, and what those strange pill-shaped things were.

But she also needed to get to the docks. No, what she needed was a calendar to see what day it was and whether the Casimirs could even *be* back just yet. Her hands continued to quiver, throbbing no differently than when one was stung by an insect, only it spanned the entirety of her arms. They hurt so terribly that she barely felt the pain pulsing down the rest of her.

She opened the door, stepped through, closed it. *One step at a time.* She tucked the key into her pocket, stifling a sneeze when fuzz from the cloth around her face tickled her nose.

Though her room had been bare and cloistered, outside was far more spacious and furnished. Round lights hung from the ceiling at intervals, none too bright, casting the beige walls in an almost sinister glow. And it was *large*, halls running every which way, rooms spreading wide.

Flick took several steps from her door and recognized the large meeting chamber nearest her, the halls extending from either end in oddly placed positions. This was the place. The location sketched in her mother's ledger. But why had Flick's sleuthing taken her to an empty lawn? She hadn't seen anything this large by the palace.

Someone bumped past her. Black-clad men were everywhere, some lugging boxes, others holding notes or reports or some such, while even more loitered in hushed conversation. The air thrummed with a sense of fear.

She saw a calendar tacked to the wall by a desk full of folders and documents organized into little bins. Much of the month had been crossed off, which meant . . . Flick blinked at it again. The tribute was in six days? That couldn't be right.

"Oi, why are you standing there?" someone shouted, and then smacked her head with the flat of their hand.

Flick whirled around to face the man, schooling her eyes before her sudden spurt of anger could give her away.

"Well?" he asked.

"Thought the days weren't rightly crossed off," Flick said as gruffly as she could. She sounded like she had a cold and a sore throat.

He squinted at the calendar. "Oh, yeah. They aren't."

He snatched up a pen from a cup on the desk and crossed off a day. *Five days until the tribute.* Then he crossed off another. *Four days.* And another.

Three days.

Flick's breath stuttered, but he dropped the pen at last.

Three days until the tribute. Jin and the others should be on their way back by now.

The man grunted as he faced her again. "Don't you have somewhere to be?"

"Y-yes," Flick said. She gestured into the direction of her room. "I'm—"

He smothered a laugh, and she noticed he was looking toward the room directly across from hers. "That boy thinks he's putting up a fight, a'right. A high captain, my arse. More manacles ought to do the trick. Have fun, eh?"

Have fun? Flick swallowed her disgust, wishing she could throw the manacles into the dustbin. She didn't realize there were other prisoners here. Then she remembered the sounds of a scuffle she'd heard earlier. She tried to imagine who else her mother would need to interrogate. *Chester!* No, it wasn't any of the boys. Whoever that was sounded older, and Chester, Felix, or Reni wouldn't allow themselves to get caught as Flick had.

Don't write yourself off so soon, love.

Indeed. She was still standing, still breathing, and as the man walked away, she exhaled in relief because she'd just passed her first test.

She looked down the hall to either side of her, wishing she could walk straight up to one of the Ram's men and ask to be escorted home. She recalled her notes from the ledger and headed in the direction of the room with the pill-shaped things, keeping her eyes from swiveling through her surroundings too obviously.

She tried the door to her right, surprised to find it unlocked. It was a storeroom, and she was about to close the door again before Arthie's voice crept into her thoughts, reminding Flick that anything could prove valuable. She slipped inside and tugged on the light.

An array of vials and chemicals were spread out across the shelves, but her hands wouldn't stop trembling to make out what they said without giving her a headache. As far as she knew, chemicals were used for cleaning and poisoning and, if one was a scientist like Jin's parents, creating. Then there were boxes filled with tubes that she first thought were pens before realizing they were stacks of dynamite. Flick's heart leaped to her throat. She shouldn't have been surprised, but what did her mother need with explosives?

A thud echoed in the shadows of the storeroom. She held her breath, listening for movement, but could hear nothing over her pounding heart. Had she imagined it? She wasn't going to wait to find out.

Flick rushed back into the hall, nearly slamming into a pair of men marching past. They gave her a strange look but didn't stop, and she didn't stop either, walking across the hall as though she belonged here.

The place was oddly built, sounds muffled, walls strangely thick. The ceilings were low, beams running every which way to hold everything in place. Flick didn't think she'd ever been in a place like this.

The door at the end of the hall opened, flooding the space with sunlight. Daylight. Footsteps thudded down what seemed to be stairs.

That was her way out, once she finished her snooping.

If she lived, that was—footsteps were heading her way. Flick froze, pressing herself as flat against the new door as she could. Shadows sliced back into the hall, outlining a silhouette in the last of the light.

The Ram.

Flick held her breath, hoping the Ram had no need for the room behind her. Or was that a better option than the Ram walking back into Flick's room and finding her gone? Flick held still, refusing to breathe, until the Ram passed her by.

Flick didn't wait; she flung open the door and, for whatever reason, glanced back at the Ram. As if she could feel the eyes of the girl she had called *daughter* for the past eighteen years, she began to turn around.

Flick leaped inside the room, closing the door behind her with the quietest thud.

And immediately knew she wasn't alone.

It wasn't the eyes that she felt on the back of her head, or voices that made it clear she wasn't alone, no. She felt the presence of others in an eerie, muffled sort of silence.

With a sinking feeling, Flick knew, before turning around, what she would find.

A sound lurched from her throat.

The kidnapped humans.

The space was as large as Flick had assumed from the ledger sketches, but there were no pill-shaped cylinders here. Only a cage, massive and dismal.

Full of girls and boys close to her age.

There were twelve, all alert, some rocking back and forth on the floor of the cage with their arms around their knees, others standing as straight as the cell bars. Their mouths were bound, but the room was blanketed, and Flick realized that it was to muffle any who might scream.

They stared with wary eyes, as though she wasn't to be trusted. *Of course you aren't*, she scolded herself. She was dressed as one of the Ram's men. Flick pulled the covering from her face.

"I'm like you," she whispered. "I was trapped in one of the other rooms."

But I'm her daughter, she didn't say. Because she wasn't anymore.

One of the girls came forward. She was saying something, crying through the binding around her mouth. Her hair was a chaotic cloud around her grimy face. Tears were trickling down her chin. Flick rushed over and squeezed her hands between the bars, whimpering when the widest part of her hand struck the metal bar. For a second, she saw stars, but she shook them away.

"You have to be quiet," Flick said, and when the girl nodded with a quick glance at the door, Flick untied the rough strip of cloth.

"Thank you," the girl croaked. "Thank you."

"What happened to you?" Flick asked, wishing she had water, food, a way to free them. "How did you get here?"

"I—I don't know," the girl whispered. "I was walking home from school when a carriage stopped beside the road and men dressed like you grabbed me."

Flick swept a glance across the others. Her heart was pounding in her ears, loud and impossible. She could barely think, barely see, panic threatening to overtake her. Another girl frantically gestured to her mouth, and Flick quickly undid her bindings too, her fingers faltering to the point where the first girl noticed and glanced at her sidelong.

At last, Flick ripped the binding free.

"She's going to turn us on the night of the tribute," the second girl cried. "Into vampires!"

Vampires? Flick took a step back, trying to understand. The others were crying, weeping through their bindings, panic spreading anew. One of the boys began thudding his head against the bars. They hadn't known. The first girl was frozen, paler than the others.

Flick glanced at the door. She wanted to get them out of here. The exit wasn't too far. A noise thudded from outside the door, reminding Flick that she was alone. She couldn't free them, but she knew who could.

Jin and Arthie, when they returned.

"Get out!" the second girl shouted. "Get out before they put you in here too."

They were trapped in a cage, hungry and parched, unable to speak, and they were looking out for *her*? It only highlighted how terrible the Ram was.

Flick pulled the covering back over her face and nose. "I'll return for you, I promise. We'll get you out."

She didn't know if it was a promise she could keep, but it was one she would have wanted to hear regardless.

Several of them immediately perked, eyes widening. Heart in her throat, Flick tied the ropes back over the girls' mouths, leaving them looser than she'd found them. She could give them that, at least. As much as Flick wanted to tear every last binding away and grant them that comfort, she didn't.

The Ram was prepared to kill her daughter. She would kill a nuisance in a heartbeat. Flick had seen in it her cell, where she'd dropped two of her own men because of words Flick had said.

Though every part of her protested against leaving the girls and boys behind, Flick inched the door open and glanced down the hall.

"There you are."

Flick froze.

"What were you doing?"

She stepped through and closed the door. It was the man who had stopped her by the calendar, and Flick didn't think her luck would work a second time.

"I was checking on them," Flick said, remembering to make her voice gruff at the last second. She didn't know who he thought she was, or how many others there were for her to blend in with, but she decided to keep her words scarce.

"When did we ever check on 'em?" the man asked, and when Flick didn't answer, his gaze narrowed, scrutinizing her.

"Maybe we should," Flick said. "They're hungry and thirsty. Can't use them if they're useless."

He started to respond, but Flick didn't hear him, for past his shoulder, she saw a terrible sight: the Ram. She was talking to someone in front of Flick's door. Her shoulders were relaxed, her pose unbothered.

Flick forced a breath. She hadn't discovered that Flick was missing just yet.

But she was about to: Flick saw the Ram pull a key out of her pocket, that gunmetal mask glinting gold in the light.

Flick didn't wait. There wasn't time to hunt for those pill-shaped objects now. She needed to leave. She eased away from the man, picking up speed as she neared the exit. Sweat trickled down her back. She ran her gloved thumb over the ridges of her brass knuckles to calm her racing heart. Pain shot through her arms instead.

"Oi, I asked you a question," the man called after her, and Flick stumbled but didn't stop.

Not until she reached the door. Then she looked back to find the Ram facing the commotion, eyes narrowed. Because Flick might have been covered from head to toe, but just as she'd instantly recognized her mother's eyes through the mask she wore, her mother recognized Flick's.

She saw it in the way the Ram stiffened. "Stop her!"

Flick shoved at the door, surprised by its weight, only to find it opened upward, not sideways, disorienting her as she hurried out. The daylight blinded her, burning through her sun-starved eyes. She struggled to see through sudden tears, and everything hit her at once—her hunger, her thirst, a gust of her pain.

Just a little farther, she pushed herself. The men shouted, the Ram's voice snarling in the midst of the chaos. Flick ripped the cloth from her face and ran for the wrought iron gate, for freedom, her legs still weak, her head throbbing.

Until everything fell silent.

She paused and looked back. No one was chasing her anymore. Strange—was the Ram letting her go? Flick's head hurt too much to wonder why.

Voices thrummed behind her—the Horned Guard. There were platoons of them, patrolling the green. Flick rushed to the cover of a tree and studied her surroundings. Stately trees rose around her. Beneath her, neatly trimmed grass. This was where she'd stood the night she'd been captured. The coordinates she'd gleaned from the Ram's sketches in the ledger *were* right.

She hadn't seen the place because it was underground. A bunker. The door was set into concrete on the ground, tucked beside a short wall, dark and inconspicuous, hidden by the lush trees.

And when she turned, she saw what was on the other side of that short wall: the palace.

The very palace where the Ram was to hold her tribute to the fallen press in three days' time. Above an underground den full of weapons, and men to do her bidding, and humans in a cage.

31
ARTHIE

When Arthie opened her eyes, Shaw was in her face, peering at her through a monocle. Sora was beside him, wringing her hands. Arthie sputtered, trying to shrink back, but her head slammed into a slab of wood and she growled. Matteo took his place, their voices muffled as if they were speaking from far away and not inches from her. Her body stung, her limbs weighing heavy and laden.

Worse, she couldn't think. Her head felt stuffed full of dirty tea rags.

"You saved us," Sora whispered. "You—silly girl, why?"

"What's wrong with her?" Matteo asked.

Wrong? There was nothing wrong with her. She was tired and beat. She had just fled a sanatorium with a Ripper vampire and endless guards.

"She was shot with a green dart," Shaw said.

Oh. That wasn't good. Did she look as terrible as she felt? She tried to speak but couldn't get the words out. The last she remembered was Shaw and Sora and a torch.

Someone said something Arthie couldn't hear, and Matteo snapped in response, "Well, remove it from her system, then."

"Where—where—" Arthie stopped. A fire was scorching her skin from the inside. The fire! Had she imagined those beautiful flames engulfing the fort and the screams as people fled to the wilderness?

She didn't realize she'd asked the question out loud.

"You set fire to it, darling," Matteo said. "And we escaped. A good number of the vampires, Jin, his parents. We're on the ship back to White Roaring."

His tone was soft, gentle, telling her the world wouldn't crumble if she didn't remain in charge. A hot tear burned down her face.

They made it. They were leaving Ceylan. *So soon*. There was a shuffle, and when Arthie tried to open her eyes to see what was happening, she saw colors, blending into one another, bursting in intermittent splotches.

"Get this out of her, Shaw," Matteo snarled.

Shaw was murmuring to himself. "The consistency of vampire blood is much thicker than that of a human's. The serum was meant to mimic a mosquito's venom—eating away and poisoning a vampire's blood faster than they can replenish it. The full dose is in her system, and she is quite small."

Arthie groaned. Her head throbbed.

"A transfusion is the only way, boy. We're nowhere near the equipment necessary for such a thing."

"A transfusion would stop it from spreading?" Matteo asked, tone perking. "Are you certain?"

"Yes." Then she heard Shaw's voice turn aghast. "What are you doing?"

"Giving her a transfusion," came Matteo's curt response. "As vampires do when we turn you humans. We don't need equipment or a fancy education for it."

"If you ingest—"

"I won't. Go take care of the others," Matteo said, and Arthie tried to protest. Her head might have been stuffy, her brain functioning at a percent of what it should have been, but she didn't like the warning in Shaw's voice that Matteo was ignoring so hastily.

Matteo lifted her by her shoulders, again with a gentle touch. She tried to pull away, to refuse whatever he was about to do.

She was powerless against him.

"Arthie, look at me," he said, his lips brushing against the shell of her ear. She thought she shivered. "No? Then tilt your head, darling."

She tilted her head. Why was she obeying him?

"There we go."

He moved closer. She could smell him, even if her eyes were refusing to let her see the smooth skin of his face, the emerald of his eyes that reminded her of the lush Ceylani trees beneath a bright sun.

He kissed her throat, so softly she thought she imagined it. That wasn't part of what a vampire did to turn another. That had nothing to do with transfusion of blood. This was his fear of losing her. Before she could ponder any further, he drew her shirt away from her shoulder and smoothed his tongue over her skin. She heard the stutter of his exhale, and it sent heat rushing through her limbs, straight to her core.

And then his fangs punctured her shoulder, right where the dart had deposited its green venom. Pain ruptured through her, building, rising, cresting like a wave until it drowned her, and the world went dark once again.

When Arthie woke, she was in a cot. She didn't feel so terrible anymore. Still a little stuffy, but the fire that was clawing its way out of her had been snuffed to cinders, leaving her empty.

The ground beneath her rocked, and she started reaching for her pistol before she remembered she was back at sea, the crashing waves returning them to Ettenia.

A terrible loneliness ached in her chest. *Loneliness?* Arthie was never good with her emotions. Perhaps it wasn't loneliness, but it felt that way, in a sense. She would have liked to see the island one last time as they sailed away. To stare at the fire she'd cast inside the walls of the fort, to see Ceylan's sandy shores and know that, this time, she wasn't a child anymore; she wasn't bereft and alone. She wasn't leaving her people to a horrible fate again.

This time, they would rebuild, restart, and replenish their losses. They could drive out the Ettenians now that they had the upper hand.

A sound scraped beside her where someone was fiddling ever so quietly.

"Matteo?" she asked.

"It's me," Jin said, and she sat up, scrunching her brow when her head spun.

"Is Matteo—?"

He nodded. "Just fine."

Arthie breathed a sigh of relief. He might have assured Shaw that he was capable of the transfusion, but it was Shaw's tone that had unsettled her.

Her eyes were working now, and she was equally relieved to see that Jin had escaped unscathed except for the bandage around one ear and the bruise swelling the right side of his lower lip.

"You're all right. I was worried."

He laughed softly "I am. I—I thought we were going to lose you."

"And that's funny, is it?" she asked, swinging her legs over.

"What's funny is that you nearly died, but you were worried about me."

Arthie shrugged. "That's what big sisters do."

He lifted an eyebrow at her. "I'm the older one, in case the Ceylani sun made you think otherwise." Then his features turned serious, his brow pinching with apology. "You nearly died for my parents."

It would have been worth it, she realized. She had always wanted to make him happy. "In case the Ceylani sun made *you* think otherwise, I don't die."

"I used to believe that," Jin said with another snorted laugh. "You came between me and death so many times I've lost count, but ever since I learned you were a vampire, you've never been more fragile."

"That's not insulting."

But he was right. She'd nearly died twice since she'd turned him and revealed, at the same time, that she was a vampire. She'd never been more in danger of dying before then.

"Are we on track to return in time for the tribute?" Arthie asked.

Jin glanced at her. *Back to business*, the look said. "We were, until we hit stormy waters. I think Vane said we'll be arriving a day later."

That wasn't ideal. Not at all.

Jin leaned back with a sigh. "I could use a streusel right about now."

"I'm sorry," Arthie said.

"That I died? I can't blame you for that particular bit." His words were light, but the bitterness was there. He was here, alive in every way, but at the same time, he wasn't. He would never age, he would never savor. He would never be human again, after knowing nothing else for years.

"I deserved your anger," Arthie said finally, for she didn't know how to speak of his new fate just yet, not when she had lived as a vampire for a decade and still hadn't come to terms with it herself. "I was too much of a coward to trust you with the truth because I was too much of a coward to acknowledge it myself."

He nodded, looking to the lantern flickering on the chest against the cabin wall. "I can understand that. I haven't . . . had a proper conversation with my parents yet."

"They love you, Jin. I see it in their eyes. You can hear it in the way they speak your name. You're still you. Vampire or human, that doesn't change that."

That, at least, she knew for certain.

"You ought to listen to that yourself."

Perhaps she did. Shouts from above deck echoed inside. "How many made it?" she asked.

Jin shook his head. "Only eighty or so. Vane helped get everyone on board. The guards were relentless. The vampires were weak to begin with, but there were others too angry to even stop fighting and escape with us."

Too angry. Their vengeance had claimed them. Arthie didn't know how she felt about that.

"What about the ones who did make it? Are they angry too?" Arthie asked, reaching into her pocket where the silver dose sat small and innocent, as though it hadn't set a worldwide operation into motion.

"Ready to tear the Ram apart, for certain," Jin said, sitting back down in the chair. "They were happy to see the fire, but they're certainly not pleased to be back on an EJC ship, and they're calling for blood."

Arthie no longer sought vengeance for herself alone anymore. This was bigger than her now. Bigger than her dead mother and father and her humanity. This was for Penn and the vampires stolen away and weaponized. This was for Jin and his parents, for Flick. For Matteo and the life he could have lived if the Ram hadn't made him into a pawn for her own affairs.

No, vengeance had steeped in her blood long enough. It had changed, grown, morphed. It was retribution now, and it would find its end with the Ram.

32

JIN

Jin wanted to sit with Arthie a little longer, but she wasn't having it. She shooed him out of the cabin to find his parents, from whom he was deliberately staying away. Jin closed the door behind him, gripping the wall as waves crashed against the ship. Using his umbrella as a walking stick, he made his way to his parents' cabin.

He knocked once. His hand was still midair when the door opened to his mother's face.

"Jin," she said, and if he closed his eyes, he could picture their house on Admiral Grove, the crackle of the fire in the hearth, the smell of chestnuts from the polish she insisted they use on every wood surface, his schoolbag full of books sitting primly on his desk.

"Ma," he said before he remembered she never liked when he did. *Mother*, she said to call her, because he wasn't a child anymore.

He had never been as old as he was today, but he didn't care. He stepped inside. His father was standing by the tiny round window. He looked as uncertain as Jin felt.

"We were waiting for you," his mother said.

"I know."

Did the years that had passed without them matter now that they were here, in front of him? He didn't know how to respond. He could flirt with a tree if it came to it, but now it felt as though his mouth were stuffed full of pastries, his tongue tied up in knots.

"Sit down, lad," his father said, taking up a seat on the cot and patting the space beside him.

Jin did as he was told. He always had when it came to his parents. He had always been able to trust them, which was a privilege that not many children received.

But what did it mean now that he knew what they'd done? He still trusted them. He still thought them to be well-intentioned people who wanted the best for vampires—but that wish hadn't come without a cost. They had dirtied their hands; they had killed.

He felt the heat of his father beside him, heard the rushing of his blood more than the sound of his breathing. Before he could stop himself, he leaned into that warmth, resting his head on his father's shoulder.

"I searched for years and years," Jin whispered as his father pulled him tight against him. His mother came and wrapped her arms around them both.

Jin felt the rumble of his father's laugh. "You always were tenacious. Though, in my experience, it was in regards to that sweet tooth of yours."

Jin couldn't laugh with him. "But when we reached Ceylan and I thought you had sided with the Ram, I"—he pulled away to look at them both—"hated you."

"I see," his father said, his features giving away nothing. "And do you still?"

Confusion pinched Jin's brow. "Well, it's not quite as simple, but no."

"Then I don't see why you're looking so dejected."

That, Jin could laugh at, and his father smiled before his eyes dropped to Jin's teeth. More notably, to his fangs. Jin stupidly closed his mouth, trying to will them away.

They knew he was a vampire. The captain and his men had made sure of it back on Ceylan, but Jin thought it had to be said anyway. He needed to get the words out of his system, out there in the open so his parents could decide if they still wanted him.

"I'm—"

"When did it happen?" his father asked first.

"Under a fortnight ago," Jin said. "You just missed the live version of me."

"There isn't a difference between the versions to us," his mother said, tilting up his chin. "What does matter is that someone killed my son."

She did not know how much those words meant to him. How high their effortless acceptance lifted his heart.

"Leaping to murder, Ma? I could have tripped over a knife."

She clucked her tongue. "I taught you better than that."

"It was the Ram."

Both his parents were startled at the new voice, but Jin only sighed, peering past his mother to give Arthie a look.

"Have you ever considered knocking?" he asked.

"No," she said. Matteo stepped in after her as though this was her office in Spindrift.

She was about to make herself at home in the single armchair when Jin's father swept her into a hug. Arthie stiffened.

"You saved my life," he whispered.

"Both of ours," Jin's mother said.

Arthie pulled away with a shrug. If she was going to say *I needed you alive*, Jin was going to slap her. "Saving the lives of your family is what I do."

He couldn't not smile at that.

His father gave her a wistful smile of his own. "*Our* family. You're Jin's sister, are you not?"

The waves crashed against the side of the ship. Muffled voices from above deck and below echoed like White Roaring's streets outside of Spindrift. Arthie remained silent. Jin saw the way her chin dipped a fraction, the way the right of her cheek twitched as she contained a gust of joy. She wasn't calculating her next words, nor was she angry—she was shocked.

"I—"

"Just answer the question, Arthie," Jin said.

She flicked her gaze to his, suddenly shy. It was adorable. "Yes. I am."

Matteo sank into the armchair. "Did you ever consider, Shaw and Sora, that you're simply joining *our* family?"

Arthie laughed. "Well, this family is full of murderers, and we're after the biggest one." She nodded at Jin. "The Ram shot him, by the way, is what I meant."

"Point-blank, if I may add," Matteo said.

Jin's father sucked in a breath. His mother bit out a curse. Jin rubbed at the spot where her bullet had made its home, burning through the layers of his clothes and his skin, tearing through his heart.

"I turned him," Arthie said. "And I know your reunion was ten years in the making, but we cannot mistake it for a happy ending. It's only the beginning. We need to plan."

She was right. Irritatingly so. Could he not, for a moment, pretend to ignore reality and bask in his victory? *Soon*, he promised himself, surprised by his optimism. Flick would be proud.

"The tribute," Matteo said. "Remind me: How many days away is it?"

"One," Arthie said. "Thanks to that wretched storm."

"How do you know?" Jin asked. "We don't have a calendar."

Arthie dangled her pocket watch. "No, but I have a clock and a brain. I've been keeping track."

"What is this tribute?" Jin's father asked.

"She's sent invitations to the rich and powerful for an event to honor the members of the press that *she* massacred, unbeknownst to the public, and celebrate a vicennial of her monarchy. It'll be anything but that. We stole her incriminating ledger that led us to you, and she's lashing out. She started with renewing chaos on the streets by kidnapping humans to stir up hatred and fear of vampires once again."

"Humans?" his mother asked. "Whatever for?"

"For a public uproar," Arthie answered. "Blaming the press massacre on vampires was the first step, but she needed to keep that thread of fear alive."

Jin's mother's lip twisted in disgust. "While she throws a celebration."

"I hadn't realized we were nearing a vicennial," his father said. "Those usually bring in officials at every level."

"Even the Council?" Arthie asked.

He pursed his lips. "Yes. If we'll be able to attend, their presence could work in our favor. What is our plan to dispose of her?"

Sora asked. "Death?"

But when Jin thought of killing the Ram, he thought of Flick. The Ram was a monster undeserving of a daughter like Flick, but she was still her mother, the woman who had raised her from a young age.

"Death is an easy punishment," his father replied. "I much prefer a suffering in which she can watch us flourish, don't you?"

Yes. Jin liked that very much.

"If we must," his mother said with a sigh. "What *is* your plan to take her down?"

"Unfortunately, we dipped into this battle long after it started," Arthie said, "but there are three parts to the Ram: monarch, businesswoman, and lady. We've burned down the heart of the EJC. We've put a dent in the monarch's plans for weaponizing vampires. Now we'll expose all three, ruining the lady's image by unmasking her in front of her handpicked audience."

"How do you plan to unmask her?" Sora asked. "The rich and the powerful might have been invited, but she won't risk standing among them."

"Perhaps Shaw and Sora can convince the Council to demand that she unmasks," Matteo suggested, looking at the Siwangs.

"The Council appointed her; they know who she is," Jin said. "Are they masked too?"

"They are indeed," Shaw said.

"Of course they are," Matteo drawled. "Still, the person they appointed isn't the person who she is today. Nor do they know a fraction of what she's done. Once they know of her deeds, they'd want to help."

Arthie worked her jaw. *That's not enough*, the set of her mouth said. "We don't want help; we want to hurt her image. Irreparably. Let's move on so I can think. Do we have to fear Ripper vampires in Ettenia?"

"Would the Ram risk deploying them?" Jin asked. "She'll have little ability to control them, and White Roaring is far more populated than the Ceylani colony."

No one responded because the answer was clear. The Ram *would* risk it. She didn't care for her people. She was kidnapping humans off the street simply to build a lie, to cause havoc.

Shaw shook his head. "The moment we caught the mutation, we contained the vampires. There are inoculated vampires in Ettenia awaiting shipment, but none of them sit there long enough for the possibility to mutate. The Ram believes it's a new serum we developed but haven't perfected and delivered yet. Once we arrive, we'll ensure the inoculated vampires are cared for as well."

"Pity we can't strap the Ram to a chair and demand the answers we need," Matteo said.

Arthie looked as though she'd considered the same. She always did like going to the source.

Shouts echoed from above deck, and Jin straightened, reaching for his umbrella before someone threw open the hatch and shouted, "Land ho!"

"Home," Jin murmured. He almost laughed at that. He didn't have a home. The home from the first decade of his life had burned down just like the second one had. And yet he was eager, for home had never been about the walls he'd stood within, but the people standing around him. Like Arthie, like his crew.

Like Flick.

"I don't say this because I doubt Flick's capabilities," Arthie said, following his line of thought, "but we need to dock with the possibility that the Ram might ambush us."

"It's a good thing we have an army of vampires down there, then," Jin said with a sigh, gesturing to the hold.

"An army that needs rest," Jin's father said.

Jin and Arthie had prepared for as much. Sidharth promised to have runners monitoring the seafront for their return, after which he'd send carriages to take the vampires to the Athereum and provide aid, care, and eventually reacclimate them into society. They'd have to tell him about the coconuts too.

"And a balm for their pain," Matteo countered. "If the Ram ambushes us at shore, we won't be able to hold them back."

"That may be true," Shaw conceded, "but it must end there. If you want vampires to infiltrate the tribute with you, we'll need allies capable of blending in with high society lords and ladies. Our vampires are too angry to hold themselves back, nor are they in the best of shape."

Jin and Arthie shared a glance, for they knew exactly where they'd find such vampires: the Athereum.

"Hold on—'high society lords and ladies,'" Arthie repeated, straightening with an idea. "We're counting on Flick to forge invites to people who aren't fond of Lady Linden, but how many of her own guests do we reckon were denied a contract with the government because Lady Linden could handle it herself through the EJC?"

Jin had never considered that. Even he and Arthie had partnered with a lord who owned multiple shipping warehouses, to store their teas for Spindrift. A country was bound to need all that and more at any given time, but if the Ram could pay herself to do what was needed, why distribute the wealth?

"Even more reason to unmask her, then," Jin said. "Make high society angry, and they'll tear her down themselves. We'll have ruined her forever."

As the Ram had ruined each of them in some way. They wouldn't even have to worry about convincing the Council. High society would do the work for them. No one was more dangerous than a rich man scorned.

"You're a clever one, Arthie," Shaw said. "See, that is a far more excellent end than death."

Arthie said nothing. She didn't voice a concern or make a comment, but Jin knew that look: She was scheming. Unmasking the Ram was well and good, but was it enough?

It was indeed a pity they couldn't sit the Ram down and get answers out of the woman themselves.

33
ARTHIE

Arthie made her way to the hold to speak to the vampires, leaving the others. Leaving Jin with his family, with his father who had decided she could be his daughter too. Arthie was overwhelmed by the warmth that rushed through her veins, the strange fuzziness.

The dark passageway enveloped her, and when she heard the *hush hush* of the sea against the side of the ship, she didn't feel that incessant guilt eating away at her with each push and pull of the waves. She felt a sense of calm. Not because she'd burned down the fort, really, but because she had gone to Ceylan and returned. Her guilt hadn't consumed her; her past hadn't swallowed her whole. No, she was closing in on the monarch of Ettenia.

They still didn't know what the Ram planned for the tribute, but the more they spoke of their own plans for that night, the more it felt as though it was a trap of their own making and the Ram would be their unwitting prisoner.

Footsteps thudded behind her, and Arthie glanced back, seeing his blood-streaked white shirt before the rest of him.

"Careful," Matteo said. "A beautiful lady such as yourself shouldn't wander alone in the dark."

Beautiful and *lady* weren't typically used on Arthie. She would have been offended by his words if they weren't spoken in that darkly teasing tone that slipped beneath her clothes like an errant touch.

"It's the dark that needs to be afraid of me," she replied.

Matteo sighed. "Just once, darling, can I be the heroic savior of your dreams?"

She gave him a look. "You know I dream of no such thing."

"And that is one of the many qualities of yours that I adore."

His eyes were soft. Arthie wanted to look away; she wanted to square her shoulders. The ship rumbled. They were slowing down and she needed to speak to the vampires, not get lost in emotions.

She turned away, because for all her snarking, he *did* save her. Once when he turned her, and then when he knocked down and *killed* a guard aiming for her, and then again a day ago on this very ship, after she'd taken a bullet for Jin's parents.

"Too busy dreaming of me, I know."

His voice came right at her ear, and her eyes fluttered closed. She knew what he was doing. He'd done it every time she'd inch close to opening her heart before giving in to cowardice. Distract her. Reel himself back. It was unfair to him.

She faced him again. Goodness, lifting her eyes to his waiting ones was harder than facing Bloodworth's men.

"I've never—I've never done this before," she whispered.

Matteo tilted his head, noticing her change. "Done what?"

"Opened up my heart to anyone."

His lips quirked with a small smile. "Darling, I've held your heart in my hands and begged it to beat for me again; what more do I need?"

He never asked for more than what she gave. Never. That was what made this scary—how readily he accepted her, applauded her, *understood* her. And to think she'd once stood on his doorstep and thought he was no more than a rich artist whose hands were only as dirty as the paint that smudged them.

Arthie stepped toward him. From the tiny, circular windows scattered through the ship's hold, the evening light cast him in warmth, placing him at home in the rich furnishings and the vessel's ornate build.

"Is that enough?" she asked, her voice wound tight.

His response was just as quiet. "To attribute the word *enough* to Arthie Casimir would be a grave offense."

And then she rose on the tips of her toes, unable to hold back her smile, and touched her lips to his. It wasn't as though she hadn't kissed him before or pressed herself against him, so why then did she feel suddenly shy? Why did this feel less like she was sating her hunger and more like she was tearing pieces of her soul and presenting them to him and asking him to be gentle?

And gentle he was. He cupped her jaw with delicate hands, holding her in place when he lowered his lips to hers. His kiss was soft, imploring, accepting. It sent shivers down her spine, lifting the hairs on the back of her neck.

He pulled away, pressing a thumb into her chin, and when he met her eyes, it scared her. *I would do anything for you*, those eyes said. He already had. He had killed for her; he had infiltrated the Athereum for her. He had sailed across the seas for her. What more would he do?

"Shall we?" Matteo asked, gesturing to the hall ahead as footsteps rushed on deck.

Arthie followed him, surprised by the quiver in her hands, surprised by how ready she was to lock away her pocket watch in a vault and ignore everything else. He opened the door, and when Arthie saw the vampires, she forced her emotions into that vault instead.

First she'd ruin the Ram, then she would have her way with Matteo Andoni.

The vampires crowded around them. Some were loitering around the space, some huddled in corners staring at nothing, others talking in groups.

Their anger was a beating, writhing thing, warped with pain and despair. Arthie thought of the humans plucked off the streets, kidnapped no differently than these vampires. For no reason other than the Ram's selfish purposes.

"Have we arrived?" one of the vampires asked, rolling a coconut between him and the vampire sitting cross-legged from him.

"Almost," Matteo said.

"Our arrival may be met with resistance," Arthie said. "There's a likelihood we will be ambushed."

Their reactions were instant, quickly heating the expanse.

Our own country!

I'm not surprised . . .

Have we not dealt with enough?

But it was Oliver who asked the question they were clearly thinking, for they fell silent when he spoke. "By the Ram?"

Arthie understood that. It was one thing to be angry; it was an acute sort of satisfaction to know where to direct one's anger. She nodded. "I wish we could return in better circumstances, but I can promise nothing."

"No better circumstance than that!" someone shouted from farther in the back. Echoes of agreement rang throughout.

"I've been waiting a long time for this moment," someone else called.

"Ever since they dressed us in these tasteless rags, really," another vampire sniped, and others echoed the sentiment.

Arthie sighed. Vampires were vampires. They'd been trapped in coffins, injected with serums and inoculations, treated as inferior, but of course terrible fashion made the list too.

"After, our friend will get you to a place where you can recoup. Food, shelter, resources. They'll do whatever you need."

"Whatever, eh? Hard to believe anyone would do whatever a vampire would need. Where's that?" Oliver asked.

Matteo grinned. "The Athereum, of course."

His answer was met with a medley of responses: relieved sighs, excited chatter, awed gasps, and even some grouses and grumbles. Arthie had shared that particular sentiment until not long ago.

Who knew the Athereum would one day be an ally? Who knew Jin would find his parents in Arthie's motherland? Who knew Arthie would one day have an army of vampires eager for a fight?

34
JIN

It was nearing dusk when Jin and the others arrived in Ettenia, the skies hanging gloomily and the clouds rolling in moody hues of gray, shrouding the sun with petulance. It was a stark contrast to the bright and sunny Ceylani shores. Captain Vane's shouts cut through the din of the crew as they berthed where the inspector had instructed. Jin was vigilant, his heart lodged in his throat.

The docks were quiet, eerily so. What did it mean if the Ram was waiting to ambush them? If Flick had failed in her duties, did that mean she was in danger? That the Ram had found her?

The waves sloshed against the side of the ship, the chill creeping up his skin in warning. *Stay away*, the waves seemed to whisper. Jin ignored them.

He was halfway down the plank when he saw her.

Flick.

She was by the docks, delicate hands on the rail, the sea breeze tossing her tightly coiled curls. Goodness, he'd been gone long enough for the girl to turn scandalous. Those diabolical trousers were cinched tight to her waist, the top two buttons of her crisp white shirt exposing a slice of her gorgeous skin.

"Friend of yours?" his father asked, taking up the rear.

"She—I—erm." Jin couldn't seem to formulate a string of words no matter how he tried. Wicked knives, where was his tongue?

His father tried not to smile. "I see."

"That's Felicity Linden," Matteo replied, poking his head around. "Yes, Lady Linden's daughter." Jin was just about to pin him with a glare before he continued, "She's also the most talented forger in White Roaring, and a crucial part of our crew. Can you hurry? I'm not fond of this thin beam of wood."

"Is that so?" Jin's father asked. Jin didn't want to talk to him just then. He wanted to see her. Hear her voice. Feel her skin.

Kiss her.

But she wasn't supposed to be here. Arthie had instructed her to meet them at the Athereum, not here at the docks, where she and the ledger would be in danger. How had she even known they were arriving? He was too far to read her expression, but the harsh line of her shoulders was telling enough.

"Not a single Horned Guard," Arthie said beside him.

"Or otherwise," Matteo said. "The docks of White Roaring would never be empty—not unless she cleared them."

Arthie had said this was possible, but that didn't make Jin feel any better. As he neared, Flick met his eyes. She didn't look excited to see him; she didn't look happy. She was shaking her head.

Warning him.

The Ram was here. Jin scanned the ghostly square behind her. But what could they do? Huddle back on board? No, Jin was ready for a fight, as were the vampires clambering on deck behind him.

"What's our plan?" he asked.

"Fight our way to the Athereum," Arthie said. "Sidharth's runner should have spotted us, and his carriages will be on their way for the vampires, but I don't want your parents here any longer than necessary."

"No one else is here," Jin said. "Not a single civilian."

"No, but she is," Matteo whispered as the Ram strode into the square and her black-clad men fanned out like bullets.

35

ARTHIE

The docks were empty one moment, then flooded with dark figures the next, streaming from the square beyond. In the center, like the eye of a storm, was the Ram, cloaked in black and masked in silver. Even from her distance, Arthie could feel the monarch's eyes on her.

She stepped onto the slatted wood of the dock and lifted her chin. She was not the same scared little girl setting foot on Ettenia for the first time.

And she was not alone.

Behind her, Matteo exposed his fangs with a growl. Flick was waiting, brass knuckles on her fingers, her expression frantic yet determined. Jin rushed forward and flung his arms around her, burying his face into the crook of her neck. Even Matteo looked shocked by his boldness. He pulled away, eyes dropping to her lips before he settled for brushing a curl from her brow.

"You're not supposed to be here, love," he said, "but we'll get to that later."

He paused to glance back at his parents, and then at Arthie. She knew what he was asking.

"I've got your parents," she promised.

"They're yours too, remember," he said, and he turned to the vampires crowding behind them and pumped his hand into the air, umbrella in his fist. "The floor's ours!"

The docks rumbled as the vampires thundered after him with shouts and growls, fangs sharp, claws long, coconuts held tight. Their pain and zeal was a veritable, tangible thing in the air. Arthie felt it in her veins. The Ram had to feel it too.

She had to know the vampires wanted her head. Would she flee?

Within moments, vampires and black-clad forces clashed on the cobblestones just beyond the docks. Shots rang out, steel clashed, for the vampires had grabbed what they could within the ship to use as weapons and shields. There were more wooden stakes than Arthie had ever seen in one place, fisted in the hands of the Ram's army.

Humans and vampires alike ducked for cover where they could, behind stacks of crates and delivery wagons, others stormed to the tops of them before launching into the throng of the battle. Even some of Vane's crew joined the chaos. A gust of wind rolled through the port and waves rammed against the side of the ship, eager to join them.

Arthie ushered Jin's parents to stay close. They ambled, both of them green from the voyage.

"Jin," Sora whispered at the sight of him and Matteo at the front of the battle, tumbling toward their enemies like steam from a fresh pot of tea.

"He'll be fine; now stay close," Arthie told them. She drew Calibore from her holster, transforming it into a knife as she scanned the battleground.

The Ram was nowhere to be seen.

"Come with me!" Flick shouted over the din. She looked torn between minding her manners by introducing herself to Jin's parents and wanting to run. At the wharf, she guided them up a short flight of steps to the cover created by the short partition fishermen used to sell their wares.

Flick spoke as they moved. "I've been hiding out here, but you were right about the tribute. She's built an entire bunker under the palace."

Arthie pulled Flick down beside her when footsteps pounded behind them. One of the Ram's men rounded the partition. Before she could react, he slashed a knife toward Sora, catching her arm. She cried out, but Shaw pulled her out of the way as Arthie knocked the knife to the rot-ridden stones and kicked him to the docks below.

Blood was gushing down Sora's arm. Arthie smelled it before she saw it, relieved when it wasn't hunger that lurched through her, but concern.

"I'll be fine," Sora hissed. Beyond the wall, the battle continued, louder than the crashing waves, louder than Arthie's thoughts.

They crept along the cover of the partition, nearing the large, open square. It would be a harrowing escape, but once they reached the cluster of White Roaring's slums, Arthie and the Siwangs could easily lose any assailants in the maze of alleyways. Because unlike Ceylan, Arthie knew this city like the back of her hand.

"How do you know there's a bunker?" Arthie asked, on Flick's tail.

"I was trapped in it," Flick said. "She somehow knew you were a vampire too. I thought very few did."

Outside of Penn and the crew, no one did. No, that wasn't right. Someone else did too.

Arthie moved past Flick and peered over the partition. The square was a bedlam of vampires and black-clad men, the Ram's carriages far beyond like a dark dam. Just up ahead, Matteo tore a man apart, crimson staining his shirt. Jin was beside him, fighting two men at once, oblivious to the one behind him.

"Jin!" his mother shouted at the same time that Flick screamed his name and raced into the fray, masterfully evading the Ram's men. Arthie couldn't protect them both. She clamped a hand over Sora's mouth and pulled back in time to see Flick pull a wickedly long knife from a makeshift sheath at her side.

"We need to keep moving," Arthie shouted, searching once more for the Ram. Not a glint of that silver mask was to be found. Arthie pointed to a cobbled wall halfway through the open square. "See that ledge? On my count, run for it. Stay on my left. Hide."

She didn't know if she could ever call the Siwangs her parents, but she meant to protect them as if they were. *Only because I need them for a job.*

"Now!" Arthie shouted, and the three of them rushed into the open. They were spotted immediately. Men broke away from the vampires, heading for seemingly easier marks. In her hand, Arthie transformed Calibore back into a pistol and swung a wide arc, driving the men back.

Two of them launched themselves at her. She fired, striking one in the arm. The third rushed forward with a knife, only to go flying when Shaw swung a rotting board of wood and caught him straight on. The man hit his head on the cobblestones and didn't rise again.

"What? I need to keep my daughter safe," he said at her look.

Arthie couldn't make sense of the emotions that rose at his words. She fired at the last of the men and skidded beside the cover of the ledge, Shaw and Sora on her heels. Sora leaned against the stone with a relieved sigh, clutching her arm beside Shaw.

Sidharth's carriages still hadn't arrived, but the slums were just paces away. If Arthie could sneak the Siwangs past the guards that were bound to be waiting up ahead, they would be infinitely safer. But the Ram was still out there somewhere, and Arthie didn't like not knowing where.

"Looking for me?"

Arthie whirled.

The Ram stood before her, gunmetal mask glinting in the wan light. She turned her bright eyes from Arthie to the Siwangs leaning against the stone ledge. It might have been just the four of them in the world in that moment, isolated from the others and hidden from view.

"Did you think bringing them back would hurt me?" the Ram asked her. "They *belong* to me. Everything in this empire belongs to me, and soon, that will include the rest of the world."

Arthie lifted Calibore and squeezed off a shot. Quicker than Arthie anticipated, the Ram evaded, swinging a shield that was as small as a handheld mirror. The bullet bounced off its surface and shot straight back at her. Arthie rolled out of the way, heart in her throat, and that was her fatal mistake.

The Ram didn't look at her again. She didn't need to. She had what she needed:

The Siwangs. Unprotected.

Shaw leaped in front of Sora, but the Ram didn't care who died first. She fired. Twice. Two bullets. One for each of Jin's parents. One for each of Jin's long-lost parents, one for each of *Arthie's* new parents. They rang in Arthie's ears as if they'd landed in her own body, and by the time she could fire back, the Ram was gone and Arthie was surrounded by a throng of her men, the last of the Ram's words echoing dully.

I'll see you at the tribute.

36

JIN

Jin heard the gunshots, and he knew. He knew that gun. He moved in the direction of the sound, but he was slow, as if wading through water. A fist connected with his jaw. By his side, Flick screamed. He couldn't fight back. The world slowed to a buzz, ringing in his ears, thrumming far away. The man hit him again. Jin stumbled. And again.

Then Matteo was beside him. He cut the man down. He was dragging Jin and Flick away, pulling them to the shadows.

Where the familiar gunshots had rang out.

"Arthie!" Matteo shouted, and Jin saw the portrait in front of him.

His parents were slumped against each other, leaning against the gray stone wall. In some twisted way, they looked asleep, as though they had finally, finally found a moment's rest after the years of mayhem.

But their eyes were glassy. Their chests unmoving. He couldn't turn them. He couldn't make them vampires. He couldn't say goodbye.

He didn't get to tell them that he loved them.

He could have sworn there were claws in his chest, tearing his heart to shreds, so great was the pain.

Not even three feet away, Arthie was surrounded by the Ram's men. Calibore was clutched in her hand. Matteo ran for her, but Jin couldn't move. *You must.* She was his sister, the last of his family.

Jin cocked the revolver and fired at the men charging her, then fired again. Again. Again. He fired until the cylinder ran out and Matteo rose from the mess of limbs and bodies, blood dripping from his chin. Then it was quiet. The world was roaring around them, but here in this moment, it mourned. It wrapped them in silence. Then his tears fell.

37

ARTHIE

Arthie could not cry. She could not feel. She stumbled away from Jin's tears and Flick's sobs beside him. Arthie could not afford that luxury.

She had failed them.

She had shut down the weaponization of vampires in Ceylan, she had torched the entire fortress, but none of those victories rang true without the Siwangs—the two people they'd sailed across the ocean to retrieve, the two people Jin had spent half his life waiting for.

They had promised to be her family.

Arthie wanted to drop to her knees. She wanted to scream. She did none of those things. How could she? She was a lighthouse at sea, unmoving, unflinching, sought out in the darkness, and the others needed her.

She needed to be strong. So why, then, when Matteo grabbed her shoulders and pulled her to his chest, did Arthie allow it? She crumbled beneath his touch. She melted into his arms. *I'm sorry*, he was whispering over and over as the battle raged just beyond the cover of the wall. The gray skies darkened, mourning with them. Arthie needed to get back out there. She needed to fight. To do *something*, but she was so tired, so weak. So—

I'll see you at the tribute.

As Arthie replayed those words in her mind, she caught the utter pleasure with which the Ram spoke them. The joy she had taken in killing Jin's parents, for she not only wanted to ruin their plans but Arthie and Jin too. She wanted to break them. It was what she'd done with Spindrift, first by threatening to close it, then when she burned it down altogether. It was what she'd done time and time again.

No more. The Ram wouldn't need to wait until the tribute. No, she would see Arthie now. Because Arthie knew exactly what they needed to prepare for the Ram's big event.

Arthie pulled away from Matteo, and when he looked in her eyes, he saw her resolve. His low chuckle stirred her blood. "There's my Enchantress."

She looked away, her eyes falling to Jin's parents, to Flick wringing her hands and Jin in shock, his umbrella lying on the cobblestones like an afterthought. She dropped to her knees in front of him, and the sea breeze stirred Shaw's scent, sending a wave of sorrow through her.

She took the Council calling card from her pocket. "Jin. Jin, look at me."

He lifted blank eyes to hers. He was that eleven-year-old boy again, stumbling out of the fire. Alone. Afraid. Hurting so much. "They're gone, Arthie."

"I know," Arthie said, swallowing the knot that lodged in her throat. "I know. Look at me. She thinks she's won. She's trying to break us."

"Hasn't she?" he asked, hysteria creeping into his voice.

"No, she's distracting us and we can't let that happen." She was aware she was calling Jin's parents' death a distraction, but in a horrible, twisted way, it was true. She pressed the coin into Jin's palm. "Your father gave it to me. Present this to a Horned Guard minister, and they'll take you to the Council."

Jin wiped at his eyes. "For what, Arthie? They're all the same."

Arthie stared at Jin's parents, and she could not disagree. "Whatever they are, they're masked. Take Flick. She can study them and forge us one, because if anyone can get close enough to the Ram during the tribute, it's them. With a mask of our own, we'll take one of their spots."

Jin's head bobbed, his eyes drifting to his parents again.

"Jin," Arthie said, her voice hard. Part of her wanted to grab his shoulders and shake him, the other part wanted to weep beside him. She had promised to take care of his parents. She had promised him and failed, and now she wasn't even letting him mourn. "I'm trusting you, Jin."

He flicked his gaze to hers then, surprised by her admission, and finally nodded.

Arthie rose with a deep breath.

Matteo narrowed his eyes at her. "What are you going to—wait, Arthie, where are you going?"

Arthie stopped beyond the wall and clenched her jaw at the chaos. "I'm going to buy us time. Get him to a minister—"

Matteo nodded. "I know one."

"Good. Don't come for me. I'll meet you at the tribute." Before he could make sense of her words, she ran from the newly minted graveyard, from the death forever seared in her mind, and disappeared into the fray.

Where she was met by a pair of men. She flipped Calibore in the air, the hilt of a dagger falling into her hand. She shoved it into the first man's leg and pulled it free. He screamed, stumbling to the cobblestones with his hand pressed to his calf to staunch the blood. She slashed her dagger across the second man's neck, walking past as he gurgled to his knees. She picked up his knife, and pushed forward, the whisper of the sea growing quieter and quieter.

Just as Shaw's heartbeat had, just as Sora's.

Around her, vampires tore out throats and limbs, feeding for the first time in weeks, months, and in some cases, years. They were the starved weapons the Ram wanted them to be, turned against her. Men fell like rag dolls; some emerged with wooden stakes. The square was a war ground.

A cleaver swung toward her. Arthie leaped away. She flung her stolen knife into her attacker's stomach with a sickening squelch.

"Not enough money in the budget for a real weapon?" she asked. He ripped it out with a snarl, and she winced. "Should have kept it in."

A chill dragged down her spine, and Arthie found what she was looking for: the Ram, standing beside her carriage just outside the chaos. She had played her part in the battle, and now she was content to watch.

Good. Watch me destroy.

Arthie fought her way forward, slicing at the men with Calibore, leaving a trail of bodies. She transformed it back into a pistol as she neared the Ram, and held her gaze when she cut the last of the men near her down, tossing his cheap knife down with him.

The Ram stared at Calibore, then at Arthie.

"We meet again," the Ram said.

Your men are losing, Arthie wanted to say, but there was a better way to say it and get what she wanted out of this moment, to make the Ram think she had won and Arthie was a willing prisoner:

"Let's not kid ourselves. It's me you want."

The Ram tilted her head. "If I did, I would have killed you with the Siwangs."

Arthie smiled her razor-edged smile. "That's exactly why you didn't. Call off your men, let mine go free, and you can have me."

The island is Arthic Casimir incarnate. It truly is. Wild, enigmatic, and goodness does it make me sweat. I can only hope the Siwangs will do our bidding. I am not a violent ma—

Map labels:
- vampire cells
- coconuts
- the dreaded laboratory
- storerooms
- overseer's office
- chandelier
- Ripper room
- Armory
- extra space?
- the vault-like door

ACT III
DASHING AND DEADLY

38
ARTHIE

Arthie leaned back into the supple leather seat of the Ram's carriage. The last time she sat here, the Ram was threatening to take Spindrift. This time, far more was at stake—far more had been lost too.

You're welcome for the dignified retreat, Arthie wanted to gloat, but she couldn't decide if the Ram thought Arthie was gullible enough to think her black-clad men had the upper hand there, or if she was playing Arthie just the same.

Arthie was where she wanted to be, and that was what mattered.

Before the carriage door slammed on her face, Arthie met Jin's eyes across the distance. She saw his rage, his pain. He started running for the carriage, shoving humans and vampires out of the way.

Why? his eyes implored.

Matteo caught him, holding tight against his thrashing. He held Arthie's gaze too, as confidently as he said he held her heart, and she pressed her fingers to her lips, remembering their kiss in their final moment of solitude.

Then the Ram rapped her knuckles on the ceiling and set her gloved hands in her lap as the carriage lurched forward. Hands that had just killed two people the Ram had known for decades. Two people who had been an important, integral, irreplaceable part of the Ram's operation for years. Her disregard had never shown itself so starkly.

Why? Jin had asked.

Because the Ram was winning, and she needed to continue believing that. She needed to continue believing she had broken them. Because she had.

Now she even had Arthie.

But the Ram didn't yet know the damage Arthie had dealt, the damage she would soon amplify. She was ruin personified, and her enemies would know it.

"You may as well remove the mask so you can breathe, Lady Linden," Arthie said.

When the light bounced in through the carriage window, Arthie saw the Ram's eyes harden. If vampires could feed off of anger, Arthie would have gorged just then.

"Quite the ruse to keep for twenty years," Arthie continued. "Do you kill the people who find out?"

The Ram's silence was answer enough. She had killed for less.

Arthie pressed on. "In cold blood, like you just killed the Siwangs?"

"The Siwangs were living on borrowed time from the moment they went against me," the Ram said. Was she speaking of the moment the Siwangs had joined Arthie and the others? Or something else?

The carriage rumbled through the heart of White Roaring. The city was still as tense as it had been before Arthie had left for Ceylan, frightfully quiet even as shouts echoed from the direction of the Athereum. "You and I are quite similar, Arthie."

Arthie didn't like the sound of her name out of the woman's mouth. She wanted to say she could never be anything like the colonizing monster sitting before her, but that wasn't true.

Lady Linden was calculating and clever. She had started from nothing and clawed her way to the top. She may not have had an establishment that doubled as something else, but her entire identity did.

"Am I wrong?" the Ram asked.

"Posture all you want," Arthie said, but the Ram *wasn't* wrong. Arthie had climbed into this carriage to learn what she could, yes, but also to do what the Ram had done to her: distract her.

"Ambition is a lonely place. What we see as growth, others see as greed."

"Or is it lonely because we work to isolate ourselves?" Arthie asked. She had opened her mouth to keep the Ram talking, but she was surprised to find that her question was a genuine one.

She *had* worked to isolate herself. From Jin, from her crew, from Matteo.

The Ram tilted her masked head, eerie and stilted, as if she pondered over Arthie's question for a moment before deciding to ignore it altogether. "In the Siwangs' case, they were always liars; it just so happened to work for my needs. But a mutation is a difficult thing to hide, isn't it?"

Arthie went still. Shaw had said the Ram knew of the Rippers, but not how they were truly coming into existence. How did the Ram know of the mutation?

"They thought they were being coy, hiding it from me. That wooden spoon Bloodworth tells me everything, every assumption they fed him, every detail he wanted to brag about until it was clear to me what was truly happening. See, a Ripper vampire is precisely what I needed. What I wanted from the Siwangs was a cure for the mutation, which would lead to a way to control it, *use* it, but I suppose I'll have to make do without," the Ram said with a shrug.

She spoke of their deaths as if she'd forgotten to place her potted plants out in a rare rainfall. She spoke of Ripper vampires as if they weren't dangerous and indestructible.

Worse, she spoke freely. Arthie wasn't even having to push for answers.

But if the Ram knew the truth about the Ripper vampires, did Arthie and the others need to fear their existence here in Ettenia?

"Nothing to say?" the Ram asked.

"What did you want me to say?" Arthie asked. The Ram had simply assumed Arthie knew about the Ripper vampires, and Arthie wouldn't give her any more than she needed to know.

"Tell me, do your *friends* know you're a vampire?"

Did the Ram see a monster when she saw Arthie? Did she see something despicable, something in need of utilizing for her own needs? She didn't appear *afraid* of Arthie.

"I'm not one for hiding who I am, unlike you," Arthie replied, lying through her teeth.

"And are you always hungry?" the Ram asked. "While walking among humans on the street, while standing in your erstwhile tearoom? Do you crave their blood?"

Arthie gave the Ram a look, unsure of her tone. It sounded almost . . . pensive. "I'm a vampire, not a rabid animal."

"Is there a difference?" the Ram asked with a derisive scoff.

Arthie once saw no difference either—it was why she had chosen to consume coconut.

But that was enough of this conversation. "Did you ever imagine your daughter choosing criminals on the street over living with you?"

The Ram didn't have to remove her mask for Arthie to see she'd struck a nerve. She stiffened as though Arthie had slapped her. Her fingers clenched, no differently than when Matteo extended his claws.

And Arthie ventured to make a guess.

"You wanted to kill her like you do anyone else who stands in your way, didn't you? Pity that was so hard. Greater pity, I suppose, that she escaped."

The Ram's reaction was instantaneous. She launched herself at

Arthie. The carriage tipped, and outside, the driver shouted, steadying the horses. Arthie had her arms up in an instant, and though she was smaller and the Ram larger, it still required far more effort to push the older woman away than she had expected. The Ram slumped back in her seat, seething as she straightened her mask.

Arthie drew Calibore. "Touch me again, and I don't care who you are. I will kill you."

What's stopping you now?

Killing the Ram in cold blood would make true her claim that they were alike, among other things.

"You think you can kill away your problems?" Arthie asked. "You think killing the Siwangs will stop me? You think killing *me* will stop anything? Your reign was predicated upon lie after lie, and I would go so far as to predict that it will soon be over."

Her words were met with the rumble of the carriage wheels. The quiet outside was broken only by the rustling trees, which meant they were nearing residential streets.

The Ram's gaze burned into her, but it was too dark to decipher. "I don't need to kill you to render you useless. I only need to keep you from the rest of your crew. Without you, they are nothing."

Arthie swallowed a smile, biting the inside of her cheek to keep the thrill of a con gone right from showing in her eyes. This was what Arthie wanted.

"They will come for me," she swore, even as she hoped they would not.

The Ram only *hmm*ed.

Arthie crossed one leg over the other. "While you're busy preparing to gloat in front of high society about twenty years of a horrible rule."

"If you were Ettenian, you would know the purpose of a vicennial," the Ram said at last. "It's customary."

If you were Ettenian. It took every ounce of Arthie's will to keep her lip from curling and letting the Ram see that she'd struck a nerve. Arthie had never cared that she wasn't Ettenian, but she had just returned from a place where she did once belong and found she'd become less rooted in Ceylan in the years away. To where *did* she belong?

She released a careful breath. She needed to remain focused.

"We must often reassert our position in a country such as this, before officials, before lords, ladies, the Council," the Ram continued.

The Council. They *were* going to be there, as Shaw had said. She only hoped Jin had risen from those bloody cobblestones with the calling card in hand. Arthie could not remember a time when she had relied so heavily on someone. They had always split tasks for a con, but never like this. Never where Arthie gave herself up, never where she relinquished control over her crew and a situation so completely.

The seat beneath her began to sway like a boat at sea, waves sloshing inside, blood at her ankles. She fought the feeling, gritting her teeth. This wasn't the same. She wasn't losing control.

She was trusting him.

"Am I right to assume you will use both the ledger and the word of the Siwangs as evidence against me in front of the Council?" the Ram asked with a smile.

"The dead Siwangs?" Arthie asked. She wasn't foolish enough to present a ledger written in code to the Council, but the Siwangs had indeed been a part of their plan.

And why, again, was the Ram talking far too much and far too casually?

Did the Ram already have the Council in her pocket? *It didn't matter*, Arthie reminded herself. They needed to replicate one of their masks, nothing more. Forging it would take Flick time, even with her skills, and they'd be cutting it close, but they would make do.

They had to.

Because between the Siwangs' death, the Ram's knowledge of Ripper vampires, and how close she'd veered to unraveling one of Arthie's original plans, the crew's chances of trouncing the Ram were growing slimmer and slimmer.

Darkness filled the walls, swallowing the dusky night sky and flooding through Arthie just the same. The carriage angled downward and eventually rolled to a stop, the brake yanked into place as the horses stomped their feet. Not a shred of light slipped through the window. They had parked inside some place.

"I thought you might want to see where I kept my daughter," the Ram said, and stepped out into a narrow hall that opened to a well-lit space at the other end.

Her underground bunker.

Arthie stepped out behind her and glanced up at the ceiling. It was stone, hewn together with care, gray and drab, but nothing hinted at this being underground.

The Ram's men marched toward Arthie, and she crossed her arms behind her herself before they could jostle her around. One of them grunted in surprise, and then she was dragged behind the Ram.

"I could have walked," Arthie snapped.

They shoved her through to the light, and Arthie was shocked by how little the bunker *looked* like a bunker. It was spacious and palatial, a lavish hideout and a milder version of the Athereum, which was to be expected, she supposed, for it was built in the vicinity of the palace for the monarch herself. The men followed the Ram, pulling Arthie behind them, passing a collection of rooms and halls.

She kept her eyes peeled for any sign of Ripper vampires but saw nothing. The Ram gestured to a set of four identical iron doors, and the men threw one open and tossed Arthie inside.

The room was a stark contrast to the rest of the bunker, plastered with sheets of what looked to be metal. It was empty, save for a single chair and several iron rings secured to the wall—for fastening shackles, if Arthie was to guess.

"Shackle her," the Ram said to one of the men.

I knew it. As Arthie was yanked toward the iron ring, she pitched herself forward, pretending to lose her balance. The man sneered as he shoved her upright, too focused on her misfortune to notice the key she slipped from his pocket and into her sleeve, nearly getting a finger stuck beneath the cuffs as they clamped them down over her wrists. The chain between them was short, a handful of inches, but it was enough for him to fasten it to the ring just above her head.

Well. She hadn't climbed into the Ram's carriage expecting sweet treats and well-brewed tea, had she?

"Comfortable?" the Ram asked.

At least she was on her feet. Arthie smiled. "Very."

The Ram strode closer, studying Arthie through the holes in her demonic mask. "I have use for someone of your caliber. It'll get you out of those chains, and your coffers refilled. Surely they ran dry after your illegal establishment's untimely end."

She couldn't even call Spindrift by its name.

And here Arthie thought the Ram was smarter than that. If they were indeed the same, she would know better than to stand before a girl in chains—whose lands she herself had stormed, pillaged, *stolen*, whose establishment she herself had threatened simply because of its success and later burned down—and offer a partnership.

Then again, they weren't the same. The Ram had reached a level of power that had rearranged the very fibers of her brain.

When Arthie blinked, she saw the Siwangs lying in a pool of their own blood. She saw the cells in the sanatorium.

"What will I get in return?" she asked.

A pair of men entered, awaiting the Ram's command. It was the first time Arthie had seen them up close in a setting where she wasn't fighting for her life. She saw their unease, the flicker of fear in their eyes as they glanced at the Ram for instructions.

"That remains to be seen," the Ram said. "We'll start with a test."

Arthie lifted a brow. She was locked in a room with her hands bound. As far as the Ram knew, she had no resources, no hidden lair of her own. There was nothing the Ram could take from her that she already hadn't.

"Give me Calibore."

Except that. Arthie froze, unsure she heard correctly, but the Ram was looking at her waist, at its otherworldly silver grip. The tribute was in a day. What did she want with her pistol?

Arthie's response was a harsh, tight whisper. "No."

The Ram hummed. "Very well."

Arthie reached for her sleeve, sliding the key free when the Ram glanced away. Her hands were in plain sight. Unless she could escape in the span of a breath, she would be caught.

The Ram's men stepped toward her. One of them pulled back the lapel of her suit jacket. They were going to take it. Derision scraped her throat. The Ram wasn't even going to allow her a moment to decide? Panic rushed through her, and Arthie thrashed against him, kicking up with her feet. The other man leaped to help, holding her down without effort.

"What are you doing?" Arthie shouted.

"Taking back what's mine," the Ram replied.

Arthie felt Calibore's absence acutely. It was a part of her, a limb she could not live without. The man held it up to the light and stared in awe until the Ram snapped her fingers.

"Give it here."

Arthie heard that precious metal barrel hitting the Ram's palm, felt the empty weight of her holster like a chasm ripping through her heart. Arthie reminded herself of why she was here: to distract the Ram, to make her believe the crew would stand still without her.

She could only hope they wouldn't prove the Ram right.

"I don't know that we can have an alliance, but I would very much like one. I've known about you since you stole this from White Roaring Square, you know," the Ram said, taking a seat in the chair in the room's center as the men scurried out like a pair of rats.

Arthie was only half herself without Calibore. "And yet you decided today was the day you needed to take it from me."

"Oh, we tried. You were a tiny, slimy little thing, and I decided to let you have it. It was one of many artifacts we've picked up over the years, and I am known to bide my time."

"Until?"

"Until I learned what it's truly capable of."

The Ram was suddenly interested in Calibore because she had seen Penn die. She'd been there when Laith fired the pistol at Penn and unknowingly killed him.

"Killing vampires?" Arthie asked. Her neck still stung with the remnants of the green dart she'd taken to protect Jin's parents. *Before they'd died.* "I've since learned you've found alternative ways of eradicating vampires."

"None as quick as this," the Ram replied as the door to the room opened again. "But it's more than that, isn't it? I didn't know it was magical, or that something as far-fetched as *magic* even existed. That's not to say I care, but it is fascinating."

Arthie schooled her features. *Magic.* Only one person knew of the pistol's origins. He had tricked her for it. He had died for it.

And he knew that Arthie was a vampire.

But he was loyal to his kingdom, even if his anger for his king blurred those lines some. He had spoken of the crown prince with fondness, his training the same. She could not imagine him giving up information like that to the Ram so freely.

The two men returned, one holding a stack of wrinkled, bloody papers in a language that did not look remotely Ettenian, the other dragging a third person between them. He was bloody and beat, the silvery white of his robes drenched in varying shades of red. His hair was matted to his brow, white strands as brilliant as the moon. Even from her distance, she could see the twin flecks of black above the curve of his left eyebrow, the strained rise and fall of his chest.

Laith.

39

FLICK

Flick had never wished for anything as much as she did now. She wished Arthie wasn't seated with a monster in a carriage. She wished Jin's parents weren't bleeding on the cobblestones of the home they'd left ten years ago. She wished the Ram hadn't ambushed them at the docks, and that Flick had been able to properly warn the others.

She didn't know why Arthie had given herself up as the Ceylani vampires were turning the tides. Arthie would say she had her reasons, but she hadn't been imprisoned for days that echoed like a lifetime. There was no telling what the Ram might do to her.

Meanwhile, Flick and the others were in the comfort of the Athereum. They were safe, but that didn't fill Flick with the relief she thought it would.

"Arthie said not to come for her," Matteo said, pacing back and forth in the hall outside their rooms.

"Well, we are," Jin replied. He didn't look sad, really. He looked numb, empty—emotions Flick didn't know how to contend with herself. He flipped the coin Arthie had given him. "And thanks to you, we're in sparkling-new outfits."

Matteo scowled.

When Arthie and the Ram rumbled away, her black-clad forces had climbed into their carriages and done the same. The slaughter was over, but the vampires were not sated, unwilling to board Sidharth's carriages that arrived a moment later. It wasn't until Matteo warned them that the Horned Guard cordoning off the area would paint them as the culprits that everyone moved.

Jin had wanted to head directly to the Council, but Matteo had gestured to their bloodstained clothes and grimy skin, and not even Jin could argue against a shower. So here they were, in the Athereum.

Flick stifled a scream now as something wet and rough ran along her arm. "Opal!"

The kitten meowed indignantly in response. Her eyes were wide, affronted at having been left alone, but her tail was high, swishing in contentment at their return.

"I know, I know," Flick replied, pulling her into her lap. Opal immediately began to purr. "I didn't mean to be away so long."

In hindsight, two days was nothing. No one would understand if she told them just how long those days had felt.

"What happened on Ceylan?" she asked, determined to forget.

One side of Jin's lips quirked into a wry smile. "I had my head shoved in a sack, found my parents, watched Arthie burn down thousands of duvins' worth of resources in the fort, and rushed back to find you."

Matteo snorted. "That's the gist of it. He also commandeered a moving carriage in the middle of traffic."

Flick gasped. Before she could berate him, a shriek echoed and Chester came tearing through the hall, Reni and Felix on his heels.

"Flick!" Chester shouted, wrapping his arms around her. He smelled like sugar and sunlight. "We were so worried, we was! We tried looking for you, but none of our runners had a clue!"

"I was underground," Flick said quietly. "Not an easy place to find."

He whirled to Jin. "We're sorry, Jin. We tried to keep her safe."

"I suppose I can forgive you," Jin said with an overly dramatic sigh, but then he looked back at Flick. "What happened?"

This time, his voice was a death sentence, spiking her blood with a promise to do horrible, horrible things to anyone who hurt her.

"I found coordinates in the ledger, and when I realized they led to a place close to the palace and the tribute, I thought I'd find out what her plans are, but her men found me first," Flick said. "It's a bunker, sprawling under the palace. I couldn't explore it in its entirety, but—"

Flick stopped. How was she meant to describe the cage full of girls and boys? How was she to talk about the helplessness in their eyes, the knowledge that their monarch was worse than the vampires she blasphemed across the country?

"What is it?" Matteo asked.

"I found the people she's been kidnapping off the streets."

"In the bunker?" Jin asked.

Flick nodded grimly. "They're caged in a room."

"But why? If she was kidnapping them under the guise of vampires slaughtering innocents on the street, she wouldn't need to worry about keeping them alive."

Flick cradled her wrists in her lap. She hesitated to call the Ram heartless when she always had been. It was Flick who hadn't been any wiser. Still, she *was* worse now.

"She's going to turn them," Flick said. "They—I spoke to the kidnapped. She's going to turn them on the day of the tribute."

Jin took a sharp breath. "And?"

Everyone knew the story of how the Ram came into power. She appealed to the masses by creating the Wolf of White Roaring and taking the reins. She was careful with her chaos and greed. Now Flick wasn't so certain she would be.

"I don't know," Flick said. "Unleash them onto the streets while the rich and powerful are safe in the palace, perhaps?"

"Not if we get to them first," Matteo said quietly. "We're not letting the Ram replicate the massacre from twenty years ago."

Sidharth brought in a tray holding several flutes filled with crimson and a cup of tea for Flick. Matteo took one of the flutes and offered it to Jin. Flick wondered if he'd taken her gift on the ship, if he knew why she'd given it to him: to tell him that she accepted him no matter what. She didn't care that his heart no longer beat, or that he couldn't walk out into the sunlight.

But at the same time, she *did*. He had lost so much of what he enjoyed. He had died, even if he had returned seconds after. That was the core of it, wasn't it? Being a vampire meant mourning one's own death forever and ever.

Flick took the flute from Matteo, doing her utmost not to let the smell of the blood twist her features, and extended it to Jin herself.

"Another gift? Felicity, you spoil me," he said, soft and despondent, though a smile wavered on his lips.

He took a dainty sip at first, his eyes brazenly lifting to hers. Heat rose to her cheeks. She wondered what it would be like to have her own blood staining his lips. To have his fangs at her throat, his tongue smoothing the goosebumps rising even now with the thought alone. He took another sip, then another, downing the rest in one quick swig. He swayed, relief and satisfaction wrapped in a deep-throated sigh.

"Much better," he said in a low tone that made her shiver.

"The carriage is ready whenever you are," Sidharth said. "My driver will take you to the Horned Guard minister, if you have his address."

"I do," Matteo said, and rose to his feet. "How are the vampires?"

"I'm glad we had the foresight to clear out a wing for them," Sidharth said. "There's a good number, eh? And I had almost forgotten how many of them were members. I can't say everyone's happy to be here, but they understand the situation. None of us ever saw the Athereum becoming well-nigh a prison, but it's only temporary."

Flick hoped so, for all their sakes.

"They're acclimating well thus far. We've given them each coconut water, as instructed, and will continue to monitor and aid as necessary. They have rooms, free rein of their wing. They'll get through. Oh, and"—Sidharth handed something to Jin—"we found these on your father's person. I thought you should have them."

It was a book, bound in leather the same deep shade of green Jin favored in his suits. It was bursting with notes and slips of paper shoved inside, wrapped tight with cords to hold everything together. Flick didn't know if they were notes from his work or a diary, but she was glad Jin had another piece of his father to hold on to.

"I am sorry, Jin," Sidharth murmured.

Jin took it, jaw clenched as if he, too, was just barely holding himself together. Then he looked at the others. "Right. Let's go meet the Council."

The Council. She froze.

"What is it, Flick?" Chester asked, tilting his head at her. "What's wrong?"

What was she to say? She hadn't forged the invitations Arthie had asked her to send out, nor could she. Flick had overheard Arthie's instructions at the docks. She knew what Arthie wanted her to do. And Flick couldn't. This was the moment she had been dreading. The need for her talent.

She stared at her fingers, at the tremor she couldn't shake. Holding anything was a pain, but holding something steady would be near impossible. She had tried. A cramp rendered her useless in moments. *She values her hands very much, and I don't see her using them to the fullest extent after this.* The Ram couldn't get Flick to return to her, so she had ensured she was useless to Arthie and Jin too.

"I can't," Flick whispered.

"You can't what?" Jin asked.

She tried to elaborate and explain, but tears crowded her throat. Instead, she tugged on her sleeves, pulling them just above her wrists.

Her skin was bruised in shades of purple and green.

"She—" He broke off with a growl and stood up, directing his next words at Sidharth. "I need a medical kit."

He didn't ask her what happened. He didn't press her for answers, and for that, she was strangely grateful.

Sidharth led them to another door without question. "This way."

She glanced back at Matteo before the door closed behind them, an apology leaping to her tongue for the delay, but his brow was creased, his expression pained as he stared at her arms. He knew what it was like, she realized. He was an artist after all.

Jin dropped a hand to her lower back, guiding her behind Sidharth to a lavish washroom complete with a bench. Sidharth pulled a kit from the vanity drawer and spread its contents on the counter before leaving with a little bow.

Flick sat down as Jin riffled through the different ointments, bandages, and creams with his back to her. He was quiet, unnervingly so. Was he upset that she wasn't going to be able to contribute to their plans in the way that they needed?

He turned back, setting an array of bottles on the bench before sitting beside her.

"Are you angry?" she asked, her voice small.

"Yes," he replied, and she *heard* his anger, felt it. "How can someone call themselves your mother and do such a thing?"

Oh.

"If we weren't already dedicated to tearing her down, I would be simply on account of this," he continued. He reached for her hand. "May I?"

She nodded, and he set her wrist on his knee, her hand just below his thigh. He was cold. He had been since he was turned, and that was okay because she was always so warm.

"The bruises don't hurt as much as, I don't know, inside," Flick said.

He nodded. "I know. This will help."

His *I know* made it sound as though he had been shackled in manacles himself. And she supposed he could have, at any point over the past ten years. He had lived a lifetime of this, she always seemed to forget. Maybe because when she was with him, she thought of days ahead, not experiences past.

"I'm sorry," she whispered. "About your parents."

The ointment stung her skin, but he was right: As he rubbed it into her wound, the relief was instant. Or it might have even been the feeling of his fingers on her skin, drawing small circles and stirring her blood.

"I—I don't know how to feel about any of it," Jin said, and she had the sense he was struggling to find the right words. "They had been missing for so long. Then I learned their hands weren't as pristine as I long believed. I accepted it because they were going to right their wrongs here, and then the Ram just— That's what shocked me the most, I think. How she killed them without a second thought."

If she'd found a way to throw the Ram off their scent, would Jin's parents be alive right now? Flick was too terrified to ask such a thing, to plant that thought in his mind.

"You're not allowed to feel guilty, you hear?" Jin asked. "For not being able to forge. Promise me."

Flick looked away. "I—I promise."

"Good girl."

With a trembling exhale, Jin took Flick's other hand and did the same, each swipe sending a zap of current through her veins. He turned to grab a roll of bandages from the other side of the bench and she traced the strain of his neck with her eyes, wishing she was bold enough to use her fingers. To touch the heron tattooed on his skin, to brush away the errant strands of his dark hair.

He straightened, unraveling the roll and gesturing for her to lift her arm so he could wrap it around her wrist, the tip of his tongue slipping out from the corner of his mouth as he focused on keeping the gauze straight and neat.

She was starting to wish she had more bruises to tend to.

"Almost through," he said, his voice low and rough. He tucked the end with a satisfied *hmm* and moved to her other wrist, winding the gauze around and around until he tucked that away too. Then he hesitated, and before she could ask what was wrong—or try to get the words out anyway—he flicked his gaze to hers and lifted her wrist to his mouth, pressing a kiss to the sliver of exposed skin.

Her exhale was a crush of a gasp, half knotted in her throat.

"The secret to speedy healing," he explained, and flashed her a smile. It was the lovely lighting washing him in gold, it was the sweet scent of whatever dusted the air, it was the romantic wallpaper behind them—something, *something* possessed her to lurch forward, and Flick stole his lips between hers.

Jin froze for a long, treacherous beat of her heart.

And then he was lifting her arms to his shoulders with tender hands and scooting closer and kissing her back. His lips were as soft as she remembered, but where they tasted bright before, they were darker now. Heady, the metallic tang of the blood he had sipped almost dangerously sweet.

His teeth grazed her lower lip with a groan, and heat surged through her, making her dizzy. He reached for her waist, tugging her even closer, adjusting his legs so they fit together in a way that made her heart soar, her pulse driving beneath her stomach.

She pulled away first, a realization sending her pulse roaring faster than the wings of a hummingbird. Jin studied her, smoothing back her hair and lifting up her chin. His eyes were glazed, and before he could press his lips closed, she saw the flash of his fangs.

"What is it?" he asked.

Did someone like Jin Casimir fall in love? Or was everything in his life temporary, lived in the thrill of the moment? She didn't know, and so, she said nothing.

"Did I hurt you?" he asked.

"No!" she said far too quickly. "It's not that, it's . . . I—" Goodness, what was she supposed to say? "I like you, Jin. Quite abundantly."

Relief washed over his features, too intense to have been surrounding this moment alone. It gave Flick hope.

"I like you too, Felicity. I cannot imagine an existence without you, much less an eternity," he said, entwining his fingers with hers.

Flick pressed her other hand to her heart, afraid it would burst if she didn't contain her emotions. Did that mean he wanted her to be a vampire too? Did *she* want that? A question for another day, she supposed.

He laughed.

"Too much?" he asked, the light back in his eyes, however faint. "I can reel back the charm at any given moment, love."

He was teasing, she knew, but she could tell from the tenderness in his eyes: He couldn't reel it back even if he tried.

40

JIN

Jin was undead, but he'd never once in his life felt more alive. It wasn't as though he hadn't kissed Flick before. He had missed her, yes, she was beautiful, yes, but the knowledge that he could have lost her as he'd lost his parents today was what made him realize how much he cared for her.

Loved her.

Bloody wicked knives, man.

And he was angry. It roiled beneath his skin, rising every time he blinked and saw the purple-and-green bruises on Flick's arms, now hidden beneath ribbons of bandages. The Ram had hurt her. Worse, she had made her feel as though she were ruined, less than. Useless. Just when Jin had thought he couldn't loath the monarch any more than he already did.

As they squeezed through the Athereum's tunnel, he was grateful for the cold air that struck him like a blow. He could barely think as Matteo relayed the address of the Horned Guard minister he knew to Sidharth's driver. The three of them climbed into the carriage, and Flick sat beside him, a vision against the moody reds and purples of the carriage interior.

"I never thought we'd be meeting the Council," Matteo said, leaning back.

Jin didn't know if he wanted to. He reached for the calling card in his pocket, an odd, weighted coin. It was rounded, compared to the Athereum marker, the shape reminding him of a piece of candy. Only this was metal, a dull, brushed gold with an engraved *C* in its center. Why had his father given it to Arthie and not him? Did he not think Jin was as capable as Arthie?

Don't be silly; you know you aren't.

"Flick can't forge," Jin said as the carriage trundled along. "So we're going to have to convince them to join our side."

Matteo looked skeptical. "They're the Council. I doubt they can be convinced of anything."

"Oh, but they haven't met me," Jin said with only half his usual charm, suddenly wishing Arthie were here. "And then we're going to get Arthie. I don't care that she doesn't want to be rescued. I'm not losing her too."

"She's likely in the Ram's bunker," Flick said. "The Ram tried getting answers out of me. About the ledger, your whereabouts, and—and Arthie's pistol, strangely. I tried not to divulge that you were even alive, but it seems she got what she wanted out of me anyway. I knew she would ambush you at the docks, so I was waiting there to warn you, but some good that did."

"It's all right," Jin said softly, and took one of her hands in his, holding it steady as the carriage hit a bump in the road. He clenched his jaw tight at the sight of her bandages. Should he not have given her the brass knuckles and a teapot full of advice?

"I—" He broke off with a cold, hard laugh. "She risked her life to save them, did you know? She braved going back to her homeland to save them, and we made an entire, now-useless journey to have them die the moment we return."

"The voyage wasn't useless," Matteo reminded him gently. "We rescued nearly a hundred vampires. We ruined the Ceylani trade route, and really, we did save your parents. They died as Ettenians, not prisoners, and they got to see that their son is alive and well, even if undead."

"They died with hope," Flick added. "Something they did not have for a decade."

Did they? Jin would never know for certain. He'd lived a decade wishing they were alive, only to see them die.

"They were supposed to help with Arthie's plan," he said softly.

"We'll figure it out, starting with the Council. And if we could free a sanatorium full of vampires, armed with Flick's findings, we can do the same to the people in that cage, turned or not. Then we will ruin her," Matteo replied as the carriage turned, and then winced, as if he'd forgotten Flick. "I'm sorry."

She rested her arms gingerly in her lap. "You don't have to be. She's not my mother anymore."

She was sure of herself and the words. There wasn't a hint of remorse on her face, not a flicker of sorrow or regret. No, at some point after Jin and the others had left for Ceylan, Felicity Linden had broken free of the mold her mother had shoved her inside. She was her own person.

The carriage rolled to a halt. Night had fallen, and Jin could only hope the Horned Guard minister hadn't left for the day. Or the Council for that matter, however they worked. The driver opened the carriage door, and Jin was surprised to find them parked in front of a tavern. A shabby one at that.

"Are you sure we have the right place?" Flick asked, eyeing the seedy establishment.

"Spindrift is turning in her grave," Jin murmured.

THE BROODING TURNIP, a sorry sign read, but the letters were fading. It was small, but even from their spot across the street, Jin could hear the raucous crowd within. He would not expect Matteo to know anyone who frequented the place.

"It's seen better days," Matteo admitted. "Shall we?"

41

ARTHIE

Laith was alive. He was in a terrible state, but he was alive. Arthie tried not to give the Ram the reaction she was waiting for, but it was impossible. No matter what Laith was now, he had been a part of their crew. He had been a part of Arthie's life.

Even if she'd shot him and left him for dead—twice. Even if he'd shot her and left *her* for dead in turn.

"Are you proud of yourself for torturing him?" Arthie asked. "Is that what this is about?"

Beside the Ram, Laith let out a quiet snort. The Ram shifted Calibore to her other hand, and Arthie did her utmost not to drop her gaze to it.

There was a bond between her and the pistol, one Arthie, despite her adamance for staying realistic, knew existed only because she acknowledged that the pistol was sentient. It cared for her as she cared for it. The Ram couldn't replicate such an alliance no matter how she tried. She could barely nurture a bond with her own daughter.

"It won't do what you want it to," Arthie said.

The Ram aimed it at her. "No?"

Laith made a sound.

"Oh, what was that?" the Ram asked. "Are you concerned for the girl I put in your charge?" She looked at Arthie. "I don't care about magic or whatever ridiculous notions you believe it possesses. What matters is its importance to the Arawiyan throne."

Its importance to the Arawiyan throne was exactly why Laith had come to Ettenia with his now-dead sister. She had been tasked with retrieving the pistol to stave off conquest, for Calibore was more than a gun, more than a shape-shifting weapon. It was one of the many artifacts the kingdom was trying to return to its own coffers, each filled with insurmountable magic, each as integral to the kingdom's survival as a skilled army was to any other.

The Ram might not care for magic, but it was clear to Arthie what she wanted just then.

She wanted to colonize Arawiya.

Her greed had no end. She had colonized Ceylan and Jeevant Gar. She had colonized parts of Qirilan and other countries too. Arawiya was one of the largest kingdoms near Ettenia, and its sheer size was likely why the Ram had never touched it.

With Calibore, she could.

This time, Arthie couldn't school her features quickly enough.

"Indeed," the Ram said with a level of smugness Arthie wanted to wipe clean. "You can thank the high captain here for that. Though, to his credit, he did try to keep his mouth shut."

How strange it was to know that a single artifact could open the door to such an atrocity.

Arthie might not have been able to stop the Ettenians from sweeping into Ceylan or Jeevant Gar or any of the other kingdoms and countries, but she could stop this. She had nothing but the silver dose in her pocket and the key she'd swiped, but she would find a way.

Laith spat a bloody mess at the Ram's feet.

The Ram *hmm*ed in response, and one of the men twisted Laith's ear until he croaked.

Arthie toyed with the key in her fingers. How easy it would be to unlock her cuffs and free herself. To wrestle Calibore from the Ram's hands and shoot her in the throat, watching the life bleed out of her.

"Now, if you'll excuse me, I've a tribute to prepare for," the Ram said. "Strap him to the chair and lock the door; I don't need another escapee."

"Are you just going to leave me here too?" Arthie asked.

"We discussed this already, didn't we? Am I going to leave the brains of the Casimir crew here, rendering the rest of that sorry gang useless?" the Ram asked. "Yes."

The men threw Laith unceremoniously onto the chair, wrenching his arms and locking them behind him. Then they knocked him unconscious for good measure.

"What about her?" one of the men asked.

The Ram regarded her, turning Calibore over in her hands. Dangling it in front of Arthie. When she'd chosen to give herself up, she hadn't chosen to give up her pistol too.

"Sit down and watch her." She glanced at the second man. "Bring him a stake too, just in case."

42

FLICK

A Horned Guard minister was a rank above high captain, one rarely seen on the streets of White Roaring, for their work primarily consisted of sitting behind a desk. Flick didn't think she would find one at a tavern such as this. She'd never *been* to a tavern before, only read about them in books and seen them at a distance.

Flick stayed as close to Jin as she could without stepping on his feet. Her shoes squelched in the mud. She felt eyes on her more than once, figures silhouetted against the darkening sky running across the narrow streets.

"Are you sure we'll find a minister here?" she asked.

Flick fought her guilt. She'd promised Jin, but that didn't stop her from feeling useless. Arthie wanted them to meet with the Council *simply* so that Flick could forge one of their masks, but if Flick couldn't hold a teacup, much less attempt to replicate a mask, how could she? Was Jin silver-tongued enough to convince the Council to unmask the Ram themselves?

He was busy scanning their surroundings like a Horned Guard himself. Funnily enough, Flick didn't see any guards patrolling this portion of the city. Nor were people here hiding away or protesting vampires.

"Certain. He goes by the name of Ward," Matteo said, pulling open the door. It squealed like the pigs rolling in the mud just across the alley.

The hushed evening exploded into a bustling den of depravity.

Flick glanced at Jin, wondering if their surroundings had transported him back to Spindrift, but instead of nostalgia, she found his upper lip curled at the cruddy space. She supposed it was wrong of her to equate such a mess to Spindrift.

The tavern was crammed full of people, some dancing to brassy tunes, others clinking heavy pints, drink sloshing over the worn floors. The air reeked of sweat and bodily fluids.

"How are we supposed to find anyone in this wreck?" Jin shouted above the din.

"Stay close," Matteo shouted back.

Flick didn't need to be told twice. She stayed on Jin's heels, keeping her head low, ignoring toothy grins and women looking over her clothes as though she had no sense of style, dressing like a boy while they dressed like they'd never seen a river.

Goodness, Flick, that was rude.

But it was true. Jin turned back and reached for her hand, and Flick felt her cheeks warm. They had kissed and touched and shared heated glances, but there was something unspeakably remarkable about being sought out and remembered even in the midst of mayhem.

Matteo led them to the rooms in the back. There was a line of them, and Flick did not have to wonder if they were occupied. Breathless sighs, low moans, and fervent commands escaped the doors. Jin's hand tightened around hers before he let go altogether, deliberately looking away when she tried to catch his eye. She held back a grin at his discomfort. The great Jin Casimir! Shy!

"I'm here for the Council, Andoni," Jin said dryly, but Flick caught the rough abrasion of his words, the huskiness in the back of his throat. "Not a show. Wicked knives, I can't believe we showered for this."

Matteo ignored him, stopping before the center door, which was wider than the rest. More . . . official, Flick felt. He knocked twice, and when a gruff voice answered, he stepped inside, Flick and Jin on his heels.

A middle-aged man sat behind a desk that had seen better days, his window open to let in the sour air from the alleyways. He had a dark beard that reminded Flick of Penn, and a collection of teacups on a worn shelf behind him. The paint was peeling off the walls and the floor needed a polish, but Ward was dressed in fine scarlet livery of a Horned Guard minister that looked out of place.

"Andoni!" Ward called. "It's been too long, my boy."

"An artist never sleeps," Matteo said with a lazy shrug. In Matteo's case, that was very true.

"Sugarplums?" Ward asked, nudging the bowl on his desk. Neither Matteo nor Jin moved to take one, but Ward looked so hopeful that Flick thought it bad form to refuse.

"Does this establishment belong to you?" Jin asked, and Flick thought he could have toned his judgment down a tad.

"My pa's, originally," Ward said with a nod, and then regarded Jin with a tilt of his head. "Why? Are you interested in buying?"

Flick wondered, for a moment, if Matteo had pulled some cruel joke on them, but he wanted to meet the Council and find Arthie as much as they did, and Ward *was* wearing the right uniform. It was simply a strange sight.

"I thought you were a Horned Guard minister," Jin said.

Ward leaned back, his amenable tone slowly slipping away. "And I thought we were allowed to work more than one job."

"Forgive my friend here. He's been wronged more than once," Matteo said.

Ward studied Jin for a long, silent moment—as silent as the room allowed them to be, for the ruckus outside thrummed in the very air—and Flick worried Jin had gone too far and the minister would turn them away.

"White Roaring is a terrifying place," Ward said finally. He set down his pen and folded a letter. "Now, care to tell me why you're here?"

"Because of this." Jin stepped closer to his desk and held out the heavy gold coin. The Council calling card.

Ward stilled. "I haven't seen one of these in a long while."

"Will you take us to them?" Matteo asked.

Ward lifted his brows, casting Flick and Matteo a glance. "And where did you get the coin? We don't produce them anymore."

Jin mulled over his reply. "From a kinsman who can't make use of it himself."

"Is that so? That's a hard truth to believe, young sir."

Matteo pursed his lips as though he knew what he could say but didn't want to. "He's a friend of mine, Ward," Matteo said finally. "Can you not trust the friend of your sister's son?"

Jin balked. Flick's eyes widened of their own accord before she schooled her features. This man was Matteo Andoni's *uncle*? He looked nothing like the tall, aristocratic vampire.

"Sister by choice," Ward corrected, rising to his feet. Ah. That made far more sense. "But you're right. And coin etiquette demands I take you there, no questions asked."

Matteo's brows flattened.

The man had already asked an *awful* lot of questions.

"Where is *there*, exactly?" Flick asked.

Ward lifted a finger. "No questions from either side, miss." Then he glanced at his pocket watch. "Bollocks. It's half past seven bells. The Council won't convene until dawn tomorrow, so I'm afraid we can't go just yet. Luckily for you, I've got spare rooms."

He looked so pleased to offer them lodging that Flick couldn't *not* smile at him, but she couldn't be blamed if it looked like a grimace.

43
JIN

When Ward said he had spare rooms, he apparently couldn't count because he only had one. It was tight, cramped, and astonishingly clean, but there was just a single bed. The three of them stood in the narrow doorway, and Jin was suddenly overwhelmingly aware of how Flick's heartbeat quickened.

Matteo heard it too and glanced sidelong at Jin before taking several steps back. "The room's yours. Fortunately for you two, I don't get cold."

He sauntered down the dark corridor toward the bustling floor without another word, leaving Jin and Flick alone. She smoothed down her trousers with her hands, saying nothing.

Jin didn't get cold either. Nor did he need sleep. He gestured in the direction of the revelry. "I'll—"

"Stay," Flick whispered. A quick volley of the word as if part of her wanted to hold it back, but the rest of her could not.

He held himself still. This was the perfect moment to tease her, to remind her that sharing a bed with a boy in a tavern was positively unladylike, but he could manage no such raillery. She was a marvel in the moonlight, and when she looked at him with those eyes of sunflowers and sunshine, of warmth in a world that gave so little, Jin could not say no.

He closed the door. He couldn't leave even if he wanted to.

"Vampires don't need sleep," he said.

"I know. Needing and wanting are two different things," she replied, and it was such a leap from the Felicity Linden he'd stolen away from her mother's estate that he couldn't help himself.

He inched forward. "Oh? And what is it that Felicity Linden wants?"

He was not expecting her to mimic him. To close the distance between them. He instinctively took a step back, his head thudding into the worn wooden door.

"She wants to be called Flick," she said, a dark undercurrent to her tone. There was a spark in her eyes he'd never seen before. Dangerous, thrilling. He felt the heat of her exhales, smelled the sugarplums she'd eaten.

"What else does she want?" he breathed.

Flick glanced at his mouth, then into his eyes for an eternal moment until something softened in hers. "She wants to kiss away your sorrows. To pluck each one from your heart and fill it with sweet happiness instead."

Jin stared at her. As if summoned by her words, he *felt* each of those sorrows, like stones weighing him down, drowning him beneath Ettenia's dusky waves. The tumultuous loss of his parents. Arthie giving herself up just after they had mended their broken bond. A soul as gentle as Matteo forced to become the Wolf of White Roaring. The damage the Ram had dealt to Flick's arms.

She threaded her fingers through his with a wince she tried and failed to hide, then tugged him ever so gently toward her until their brows touched.

"I want every part of you here with me, present, *bare*," Flick whispered, and then her gaze swept downward with a tiny, anxious giggle. "Not that kind of bare. Not that I don't want you to be bare—oh, goodness, I didn't mean—I want—"

He kissed her quiet. She gasped against his mouth, tightening her fingers around his, tilting her head and deepening the kiss with a hitch of her breath, her curls brushing his brow as soft as her words. He could feel her heartbeat, racing faster than a bullet out of a barrel, the pitter-patter rising until it was as loud as the tavern din.

She pulled away, cheeks flushed, and then she turned to the bed, still holding his hands but too shy to voice her words.

He followed her. Sat down when she released him. The bed was more of a cot, really, barely enough for a single person, let alone two. It dipped beneath her weight, rocking as she shimmied back and made herself comfortable.

It took an excruciating moment before he could turn and face her. She was waiting, tilting her head so the moonlight caught one side of her face, her white shirt framing that vee of skin, sleeves folded to her forearms, bandages wrapped just above her wrists, those infernal trousers teasing him. She was leaning against the plain headboard, a pillow propped behind her back.

When she patted the space beside her, Jin could only oblige, unsure of how she wanted him. He started to lie down, but this was a new Flick, one who knew what she wanted. She pulled his head into her lap, and Jin felt the warmth of her skin through the soft fabric of her trousers. Matteo had lied, for vampires did get cold. Achingly so.

"Are you snug?" she asked.

Snug. Jin almost laughed. It was an odd question, but Flick was no ordinary girl, and this was no ordinary moment.

"Are *you*?" he asked.

She nodded with a sweet smile, staring into his eyes. He knew what she was searching for: to see if he was present. To see if he was trying to distract himself with *her* presence.

And she was pleased with what she found.

She traced the lines of his face with a gentle, barely there touch. His breath shuddered, surprising him, and he heard her lips curve into another smile before her fingers moved to his hair, running through the strands, nails scraping his scalp until Jin drifted off to sleep.

44

ARTHIE

Arthie tracked the passage of time by the way Laith dozed in and out of sleep in his chair. He barely seemed to notice her, or the black-clad man sitting in the chair and watching them with a stake in hand, slipping into a state of delirium every time he jolted awake before nodding off again. Arthie pretended the same, letting her head loll and hang until the man eventually grunted, drew out his pocket watch, and left, the lock turning behind him.

Laith stirred when the door slammed.

"Casimir," he wheezed.

Arthie toyed with the key in her sleeve. What would she do? Run to him and finish the job? Try to help him? She didn't know what would happen if she touched him.

"You're alive," she whispered, her chains rattling.

He started to laugh but broke into a series of wretched coughs instead. "Don't act so surprised. If you wanted me dead, you would have ensured it."

Matteo had said as much himself. At the time, Arthie had wanted to refute him, but it was true, wasn't it?

There was no telling when the guard might return, so Arthie wasted no time. She finagled her stolen key into the lock, turning until it clicked and the cuffs fell away, dropping her arms. The chain remained locked to the iron ring on the wall, scraping back and forth in her wake.

Laith looked up with a weary chuckle. "There's the Arthie Casimir I know."

She pulled out her pocket watch—it was just pushing dawn. She'd been locked to the wall for hours now. Had Jin met with the Council? Was Flick forging a mask? Had she sent out the false invites to her list of people at odds with Lady Linden?

"I know you hated your king, but I didn't know that extended to the point where you'd sell your kingdom," Arthie snarled to Laith. "Whatever happened to the Ram having too much power?"

"Sell my kingdom? Do I look as though I've gained anything?" he asked. He sounded tired. Empty. There was grime on his fair face, a streak of blood dripping down his brow. "I said nothing, not even when they threatened to desecrate my sister's grave."

"And yet, she walked out of here with Calibore and a plan."

Laith remained quiet, shuffling his hands with a mangled breath.

Arthie scoffed. "Liar. You even told her I was a vampire."

She should have finished the job that night, but some part of her couldn't aim for his heart. He had betrayed her, used her, tried to manipulate her, and yet, there was something more between them. Something that hinted at change, something that had whispered against her skin when he'd touched her oh so tenderly, when he spoke of their shared pasts and sufferings.

Laith lifted his chin and looked into her eyes. For a moment, they were clear of pain. For a moment, they were back on top of the Old Roaring Tower again.

"I had foolishly saved my sister's missives from the king because I couldn't bear to part with them. The Ram found them, ruined them, and then she started interrogating me. By threatening you."

Arthie refused to accept the honesty burning in his gaze.

"You believe me to be lying," he said in defeat.

She laughed without mirth. He was foolish for thinking otherwise. "Forgive me for being unable to trust a word you say."

He looked ashamed. If regret had a portrait beside it in the dictionary, Laith would be the perfect candidate.

But forgiveness, for Arthie, was not an easy thing.

"I know," he ceded. "But I gain nothing from telling you."

She supposed he was right.

"The Ram suspected you were in Ceylan. I told her you'd confided in me otherwise. It didn't take her long to learn I was lying."

"Were you hoping for a thank-you?" she asked. "For me to pull you into my arms for watching over me?"

Laith recoiled as if she'd slapped him.

She walked over to him, staring down her nose to where he was dripping blood, his cuffed hands scraping the back of the chair with his labored breathing. The sound of his exhales, the sight of his skin, those twin flecks above his brow—everything sent her off-kilter. The press massacre felt far away, another time, another her. She blinked, certain this was some strange hallucination.

"Is my cat alive?" he asked.

"And well," Arthie replied. "Her name is Opal now."

Laith laughed. "Flick. She always was concerned that I didn't name her."

But Arthie didn't want small talk. She didn't want his laughter. She didn't want to stand in this room any longer.

"Threatened me how?" she asked suddenly. Laith tilted his head in question. "You said you spoke because the Ram threatened me. How?"

"She was going to turn you into some other type of vampire. I forget the name."

Arthie pinched her lips tight. "Ripper."

Now that the Ram knew Rippers were a result of a mutation and not a serum she had yet to hold in her hands, would she attempt to create them herself? Arthie wondered if that was even a concern she needed to have. The tribute was soon. The Ram had far more to contend with than navigating the difficulties of uncontrollable, insatiable Ripper vampires.

Arthie glanced at the door. She had no lockpick, no Calibore, and there was every likelihood a guard stood on the other side.

"Give me a chance, Arthie," Laith whispered. "Let me prove my worth to you again. I'll help you get Calibore back."

"Why?" she asked, her voice a harsh whisper. She had betrayed him as he had her. Why was *he* so quick to trust *her*? She had nothing left to steal, and she supposed he didn't either.

"And—and then we'll be done. Even," he said, not answering her question.

Just like when she'd saved his life and he'd saved hers. Just like when she'd betrayed him to the Athereum and left him for dead, and he'd done the same to her after she'd bared herself to him and feasted on his blood. Returning to the Athereum hall after she'd sent him away was the final tally that remained. It had resulted in Penn's death. It had resulted in hers.

"Because you need help escaping?" she asked.

He croaked a laugh, panting as he struggled with something behind him. He rapped it on the back of the chair and gestured for Arthie to look. It was a key, and not a small one meant for shackles. "Do I? I took it from the guard who twisted my ear."

There was the Laith Sayaad she knew.

Arthie uncuffed him, ignoring the deep lines the iron had carved into his wrists. His skin was pale. He struggled to his feet, and Arthie heard that wheeze in his breathing that hadn't been there before, likely from the bullet she'd fired into his chest.

She felt sorry for him, though she couldn't summon remorse. He had stared into her eyes, spoken of love, and pulled the trigger on *her* gun. And yet, she could not hate him either. He had been on the path that he was because of his sister. Arthie would have done the same for Jin ten times over.

So why was Laith helping her now?

Arthie didn't know, but she would take every ally in this moment.

45
JIN

When Jin opened his eyes to the dawn sun, he hadn't the faintest clue where he was for a moment. He felt something warm and uneven beneath his head, and then a sound. He looked up—he was in Flick's lap. The night before came rushing back. She was snoring softly, leaning against the headboard and startled awake when he stirred, blinking wearily.

"Hello," she whispered shyly, and Jin remembered her fingers in his hair, coaxing away his sorrows, lulling him to sleep.

"Hello, Flick," Jin replied, and she ducked her head when he said her name. A knock sounded on the door, and the two of them rose as the cot creaked, begging for them to stay.

If only. The tribute was tonight, and Jin had little time to waste.

Matteo was on the other side of the door. He glanced between them dubiously. "I take it you two rested well?"

"We did, actually," Jin said, throwing Flick a wink. She sputtered at the insinuation.

Matteo sighed and turned straight for the corridor without another word.

"See, that's how you deal with nosy people," Jin whispered.

"But he's going to think—I—Jin!" Flick stammered out.

Jin glanced at her sidelong. "Is that a terrible thing?"

She paused because she clearly hadn't considered that. She was still troubled with the whispers high society would toss back and forth while having tea. But Flick didn't have to worry about that anymore.

They had far worse to be concerned about, really.

Ward kept his word, leading them from the tavern without complaint. It was far more tame during the daylight hours, the ruckus replaced with the lonely sound of a mop sopping the wooden floors. After zigzagging their way through the district filled with places just as shabby as The Brooding Turnip, from teetering inns to rotting shops, Ward led them in a direction Jin didn't often frequent: near the academies of White Roaring. The paved walkways were empty here, the schools closed due to the unrest and fear teeming in every shadow. It was a stark contrast to the tavern last night. In many ways.

Was the Ram truly planning to unleash a veritable army of half vampires onto the streets while the rich were safe with her? What did she stand to gain from killing innocents, other than stoking more fear into the very heart of White Roaring?

At last, Ward stopped at a turreted building. It looked like someone's house, not where one would find the Council in charge of electing and discharging a monarch over Ettenia.

"Through there," Ward said. "Be prepared to hand over your calling card."

Jin tightened his fingers around the coin in his pocket.

"Are you sure this is the place?" Flick asked.

Ward tipped his hat, turned, and left.

"Helpful fellow," Jin remarked, and he, Matteo, and Flick walked up the wide steps to the arched door, which opened to the face of a woman as dark-skinned as Flick.

"May I assist you?" the woman asked.

She was wearing a housedress, and the place looked even *more* like a home inside.

Still, Jin held out his coin, and the woman's face changed, features rearranging from *Welcome to my house where I've just made fresh tea!* to *Fill out these forms and I'll take you to the vault.*

She looked from the coin to Jin with a furrow of her brow, then at Matteo and Flick. "Where did you get this?"

She was as surprised as Ward had been, and Jin wondered how few of the coins had truly been made.

"An . . . old friend of the Council's," Jin said.

The woman *hmm*ed but asked no other questions. She took the coin and invited them inside, and Jin held himself still as a piece of his father disappeared into her pocket.

This had better be worth it.

As the woman led them farther into the house, Jin noticed the pieces that made the house homely slowly disappear. The fresh flowers, the blankets, the cozy armchairs. It turned more stately, more distinguished, until the woman stopped before a grand set of doors.

The three of them paused when she swung the doors open and gestured them through. It was as if they'd stepped into a different building altogether. The walls were a washed gray stone. The floors matched, echoing every footstep and sound. Fluted columns rose high to an arching hallway that widened to a domed ceiling looming over a spacious atrium quite like the kind one would find in a university.

At the center was a round table in which seven people sat.

Each of them wore a mask. One of them was still securing it behind their head.

They were gilded, shimmering in antique bronze. Unlike the monarch's, their masks weren't animalistic, but darker. Faces that looked eerie, almost. Beside him, Flick made a sound. They set down their work and fell silent at Jin's approach, Matteo and Flick on his heels.

There were stacks and stacks of paper, ink staining the tables, books lined along the floor. Jin, like many in Ettenia, knew very little about the Council. They appointed monarchs and discharged them, but they did more than that too. They reviewed laws before they were put into action; they monitored the happenings across Ettenia.

"Thank you, Clara," one of them said.

She bowed her head and left without another word.

"State your business," said the mask in the center.

Well, that was a warm welcome. This was already off to a splendid start.

Jin had rehearsed his words, but that didn't stop the rush of uncertainty as they stared at him with cold eyes. He had one shot to convince them, one chance. If he failed, Flick might attempt to forge a mask, but he'd seen how gingerly she held her hands, how difficult it was to hold anything.

Arthie was counting on him. His dead parents were too. *Everyone* was.

"My name is Jin Casimir," he began, and the murmurs were instant. "You may know my sister and me from the tearoom that we once ran, Spindrift."

"Yes. A criminal," one of the Council members said.

Jin laughed softly. "Aren't we all? I'm sure you're aware that the Tribute to the Written Word is tonight."

Seven eerie masks stared back at him, and Jin didn't trust a single one, suddenly grateful he wasn't here alone, acutely conscious of how alone Arthie was in the Ram's underground bunker.

"The Ram wishes to honor the fallen members of the press in the palace, but I was there that night. It was the Ram's very own men who killed them."

Three of the Council members protested his claim.

"If you're alarmed by that," Jin continued over them, "then I'd like to let you know that the Ram is also responsible for the humans disappearing off the streets. She has them caged."

"Caged? That is preposterous," one of them exclaimed.

"Are you blaming the monarch for the actions of rogue vampires?" another countered, parroting the response as if he'd read it off the newspaper folded on his desk.

Jin didn't know how much longer he could tolerate this pretentiousness. "Oh, the Ram's done worse, but you knew that, didn't you? You know what our monarch is capable of, and yet you allow it."

"Do you know who you speak to?" one of the members snapped.

"Do *you* know who you speak to?" Jin asked. "I am the son of Shaw and Sora Siwang. A pair of scientists you once applauded before the Ram stole them away for purposes you blatantly disregarded."

Jin didn't know if his words were true. The Council may well be unaware of the Ram's affairs, but how ignorant could someone so close to the monarch truly be? At some point, one *had* to look the other way to allow such atrocities to continue.

"Words are easy," one of them said. "How are we to believe you are their son?"

Jin was relieved they didn't call his parents traitors. That meant the Ram hadn't fed them that particular lie. Just paces away, Flick wrung her hands, holding herself back from reaching for him.

"I came with a calling card you had given them."

"And are we to believe the word of a boy over the monarch themself?" one asked.

"You don't have to believe me," Jin said. "You can question the

Ram yourself if you'd like. As an Ettenian, my duty lies in telling you, and warning you that worse might happen tonight."

"Tame yourself, Jin," Matteo hissed behind him. The Council members murmured among themselves.

"That sounds quite like a threat," one of them said.

"Precisely," Matteo whispered.

"Or a warning," said another, glancing at his brethren. His mask had beautiful eyes.

"You take the word of a child?" asked another.

"I take the word of a troubled citizen when it concerns his empire."

"And is that why you came?" another asked. There were indents along the bridge of the mask's nose, making it appear as though it was studded in jewelry. "To warn us?"

Jin's head was beginning to hurt.

"To implore you that the Ram is not the person Ettenia needs. We need a new leader. The people are divided, some scared, some brimming with hatred," Jin said. "I want you to demand that the Ram unmasks in front of the audience tonight. If our monarch has no wrongs to keep hidden, it won't be a difficult request to heed."

To say this was faring poorly would be an understatement. Arthie was trusting him. After a decade, she wasn't only trusting him to see this through, she was trusting him with her *life*.

Jin could not fail.

"You've come to ask us to discharge the Ram of their seat of power?" the Council member in the center asked.

Jin could hear the derision in his tone, and he decided then and there that he did not need the Council. He didn't need their snobby words and ridicule. He didn't need Flick hurting herself any further either by trying to forge a mask.

He would be the criminal they said he was. He would steal one.

"I will leave you with one last question: How long will it be before you become the enemy when the Ram tires of demonizing vampires?" he asked, skimming the room while he spoke.

There was a window farther down the wide atrium, tucked between two whitewood bookshelves. The Council was bound to rise from their round table at some point, and Jin had seen one of the members donning their mask only after their arrival. They didn't wear them all the time.

He would sneak in before they left for the tribute and snatch one for himself.

Because he was done trying to appeal to a table of snooty old folks. Jin turned on his heel before they could speak another word. He didn't know if that was how one should *not* leave a high-and-mighty Council, but he certainly hoped they were miffed and disrespected. Matteo and Flick hurried after him, and Jin could hear the Council dispersing in their wake, feet shuffling, voices rising and falling as they likely mocked him behind his back.

"Halt!"

Jin was unsure he'd even heard the voice for how quiet it was. Matteo and Flick hadn't, only realizing when Jin stopped and turned. It was the Council member with the beautiful-eyed mask. The only one who'd spoken somewhat in their favor.

"Are you truly the Siwangs' son?" the man asked, then he tilted his head and stepped closer. "Great seas. You're a spitting image of Shaw, aren't you?"

Jin nodded, wary.

"I gave your father that calling card," the Council member said, tilting their head. It was only then that Jin caught the slight hint of an accent. "Your parents were good people, and I always suspected the Ram had something to do with the fire that burned down their house."

He'd suspected, but had done nothing? Jin bit his tongue against a snide remark.

"I cannot stop the Council from attending the tribute," the Council member continued, "nor can I strip the Ram of power, not unless we are shown tangible proof of the monarch's crimes."

That, Jin could understand. It was why Penn had been moving so slowly—to gather what the Council required would take far too long. And require far too much patience.

Jin found that his own patience was running thin, and there was also the small issue of the longer the Ram remained in power, the higher the dead bodies piled.

"I can, however, aid in your efforts on my own, if your requests are within means. How might I assist you?"

Jin studied him; the eyes that stared back at him through the mask were as dark as Arthie's, the skin the same shade, wrinkles crowding the edges.

"How can we trust you?" Matteo asked.

After a fleeting glance back to the winding walkway, the Council member nudged them to a corner, where he hesitated before deciding upon something.

He removed his mask. "The same way I trust you: out of choice."

He was an older gentleman Jin had never seen before. Nor had Flick or Matteo, by the looks of it. He was brown, possibly from Jeevant Gar or even Ceylan. Jin hadn't expected anyone but a peaky to be on the Council. It gave him hope.

"Are you allowed to show us your face?" Flick asked, aghast.

"No," he said simply. His eyes were a light shade of brown, keen in the shadows. "Nor am I allowed to tell you my name. Rayan. If I were to walk in public, no one would know who I am, but I quite like the idea of three champions allowing me to be a part of their victory."

"We're talking of toppling the Ram," Matteo said carefully, as if the man might have misheard.

"I'm aware, and I ask again. How might I assist you?"

"Well," Jin said, tossing a glance at Matteo and Flick, then down to the mask clutched in Rayan's hand. "Since you insist, there is one thing."

46
ARTHIE

Arthie unlocked the heavy door with the key Laith had lifted and carefully opened it, heart in her throat. She rarely feared for her life, but she felt bare without Calibore, not as whole and not as strong. She imagined Matteo beside her, telling her otherwise.

"Plotting my death?" Laith asked behind her.

"I don't need nearly that much effort," she whispered back. She could hear voices out in the hall.

"I count nine," Laith said, and Arthie scowled when she saw his head peering through the gap above her. She scanned their prison one last time for anything that might aid their escape, but the Ram had left them nothing. No, she'd *taken* from Arthie instead.

With a nod, Laith darted through and flattened himself against the opposite wall beside an open doorway. A light flickered from the sconce above his head, casting a wavering shadow beside where two men were in conversation.

Arthie gestured to his shadow, but Laith was clearly not acting at his finest, for he didn't comprehend quickly enough.

One of the men spotted it.

"Oi, who's there?" the man asked, and Arthie quickly closed the door, leaving it a smidgen open so she could see.

Laith straightened, watching Arthie. The man kept walking toward them, and when he reached the corner, she nodded. Laith swung forward and locked his arm around the man's neck. Arthie rushed into the hall before the other man could shout, throwing a palm strike to his chin and dropping him immediately. He fell with a thud, his deadweight knocking a mug off the counter behind him before Arthie dove and caught it.

"Not bad, Casimir," Laith said, dragging the other man inside. It was a dining space, and together, he and Arthie rolled the men beneath the table, arranging the chairs so that the men were tucked out of sight.

Arthie peered down the corridor. The place was a labyrinth. She couldn't imagine how much time and effort it would have taken to build out such a thing.

"Do you know where any of the rooms are? The exit?" Arthie asked.

"I was dragged around with a sack over my head, so no," he said, but he was an assassin, and a sack over his head shouldn't have hindered the rest of his senses. As if on cue, he continued. "I did enter through the palace doors, however. They took me through to a door in the back, which is connected to the bunker through a tunnel. A long one at that. I'm guessing we're not directly beneath the palace, but the lot beside it."

That was more information than she thought he could provide.

"I came in directly from the outside," Arthie said, gesturing to the right. "Through a carriage park. This way."

Arthie snuck back to the hall, staying close to the wall, Laith on her heels. They tiptoed past a room where a number of the Ram's black-clad forces were meeting in low voices, then another armory-type room with knives lining the walls, which would have been greatly convenient except for the fact that there were people there too.

Laith clutched her arm, holding her in place. She turned her head to him sharply, and he nodded to the large, open chamber up ahead. It was full of black-clad forces. There was no chance Arthie and Laith could sneak past, not without alerting them.

"I came from that end," Arthie whispered. "There's a short stairwell leading to the door."

"We can run for it," Laith suggested, even though he limped with every step. Then he froze, pressing a finger to his lips.

Arthie held herself still. Muffled moans. Stifled cries. They were coming from behind the door across from them. Laith snuck across and tried the handle. Locked. Arthie froze when a grating laugh echoed down the hall, but no one was coming their way.

"Try this," Arthie said, handing him the key for their room. He slid it in. The lock gave way with a quiet click.

They exchanged a look before he carefully turned the handle, keeping sound to a minimum. He disappeared inside. Arthie hurried in after him.

To find a cage.

It was placed front and center in a large room, like an attraction at a circus. Sconces on all four corners of the large room illuminated the silver bars and what was within.

Humans.

Girls, boys, hair hanging in clumps, clothes coated in grime and blood. Some were bleeding and scarred, others bruised. Arthie counted twelve, her pulse rising. Anger burned hot and red behind her eyes. She knew without a doubt that these were the humans the Ram had kidnapped off the streets in the span of a week, claiming it was the work of violent vampires.

They rushed to the bars, screaming behind their bindings, eyes frantic, and when Arthie approached, they began shaking their heads, as if . . . as if warning her.

That was when Arthie registered the other presence in the room. Outside the cage.

"Arthie!" Laith shouted, but it was too late.

Something heavy slammed into the side of her head with a resounding clang, and then her vision went dark.

47

JIN

As far as Jin knew, Arthie was sitting in a chair and keeping a close eye on her pocket watch, awaiting the moment the tribute began and their retribution could finally run its course. But with three hours left, he couldn't let her remain there any longer.

He had detoured to the ledger's hiding place in White Roaring Square with Flick and retrieved it on their way back to the Athereum. It was like a bomb that had turned inert—dangerous and valuable once but fairly useless now. It was written in a cipher, which made it near impossible to be used as evidence in front of the Council, but incredibly of service to Jin and the crew. It had led them to Ceylan and his parents—and the Ram's bunker too.

He tucked the ledger into his vest and smoothed down the lapels of his coat with a sigh. It was his first time dressing for a special occasion since being turned into a vampire, and without a mirror to see himself in, he hadn't the faintest clue how well he was doing.

Nor did he find much joy in wearing a suit as he once did: He'd worn them because of his father. For years, when Jin closed his eyes, he would see his father as he did when he was a little boy, sitting in his study, legs crossed, back straight, jacket crisp.

Now Jin saw his father's glassy eyes and slumped-over form. He saw his dead body.

A knock sounded on the door. It was stilted, like someone was using their elbow instead of their knuckles. He knew exactly who it was, which gave him pause.

"I know you're in there, Jin," Flick said from the other side. "And I—I can help."

"How do you know I need help?" he asked.

She said nothing.

He growled beneath his breath and opened the door. His jaw dropped.

She was wrapped in the most stunning shade of crimson. It was dark and rich, the hue painting a lively flush on her already gorgeous skin. It hugged her chest and middle, the neckline shaped like a heart, cupping her curves while the skirt flowed wide. A necklace was cinched tight around her neck, made of tiny red beads, a rainfall of red along the side of her neck, large jewels hanging off the end of each one. Jin knew what the necklace was meant to represent: blood trickling down the bite of a vampire. It taunted him no differently than the sheen on her lips.

He had grown so accustomed to seeing her in trousers and a shirt that the sight of her in a dress tugged at every fiber of his being.

She was waiting with lifted eyebrows. Somewhere since escaping the prison of Lady Linden's estate, Flick had picked up a good bottle of sass and gulped it in one go.

"Do you approve?" she asked. "There wasn't time for the tailor to make me anything custom."

"Are you aware that we have somewhere to be quite soon, Felicity?" he asked in a slow drawl. "We haven't time to find another bed and get snug."

The way he spoke the words *get snug* made it clear he had no intention of doing anything as sweet as they had the night before.

She swallowed. Jin smirked. Her eyes drifted down his outfit, lingering on his trousers and then his double-breasted ivory shirt and the dark teal tailcoat that tied it all together.

"I see that you didn't need help," Flick said quietly.

"Hmm," Jin drawled. "I wasn't sure I didn't until that reaction, honestly."

She looked like she wanted to throw something at him. "You really are infuriating, did you know?"

He pouted, and she sighed, watching as he ran his fingers through his hair, wishing it was hers again. "Good?"

This time, she smiled softly and replied with a nod.

He held out his arm. "Shall we save my sister and ruin the Ram's night?"

"Please," Flick said.

Out in the hall, Sidharth was already waiting, as was Matteo. Impatiently. He still couldn't find his buttons, it seemed, but his hair was tied neatly at the base of his skull.

"Ready? Good. Let's go," Matteo said. He was holding the Council member's mask in one hand, a bag in the other. A gift for Arthie, he said, as if this were any time for gifting. "What does Arthie usually say? Time for mayhem, charlatans."

"That's not even remotely close," said a new voice. "She's had her tea; now she's out for blood."

The four of them whirled to the hall entrance. A Horned Guard stood by the door, one Jin didn't think he'd ever see again.

"You're alive?" he asked.

"Unlike you," Laith replied.

"I'd almost forgotten how little I like you."

Laith tilted his head. He was panting, bloody and bruised, and his clothes had seen better days. "I am sorry for what transpired that night."

"What happened to you?" Flick asked.

"The Ram," he replied, which was answer enough.

"*You.*"

Matteo stormed past Jin and flung Laith against the wall. The boy was already bleeding, his hair a dull matted mess on his brow. "You killed him."

"And if you don't let me go, the Ram's going to kill Arthie," Laith said.

Matteo dropped him immediately. "What?"

"We were trying to escape and found a cage full of people," Laith said. "They're—"

Flick cut him off. "We know about them. What happened to Arthie?"

"The Ram was in the room too. Preparing something, I don't know."

"Preparing to turn them," Flick answered. "I spoke to two of the girls on the day I escaped."

"And now she can use Arthie to do it," Jin whispered.

Laith looked like he hadn't considered that. "How do you know?"

"I know," Jin said. The Ram was full of twisted ideas, and it was as Arthie said: She wanted to break them. He looked to the time. The tribute didn't begin for another four hours. "We need to go. Show Laith the sketch of the bunker. You, tell us everything you know, and if you think you can lie and get away with it, I will kill you."

"I don't doubt it," Laith said quietly, following them to Matteo's sketches that he'd made using the Ram's terrible artistry and Flick's recollection of the place. "There are two entrances. One here—"

"Where I exited," Flick said. "It leads to the outside."

"And another here," Laith said, pointing to a corner at the top of the other end. "Connecting the palace to the bunker. The door leads to a tunnel, at—"

Matteo didn't move to make note of it. "Forgive me for not trusting a traitor."

Laith crossed his arms. "Am I a traitor if you never trusted me to begin with?"

"And a murderer."

"Aren't we all? The tunnel is at least thirty feet long, and if we enter through the palace, it'll take us close to the room with the cage."

"Us?" Matteo asked. "There is no *us* after what you've done."

"Be that as it may, you haven't seen the bunker to navigate it on your own," Laith said.

Jin shook his head. "We need to get to Arthie before the tribute begins. One, that means there won't be an audience loitering in the gardens for us to use as cover. And two, the palace doors won't be open yet to even access that entrance to the bunker."

"I'll lead us through the other entrance then," Flick said.

"You need to stay safe. Aboveground," Jin said.

Flick furrowed her brow. "No, I do not. I promised the humans I'd be back for them. Even if I hadn't, I'm not letting the rest of you go in there while I sit outside."

Jin wanted to lock her away and keep her safe, but she was right. He had trusted her before; he couldn't stop simply because she was hurt. Flick could handle her own. She *had* handled her own when they were leagues away in Ceylan.

"The Ram's men outnumber us by a large shot," Flick added. "Plus, we have to prepare for the humans to have been turned, and possibly free of the cage. We need all the help we can get. That means Laith's too."

"Very well," Matteo said, the look on his face making it abundantly clear he was ceding only because of her.

"Sidharth, get the assassin armed and cleaned up, please," Jin said. "Your vampires?"

"Thirteen Athereum members were invited," Sidharth said. "A few more managed to get invites through friends and other means, but fewer and fewer of us are able to keep our identities a secret. I have twenty vampires total, nicely polished and dressed for the event."

Twenty powerful Athereum vampires. That was more than Jin thought they would have.

"We'll take two to accompany us through the bunker," Jin said.

Sidharth nodded. "The rest of us will remain aboveground and await the tribute then." He gestured to the hall. "Shall we?"

"What about the Council mask?" Flick asked Jin as Laith and Matteo followed Sidharth out.

Jin turned it over in his hands, running his fingers over the bronze ridges and lines. "It's for Arthie. She deserves to unmask the Ram more than any of us. I just don't know where to put it."

Flick took it from him, lifting the hem of her skirt and securing it beneath the buoyant folds of her dress. She didn't wait for him to turn around. She didn't move to hide every inch of her skin.

Jin averted his gaze from her leg and directed it to her eyes, only to find her already waiting for him. Goodness, this girl. She grinned and held out her arm. "Let's go save your sister."

48

ARTHIE

Arthie's vision blurred when the Ram forced her upright. She swayed, gripping the bars of the cage to remain on her feet. Laith was . . . gone. He had left her. The reverberation of the Ram's strike still echoed through Arthie's core, long after the woman had dropped the metal beam. The girls and boys inside the cage had stopped moving. They looked at Arthie with sympathy, remorse.

For they were in a cage, and Arthie was in front of a gun.

Her gun.

Arthie lifted her eyes from Calibore's barrel to the Ram's eyes that were thrilled behind her gunmetal mask.

"Here I was, ready to turn them into vampires by other means, but you arrived at a most opportune moment," the Ram said.

Other means? Opportune moment?

"Turn?" Arthie asked. The Ram had kidnapped them under the guise of blaming vampires, but she was going to turn them herself? How did she even plan to turn them?

One of the girls shook free of the rope binding her mouth.

"She's going to set us loose on—" she started to shout.

A gunshot cut her short. She fell in a lifeless heap.

For an eternal moment, Arthie hung suspended in disbelief at the sight before her. The girl was . . . dead. The Ram *shot* her.

The air rushed from the room. Blood sprayed everywhere. The

remaining eleven girls and boys screamed, the sounds muffled by their bindings.

"You killed her," Arthie whispered.

"What's one less?" the Ram asked, and then turned Calibore around and held it out to her. "You asked me what's in it for you, so here is my offer: I'll give you Calibore if you turn each and every one of them."

Arthie looked at the humans. They weren't dying. They weren't anywhere near death. Turning them now would mean turning them into half vampires. Like the Wolf of White Roaring. Like Arthie. The Ram wanted vampires that were powerful, difficult to control, yet still thwartable, unlike the Ripper vampires on Ceylan.

Calibore for a small army of half vampires.

A small army for a piece of Arthie the Ram had stolen and dared to flaunt.

Arthie couldn't pretend now. She couldn't stifle her anger anymore. There was blood on her clothes. The blood of an innocent girl who tried to warn her. It was on her lip, luring her, coaxing her for a taste.

The Ram saw.

"Unless that deal includes shoving the barrel down your throat, I'll pass," Arthie said.

The Ram smiled and fired Calibore again.

49

JIN

Jin had never been to the Ettenian palace. He'd walked the street outside the palace on errands at times, but rarely and only when it couldn't be avoided, for it reminded him of his father. Shaw Siwang would often recount tales of the times he and Jin's mother had visited the halls, experiencing the extravagance as they'd sipped tea with the Eagle.

Never again, because of a choice the Ram made.

One she would pay for—not for Jin's own sake, really, but because it was what his parents were owed after what she'd done to them. He didn't realize his hands had begun to shake until Flick reached over and gripped them in hers, tightening her fingers through his. He squeezed back, forcing himself to remain present.

As they neared the palace, the dim, gaslit streets turned brighter, packed with throngs of people walking to the gardens before the still-closed doors. Carriages trotted away after dropping off their hires. Laughter echoed with hushed voices. The mood wasn't as somber as Jin would have expected.

"So much for arriving early," Matteo murmured.

"This is good," Jin said. "Plenty more cover for us."

The palace sat on a slight hill, sprawling with poise, its turreted spires matched by the intricate corbels, accents as dark as the night sky, lending an eerie, sinister air to the place. Still, opulence oozed from every inch, and Horned Guards were everywhere. Set beneath an arch carved with thick florals, the double doors were closed, but they looked familiar somehow.

"Do those not remind you of the one from the sanitorium?" Matteo remarked.

That was it. Odd.

The carriage rumbled to a stop beside a long line of others, and Jin leaped out, umbrella clutched in one hand, the other checking on the two knives he had tucked away. There would be no guns tonight, for stealth was of utmost importance. He helped Flick down, careful not to put pressure on her hands and arms. "Are you sure you're up for this?"

Flick nodded, her sunflower eyes intent. It was less of a decision for her, and more of a need, Jin realized. She would not allow her mother to think she had won in any regard.

"This is it," Laith said, his hair damp from a quick shower—so quick, he had missed an entire streak of blood. Two of the Athereum vampires joined him, burly men in fitted tweed frock coats. The six of them made their way up the gravel pathway that wound around the palace until they reached a short wall with a hatch-like door set into a square of concrete in the winter-stiff grass.

"There it is," Flick said.

"That tiny thing?" Matteo asked.

Flick nodded. "It will take us to the bunker."

"—And she had the gall to wear such a thing to *my* dinner function," a woman said as she passed with another, and the six of them straightened as though they were having a frivolous conversation of their own.

Goodness. The snobbery of high society was a level not even vampires possessed.

The moment they passed, Jin dropped to his knees as the others covered him. He pulled out his lockpick. There was no turning back now.

50

FLICK

Flick wanted to be strong. She *was* strong, but fear ricocheted through her like an errant bullet the moment she stepped through the bunker door ahead of the others. The air was different from when she'd first arrived. Outside, it thrummed with excitement at the festivities. In here, it was frantic and anxious. Even the Ram's men were afraid.

Understandably, Flick supposed, seeing how swiftly the Ram disposed of them. She wished she could sit them down and ask what the Ram had in store, but something told her not even they were fully aware.

Flick paused at the corner with Jin. Laith and Sidharth's vampires followed close, Matteo taking up the rear and still unhappy to have the high captain along. Flick peered around the corner, half expecting to see the Ram on the other side, blue eyes waiting. She wasn't there. Her men, by contrast, were everywhere, clothed in black, armed to the teeth. Many wielded machetes. Others marched with knives strapped across their chests.

"This way," she said.

"The Ram might still be in the room with Arthie and the others," Laith murmured. He was dressed in dusky dark-blue robes that she didn't know where he'd found.

"Let's hope not," Jin replied as they crept along the shadows. He tilted his chin. "Two men ahead."

Laith nodded and sprinted forward, dropping one with a blade through his throat and another with an arm around his neck. Flick held her breath tight and opened the door to a storeroom beside her. Sidharth's vampires dragged the two men inside, but not before Laith dug through their pockets, rising with a smug smile and a ring of keys.

"Oi!"

Footsteps pounded toward them, and a knife arced toward one of Sidharth's men, tearing through his coat, the blade sinking down to its hilt.

Flick covered her mouth against a scream, but the vampire only stared at the torn fabric and growled, grabbing his assailant with both hands and throwing him into the storeroom too, where he hit his head against the wall and fell without another twitch.

That was one way to do it.

The amount of blood and carnage Flick had seen since leaving the Linden estate was a comical contrast to the occasional papercut she'd dealt with before. She focused on putting one foot in front of the other. For Arthie. For the girls and boys locked in that cage. For taking down the Ram.

"Which way?" Jin asked.

"Straight ahead," Flick said as Matteo pulled the storeroom door closed behind them. The five of them moved with a fluidity Arthie would appreciate, quick and soundless, outside of Flick's hem whispering with her every step.

Flick led them through corridors and shadowed walkways until they reached a large hall, the one where she'd seen that calendar, and felt her heart drop.

It was not empty.

"The cage is in the room just on the other side," she whispered.

"Past an awful lot of men," Jin murmured.

"We can handle them," Laith said.

"Give me the keys," Flick said. "I'll get to Arthie and the others."

Jin glanced at her, concern etched into his features. He clearly wanted to do nothing of the sort, at war with not wanting to treat her any differently. She saw Matteo's discreet nudge, his nod, and then Jin reluctantly handed her the keys. He met her eyes, and though he said nothing, she heard his words: *Be careful. Stay safe.*

Flick didn't know if she imagined more than that in the heat of his gaze.

He adjusted his grip on his umbrella, pulling a knife from his coat and turning to the hall full of the Ram's forces. "Wait until they're distracted."

With a nod, Laith moved first, tearing like a whip into the room, felling four in one smooth dance before he was noticed. Shouts rang out. Black-clad figures leaped to attention, weapons drawn, but Jin and the others were faster. They rushed in, the Athereum vampires using their size to their advantage while Matteo clawed his way through. Jin threw up his umbrella as a shield—and a guide—drawing men to his knife as Laith did the same with his gauntlet blades. Men fell. Knives clashed. Somehow, Matteo kept his shirt clean.

Flick wasted no time. She raced across the hall, breath held to listen for any sign of the Ram on the other side. She heard nothing but muffled cries and sobs. The girls and boys. Were they still human or had they been turned?

It took three tries before Flick found the right key in the heavy ring Laith had pilfered, doing her best to ignore the pain still throbbing through her arms, weighing her muscles with infuriating fatigue.

With one last look down the hall, Flick turned the handle, and the door creaked as if in warning. It took several seconds before Flick made sense of the sight in front of her.

Her heart halted, stuttered, and despite her every attempt to remain quiet, she could not. She screamed.

51
JIN

Jin ducked as the whisper of metal sang by his ears. The machete swung for him again, arcing toward his nose. He threw up his arm, knowing he couldn't move fast enough, bone-chilling dread washing through him before the man dropped like a sack.

Laith was standing behind him, blades dripping blood.

And in that split second, Jin's limbs froze as a new sound rocked him to his core.

Flick's scream.

"Go!" Laith shouted. Jin didn't need to be told twice. He ran from the fight, slamming his umbrella into the knees of one more attacker before he tumbled into the hall. Flick was frozen at the door. She was unharmed, which meant Arthie—no.

Jin refused to finish that thought.

He pushed past Flick, and his brain registered everything in parts. The cage was even more sickening in person, as wide as the ones the circus sometimes flaunted with trapped tigers. Blood drenched the silver rods and the floor around it.

Girls and boys were inside, begging through bindings around their mouths, reaching out between the bars. The Ram was nowhere to be seen, but Arthie was there.

Oh, Arthie was there, all right.

Seated in the middle of the cage. Coated in blood.

"She's—she's—" Flick stammered.

"She's alive," Jin assured her. He didn't know how his voice sounded as stable as it was. "Give me the keys, love."

He pried them from Flick's white-knuckled hands. Inside the cage, he counted nine others, each giving Arthie a wide berth.

Because there were three dead bodies around her.

A roar broke the hushed quiet—Matteo. He shoved past Jin to the bars. "Arthie? Arthie look at me." His fangs were extended, his claws sharp. He looked at the people in the cage. "What happened to her? Oi! Did you not hear me? Speak!"

The captives stared with wide eyes. They were still bound; they couldn't speak if they wanted to.

"Matteo, stop shouting at them!" Flick cried.

Jin tried key after key. None of them fit. He threw the ring aside and drew out his lockpicks, working the lock until it finally snapped open. Jin swung the door wide. The hinges groaned. The caged girls and boys didn't move, frozen in fear.

Matteo only saw Arthie.

"You came," she whispered.

He rushed inside, dropping in front of her, running his hands over her face, her neck. He was looking for a bullet hole, for the jagged edge of a stake. "Laith found us. Are you hurt?"

Arthie shook her head. "She's coming back. I need to turn them for Calibore. I need to turn them so they'll live. She—she took Calibore and shot them." Her voice was a rough, broken whisper. "I didn't do it."

She was staring at the dead. Two girls, one boy. Three bodies. And Jin knew she wasn't here in the cage anymore, no. She wasn't in the bunker, or even White Roaring. She was a young girl adrift at sea, in the little boat that was no different than a cage, surrounded by the bodies of the three people she had mutilated.

Arthie might not have killed them, but in her mind, she had.

"She's not going to kill them," Jin said. "We're getting them out before she returns."

And for that, they needed to move quickly.

"Calibore," she kept saying over and over, barely acknowledging their presence.

Matteo helped her to her feet. "We'll get Calibore back. Right now, we need you." He paused, looking at the captives, but Flick handed him the Council mask.

"We'll take care of them," she said softly. "You need to get her masked and ready for the tribute."

"Laith, cover their exit," Jin said when the Arawiyan stumbled inside the room. He nodded, leading Arthie and Matteo away.

Arthie looked small. Like the child she had never been allowed to be because of the Ram. Because of the EJC.

"Jin," Flick murmured, brushing his arm.

He nodded. Right. They had work to do.

Flick turned back to the cage. The captives regarded her warily, and Flick lifted her arms, as if to show them she was unarmed.

"I promised I'd come back for you," she said gently. "And I did. We're here to get you to safety."

Jin was yet again amazed at how a woman like the Ram raised a girl like Flick, whose very nature was nurturing, kind. Caring.

"Were any of you turned?" she asked.

The girls and boys shook their heads, sharing glances that made it clear they feared more than once that they had been close.

"There's nothing wrong with being turned, but never against one's will," Flick said.

She didn't care about the hem of her gown soaking up the blood in the cage. She didn't care that there were dead bodies mere feet away from her; Flick climbed into the cage and began untying their bindings, freeing their arms first before the ropes around their mouths.

Jin moved to help, approaching them as carefully as one would a spooked animal, even as every inch of him itched to hurry, to check on Arthie, to rush back to the palace gardens in time for the doors to the tribute to open.

"The Ram," one of the girls whispered. "The Ram will come back for us."

"We're going to get you out before that," Jin said. "You don't know me—"

"I do," one of the boys said. His voice rough from unuse. "My sister fancied you years ago." He stopped to hack a dry cough, and Flick looked around for water, coming up short. "You're that Casimir bloke."

Jin held back a groan, certain he knew where this was going. Now wasn't the time to get a beating for breaking a girl's heart, but was there ever a right time?

The boy narrowed his eyes at Jin. "Eh, he's all right. I say trust him."

Flick hid a smile but hurried them out of the cage. "The Ram's having a party aboveground, which will give you the perfect cover to escape."

The group looked at one another, skeptical.

"Just like that? And go home?"

Jin hadn't thought that far, but an idea struck right away. "I have a friend waiting by the palace gates."

"He will take you to the Horned Guard headquarters," Flick said. "Where you can tell them what the Ram did to you. Because right now, the city thinks vampires are responsible for your disappearances."

The girls and boys conferred among one another.

"No one will believe that," one of the boys said, and Jin understood why he spoke with ironclad conviction: They had lived their own lives believing vampires were at fault for everything. It was their first time standing on the other side of it.

"They will soon enough," Flick promised, locking eyes with Jin. "We're going to make sure of it."

52

ARTHIE

The bodies of the three captives were seared in Arthie's mind. It was one thing to know what the Ram was capable of, to see the effects of her monstrosity in the very bones of society, but it was another to witness it confined in so small a space, diluted to the essence of what the Ram was: evil.

Those three shots rang out in her ears over and over again, even as Matteo snuck her to an empty storeroom and locked the door shut. It was a narrow, musty space, lit only by the lantern he had grabbed on their way in and set on a barrel of what seemed to be gunpowder.

Arthie wanted to tell him they didn't have to worry about the Ram now. She was out there, readying to meet her handpicked audience, masking her identity, masking her cruelty, masking away the heinous person that she truly was.

In the dark, Arthie saw the pleading in the captives' eyes. She heard the girl's warning, cut short by a gunshot. Calibore's bullet, the pistol gripped tight in the Ram's hand.

Arthie might as well have done it. Shot and killed three innocents in cold blood. And unlike the first time she'd slain three, she was lucid and sober, not inebriated by half vampirism.

"Arthie," Matteo said softly. She lifted her eyes to his. "It wasn't you. Those dead bodies inside that cage? It wasn't you."

"It may as well have been," Arthie whispered. "Why do you think the Ram put me in there? She was waiting for me to succumb."

The Ram didn't know what Arthie had done as a child fleeing Ceylan, but she had seen the way Arthie's body reacted to that spray of blood before she'd made that decision. She had assumed in a strange way that vampires were perpetually hungry—she had asked Arthie as much in the carriage.

Matteo pursed his lips. "Then she sorely underestimated you, but then again, she always has, no?"

It was true, Arthie wasn't new to being underestimated. She was, however, new to being so thoroughly understood. She wrenched her gaze away from his. The room seemed to shrink, the distance between her and him taut, suddenly abuzz.

"Remember when I said I held your heart?" Matteo asked. "It's how I know your strength. She can't break you."

He was waiting for a response, so she managed a nod, a trill shooting through her at his pleased smile. He licked his thumb and wiped a smudge of blood from her chin, the lantern drawing him in sharp relief. His hair was knotted at the base of his skull. She liked when he wore it that way. She liked when he wore his specs too, which she'd learned he actually needed for reading but didn't always wear because he clearly thought them ugly. He was still dressed like a rogue, despite being in a palace, and he still couldn't find his buttons. How he'd managed to keep the white of his elegant shirt spotless would remain a mystery.

"You're right," she said with a sigh.

"I usually am, darling," he drawled.

She rose and winced at the squelch of blood. "I'm not exactly presentable for a tribute, though." She spotted a rag on the barrel beside the lantern, and wiped the last of the blood from her hands. "It'll have to do. I'm sure the Ram will understand."

"You must know by now that I'm a man who takes care of his woman," Matteo said grandly.

Arthie lifted an eyebrow. "Am I your woman now?"

He said nothing as he handed her a bag, narrow and dark. It was wrinkled from being tucked into the waistband of his trousers. Arthie took it and waited for an explanation, but when he remained quiet, she glanced inside to see something in purple—no, gray. She tilted it to the storeroom light.

It was mauve, the color of her hair, in a fabric she recognized.

"A sari," Arthie whispered.

"You've never once skimped on appearances. The woman at Hira House had your measurements from the last time you ordered and assured me this was the latest style."

Arthie couldn't contain her shock. "You went to Hira House."

"Of course. We're exposing the Ram, and I know you like your statements."

Arthie gave him a look, because *he* was the one who cared about making a statement. It was stunning, the fabric lustrous and silky.

"*Plus* it's your color, *and* it has pockets."

"Pockets?" Arthie asked, unsure how such a thing could exist on a sari.

Matteo nodded, utterly pleased. It was almost endearing.

"Thank you."

The words were foreign in her mouth, like she was attempting to talk through a mouthful of stones. She meant them though. It *was* her color. She had chosen red for her sari for the Athereum meeting to match the one her mother had worn to her death, and it had become Arthie's death shroud in turn.

But this—Arthie opened the bag and pulled it out. This was hers and hers alone.

She had almost decided to never wear a sari again, but that was wrong of her. She was Ceylani. She would be Ceylani forever—as Ceylani as she was Ettenian, which was a strange thought when she'd lived her years thinking she could be only one or the other.

And a sari was exactly what this Ettenian vicennial and tribute required.

Matteo turned away to give her privacy, and Arthie bit her cheek, wondering what would happen if she asked him to turn back around. If she were to ask him to help her undress. She couldn't fathom saying anything of the sort, but it was quite the thought to have when one was cold.

Arthie made quick work of donning the sari, emptying what little she had in her pockets and transferring it to the far smaller ones. It felt even more luxurious on her body, the fabric a decadent weight as she gathered it around herself, adjusting it several times to align the pockets just right, the mauve turning iridescent in the light. It felt like petals brushing her skin, like kisses whispering against every inch of her.

Matteo inhaled sharply, and the sound shot straight to her core.

"You look—"

"Don't say pretty," Arthie said.

"Don't insult my creative prowess," Matteo said with a sniff. But she didn't need to hear his words to know what he thought of her. It was written clearly in his green eyes. "I have not wished to paint for a long while now, but I would love nothing more in this moment."

She smiled and couldn't think of what to say, shocking herself with her own shyness.

"No response?" he asked. "Have I thwarted the great Arthie Casimir again?"

"What am I supposed to say? I would pull off a heist for you if it meant you were the prize?"

He laughed. A full-bodied laugh that Arthie had never once heard from him before. He threw back his head, fangs in full display, throat like that of a sculpted statue. And the sound—goodness, the sound of his laugh was enough for a vampire to subsist upon for a century.

Arthie didn't want to leave. She didn't want reality to rush back into their lives, and it was a harrowing realization: She wanted to live. If only for a day, if only for a moment. She had spent so many years tied up in her need for vengeance, in her need to keep Spindrift running, in her need to keep her head held high in a country that wanted to squash her.

She hadn't known how truly tired she had become.

Matteo stepped close to her, glancing from his outfit to hers. "We make a good pair, you and I."

"Oh, do we?" she asked.

"Dashing and deadly," Matteo said with a nod, the motion rubbing his arm against her bare skin. He noticed. "Oh, my apologies." He pulled away. "Here, this would be better."

And he lowered his lips to the hollow of her shoulder without warning.

Arthie drew in an unsteady breath. Matteo's mouth curved against her skin, and she felt the tip of his tongue, just barely, as if he wanted to taste her but wasn't sure he'd like it.

But he did. He straightened with a lazy grin and hooded eyes. She knew he did.

Arthie locked her hands at the nape of his neck and tugged him toward her. He offered no resistance, his nose brushing hers, the soft strands of his hair teasing her brow, his lips soft and insistent on hers.

He pulled back. "Not yet. I see the light at the end of the tunnel, darling."

"And then?" she asked, her lips abuzz.

"And then it'll be an eternity of you and me," he said, and pursed his lips. "Jin and Flick too, I suppose. We'll open a new Spindrift, half bloodhouse, half tearoom, both at once. Because you really ought to give your employees the nights off."

Arthie laughed at that.

Matteo handed her a mask and the folded cloak tucked in its recess.

"Flick did it," Arthie said. "And very well at that."

Matteo shook his head, the light disappearing from his eyes. "The Ram ruined her hands. She can't forge."

Flick couldn't forge. The Ram had gone out of her way to hurt each of them in any way she could. Arthie's anger spiked in her blood once again.

"Indeed," Matteo said, noticing. "Jin attempted to sweet talk his way into the Council members' hearts, but he wasn't in the greatest of spirits himself, and they weren't very receptive. One of them was fond of his parents, however. That's his mask."

Arthie flipped the mask over in her hands.

"Am I right to assume Flick didn't forge the invites, then? I never had the chance to ask."

"She did not."

Arthie would have been irritated once, annoyed at a failed task, but she couldn't summon those emotions now. Those emotions felt *wrong* now. She nodded. They would manage. They had to. The Ram had ruined far too much for them not to win.

She pulled the cloak over her shoulders and tossed her hat with the pile of her ragged clothes before twisting her hair into a bun. If she had Calibore, she would turn it into her bladed hairpin and hold the errant swoops in place.

"I still can't believe she was trying to send an army of half vampires out on the streets," Matteo said.

"On the streets?" Arthie asked.

"So I assumed," Matteo said. "Where else? Monarchs have long celebrated vicennials to rekindle support and commendations. Why wait until the tribute when the upper echelon is safe in her palace if not to unleash onto the streets half vampires who will cause the chaos she needs to gain the favor of those people of importance?"

Where else indeed.

53

FLICK

Though the night was cool, Flick was anything but. She had stepped free of the bunker, but still saw the trembling shoulders of the kidnapped girls and boys. She saw Arthie covered in blood. The very smell of the bunker—a little damp, a little earthy—made her limbs throb as if she were trapped inside that room again.

She took a fortifying breath and turned to the guests loitering in the gardens. Flick knew some of them from debutant balls, others from meetings with Lady Linden. None of them paid Flick any attention, and she was intent on keeping it that way.

She wished she had been able to forge those invites for Arthie, but she was surprised to find two of the lords she had wanted to invite stepping through the gates. *Strange*. Why would the Ram invite people she disliked to a vicennial? Then again, the Ram didn't know Arthie planned to unmask her.

The palace loomed, stunning even beneath the moonlight. It was nowhere near the dark opulence of the Athereum. Where the vampire society was sultry and sensuous in comparison, the palace stood sinister. As if evil was what held the bricks together. The suffering of others, from the vampires of White Roaring to the colonies across the sea.

Flick had never seen the inside of the palace, despite her mother wearing the mask of Ettenia. Family rarely had a place in the monarchy when the identity of their rulers was a secret.

With Laith and Jin, Flick had escorted the captives to one of the Athereum carriages, thankful for the darkness that shielded them from view. Flick didn't want to let them go on their own, but Sidharth assured them the driver would escort them himself to the Horned Guard headquarters.

There was always the concern that the guards wouldn't believe the voice of the victims, but once the crew unmasked the Ram and bared her sins to the capital's elite and the Council alike, the Horned Guard would understand. Flick and Jin would go there themselves and ensure it after, if they had to.

When the Old Roaring Tower rang in the hour, Flick was alone. Jin had rushed back to help Matteo and Arthie. Laith was with Sidharth, discussing their plan of attack. The palace doors swung open, groaning with a sense of finality. A buzz rose from the guests, and they began migrating inside.

Though this was a tribute and supposedly a more somber affair, the air was no different than a lavish ball. Flick didn't blame the attendees as much as the Ram who had decided a celebration was in order when throngs of the press had died—mutilated and butchered in their pursuit of the truth.

Calling it a tribute was a cruel joke. It was a vicennial through and through.

The walls oozed opulence, and the more Flick looked, the more she noticed her mother's touch—the *Ram's* touch—throughout. It felt like she was in the Linden Estate again.

Some of the guests had gathered in groups, some drifted on their own, others in pairs. The Athereum vampires dispersed into the crowd, exchanging nods and pleasantries. They were stunning as ever, well-dressed and elegant. Flick thought it strange that the very people who turned their noses up at vampires greeted them by all but slobbering. Then again, that was what people across White Roaring did to Matteo too.

A stage was erected up ahead, and several chairs fanned out behind a podium. *For the Council.* Dread coiled tight in Flick's belly, knotting itself over and over with each passing breath.

A string quartet began to play, and several of the ladies near her commented on the Ram's choice in music. There were lords dabbing at their lips after sampling the night's nibbles, and couples already gossiping about other couples. A familiar bronze glint caught her eye, and Flick peered through the mingling crowd and saw one of the members of the Council.

They'd arrived.

"Hello, Felicity," a voice said.

She turned in a panic and slammed into a warm, solid chest. "Jin!"

"Did I do something wrong?" he asked, pulling away.

"I—no! I didn't realize it was you."

"Ah, yes, my voice does sound different when I'm among the rich. The disgust is harder to keep at bay."

"I'm being quite serious. Where's Arthie?"

"Arthie is fine. She'll be here, worry not. The Ram's men might come looking any minute now, but it'll be a decent while before they find me," he said, and then he tilted his head.

"What?" she asked, suddenly shy.

"This feistiness is a good look on you," he whispered, and a lord and lady nearby began to point at their closeness.

Flick seized up, her spine going rigid. She struggled to calm herself down. She didn't need to worry about rumors spreading or her mother getting angry.

Jin ran his hands up and down her gloved skin until her breathing slowed and then quickened for another reason entirely. It was a welcome distraction from the nosy guests and the evening to come, for the last time she was dressed just as lovely, the floor ended up covered in blood.

Voices dropped to hushed tones, silence weaving like smoke through the White Roaring clouds as the Ram appeared. She walked to the podium, her footsteps ringing sharply on the lacquered stage. Her mask gleamed in the light of the many chandeliers, figure obscured by her cloak.

She rang a small, tinkling bell, as if every eye wasn't already upon her.

"Welcome, my friends," the Ram said. "Thank you for taking time to attend this tribute on the night of my vicennial. I understand that this is a most daunting time for us, and yet you braved the deadly streets."

Deadly because *she* made it so, Flick wanted to tell them. Beside her, Jin scoffed too.

"Two weeks ago, charlatans attempted to disrupt our peace," the Ram said. As she spoke, one by one, the Council members began to take their seats behind the Ram, including the mask with the beautiful eyes.

"Is that . . . ," Flick began.

"Yes," Jin murmured. He felt a spike of pride as he watched Arthie join the six others with her borrowed mask, a black cloak shrouding her attire and figure at once.

Nearby, tucked away from the rest of the Council's view between guests, Jin spotted Rayan, the man whose mask Arthie now wore. He gave Jin a slight nod.

"They gathered our finest reporters," the Ram continued, "men and women dedicated to the truth of our flourishing, growing empire. Perhaps they were jealous. Perhaps they feared our success. Whatever the reason, they sought to cause chaos, and so they did. They marched into our meeting hall and slaughtered them. I'm lucky to have escaped with my life."

Flick held back her scoff.

"Who did it?" someone asked in a nasally voice.

"Vampires, of course, with their human underlings. The sort threatened by our stature, for they do not realize that the victory of one class is a victory for each and every one of us. But the sacrifice of our brave pensmiths was not in vain," the Ram continued. "We will usher in a new time for Ettenia, a new age."

A hum echoed through the crowd, rife with excitement.

That was when Arthie stood.

54

ARTHIE

Arthie's heart was in her throat when she stood with the cool, bronze mask over her face, her shoulders squared. Beside her, the Council members asked if something was amiss. The Ram was barely feet away, basking in the cheers of her people. What did they cheer for? The Ram had promised nothing tangible.

Arthie, on the other hand, would give them something tangible. She took two steps toward the Ram, her hands inching higher and higher.

Until she froze.

For the Ram rang that bell one more time, ensuring every single errant eye was on her.

Then she reached behind her head and removed the mask of the Ettenian monarch herself, dropping her cloak in one fell swoop, and revealing her identity as Lady Linden to each of her handpicked guests.

55

ARTHIE

Arthie had known since she'd met Flick that Lady Linden cared deeply for her image. Arthie had counted on that, counted on high society to shun her, destroy her, and ultimately force her to step down from the role of monarch.

She never once imagined an outcome in which the Ram would unmask herself.

The Ram had to know her guests wouldn't applaud her. Arthie could already hear the whispers of shock and dismay, which meant the Ram could too.

Is that—dear me, that's Linden! Of the EJC!
Hold on a moment now! It's no surprise my requests were denied.
That's *why Elizabeth was turned away. Linden never did like us.*
Now we know why our contract ended shortly after her coronation.

Scorn heated the room more than the Ceylani sun ever could. Whispers began to mount. In the stirring crowd, Jin and the others looked as confused as Arthie felt. Why would a woman obsessed with her image, a woman consumed by the public's view of her, do such a thing before an entire class of people?

Arthie thought of the common criminals who ran the streets while masked, only ever removing them for one reason. She thought of the moment in the carriage when she had asked the Ram how she kept the ruse for twenty years, splitting her identity as two powerful Ettenian figures.

She killed the ones who knew.

Matteo was wrong, the Ram hadn't meant to unleash an army of half vampires onto the streets. She had meant to unleash them *here*. It was as the lords and ladies claimed: Every contract went to the EJC. The Ram didn't need them any more than she needed the Council seated behind her.

But would the Ram go to such lengths?

In answer, her black-clad forces sealed the doors closed, and only then did Arthie realize they were quite like the vault-like door they'd encountered in Ceylan. But the crowd was too caught up in the Ram's reveal to pay attention to their surroundings—and really, when *did* the rich pay attention to anything but their own person? They thought themselves as immortal as vampires.

Arthie watched as the Ram lifted her little bell and rang it again—three short bursts in a row. That wasn't an attempt at getting attention.

It was a signal.

But there was one large problem with her plan: Her vampires would not come. Jin and Flick had freed the captives before they could be turned. Before *Arthie* could be forced to turn them.

"It seems we truly are quite similar," Arthie said behind her, removing her borrowed mask and dropping her cloak. The Ram didn't look shocked in the slightest, almost as though she had expected Arthie to be here. The Council gasped, several of them scolding her as if she were a child.

The lords and ladies recognized her in an instant.

That's the Casimir girl.

The one who ran that tearoom!

Spindrift?

Slowly, quietly, the Ram's men inched toward the guests. They were being careful. They wouldn't risk a stampede or a mob. Sidharth and the Athereum vampires saw, vigilant as they were, for they knew what it was like to live ever aware of one's surroundings.

"Are we?" the Ram asked her.

Arthie ignored her. She didn't know how much time they had before the men convened and chaos descended, but she intended to make the most of it. She shoved a finger in the Ram's direction.

"You see what you trusted for a vicennial?" Arthie asked the guests. "Do you see what she's done over the past twenty years and beyond? You came here to honor the fallen members of the press, but like the Ram's identity, she lied about the true perpetrators: It was her and her men."

The shouts settled to an awful quiet. Whispers swirled through the people. They lowered the flutes in their hands. There were more of the Ram's men now, despite the closed doors. Were they coming through the tunnel? The room was a powder keg, waiting to explode.

"Is this true?" one of the Council members asked behind the Ram.

The Ram, unmasked and unchecked, didn't look fazed or caught. She didn't look trapped in that moment, nor the slightest bit defeated because of her missing would-be half vampires. There was a calm about her, one that sent Arthie's thoughts into a sudden frenzy.

"Do you remember, Casimir, when I told you my only wish was that the Siwangs had found a cure for the Ripper mutations? I decided I can make do without. A pity you didn't see them when you were underground."

The Ripper mutations.

The Ram—the Ram had Ripper vampires underground. No. Unstoppable, unkillable Ripper vampires. How had she created them when Shaw had been so certain it wasn't possible? That didn't matter now. Ripper vampires were *here. Now.* That meant the caged humans were no more than a distraction from her real weapon.

Arthie didn't even try to contain her shock.

"Don't do this," she said. "They will kill everyone. They will not stop."

They would never stop.

The Ram ignored her. She rang her bell again. Twice this time. The crowd held their breath, looking to Arthie with growing panic. And in the deathly silence, Arthie thought she heard glass shattering.

Like the cylinders the Siwangs had used to contain the Rippers.

That was when Arthie realized it: The Ram didn't need a way to control the Rippers, only a way to stop them. In this case, the doors, the very same from the sanitorium on Ceylan. The walls were already fortified—it was a palace after all.

No, this was no longer a palace. It was a fortress. And the Ram was going to kill everyone inside: every last lord, lady, and Council member present.

56
ARTHIE

Arthie had always thought the monarchs of Ettenia held too much power, for she had only ever seen the Ram's rule, but the Council was not pleased by her antics.

"Who are these people?" asked one of the Council members, seeing the encroaching line of black. It was a testament to how little they knew of what happened on the streets.

"Mercenaries," another said. "After we limited her manpower."

"First you press for the colonies, now we find out you're running a monopoly?" a third thundered. Of course that was more concerning than colonization.

The Council was confused, but one thing was clear: The Ram had gone to great lengths to get her way. She had lied to the Council, she had lied to her people, but it appeared she had grown tired of working around both.

She wanted to rule supreme. To stand as Ettenia's dictator.

How better than by removing the ones who stood in the way of that? And she was going to use the Ripper vampires to do it.

Arthie raced off the stage and into the panicked crowd, finding the others. Matteo, Jin, Flick and Laith lingered with the crowd, wide-eyed and confused. "She was never going to use the half vampires. She's using Rippers."

"Rippers?" Jin asked. "*Here?*"

Arthie pushed past them in the direction of the interior bunker entrance. "Get to the bunker. They're underground."

"For what? We can't fight them, Arthie," Matteo said.

"We'll have to think of a way—now, everyone, move!"

Shaw had a fail-safe. It had died with him. Arthie didn't have Calibore to slow them down. Around them, the Ram's forces were pressing closer, tangible black shadows creeping to the gaudy, eye-catching gowns and sleek attire of the rich. The Athereum vampires were too, waiting for their enemies to make the first move.

Arthie wove her way through the guests, ignoring any who tried to stop her. She didn't have time to answer their frantic questions, not if she wanted to keep them alive. She stumbled through the rabble of the rich and reconvened with the others just outside the din.

"There might be a chance the Rippers are still in their cylinders. Can we stop them from opening?" Matteo asked.

"The tunnel," Jin exclaimed. "If we can collapse it while the Rippers are trying to escape, we can bury them. They might not die, but it will at least buy us time to get everyone out of the palace."

"Collapse it, how?" Matteo asked.

"Dynamite," Flick and Laith said at the same time. Laith gestured for her to continue. "There's dynamite in one of the bunker's storerooms."

Jin was nodding. "If we can line the tunnel and set them off, it'll work."

It was reckless, it was destructive, but Jin was right. It *would* work.

They dashed down the hall. The lights dimmed, the extravagance fading as they reached the back of the palace. Black-clad figures were everywhere. Surprisingly, not a single Horned Guard was present.

"A kitchen!" Jin said as they ran, detouring inside and returning with knives and a heavy iron pan.

"A pan?" Laith asked.

"It's for me, assassin," Jin said, handing them each a knife.

Arthie gripped hers tight, wishing, once again, she had Calibore by her side.

"You don't need it," Matteo said softly. He was watching her. How, in the midst of this mayhem, did he know what she needed to hear?

"You don't need it," he repeated. "You are our greatest weapon, Arthie. Look at what you've done."

What she'd done was misjudge the Ram. She'd underestimated, yet again, how far the Ram would go. Arthie shook her head. "This is a mess; it's not—"

"Artists know to trust the process, darling. For twenty years, she worked her infamy in the shadows. This is the first time someone's forced her to show her hand." He extended his arm toward her. "Now give me yours, and let's stop the Rippers and give her the end she deserves."

Arthie took it. But what was the end she deserved?

He closed his fingers around hers, and she realized she'd asked the question aloud. "The end you wanted to give her. Save those high society snobs you loathe, and they'll do what we hoped the press would in the Athereum. They'll spread the word. Her image will be thoroughly ruined. She can't wear that mask again, nor could the Council allow her to."

No, they could not. Arthie gripped the knife Jin had given her and ran, her shoes skidding on the polished floor, her hair coming undone. Until she came face-to-face with a man carrying a stake.

She had a sudden, sinking feeling when Matteo shifted, knowing with utter certainty that he would step in front of a thousand stakes to keep her safe so that she would see the Ram's destruction through.

It froze her in place, even when Matteo stepped in front of her, even when the man tightened his grip around the stake, his aim clear and true.

A loud clang rang out.

The man wobbled and fell. Jin was standing behind him, pan raised in his hands as if it were a bat. Arthie snatched up the fallen stake, shaking away whatever had locked her limbs in place and caused her to freeze.

"You're welcome," Jin said, Laith behind him. "The bunker entrance is just up ahead. Where's Flick?"

"She must have stayed with the guests," Arthie said.

She would have too, if that was her mother who was about to be ruined in front of high society. Jin pulled open the heavy door. A gaping abyss lit by scant sconces stared back, and Jin disappeared inside without a second's pause. Arthie, Matteo, and Laith followed. The tunnel was deceptively long, and when they emerged on the other side, they were met with men shouting, calling orders back and forth, footsteps pounding. Arthie heard weapons being tossed from hand to hand.

"This way," Laith said, steering them to the shadows until they reached the storeroom. It was stocked with everything the Ram could need in an emergency such as this, from preserved foods to even the green darts they'd seen on Ceylan. Laith grabbed several bundled sticks of dynamite.

Arthie snatched a lighter from the shelf, and the four of them stacked as much dynamite as they could hold and circled back, footsteps as light as could be.

"There they are!"

A score of the Ram's men stood between them and the tunnel.

"We don't have time for a fight. Cover me!" Jin shouted.

Laith and Matteo leaped into action. Arthie gripped her knife tight. They dropped two men, squeezing a gap for Jin to get through. He dropped to his knees to line the dynamite.

"I think we're past the need for subtlety," Matteo said, pulling out the revolver Arthie had given him. He fired, hitting one of the men square in the chest. Laith ran forward and slashed his knife through another's neck.

Arthie grabbed a bundle of dynamite and dropped to the other side to help. Laith and Matteo continued fighting, slowly retreating with Jin and Arthie to the tunnel entrance.

Screams rang out from deep within the bunker, the wet spattering of blood chilling Arthie's bones.

"What is that?" Laith whispered.

"Ripper vampires," Matteo breathed.

Arthie looked up from the middle of the tunnel. More than a dozen vampires were barreling toward them, teeth bared in angry snarls, eyes void of life.

Jin dropped to the floor to light the wick, but the fire didn't take. "It's too cold!"

"They're getting closer," Arthie warned, snatching the lighter from him.

The flame took. The wick hissed. She hurried from one to the next, lighting them as Matteo and Laith stopped their fighting—letting the Ram's men act as a barrier between them and the Rippers. She lit the last wick and clicked the lighter off.

"Done. Let's go!" she shouted. They rushed to the mouth of the tunnel, but the Rippers had already barreled through the Ram's men. They were moving fast. The wicks were burning far too slowly.

The Rippers would escape the tunnel before the explosion could bury them.

Arthie wanted to laugh. She wanted to scream. Was it all for nothing? The journey to Ceylan, the fall of Spindrift, the death of the Siwangs and Penn and members of the press? For a moment, she and the others could only stare. What more could they do? The Rippers would tear through them, wreak havoc through the palace, and then what?

No one would be left to stand in the Ram's way.

"Go," Matteo said in their strangled silence. It was no more than an exhale. He cleared his throat and repeated himself. "Go! I'll hold them off."

Arthie wasn't sure she heard him correctly.

"That—the dynamite will collapse the tunnel, Andoni," Laith said.

Matteo nodded, avoiding eye contact. "I'm aware."

"It will collapse on you too," Jin said. "Unless the Rippers kill you first."

Matteo nodded again. "That is the idea."

The vampires were getting closer, shouting, snarling. Arthie didn't hear them. She was in a glass case, where everything was muffled, even her emotions. She didn't have Calibore to slow them down, nor the strength to fight. Jin's pistol and pan would do little. Laith was human; he'd die in seconds.

"Please," she whispered.

She could say nothing else. They were supposed to see this through together. It was supposed to be an eternity of him and her, dashing and deadly.

A new Spindrift. A new dawn. A new life.

"No," Matteo said, hearing her every protest. His hands dropped to her shoulders as mayhem roared around them. He pressed a kiss to her brow, and the tenderness in his emerald eyes tore at her heart.

When had she begun to feel so much? He kissed her nose, then the side of her mouth, and Arthie tilted her chin to kiss him fully.

It didn't flood her with heat. It didn't fill her hope. It tasted of remorse and longing, sorrow, and farewells.

"We did have a good love story, didn't we?" he whispered.

She was shaking her head, tears dripping down her chin to her sari. She wanted to shoot him again. To see him shake with laughter at her antics. To feel his smile curving against her skin.

"I had forgotten what it was like to live until you," he said. "I forgot what it was like to have purpose." He looked behind her. "It was a pleasure, Jin." Then tilted his head to the side to look at Laith. "Can't say the same."

Laith dipped his chin. "Thank you, Andoni."

"I'm not doing this for you."

"I know."

No, he was doing this for her. Hadn't he told her as much? *I would die for you, darling.* She had simply never imagined a world in which he would have to, for Arthie always saved herself.

Matteo met her gaze one last time. His green eyes were bright, at peace.

Then he pushed her toward Jin and Laith and leaped into the fray. Arthie ran for him, her sari shimmering cruelly out of the corner of her eye. Jin caught her, held her, even as she heaved and thrashed against him. The vampires roared as Matteo reached them. He toppled two in one fell swoop, only for them to rise back up again. He tore his claws down another's chest with a snarl. They were fighting back. They were hurting him. Each gash across his skin was a bullet through her, each one numbing her to the bone.

But it was working.

He was slowing them down.

"Jin! Arthie!" Laith called behind him as the dynamite hissed and popped.

"No," Arthie whispered, tears blurring her vision.

"I'm sorry, Arthie. I'm sorry," Jin was saying, over and over again, his voice cracking when he saw her face. He pulled her behind him, forcing her to run. They reached the bunker door as the dynamite fell quiet, and Arthie turned back one last time to see the Ripper vampires overwhelming Matteo, climbing over him, she saw them rip through his chest, and she found a strange, sick sense of comfort that he wouldn't live, that he wouldn't suffer beneath that rubble for an eternity.

Then Jin was pulling her through the door and sealing Matteo inside as the explosion rocked the earth and the tunnel collapsed, her heart crumbling with it.

57

FLICK

Flick stayed back. She wanted to watch Lady Linden's face when the explosion went off and terror froze her features. The lords and ladies of society were pointing fingers. The Council was turning their scorn toward her. Would they oust her on the spot?

What would *she* do?

Flick's answer came soon enough. She almost laughed when Lady Linden pulled out her tiny revolver, the very same she'd killed Jin with. What was a pistol against the masses? But Flick knew better than to underestimate the woman she once called mother. The Ram had killed Arthie's parents and Jin's, she had ruined Matteo's life, destroyed Laith, stolen a mother from Flick.

She wouldn't let her ravage anything else.

As the Ram's black-clad forces fell upon the guests, and the Athereum vampires launched into battle, Flick threw herself at Lady Linden. She screamed, but Flick held on tight, struggling until she toppled her to the floor. Lady Linden jabbed her elbow into Flick's ribs, digging deep until Flick was gasping for air, turning a pained and panicked gaze to hers.

Her mother faltered for the barest second. She looked different, somehow. Younger, almost, than when she'd lather on every cosmetic before ever leaving her room. As if her makeup worked in reverse, painting her older.

No, she looked like she was sculpted from stone. Realization sank into Flick's chest, throwing her off-kilter.

She tried to move, but Lady Linden yanked her again with staggering strength. The revolver was trapped between them. Flick wrenched away, struggling with both hands to stop Lady Linden from pulling the gun free. She wrapped her legs around Flick's, flipping them so Flick was on top of her. Then she threw Flick off, brought her finger to the trigger—

And fired.

58

JIN

Jin had never seen his sister cry. He had never felt so deep a pain ripping through him as when he saw the tears tracking down Arthie's face. For she was the strong one, the put-together one, not him. He pulled her behind him, knowing their work was not over. Knowing they could not let Matteo's death go in vain.

Then he heard the gunshot.

He knew that sound: the Ram's tiny revolver that had killed him, that had killed his parents. He barreled around the corner and wrenched to a halt. The Ram was rising to her feet, a body in front of her, wrapped in crimson splendor and white bandages.

Flick.

Jin heard a roar of anguish, only to realize it had come from him, from some dark part of his soul. He tore through the shocked masses and dropped to his knees in front of Flick, in front of *the Ram*, but he didn't care. His meadow was dying, sunshine fading, sunflowers wilting.

But just as he touched her, she began to rise, her eyes wide.

She was uninjured.

"Jin! I—"

She was alive, rubbing her head but alive. A bullet hole scorched the wood inches away from her. The Ram raised her revolver again, aiming for the Council this time. Jin threw himself forward, knocking into her arm as she fired, killing one of the Council members instantly. She growled and slammed the revolver into Jin's jaw, knocking him to the ground with a force he didn't know someone as old as her could possess.

Old? He stared at her. She didn't look a day past twenty-seven. He could have sworn she'd looked older before. No, he'd never seen the Ram without her mask before.

He struggled to rise. His head was spinning. People were screaming, running from the Ram's men. Outside of Sidharth's vampires, only a handful of guests were armed, for no one thought to bring a weapon to a party.

And there, in the midst of the mayhem, Lady Linden's tiny revolver fell to the floor. She froze as someone held a stake to her heart.

Arthie.

Her eyes were empty, hollow. Her cheeks were stained with tears, and she moved as if she could barely find the will to do it.

"I should snap this in two," Arthie said, her voice deathly still. "It would hurt a lot more going in, you crooked wretch."

A stake? Jin's brow furrowed. Beside him, Flick looked as if she suddenly carried a heavy weight on her shoulders.

Lady Linden threw up her arms. Arthie reached into the woman's pocket, pulled out Calibore and fired at the ceiling.

The silence was immediate.

It settled like a blanket over the guests and black-clad men alike as they turned to watch her. Arthie tossed the stake to the floor, where it clattered in the hushed silence. Arthie circled behind Lady Linden, giving the Council, the vampires, and the rest of the attendees a perfect view.

Arthie pressed Calibore to the back of Lady Linden's skull, and Jin heard the tap of her finger on the trigger. Her voice was quiet, barely audible to even Jin's ears.

"Might I remind you, Lady Linden, that Calibore kills vampires?"

59
ARTHIE

At some point between putting a bullet in Matteo's chest and now, Arthie had made room in her heart for him. She didn't know why. She didn't know when. Only that he had swept in and taken it, nestling into her veins even as she taunted and groused and pushed him away.

And now he was gone.

She knew, now, why the Ram had devised this night. Arthie should have seen it—the fact that Lady Linden had turned Matteo so many years ago, having known about vampires when few others did. The desire to own Calibore. The ease with which she decided to wipe out the entirety of high society and the Council.

Her actions would have dismantled an entire system that had been in place for more than a century. High society wasn't easily replaceable. The Council aside, it would take years for a new line of wealthy, influential people to take the place of the current lot. Decades, even.

Only a vampire had that much time on their hands.

But it was her hatred of vampires that should have given Arthie the clarity she needed. Lady Linden had no real reason to hate them, especially not to the extent she had taken her hatred—from fearmongering to weaponizing them.

Lady Linden was the thing she hated: a vampire.

And so, Arthie pressed Calibore's barrel into the back of her skull. For her parents, for Ceylan, for the colonies.

For Matteo.

She exhaled, nudging the barrel deeper into the blond strands of her hair. Her finger wavered on the trigger, the bullet poised to give the Ram what she desperately deserved.

And Arthie—Arthie couldn't do it. She could not kill her. It would be easy. Pull the trigger and watch her bleed to death. The lords and ladies would not be opposed.

But Arthie was not the Ram, and in that moment, she remembered she could do far worse. As Matteo had said she could, for she was a weapon as worthy as Calibore. She would make Lady Linden wish for death, as Arthie had once. As Matteo had too.

Arthie shoved the Ram to her knees. Scant snickers echoed in the anticipated silence. She felt no such rejoicing, for as she stared at Lady Linden, she saw the Ceylani. She saw the innocents in the cage. She saw Jin's parents. Matteo. Flick.

That little girl on a boat.

And the one who had gotten a second chance at being a daughter.

The Ram had only ever taken, and that was what she expected in this moment too. It was what she would want.

"Remember who spared you," Arthie whispered, tears crowding her throat, and reached into her pocket for the silver dose something had compelled her to pocket in Ceylan.

She shoved it into Lady Linden's neck.

Lady Linden looked up, horror freezing the icy depths of her blue eyes. She knew the risks of the silver inoculation. For the rest of her days, she would be forced to consume that which nearly a hundred vampires would need due to *her* decisions.

Or she would become a Ripper herself.

"No. Please," she whispered to Arthie, and why wouldn't she beg?

She had exposed herself to the people she wanted to murder in cold blood. Her guests were sneering, looking down on her, calling for justice for their own lives. She had no allies; she had no dead bodies who would take the happenings of this night to the grave.

She had nothing, and that, for a woman like her, was a fate worse than death.

The silver worked quickly: In seconds, her eyes rolled to the back of her head and she collapsed. The lords and ladies gasped. Arthie tucked Calibore into her hair.

"Did you kill her?" a lady asked.

"As much as she deserved to die, no. Vampires are not the heartless savages she's allowed you to imagine we are. I will leave what happens to her for you to decide, but I suggest you stop blaming us."

Murmurs passed through the guests. She heard more than one instance of *Arthie Casimir is a vampire?* and a part of her seized up before she thought of all that she had done, all that she had accomplished, all that she *would* accomplish.

Arthie Casimir *was* a vampire. She was also a girl. An immigrant. A businesswoman. She had pulled Calibore from White Roaring Square, and become the savior those legends said she could be.

As that sergeant had said long ago in Spindrift, she was a king.

"Is that a threat, Casimir?" a lord called, and several echoed the sentiment.

Arthie paused. She was so accustomed to issuing threats that she was surprised to find that wasn't the case this time.

"No, I'm trusting you."

The doors groaned open, and Arthie saw a pair of Athereum vampires holding several of the Ram's men at gunpoint by the mechanism that had sealed it in place. People began making their way to the exit, vampires keeping them orderly.

Jin turned to the Council and handed them the ledger. "A bedtime story for you, though it might give you nightmares." He rubbed his neck. "Perhaps we'll have a Heron for a monarch next, eh?"

"It's over," Flick whispered, staring at the woman who had raised her, the woman who had nearly ruined her. It was indeed over, but Arthie found little satisfaction in the fact.

60

ARTHIE

It was a quiet morning, one Arthie hadn't seen too often as of late. The paper announcing the Ram's removal from office, her numerous scandals, and a recounting of the Tribute to the Written Word three weeks ago sat on a table beside a collection of paints and brushes soaking in a glass, awaiting their master.

He would never return.

Arthie spent most of her days here in the studio inside Matteo's house. Turmoil still lingered on the streets and Sidharth had warned her it might not be safe, but Arthie could handle herself.

The Council had resumed control in the Ram's ousting until they could appoint a new leader. They had agreed it best to keep the Ram's identity as a vampire from public knowledge, for it was hard enough washing away the stain she had placed upon vampires as it was.

The humans she had kidnapped returned to their homes, the truth revealed, but despite the Council's attempts to curtail the public's anger, it lingered. It had stemmed from debilitating fear, making it easy to sell one's sanity to the Ram's cause. They wouldn't so quickly believe vampires to be safe any more than they would see the wrongs in colonizing countries beyond Ettenia.

Arthie wasn't worried. Like all things, their fears would settle with time as new ones arose. Such was the nature of man. She had seen it in Spindrift day after day as the posh and the privileged sat down for tea despite the open secret of what happened there after-hours.

She rose from Matteo's armchair by the window, drawing a breath full of that nutty, chocolatey warmth. She saw him everywhere: in the crisp white shirts she had found in his drawer that made excellent loungewear, in the flutes of blood she now drank without complaint, in the future that didn't loom with a cruel, masked shadow.

"What are you going to do to his paints?" Chester asked Ivor as he dusted the room.

"Leave them," Ivor said honestly. "Master Andoni had not painted with such vibrancy in a near decade. I quite like that his work was in bloom after many long years of winter."

There was a canvas still on the easel, a black backdrop with a single, sweeping stroke of color in its center. A masterpiece never to be finished.

Chester was looking at it, head tilted. "It's the same color as your hair, boss."

Arthie knew. "Don't you have work to do?"

He sighed and pulled Reni with him out of the room. They were in charge of a shipment due from Ceylan soon, an EJC ship helmed by one Captain Silas Vane, its hold full of coconuts for the vampires still recovering from imprisonment on the island.

The presses ran endlessly. They spoke about the Ram stoking the fear of the public unjustly, of weaponizing vampires, and kidnapping humans. They spoke of Matteo Andoni, the prestigious painter who happened to be a vampire, meeting his demise as he saved the day. They spoke of the Casimirs who were at the forefront of it all.

Linden was now housed in the deepest, darkest cell the Athereum had to offer. The public might not know she was a vampire, but it was a test of their faith in the Athereum. Those who knew she was a vampire didn't want to risk placing her in a mortal prison.

Arthie picked up Calibore and crossed the room. Jin had taken Flick to the local bakery for pastries. He wouldn't eat them, of course, but he would revel in the scents and sate his eyes. Every few days, Flick would send her mother a gift: the newspaper.

For Linden, lady no more, deserved to see what the papers were writing about her "utterly atrocious behavior," as Flick would say. Her next gift was to be a coconut, which Linden would accept with zeal if she wanted to avoid possibly becoming a Ripper.

By her desk, Arthie turned Calibore over in her hands. The door opened almost soundlessly, and she closed her eyes for a beat, wholly aware of who it was.

"What are you doing?" Laith asked, greeting Opal and rubbing her ears. She purred, curling her tail around his arm.

He had healed from his wounds and was dressed again in robes as white as his hair, only there was no insignia of the Horned Guard embroidered upon them anymore. Nor did he carry his sister's snake cuff any longer. No, he was a free soul now, untethered from the past, and Arthie was gradually beginning to look forward to his daily visits.

She opened the box in front of her and nestled Calibore inside. "Returning it to where it belongs."

To the Arawiyan king.

It was never hers as much as it was never Ettenia's to flaunt. It had become a crutch, but Arthie never needed it when she was a weapon herself. She smiled at the reminder. The door opened again as Jin and Flick returned, her cheeks pink and his eyes glazed. Arthie closed the box up, and they watched as she sealed it with a sigh.

"Now what?" Jin asked.

"Well, I have a proposition for you," Arthie said, handing him a card. He unfolded it and read the words, Flick peering over his shoulder before she let out a gleeful shriek.

"*Arthie, Jin, and Flick,*" Jin read, "*purveyors of blood and tea, present Spindrift at 337 Alms Place.*"

He looked up at her with a grin, and Arthie lifted her brows in question. Jin said not a word, only strode close and rapped his knuckles against hers.

It was all the answer she needed.

EPILOGUE

On the second day of spring, the doors opened with a tinkle of bells and a meow of greeting from the splotched kitten sitting on the windowsill of 337 Alms Place, otherwise known in the capital of White Roaring as Spindrift.

Patrons had gathered for the ribbon cutting outside the entrance, a long line curling around the street drawn by the posters plastered across the city and invitations printed in the papers:

SPINDRIFT RISES FROM THE ASHES.

Jin read the menu one last time. Flick's elegant penmanship was faultless, set aglow by the lights angled toward the blackboard hanging above the bartop, illuminating their extensive offerings. A list of teas to the left, starting with his once-favorite Lady Slate, and a list of bloods to the right, for he'd learned in his weeks-long taste-testing excursion that blood came in several flavors too.

"Arundel's Ace? Painter's Pleasure?" Arthie asked, reading the list of blood offerings.

"You know you're proud of my naming talents," Jin said, lifting his chin.

Arthie only rolled her eyes, though he saw the way her gaze softened. She missed him. She turned to the crew, gesturing to the thrum of the crowd waiting behind the ribbon.

"Ready?"

Matteo's house had needed updating for a tearoom that doubled as a bloodhouse, but Arthie had ensured those changes remained at a minimum. She added a second door but kept them both the same fervent red of Matteo's original. She merged the parlor with the foyer for space, but let no one touch his studio. There were tables arranged for tea, but Matteo's settees prevailed for those who wished to stay awhile, shelves of books and a fireplace crackling with welcome warmth.

"Ready, boss!" Chester shouted from the second-story balcony.

"Oh, not yet," Arthie said, and rushed to a wrapped, flat square frame propped against the counter, unraveling it to reveal a piece of art. A black canvas with a swoop of mauve brushed across with artistic flair. She set it over the hearth with a wistful smile. "Now we're ready."

"It's perfect," Flick said, stepping behind the bartop to lace her fingers through Jin's. Her grip was stronger than ever. At each of the tables scattered throughout the floor, Laith was arranging flowers in tiny vases, slowly earning back Arthie's trust with the bloom of each new day.

Arthie stepped to the doors. She looked back at her crew, at their waiting smiles, and snipped the ribbon.

Mauve silk fluttered in the breeze.

People cheered as Reni bowed and began welcoming them through the doors, Chester leading patrons to seats and taking orders. Servers carried trays with pots of tea and decanters of blood. The living walked in beside the undead, some wholly unaware, some with a glint in their eyes that said they were willing to give harmony a try.

Jin drew in a deep breath, and as the scent of tea warmed his heart, he thought of his parents, of his father's research on the mutations that Jin had decided to continue, he thought of Flick who had found a home for herself, and he thought of Arthie who meandered through the bustling floor to the bartop now.

Her dark eyes were bright. "I suppose we can save the world and have tea."

ACKNOWLEDGMENTS

As many authors can attest, sequels are the bane of our existence. It's simultaneously much like herding cats and pulling teeth, and while I, like Arthie, imagined I needed no one else's help, I'm now grateful I didn't have to do it alone. Scratch that—I *couldn't* have done it alone. *A Steeping of Blood* tried me and tested me, and while I emerged on the other side, it is a victory I share with a list of names.

To Cayce, an (evil?) mastermind who can be blamed for that heartbreaking ending. I know I had a choice in this decision, dear reader, but to my credit, I did cry when he made the suggestion, so it's not my fault. In all seriousness, I would have floundered without you, roohi, without your support, without your wit, without you drumming up lines and motives and ideas at the drop of a hat. Thank you for being the selfless man that you are, here for me at every turn. Thank you for accompanying me to every event, for always giving me your fullest despite your own busy schedule. I would say I love you, but the words for what I feel for you do not yet exist.

To Asma, for staying up late hours and reading the many drafts of this story with a keen eye. For cheering me on and celebrating my wins, for being happy for me when so many are not. You've been here for every book of mine, for every literary journey from start to finish, and when I say I appreciate every facet of your help, I do not mean it lightly. To Azraa, for loving these characters from day one.

To Josh Adams, agent extraordinaire. I cannot imagine navigating the world of publishing without you by my side. Thank you for diligently working to bring my words to readers around the world, for championing me through my doubts, and for being the amazing ally that you are. To Tracey Adams and the rest of the Adams Literary family, thank you. Working with you is a dream.

To Janine O'Malley and Melissa Warten—where do I even begin? This book was a nightmare of a time. I'm certain we crammed several years' worth of brainstorming and editing into a handful of months, and I'm not sure any of us emerged unscathed. Thank you for the many phone calls and video chats and unending discussions. Thank you, Melissa, for the daily check-ins and encouragement, the morning texts cheering me on. Thank you, Janine, for your dedication to making sure this book was in the best shape it could be, despite the time constraints. I'm sorry for making you sick by the end of it.

To the rest of the team at Macmillan, thank you for bringing my work to readers. To Chantal Gersch, sweet soul and powerhouse publicist. Our emails and events are always a treat. I will always adore your tea puns. To Samantha Sacks, for being just as amazing. To Molly Ellis and Allison Verost, incredible, powerful women I'm proud and honored to have by my side. Molly, thank you for always being ready to fight. Allison, we must meet again soon!

To Melissa Zar, Gaby Salpeter, and the marketing team: thank you for handling everything Arthie, from commissioning art to building email lists. Thank you to Elysse Villalobos, Alexandra Quill, and the rockstar S&L team. To Helen Seachrist—I'm sorry I use the word *hiss* even when there's no sibilant sound. To Aurora Parlagreco, who understands my designer anguish and accepts my lengthy emails without complaint. Special thanks to Jon Yaged, Jen Besser, and Asia Harden too.

To Cate Augustin, Cheyney Smith, and the team at Pan Macmillan

ACKNOWLEDGMENTS 437

in the UK, thank you. The enthusiasm for Arthie across the pond has been nothing short of incredible, and I appreciate all that you did to make that happen. From your stunning animations to everything Waterstones, thank you.

To Carrie and Len, for cheering me on to the finish line—and beyond. To Valentina Remenar for a cover worthy of standing beside your first one. To Kelly Andrew, Joan He, and Joanna Hathaway, authors and friends who are always ready to lend an ear and hold out a hand. To the amazing family at Bookmarks in Winston Salem, for managing my preorder campaign with such care. To Azanta, Basma, and the Zumra discord, I appreciate you so very much.

As for you, dear reader, who has been waiting since the brutal ending of the first book: thank you and sorry. I could not do this without your support and love. Thank you for giving my books a home and cherishing my stories.

Until the next one. ♥

Set in a richly detailed world inspired by ancient Arabia, The Sands of Arawiya duology is a breathtaking story of magic, conquering fear and taking identity into your own hands.

Darkness surged in his veins.

Power bled from her bones.

WE FREE THE STARS

HAFSAH FAIZAL